In Sam's Shoes

Book Design by Logotecture

First Edition

Printed in the U.S.A.

To the *special* man who helped me create an
unforgettable chapter of my life.

In Sam's Shoes

A NOVEL BY

BROOKE HORTON

Prologue

The grand, mahogany casket loomed large ahead of her, topped by a massive cascading bouquet of pink roses. Around the perimeter of the room, display tables dressed in white linens bore artifacts of a life well lived, from golf memorabilia to seemingly trivial trinkets. The focal point of the entire collection was an exquisite eight-by-ten crystal frame bearing a formal wedding photo of a bride and groom in happier days. To the casual observer, the smiling couple represented an ideal – the beautiful, wholesome wife and the handsome all-American groom dressed in the finest attire befitting the occasion, their pedigree, and their lifestyle. On either side of this centerpiece, smaller and much plainer frames told the story of a father's love for his sons, with images of the recently departed engaged in various activities with them like playing basketball and camping out in the woods.

As the funeral home worker entered the room, Sam stood at a distance with her back turned to the unfolding scene a few feet away. She could hear the rustling of the flowers and the barely audible sound of the casket lid moving against its hinges to reveal the body at rest inside. She trembled at the thought of laying eyes upon his still, lifeless form and doubted she had the strength to confront the reality of this devastating, unexpected loss.

Consumed by torturous thoughts, she continued to stare out at the hallway minutes after the woman had left her in privacy again. How was she going to handle the sight of his hideously disfigured face? The thought of staring at a nasty patchwork of scars stubbornly protruding through a heavy layer of funeral parlor make-up was just too much to bear. Her entire body convulsed as she broke down in uncontrollable weeping.

Why? Why did this have to happen? Why now? Why at all?

"Sam?" She heard Shannon's soft voice behind her. "I have to tell you he looks normal. I think you're going to be OK looking at him."

She slowly turned to face her sister. "You really think so?"

Shannon put her hands on Sam's shoulders in a gesture of comfort and confidence.

"Yes, yes I really do. I'd never tell you that if I didn't believe it. But I can stay here in the room with you if you want; I'll just hang out in the back."

"No, no – I have to do this alone. Please."

Sam drew her into a hug, appreciative of her unwavering support. She then watched until the door closed behind Shannon, leaving her alone with her soulmate for the last time.

She clutched her tissues in one hand as she strode past the oddly arranged folding chairs that appeared as if they'd been set up for a round of the classic children's musical game. Instead of facing the front of the room, they faced the side walls, as if unwilling to confront the reality of death.

Filled with determination and resolve, Sam took a gulp of air and reached out to touch the side of the casket to steady herself. Then she opened her eyes wide.

Oh, my God, not a scratch. A dried-up creek, two inches of water. How can this be? How can he possibly look like the sweet manly man I loved?

She was dumbfounded as she gazed at his perfect face. For a few moments, all she could do was stare at him in silence and wish that the entire scene was nothing more than a nightmare from which she'd awaken at any second. She placed her hand on his cheek and reacted to its icy coldness as a fresh wave of sorrow engulfed her.

"Baby, I love you! I love you so much. What the hell happened? Why? Why did you get on that bike? Why? How could you just leave me like this!"

She dropped to her knees and prayed out loud through staccato breaths. "God, I need you. I have nowhere else to turn. I don't know how I'm going to get through this. Please, give me the strength to focus on my kids. I promise, I'll spend more time praying and appreciating the good things in my life. Just please, help me."

Sam pleaded and cried until she was utterly spent. Then she wiped her face and got back on her feet just as Shannon re-entered the room to check on her.

"Let's go," Sam ordered.

"But the lady said we could stay as long as you need. You don't have to rush; there's plenty of time before the funeral – "

"I'm done. It's time to move on and heal."

"Ok, whatever you want."

Shannon followed her big sister out to the hallway, hoping this little episode signified the beginning of her new life. God knew, she'd been through enough heartache for one human being.

Keesler Air Force Base
Biloxi, Mississippi
1994

Chapter One

The November morning greeted Sam with a cool, steady breeze and bright sunshine as she walked out of her dorm building hauling a bloated bag of dirty laundry and a smaller handbag filled with blank notecards and stationary. It was Saturday on base and as per her routine, she was headed to the laundromat for the dual purpose of washing clothes and writing letters back home. Dressed in her most comfortable jogging pants, tee shirt, hoodie, and sneakers, she'd pulled her long, brown hair into a ponytail, which swayed back and forth in response to her fast-paced movement. As usual, the campus felt like a ghost town since most airmen took advantage of their free weekends by heading off base to party in Biloxi or nearby New Orleans – just over an hour away by car.

Sam stopped briefly to adjust the headphones of her Sony Walkman to better hear the soulful voice of Pam Tillis serenading her with songs from the *Sweetheart's Dance* cassette, one of her current favorites. She chuckled to herself at the glaring absence of her peers, or any other human being for that matter, along her path. *My title for nerdiest girl on campus remains intact*, she thought. Upon arriving at her destination, rows of silent white washers and dryers stood at attention, ready to perform their duties on her behalf.

"Let's see, who will the lucky winner be," she joked as she tossed her bags on a nearby table. She selected two side by side washers, throwing a load of color into one and a load of whites into another. Then she inserted the right amount of coins into the slots, threw in some detergent, and pushed the start button. "Another exciting day in the life of Samantha Townsend," she sighed before settling in at her designated spot. She pulled out her favorite pen and a sheet of floral writing paper and started to compose a letter to her younger sister in Vermont.

Ever since arriving at the base in August, Sam had made it a habit of mailing weekly letters home to Shannon. It had already been six years since their mother was killed in a car accident, an event that had drawn the two even closer together. While their dad Walter had stepped up as much as he could into the role of both mother and father, long hours devoted to his thriving photography business in their hometown of Morristown and surrounding Lamoille County kept him out of the house most of the time. Sam almost felt guilty for leaving but knew if she wanted to forge her own way in the world she had to get out of her comfort zone. Still, in her absence the friction between her strong-willed, rebellious sister and their stubborn, protective father had increased, exacerbated by the fact that at sixteen years-old and in possession of a driver's license, Shannon had erroneously assumed easy access to Walter's coveted black Corvette Stingray.

She smiled to herself as she wrote.

Dear Shannon,

Well it's another Saturday morning on base and here I am alone in the laundromat. Been thinking of you and wondering if you've asked Derek to the Snow Ball yet. Knowing you, you already did and he's already said yes. I'm sorry I won't get to be there for your big night but you better send me lots of pictures. I have no doubt you'll be voted Lamoille Union High School's hottest chick at the dance. I just wish I could help you pick out a dress. On second thought, maybe it's a good thing I'm not since you and I aren't exactly on the same fashion wavelength. How's –

Suddenly, the glass doors burst open and interrupted her train of thought. She glanced up briefly and noticed a handsome airman walking by dressed in full uniform, a clear indication he was being reprimanded for some sort of offense. At first, his presence had little effect on her beyond a cursory observation and she went back to the business of penning her letter, determined not to let him make her feel self-conscious.

Hey guess what? For once, I'm not the only one in the laundry room today. A cute airman just walked through the doors. I bet he's being punished for something because he's dressed in uniform. Wonder what he did? I have to say, he's really handsome. I think he's the guy –

"Hey, what's up?" a deep, masculine voice addressed her.

Oh, my gosh, he's even better looking close-up. A wave of insecurity washed over her, remembering her disheveled wardrobe and un-made-up face.

"Oh, hey," she acknowledged shyly.

"Aren't you Keith's friend?"

"Yeah."

"Well, I'm Russell."

"Oh…well, I'm Samantha."

So…how's school going Samantha? What week are you working on?"

"Circuitry."

"Ah, that was a tough one," he replied.

"Yeah, I can't believe how grueling this whole course is. I keep in touch with some of my high school friends who went to college and they're blown away by how much we have to do in a week."

"Yep. We're cramming an entire semester into seven days, week after week. Gotta love condensed, high-tech training," he quipped. Sam's heart skipped a beat as she took note of his full lips and perfect white teeth. *Here I am talking to this hottie and I look like a hot mess.*

"So, Saman – "

A loud booming voice cut him off and caused a startled Sam to drop her pen on the floor.

"Airman Russell!" the drill sergeant bellowed as he strode up beside him. A big, burly guy in his early forties, he was dressed in full uniform and demonstrated an unyielding commitment to discipline.

"Yes, sir!" he jumped to attention.

"What are you doing in here? Get back to your assigned duties outside; you need to be pulling weeds!"

"Yes, sir!"

Sam watched the interaction awkwardly, feeling somehow responsible. As the sergeant hustled her new friend out of the building, he turned to look at her once more. "It was good talking to you," he complimented. "You too," she mouthed with a grin, as if afraid to anger the sergeant any further.

"God, he's so cute. I hope I didn't get him into trouble. He's probably never gonna talk to me again," she sighed to no one in particular, now that the room was empty again. Then remembering her letter to Shannon, she resumed writing.

Oh, my God, you're never going to believe what just happened….

ॐ

Sam picked up a brown tray from the stack and began walking through the cafeteria line, surveying the day's offerings. After marching the half-mile from the Learning Center to the Dining Hall, she'd acknowledged her two friends, who were already set up at a table, with a smile and a wave. They were planning to study together that afternoon in preparation for their weekly Friday test once they'd eaten and caught up on the latest gossip. Her sole focus was to move through the line as quickly as possible once she decided on a cheeseburger, fries, and a Coke.

She'd just placed the hot items on her tray when she felt a presence behind her. Her heart fluttered as she turned around to see Airman Russell again, dressed in full uniform.

"Hey Samantha." He flashed his movie-star smile and she felt a shiver go up her spine.

"Hey there, Russell," she tried to sound nonchalant, yet cordial. Standing amid the flurry of activity in the dining hall in regulation dress, coupled with the fact she'd shampooed her hair that morning helped her feel a bit less self-conscious than the first time they'd met.

"Oh, you can call me Alec."

Ok…Alec. You can call me Sam. How's it going?"

"Alright. How's circuitry class?"

"Going well. I'm studying with some friends later this afternoon."

"Well, I just wanted to ask if you'd like to see a movie with me this weekend."

"What, you're not stuck on work duty?" she teased.

"Ha-ha. *Fun-ny.*" They both laughed before he continued. "Seriously, *Forrest Gump* is playing at Welch Theater. Did you see it yet?"

"No, I wanted to when it came out this summer but I was so busy getting ready to come down here I never did."

"So, how about it?"

"Um, sure," she accepted with what she hoped was just the right amount of enthusiasm. No reason for him to know her heart was pounding in her chest….at least not until she could be sure where this was headed. Sam was no psychic, nor was she an expert when it came to guys and relationships, but she did sense something special was about to happen.

"So, when do you want to go this weekend?" she asked.

"Well that's the thing," he explained with a twinge of embarrassment. "I actually do have work duty Saturday night so I figured we could go out for breakfast on Sunday then see the movie later? Are you OK with motorcycles?"

"Uh, sure. You do have a helmet for me, right?"

"You nervous? Don't be. You're gonna love my Kawasaki Ninja. And I promise, I'll be super careful."

"Well OK then. What time do you want to go?"

"Meet you outside of your dorm at nine?"

"Sounds good."

"Oh, and hey, looks like your friends approve." He winked and nodded in the direction of her two pals who had been watching their interaction with interest. Sam let out a nervous chuckle and felt the hot blush in her cheeks.

"Ok, see you later Russell," she blurted before turning around and walking away. He grinned as he watched her rejoin them at the table.

"Oh, my gosh, Alec just asked me out!" she squealed preemptively as she put down her tray.

"He did? Sam, you are so lucky; he's such a cutie," Meredith enthused.

"Yeah, all the girls on campus have the hots for him, including me," Brittany added.

"Hey, you're a married woman," Sam teased.

"Doesn't mean I can't look at the menu," she retorted. "Now stop stalling and give us details."

Sam shrugged. "There's not much to tell. He asked me to breakfast on Sunday and I accepted. I just hope I'm OK with riding on his bike; that's more my little sister's style than mine. I've never even been on a motorcycle."

"Ah, you'll be fine," Meredith declared. "Every girl on campus is gonna be jealous. I mean, he could have anyone and he chose you…oops, I'm sorry Sam. I didn't mean that to come out the way it sounded. I need to engage my brain before I engage my mouth."

"No worries," she answered sincerely. Although she didn't articulate it, the thought had crossed her mind more than once.

Trying to lighten the mood, Brittany offered suggestively, "You know, Sam, I may be getting a little ahead of myself but I just wanted to remind you as a married cadet I *do* have an apartment off campus. You and Alec can use it anytime you want."

"Ooh, Sam, I bet he's *amazing* in bed," Meredith opined as the two girls dissolved into giggles.

Sam laughed along with them, concealing her palpable anxiety at the mere thought of sex. If this relationship progressed as she believed it would, inevitably she'd have to have a heart-to-heart with Alec about her non-existent experience. But right now, she dreaded the conversation, necessary or not.

Whoa! Slow down, girl. It's breakfast for goodness' sake. No need to freak out, she thought.

"Sam?" Brittany addressed her.

"Yeah."

"I have a really good feeling about this."

"Me too," Meredith chimed in.

Despite her nervousness, Sam couldn't help but feel exhilarated as she imagined herself and Alec as a happy couple.

∽

Sunday morning dawned bright and chilly. Sam awakened early after a fitful night's sleep thanks to her jittery nerves. As she stared at her reflection in the mirror, she wondered what Alec saw in her – a "Plain Jane" who played by the rules and would be horrified if she'd ever ended up on work duty for some infraction like talking back to an officer.

Would he be bored with her after one date and dump her for a hot girl with more experience?

With Patty Loveless playing in the background, she slid into her favorite jeans, cowboy boots, and a blue cashmere sweater. Then she picked up her large hairbrush and carefully moved the natural bristles through her long, brown hair until it had just the right amount of shine and smoothness. After a quick application of lip balm, she grabbed her jean jacket and headed out to the main entrance before she chickened out.

Her heart skipped a beat when Alec pulled up in an old Pontiac Firebird, which he explained was on loan from his roommate until noon. Since the weather was too cold for a motorcycle, he'd managed to secure alternate transportation, much to her relief. Although she figured he was a skilled cyclist who would never do anything crazy with her holding on behind him, she was glad their first date was following a more traditional path – or at least as traditional as a Sunday breakfast date could be.

Even at this early hour IHOP was bustling with activity, but the hostess managed to find them a booth by a window, though somewhat close to the noisy kitchen. Alec seized upon the opportunity.

"Do you mind if I get in next to you? That way, we can at least hear each other."

She blushed involuntarily as she nodded her head, noticing for the first time the fullness of his lips. For a brief second, she wondered what it would be like to feel them on hers. Then, she brushed the thought aside and slid into the cushioned blue seat. The sweet aroma of syrup, pancakes and waffles mingled with the strong smells of coffee and grease as harried waitresses rushed back and forth bearing trays piled with pancakes, eggs, sausage, and bacon.

After placing their order, he shifted his attention back to her.

"So, Samantha, what got you into the military?" he asked.

"Well…believe it or not, it was actually a bet I made with my dad when I was eight years old."

"Really?"

She laughed.

"Yeah, my dad's a Vietnam vet. One day my little sister and I were riding along in the car with my parents and I just started asking them all kinds of questions about what they did when they were younger. You know, just being a curious little kid. When my dad told me about being in the Army, I said, 'You know Dad, I'm joining the military, too. I'm going into the Army!'"

"Out of the mouths of babes," he laughed.

"Yep. My dad was like, 'No way Samantha. You are *not* going into the military,' but I kept insisting until finally he said, 'Alright, I'll bet you $50 that by the time you grow up, you'll forget all about enlisting in the Army and go to college instead.' And I blurted out, 'Deal!' I think we even shook on it. Believe it or not, it became a running joke in my family for years."

"C'mon, is that the only reason you joined?" he countered with obvious skepticism.

"OK, it was a little more involved than that," she chuckled. "I don't know what it was like for you in New Hampshire, but in my little town in Vermont there wasn't a whole lot to do. Everyone knew my dad as the best photographer in the county and I saw how hard my parents worked at that business. At least, up until my mom died and my dad had to run it alone and raise two girls about to hit puberty."

"I'm sorry to hear that," he replied sincerely as he placed his hand on top of hers.

"Thanks," she whispered, affected as much by his genuine expression of sympathy as she was by the memory. "Anyway, I didn't really like being a student and I hated studying even though I usually brought home B's and B+'s. I was more into athletics and loved playing soccer. Then one day during junior year, my girlfriend Brandi and I were walking through a mandatory career fair in the gym when this Air Force recruiter named Leo started talking to us. He lured us in with these monthly social gatherings in Burlington, where we could at least hang out with some guys we weren't related to."

Alec cracked up.

"Hey, it's true," she insisted. "I'm probably related to eighty percent of the male population of Lamoille County. Brandi and I were like, 'Why not? Let's go have some fun one Friday a month.' One day on our ride back to Morristown, I asked her if she'd been paying attention to the Air Force stuff and told her I thought I was going to do it. She felt the same way, so we both decided to enlist."

"And your dad handed over the fifty bucks?"

"Yeah, well…it wasn't quite that easy," she sighed. "At first, he was totally against the idea, you know, of his daughter – a girl – going into the military. But it was more from a worry perspective; my dad isn't sexist or anything. And because he'd lost my mom a few years before, he was even more protective of Shannon and me. Deep down he knew he couldn't handle it if something bad happened to me; he kept trying to convince me to go to the local community college for two years to build up some credits to then maybe transfer to a better school nearby. Walter definitely wanted me around."

"Walter? That's a cool name," Alec observed.

"Yeah and he's a cool guy," she agreed with a smile. "I did feel a little guilty for wanting to leave him but the idea of being paid to go to school and travel the world was exciting. During junior year, it seemed like I might get a soccer scholarship to a small women's college in North Carolina but I never even bothered to go for it because I just didn't want to go to school anymore. Now, here I am, cramming in a semester a week at Keesler."

They both cracked up.

"But at least it's over in less than a year and then you get to move on," he noted.

"Exactly."

"So? What made him change his mind?"

"Uh, I think he just realized I was serious. And he respected that I didn't want him to waste his money on college when I had no idea what I even wanted to do. I mean, how does anybody know at seventeen? So, in the end, he signed my papers, gave me a big hug, and told me how proud he was."

"And what about the money?"

She giggled. "Yes, Walter made good on his bet and gave me my fifty dollars."

Alec laughed and high-fived her before their conversation was briefly interrupted by the waitress, who placed two generous plates of pancakes in front of them. He wasted no time smothering his portion in maple syrup and digging in.

"How'd you end up here?" he asked after swallowing a mouthful.

"Well, at first I thought I wanted nursing training but since that meant waiting until December after graduation in June, I agreed to a general program so I could start in August. I knew the longer I hung around Morristown helping my dad with his business, the harder it would be to follow through. And I didn't want to get stuck in my small town, wondering what could have been. So here I am."

"And I'm *really* glad you are here Samantha," he stated with a wink. Her heart leapt in her chest.

"So, what about you? Why are you here Mr. Work Duty?"

He rolled his eyes at the reference, then shrugged. "Kind of the same thing as you. My parents have their own construction business they are still rebuilding after one of their employees got into drugs and almost cost them everything. It's a long story, but we lost our house and had to seriously downsize. I had gone to a private Catholic boys' school before but after this happened I had to switch to public, which probably made the nuns happy since I used to drive them nuts. No joke, I bet they called my parents into a conference at least once a week because of some stupid thing I did. I gotta admit though, I didn't like public school, either. I'm smart but sitting in a classroom bores me; I'd rather be out doing things. I've always had a rebellious streak so when I announced my plans to enlist, my parents were happy because I needed the discipline. I guess I could have worked for my father but I didn't want to get stuck in New Hampshire my whole life, either. So, here we are."

He raised his orange juice glass for a toast. "Here we are," she repeated, returning the gesture.

"I, for one, am looking forward to getting to know you better Samantha Townsend," he declared as he placed an arm around her. Anticipation of what was to come consumed her as she inhaled the scent of his spicy cologne and savored the warmth of his strong, muscular body.

∾

"Hey, do you still want to see *Forrest Gump* tonight?" Alec asked.

They'd returned to base just in time for him to honor his promise to his roommate and now stood face- to-face at the entrance to Sam's dorm building.

"Sure," she accepted.

He broke out into a grin. "Ok, then, I'll come by around 6:30 and we can walk over to the theater together."

"Sounds good."

"I had a great time this morning, Sam. Thanks for having breakfast with me. Someday it'll be dinner, I promise." He leaned down and placed a soft kiss on her cheek.

"No worries, Alec, I had a great time. Thank you," she replied. He began to walk away, then turned around to look at her again.

"Sam, I don't know why you don't think you're pretty. I sure do. I'll see you later."

Wow, were her insecurities about her looks on full display? Why would he even say such a thing after one brief, casual date?

Her heart fluttered in her chest as she made her way back inside, where she planned to contemplate the possibilities until she saw him again. She'd barely closed her dorm room door behind her and plopped down on her bed before she heard a loud knock, followed by the familiar voices of Meredith and Brittany.

"Sam, open up!"

She sprang from the mattress and greeted them with a telltale grin.

"Ooh, that good, huh?" Meredith inquired, studying her face.

"I think he's a keeper, Sam," Brittany chirped.

But after the merriment died down, her expression changed from elation to worry.

"What's wrong? You just had a breakfast date with the hottest guy on campus, and you have plans to see him later. You should be jumping up and down for joy," Meredith chided.

Although it felt strange to confide in two friends she'd only known for a few months, Sam bared her soul out of necessity. After all, Brittany was married and presumably knew what life was all about; she had to have some good advice to share. After she finished her confession, she exhaled when neither one of them laughed upon discovering she was still a virgin.

"It's nothing to be ashamed of," Brittany consoled. "I think it's kind of nice."

"You know, it's not that I'm a prude," Sam began. "It's just that I know he was a high school stud hooking up with girls all the time. He never had a real girlfriend. I don't want to be just another conquest and I'm afraid if I give it up too soon that's what will happen. And I'm not exactly Niki Taylor, either."

"What's that supposed to mean? Sam, you are an attractive girl in your own way," Meredith countered. "Remember, Alec approached *you* in the laundry room, not the other way around. He must've seen something he liked."

"That's right," Brittany chimed in. "The guy talked to you when you were feeling your worst, even though you look great without makeup. Hell, I wish I looked as good as you do without it. And don't get me started on your hot body."

Sam choked up. "You know, until Alec, no one, not even my own father or my mother when she was alive, had ever told me I was pretty before."

"Wow, I'm sorry to hear that but I gotta believe it means something. Like we said, Alec could have any woman on this campus but he chose you. He found you in line for lunch that day and asked you out. Why would he do that if he wasn't interested?" Meredith opined.

"Yeah, I guess you're right," Sam conceded. "Still, I want to take things slow. And if he's not OK with waiting until I'm ready, I'll have my answer."

∽

The movie ended to enthusiastic applause as Sam and Alec made their way out of the theater holding hands. It felt natural as she strode along with him, relishing the human contact and anticipating what might happen when they reached her dorm building. Despite her fears, she had no doubt she was falling fast for the charming, muscular airman with the mischievous streak and soulful brown eyes. Little did she know she was about to discover something else about him to complete the package.

"Did I tell you I play guitar and sing?" he asked.

"Get out! What do you sing?"

"Mostly country. Merle Haggard, Johnny Cash, and Garth Brooks are my favorites. Been playing since I was a kid."

"Have you ever thought of pursuing it as a career?"

He shrugged. "Yeah, when I was younger and my parents' business was thriving. Before they lost everything and I had to give up guitar lessons. Then everything became about survival. I still love to play, though."

"Maybe you'll play for me sometime? I love country music. I remember when I played soccer in junior high, my dad would pick me up after practice and we'd sing along to Garth Brooks on the ride home. Seemed to help us heal after my mom died."

"Music can do that," he observed. "And yes, I would love to sing for you sometime, Samantha." His promise ignited a rush of excitement through her body.

The stars twinkled overhead in a panoramic sky as they lingered at the main entrance of her dorm building. For a fleeting moment, she felt a bit awkward as they stood in the silence but then Alec gently placed his hands on either side of her face and looked down at her, his brown eyes gazing deeply into her blue ones.

"You know, you really are beautiful Samantha," he whispered hoarsely before pulling her into a mesmerizing kiss. It began softly, then gradually increased in passion while Alec's fingers played with her hair and his artful lips and tongue engaged hers in a tantalizing dance. Maybe it was due to their shared New England upbringing and mutual love of country music, but whatever the reason, their first kiss unfolded with as much ease as that first encounter in the laundry room – this time without the angry drill sergeant. In fact, there was no one lingering around the outside of the building, since by Sunday night most recruits had retired to their dorm rooms in preparation for another busy week.

Sam lost herself in the exquisiteness of the moment, reveling in his broad, firm chest; soft, wavy, black hair; and sensual touch. If this was an indicator of what was to come, she knew she had nothing to worry about. Even with a sweet goodnight kiss, Alec demonstrated remarkable maturity and finesse that belied his young age and set him apart from his peers. And he awakened new and intriguing sensations within her. Still, she planned to let things unfold organically; the last thing she wanted to do was rush into an intimate physical relationship before she'd gotten a chance to truly know and understand his character.

When they finally pulled away, he gently placed his forehead on hers and whispered, "You are beautiful, Samantha. Don't ever forget that."

∽

The next few months were a whirlwind of romance intermingled with study and discipline as Sam and Alec naturally fell into a committed relationship and became known as an "item" around campus. Her initial anxieties forgotten, she was fully enamored with her cute yet sincere boyfriend, who treated her with respect and kissed her with an intensity and passion she'd never known before. Since their initial breakfast date, they'd gotten into the habit of studying together. These sessions greatly assisted her in absorbing the material, thanks to his remarkable intelligence and the fact that he was a few weeks ahead of her in terms of course curriculum.

Although Meredith and Brittany often teased her for "dumping" them as study buddies, they remained supportive of Sam's relationship, with Brittany regularly reminding her about her offer to let them use her apartment anytime they wanted. As her relationship with Alec progressed, Sam knew it was only a matter of time before she'd find the courage to take her up on it. One telltale night, she realized that moment was imminent.

They'd been holed up alone in her dorm room, alternating study time with musical interludes where Alec would strum his guitar and serenade her with some of her favorites. Inevitably, following his soulful rendition of John Michael Montgomery's *I Swear*, the two gave into passion and started making out on Sam's bed. Every part of her tingled as he kissed her lips and moved his hands seductively over her body. But by the time they ended up bare-chested and lying skin-to-skin with Alec placing a trail of soft, wet kisses from her neck downward as his hand gently explored her bare breast, she snapped back to reality, notwithstanding the pleasurable sensations that consumed her.

"Alec, stop, please," she whispered firmly as she extricated herself from his arms and reached for her sweatshirt.

"Honey, I'm sorry," he replied softly. "I thought you liked it. And I'm so attracted to you, I can't help myself."

"No, no, it's not that," she assured him. "I mean; yeah, I did like it. Very much. It's just that..."

"What?" He sat on the bed next to her and turned her face toward his. "Please, tell me."

She sighed. "Alec, I've never…what I mean is, I've never…" She couldn't say the words as she stared into his big, brown eyes.

"Sam, are you a virgin?" His voice was kind and understanding. She said nothing, just nodded her head and braced for the worst.

"Baby, it's ok. It's nothing to be embarrassed about." He pulled her into a hug and buried his face in her sweet-smelling hair.

"Oh, my gosh, I feel like such an idiot," she confessed. "I mean, here you are, this amazing, hot guy who can have any girl he wants – "

"Stop!" He moved back a bit to look at her directly. "Samantha, *you* are the girl I want. And not just in a sexual way. I think *you're* amazing, you know that? As soon as I saw you in the laundry room, I knew you were special. And yeah, I want to be with you, all of you, but we can go as slow as you want. I would never pressure you into doing something you're not ready to do. That's the last thing I want. Whenever we are together, I want it to be special for both of us."

"Really?" She could hardly believe what she was hearing, though it made her love him even more. Neither one of them had articulated the "L-word" yet, but by his actions tonight, she realized it was just a formality.

Alec softly wiped away her tears before touching his forehead to hers. "Really," he whispered. "I'll wait for you for as long as it takes, Samantha. I'm crazy about you."

"I'm crazy about you, too," she cooed, before their lips met again.

§

"What are you making your stud for dinner tonight?" Brittany teased as she and Sam pulled out of the base in Brittany's car, headed for Food Giant.

"Uh, I think I'm going with chicken parm. It's easy to make and it's always good."

"Ooh, mind if I join you?" she joked. "I love Italian food!"

"Maybe next time," Sam laughed.

"So, girl, is tonight the night?"

"Who are you, Rod Stewart?" she teased. But before Brittany could respond, Sam added, "I think so. I just want to see how everything plays out. Alec has been so understanding and supportive, I don't want to make him hold out much longer. And honestly, I don't want to make *me* hold out much longer, either. I just want it to be right. I won't get a second chance at my first time."

"Girl, let me give you a piece of advice, whatever it's worth," Brittany answered as she pulled the car into a parking spot in front of the grocery store. "Yes, it's your first time but it's also Alec's first time *with you*. That makes it special. Don't put all kinds of pressure on yourself about what's supposed to happen or how it all should go down. Relax and enjoy the moment. He obviously cares for you if he's been willing to go at your pace. It's not so much about technique as it is about being with someone you love. And I know you love him and he loves you. That's pretty obvious."

Sam blushed. "Thank you, Britt," she whispered as she embraced her. "You've been an amazing friend."

"Yeah well, don't forget I want details," she teased. "That and some good Italian cooking."

"It's a deal," Sam laughed. "Well, the Italian food part is, at least. Guess I got good at cooking after my mom died. Good thing or my dad would've probably fed us frozen dinners for the rest of our childhood."

After following Sam through various aisles and taking note of her purchases, Brittany dropped her off at the apartment with a final appeal to "have fun and let nature take its course." Once alone, Sam busied herself with food prep while singing along to her country music cassettes. Soon, the space was infused with the enticing aroma of seasoned tomato sauce bubbling in a pot and chicken cutlets sizzling in a frying pan of olive oil. Once the main course was in the oven, she got to work on a crisp salad of romaine lettuce, tomatoes, cucumbers, red onions, and croutons to be tossed in an Italian vinaigrette dressing just before it was time to sit down to eat.

With dinner handled, she moved into the bedroom to freshen up and change. Now that it was early March, temperatures had warmed a bit, making it possible for her to slip into a simple, short-sleeved burgundy dress. Its long skirt had a tasteful slit which showed off just a hint of leg while the scooped neckline accommodated a simple gold necklace she paired with matching gold stud earrings. After washing and moisturizing her face, she applied just a hint of rosy lip gloss and stared at her reflection in the full-length mirror.

Tonight's the night, she vowed silently. Butterflies fluttered in her stomach when she heard a knock on the door. She smoothed her dress one last time before rushing out to greet her man.

"Wow, you look gorgeous," Alec complimented before planting a kiss on her mouth.

"You look pretty handsome yourself," she chirped, taking note of his pressed, khaki pants and white, buttoned-down shirt.

"Man, what smells so good?"

"Chicken parm. I hope you like it."

"I'm sure I'm gonna love it," he enthused. "Oh, and I brought my guitar with me. Thought we could indulge in a little after-dinner music."

"Sounds perfect."

She took his hand and led him to the dinner table, where she'd carefully arranged two lit candles, a bottle of Merlot, and wine glasses.

"Look at this," he enthused. "You really went all out."

She felt her cheeks blush. "Well, I just wanted it to be special. We're finally getting to spend some time alone with no chance of someone walking in on us. How cool is that?"

"Sam," he began, sensing the nervousness in her voice. "You know; we don't have to – "

She shushed him with a passionate kiss that might've served as a prelude to their first lovemaking encounter had it not been for the obnoxious sounds of the oven timer's buzzer.

"Oops, sorry. I gotta get the chicken out of the oven. You can pour the wine for us," she suggested with a smile. As she made her way back into the kitchen, he stared at her fit body, showcased by her form-fitting, crushed velvet dress, with appreciation while he anticipated what he hoped would be a memorable evening for them both.

෨

My Love by Little Texas played in the background as Sam and Alec held each other close and moved to the music. They'd spent the evening laughing and talking about everything from humorless drill sergeants to their future dreams. While he savored every bite, Alec complimented her on her cooking, with genuine gratitude for the effort she'd put into creating a magical evening. By the time they'd finished dessert, chocolate mousse topped with real whipped cream, any previous apprehensions she'd harbored had been replaced by eager anticipation.

As promised, he had serenaded her with his own renditions of country love songs like Restless Heart's classic, *I'll Still Be Loving You* and John Berry's *Your Love Amazes Me*. It felt like a dream, one from which she never wanted to wake up. She thought back to the cold November day when she'd set out for the laundromat, never imagining it would lead to her to meet and fall in love with such a wonderful man. *Who'd have thought her boring routine would have resulted in this perfect, romantic moment?*

Now as they swayed to the music, she buried her head against his chest and closed her eyes to be fully present. She wanted to imprint every detail into her memory – the hardness of his muscles, the sexiness of his voice, the warmth of his embrace, the joy of just being together. No matter how their first time unfolded, she had no doubt it would be perfect.

And when Alec at last leaned down to draw her into a kiss, she responded with an eagerness that assured him she was indeed ready to be with him in every sense of the word. Still, he wanted to be certain.

"Sam," he whispered. "Are you sure?"

Overwhelmed with emotion, she just nodded her head. He smiled as he placed his hands on her cheeks and touched his forehead to hers. "I promise; I will make it special for you. I love you, Samantha Townsend."

"I love you too, Alec Russell."

He took her hand in his and led her to the bedroom. With the music providing a soulful backdrop, he fulfilled his promise exquisitely. Alec displayed a noticeable maturity, as if his wild escapades in high school had provided a foundation of knowledge for how to make love to a woman – not just have sex for its own sake. Far from the stereotype of a teenage guy ruled by hormones and a sole focus of "getting off," he'd grown to appreciate the art of lovemaking, thanks in part to his deep, abiding love for Sam. He could hardly believe he'd found the woman he wanted to be with for the rest of his life. Though he'd fantasized about how good it would feel to fully experience her, tonight his main priority was her comfort and pleasure. There was so much he wanted to teach her, but for now, it was all about making her feel cherished. They had plenty of time to grow as lovers.

He stood behind her in the darkness, moved her silky hair to one side, and seductively kissed her neck. She felt goosebumps from head to toe as his touch ignited her passions. His hands moved over the fabric of her dress, reveling in the contours of her body until he couldn't contain the desire to feel her soft, bare skin. Slowly, he unzipped it and slid it down until it pooled around her feet. Far from being fearful, she sighed as he placed soft wet kisses on her exposed shoulders, savoring the warmth of his touch and longing for him to undress her completely.

At last she stood before him in the moonlight, completely vulnerable, as his eyes feasted on the sight of her breathtaking, naked form. She smiled as she began to unbutton his shirt and release his broad, muscular chest from the constraints of fabric. Placing her hands on his rock-hard torso, she felt the heat emanating from his body and moved onto the business of unfastening his belt. Alec groaned as she freed him from the rest of his clothing. Then he pulled her close to him as his mouth came down on hers, probing her with his tongue as desire consumed them. Finally, he scooped her up in his arms and carried her to the bed, where he tenderly made love to her until the early morning sun filtered through the blinds.

∽

"Dad!" Sam threw her arms around Walter Townsend as he stepped out the car. He'd taken a road trip down to Biloxi from Morristown to deliver her teal, two-door Mitzubishi Eclipse and meet the young man who'd captured his daughter's heart. Brittany had dropped her off in the parking lot of the Holiday Inn, where Walter and his new lady friend would be staying for the duration of their visit.

"Sam, it is so good to see you!" he enthused, pulling her into a bear hug. "Home just isn't the same without you."

"Is Shannon making you crazy?" she teased.

"Let's just say she could benefit from the presence of her older, much more responsible sister," he laughed. "But I can see military life is treating you well…or should I say your new boyfriend. You sure look happy."

She blushed as she smiled, filling his heart with joy.

"And where is this handsome airman?" he queried.

"Oh, ah, he had some stuff to do on base," she explained sheepishly. Truth be told, Alec was back on work duty for challenging one of his instructors.

"I see," Walter replied with a raised eyebrow. But before the conversation could go any further, a slightly frumpy woman who appeared to be in her mid-fifties walked over and stood next to him. Walter placed his hand on her back in acknowledgment.

"Sam, this is Patricia."

"Very nice to meet you," Sam said, offering a handshake and a smile. "My dad has told me a lot about you. Thanks for making the trip with him."

"My pleasure," she replied politely. Although pleasant enough, she seemed a bit aloof, which Sam attributed to fatigue after spending 24 hours on the road. Even with an overnight stopover in North Carolina, such a long distance was enough to wear out a driver half her age. And considering she'd spent the entire time in a cramped, old sports car, Patricia had every right to be grumpy. Sam just hoped it signified that her father had finally found decent female companionship; he'd been alone for way too long.

"Your sister tells me you've gotten over your fear of motorcycles," Walter announced. "I hope Alec is careful."

"Oh, don't worry Dad. He is. And he always makes me wear a helmet."

"Good."

While her father seemed to enjoy hearing about her adventures, Sam got a distinctly different vibe from his girlfriend. Maybe she was just being paranoid, but she sensed the woman's coldness stemmed from more than just road fatigue; she could almost feel the disapproval in her body language and facial expressions. Not that it mattered. Sam was an adult who could make her own decisions. Even if her own mother were here, exhibiting the same kind of behavior, it wouldn't change her love and devotion to Alec. Not Patricia, nor any other woman her father might date in the foreseeable future had the right to cast judgment on her choices.

After joining them in the lobby to chat for a bit, Sam left them alone to rest and rejuvenate before heading out to dinner. She felt pure exhilaration as she slipped in behind the wheel of her Eclipse; it seemed like an eternity since she'd experienced the freedom of the open road in her own vehicle. Even better, now she and Alec would have a back-up for those occasions when the weather or their own preference demanded four wheels and a roof. They'd spoken often about taking a weekend drive to New Orleans, a place Sam had never visited, once she had her car again. She was excited by the thought of spending time alone with her man in the Crescent City, taking in the sights, listening to jazz music, strolling around the French Quarter, and making love in their own hotel room. Each week, she'd been careful to put away as much money as she could toward that goal.

A few hours later, Sam arrived back at the Holiday Inn, where Walter and Patricia were waiting out front, looking refreshed. Their destination, McElroy's Harbor House Seafood Restaurant, a Biloxi landmark on the Gulf, had been highly recommended by Brittany and Meredith for its Southern charm and succulent seafood. Sam hoped it would be the perfect backdrop for giving them an authentic experience of the town, but more importantly, for getting to know Alec, whose plan was to meet up with them once he was free.

The hostess led Sam, Walter, and Patricia to a waterside table. As she took in its authentic, relaxed atmosphere, Sam understood why the girls had recommended the place, which sat high up on stilts and featured indoor-outdoor dining and water views that made you feel as if you were on vacation. Yet it was conveniently located just a few miles from base. Her mind wandered for a moment as she envisioned a romantic date here with Alec, sipping tropical drinks and listening to live music while the balmy breezes rustled their hair and the setting sun streaked the sky with gold and orange hues.

But for tonight, she hoped its rustic appeal would facilitate a pleasant interaction between the two men she cared for most in the world. Just as they ordered their initial round of drinks – Sam careful to request a regular iced tea with lemon – they heard the loud, *vroom* of a motorcycle engine below. Her heart raced in her chest, recognizing the familiar noise. Looking at Patricia's horrified face, she stifled a giggle while Walter's eyes sparkled with curiosity. A moment later, Alec approached their table, looking every bit the all-American guy in his pressed khaki pants and red golf shirt. He bent down to plant a kiss on Sam's cheek before addressing her father.

"Hi, you must be Walter," he greeted him with an outstretched hand. Although a little surprised by his casual use of his first name, Sam's father shook the younger man's hand with gusto and offered a bright smile.

"So, you're the man who's made my daughter so happy. Pleased to meet you."

Patricia looked on in disapproval, convinced that this cocky teenager had nothing but trouble to offer. When it was her turn for an introduction, she gave him a limp handshake and a barely upturned smile. However, when Alec brazenly ordered a beer in response to the waitress's question, she could no longer hold her tongue.

"Young man, aren't you underage?" she demanded. Sam kept her eyes focused downward on her plate as she spread some soft butter on a warm, Southern biscuit. Walter cracked up.

"Oh Patricia, leave him alone; he's with us. In Mississippi, it's ok for a kid who's at least eighteen to drink in the presence of a parent or guardian."

"Wow, Dad, you've done your homework," she noted, clearly impressed.

"Well you know me, sweetheart. I made sure I knew everything about the area once I knew you were being stationed here." He grinned at her, obviously pleased with himself.

Unmoved, Patricia took a sip of her Arnold Palmer and continued to peruse the menu. In a show of solidarity, Walter advised their server, "You know, I think I'll join Alec in a beer here too. Whatever you have on draft is fine."

Sam looked on with elation and relief as Alec responded to her father's gesture with a high-five. From that moment on, he and Walter forged an easy friendship. They spent the rest of the evening discussing life in the Air Force, Walter's Army service in Vietnam, and Alec's aspirations. What she remained unaware of as the evening progressed, however, was that despite the lighthearted conversation, her dad never once entertained the idea of her and Alec as a long-term, committed relationship.

"I can't believe we got assigned on opposite coasts," Sam wailed to her sister. "Why? With all the bases all over the country, why do we have to be so far away from each other?"

"I know, that sucks," Shannon sympathized as she sat beside her on the canopy bed in Sam's childhood room. It was early June and she'd just arrived back in Morristown for her two-week leave before the Air Force was shipping her off to the Seymour Johnson Base in Goldsboro North Carolina. When she and Alec received the news that he'd be sent off to Travis Air Force Base in San Jose, California, they were devastated. After spending just about every waking moment together since their fateful meeting in the laundry room almost a year before, it was hard to imagine living and working so far apart.

Could their relationship survive the distance?

Shannon proceeded to pull out a cigarette and lighter from her denim short-shorts but Sam grabbed her arm before she could go any further.

"You know that stuff'll kill you right?"

"Ack! You sound just like Dad."

"Well, it's possible he can be right about something, you know."

"C'mon Sam, don't lecture me! We've been apart for almost a year. Can't we just have fun before you have to leave again?"

"Dad doesn't like smoking in the house," Sam insisted.

"Well then, I guess it's a good thing he's at the studio," Shannon retorted. In a characteristic move of bold defiance, she lit up the cigarette and inhaled deeply.

"Fine. It's your life," Sam shrugged. "But if he comes in here and smells smoke, I'm not defending you."

"Fine."

Before their argument could escalate any further, Sam's cell phone rang.

"Hello?"

"Hey, beautiful!"

"Alec," she exclaimed. "What's going on? I thought you were working with your dad today?"

"I was, until I talked him into letting me drive up to Morristown to see you. I thought we could spend a couple of days together before they send us to opposite sides of the country. He gets it. He and my mom were high school sweethearts, remember? Do you think Walter will mind?"

Sam glanced at Shannon, who was glaring at her for answers.

"Uh, well I don't know. I mean, I don't think he'll mind, but I do have to ask him. He's at work right now. Can you give me a few minutes and I'll call you back?"

"Sure, but either way, I'm coming. I need to see you. I don't care what it takes. I miss you so much."

"I miss you, too," she sighed as Shannon rolled her eyes.

"What?"

"Uh, Sam, do you really think our father is going to let Alec drive up and *sleep* here? You're dreaming."

"Well, why not? He *is* my boyfriend. We've been together for over nine months now − "

"Nine months – ha! Thank God, you're not pregnant. Patricia would have a cow." Shannon burst out laughing.

"You don't think I'm smart enough to prevent that? Besides, even if it did happen, Patricia's not our mother."

"Wow, you really have been away too long. Don't get me wrong; I'm glad dad has someone in his life. It's just that she's a stick-in-the-mud. The lady never smiles or laughs, she always has this stupid scowl on her face. I mean, I can't even picture her having sex – "

"Shannon!"

"Well, it's *true*. And she's dragging dad down with her. He used to be more fun. I bet if not for her, he'd let me drive the Stingray."

Sam raised an eyebrow in disbelief.

"Well, I might stand a better chance if not for her," she insisted. "Besides, if I were you, I wouldn't be defending her right now. The other night, I overheard her and Dad talking. She was telling him how she thought it was a good thing you and Alec were being stationed so far apart."

"Seriously? Why didn't you say something sooner?"

"I just figured I'd wait until you got home. And you were already bawling on the phone about it anyway. I didn't want to make it worse."

"What else did she say?"

"That you and Alec were too young. It wasn't going to last once you were separated and she thought it was good that the Air Force did that. You know, she doesn't think much of him. Told Dad he's a player, a bad-boy who thinks his shit don't stink."

"Shannon."

"Fine, she didn't say it like that, but that's what she meant, Sam. Guess she's not impressed that he can play and sing country music, or that he's had how many speeding tickets so far? I lost count."

"Well, I knew from the start she didn't like him. You should have been there when he ordered a beer at the restaurant in Biloxi. But you know what? Who cares? She doesn't get a say in who I date...and really, neither does Dad."

Shannon burst out laughing. "Says *Little Miss Goody Two Shoes.*"

"You don't think I can stand up to Dad? Just watch me." With that, Sam dialed his work number on her cell.

"Hey, hon! Enjoying your time back? Sorry I had to leave so early this morning," Walter greeted her.

"It's OK, Dad, I know this is your busy season. I just called to ask you a favor."

"Ask away." Sam felt her stomach twisting in knots, but she put on a brave face for Shannon's sake. She didn't want her to know how terrified she was of making the request – especially knowing that Alec was most likely in transit as she spoke.

"Alec wants to visit for a few days. He wants to drive up from Manchester."

There was an uncomfortable silence on the other end of the phone. Shannon shot her an *I told you so* look.

"Really," Walter finally replied in a flat voice. "And where does he plan on staying. With us?"

"Dad, please. We're not going to see each other at all once we head out to our assigned bases. We just want to spend a little time together before that happens," she pleaded.

Walter took her words into consideration as he contemplated the numerous conversations he'd had about the matter with Patricia. The more he thought about it, the more he realized it was a harmless request. Soon enough, the Air Force would put 3,000 miles between them, Alec would get bored with a long-distance relationship and hook up with someone else, and Walter would be there to heal his daughter's broken heart. Then, when she was old enough to handle it, she'd marry a more respectable guy. Someone responsible. Someone who would make a great father.

"Ok, Samantha, as you wish. But he's sleeping in the guest room. My house, my rules. Got it?"

"Yes, yes, I understand. Oh, thank you, Dad," she squealed with delight. She couldn't wait to feel Alec's arms around her again.

৽

"Alec, please," she whispered. "Shannon could walk in at any minute." They'd been making out on the couch in the family room while the daytime soap *Days of Our Lives* played on the television screen. Inevitably, one touch and kiss had led to another and ignited their sexual chemistry. While Sam fought to maintain control, an emboldened Alec begged her to go upstairs to her old bedroom, where they could once again enjoy each other's company in every way. Whether driving too fast, challenging authority, or breaking the rules, he relished the adrenalin rush that came from living on the edge.

But as much as she was tempted, Sam's respect for her dad won out over pent-up passion. After he'd given in and allowed Alec to visit, there was no way she'd break her promise. It just wouldn't be right, especially since Walter was out of the house all day shooting the Lamoille County Annual Summer Horse Show. And although Shannon was with her friends, most likely raising hell in her own inimitable way, there was no telling when she'd saunter through the front door.

"Are you sure, *Fancy Face*?" he teased. "I really doubt your little sister would care or even tell Walter if she caught us. And he's gonna be gone all day taking pictures at the horse show. He told us last night."

Alec caressed her back and stroked her hair as he planted kisses down her neck.

"Yeah, well, I promised we wouldn't," she replied, ignoring the pleasurable sensations that pulsated throughout her body. "And I already feel bad enough for skipping out on the horse show. I used to help him with that every year."

"But he has Patricia now," Alec reasoned. "And hey, we consummated things between us a long time ago, so what does it matter? You kinda broke that promise already, if you know what I mean." He winked at her.

"Well that was at Brittany's apartment, on-base, or in a hotel room in New Orleans, not my father's house," she countered. "Please, I don't want to disrespect him. He's a good man. And this is *his* house, *his* rules. Please, honey, try to understand." She looked at him with her big, blue eyes and there was nothing more he could say or do.

"Oh, ok, I get it," he acquiesced. He settled back against the cushion and let out a deep sigh, still holding an arm around her. Then he pointed to the screen. "That's us, you know. We're Bo and Hope…even down to the visit to New Orleans. They did that back in the 80s, we did it in the 90s."

"You're my handsome Beauregard," she drawled in her best *Deep South* accent, cracking them both up.

In the next moment, Alec's mood turned serious. "I'm going to miss you so much," he lamented, pulling her close. "I love you, Sam."

"I love you, too," she whispered as she buried her head in his chest.

Then it happened: the front door's violent slam was followed by loud footsteps, angry yelling, and Shannon's unmistakable sobs.

"Oh, my God!" In an instant, Sam sprang from the couch, adjusted the buttons on her cotton shirt, and smoothed her white shorts. "Something's going on. My little sister must've gotten herself into another mess." Alec followed close behind as they moved in the direction of the kitchen.

"I told you; you were never to drive the Stingray! Do you have any idea how much that thing cost?" they heard Walter scream uncharacteristically. "You're too irresponsible to be trusted with something so valuable. And look what you did – the whole bumper is ruined and God only knows what else. I didn't even want them towing it to shop because I'm sure I can't even afford the parts to fix whatever is wrong with it, thanks to you!"

"I-I'm so sorry," they heard her blubbering.

Sam and Alec entered the kitchen to the sight of Shannon seated at the table with her head in her hands and Walter pacing back and forth in front of the refrigerator. His usual jovial expression was replaced by a combination of frustration and rage.

"What's going on?" Sam asked superfluously.

"Your sister thinks she can just disobey me without consequences," he began. "She knew I didn't want her driving the Corvette, but at the first opportunity, she went behind my back. She knew I'd be gone all day and night at the horse show, so she figured she take my car to go joyriding with that irresponsible Derek. Now, it's all dented up. It's probably going to cost a fortune to fix it and the worst part is, I had to leave Patricia alone after the cops called me. Now she's working by herself until I can get back there."

"You got into an accident?" Sam approached her sister and placed a hand on her quivering shoulder. "Are you alright? Was anybody hurt?" Shannon shook her head.

"Well thank God for that," she noted, looking directly into her father's eyes. That seemed to soften him up a little. Although the thought remained unspoken, they both reflected upon the auto accident from years before; the one that had altered their lives forever. For a moment, the entire room was silent.

"Where is the car?" Sam finally asked.

"In the driveway. I had the tow truck follow us home."

"Uh, Walter, do you mind if I take a look? I'm a pretty good mechanic," Alec explained. "I mean, I don't do body work, but I can make sure the rest of it is OK."

"Sure, go head." He tossed him the keys.

While her boyfriend tended to the vehicle, Sam did her best to reconcile the tension between her father and sister. She discovered that a resourceful Shannon had planned to take the car once her father had left for the horse show at the crack of dawn. She'd deduced he'd never be the wiser, provided she returned his prized possession to the garage before sundown. What she hadn't planned on was getting into a minor accident as she and her boyfriend sped through Morristown's scenic country roads with the radio blasting. Not surprisingly, Derek had left her all alone to deal with the fallout.

It was a difficult line to straddle, especially since Sam understood both points of view. Walter's rules were clear on the matter; Shannon had brazenly disobeyed. On the other hand, she recognized that her younger sister was crying out for attention. Shannon had been somewhat of a lost soul ever since their mother had been killed, and Sam suspected that at least some of her father's anger stemmed from his fear of losing another loved one.

For a while, they sat in silence until the creak of the screen door alerted them to Alec's return.

"Hey, Mr. Townsend," he began, sensing a need for formality, "I think the car is fine. It needs some body work, obviously, but it's running well. I just drove it around the block."

"Thank you, son."

"Oh and Mr. Townsend? I know it's none of my business, but I kinda understand Shannon. I mean, God knows, my parents put up with all kinds of hell-raising from me. When I told them I was joining the Air Force, I think it was probably the happiest day of their lives…well, next to their wedding, anyway. I'm just sayin', don't be too hard on her. If I had a car like that in my parents' garage, I'm sure I would have wrecked it a long time ago."

Sam looked on in trepidation as Alec gave his speech, still holding a comforting arm around Shannon. By now, her sobs had subsided, leaving smudges of black mascara under her eyes as evidence of her teenaged angst. To Sam's surprise, Walter listened with intention as her boyfriend attempted to broker peace. She cried tears of joy when Alec's efforts were finally rewarded with her father and sister standing up to embrace each other tightly.

This guy's a keeper, she smiled to herself.

ॐ

"What do you mean, you're flying to California for Labor Day weekend?" Walter demanded in an angry tone. "Your cousin is getting married, Samantha."

"Dad, I hardly even know her. We never spent much time together as kids," she explained. Although her heart was racing, her mind was made up. She and Alec had been running up $200 cell phone bills every month in a constant effort to nurture their bicoastal relationship. Still, she had somehow managed to save enough money to buy herself a plane ticket to California and was determined that no one was going to interfere with her plans. If that meant living with her father's disapproval, so be it.

"Dad, I've made up my mind. There's nothing you can say."

"Fine. I don't like the idea of you skipping out of a family event, but you're an adult. You can make your own decisions."

"Thanks Dad. I love you."

"I love you, too. And Sam?"

"Yes."

"Please don't make any life-changing decisions while you're there. You and Alec are still young. If you're meant to be together, it will happen."

She pondered his words for a moment, but didn't dare verbalize her suspicions that Alec might propose to her on this trip since the only way to get stationed together in the military was to get married. Because it usually took an entire year to process the paperwork, he'd be driven by a sense of urgency.

"OK, Dad, I promise," she finally said before hanging up.

A month later, she sprinted through the gate at Sacramento International Airport, too excited to see her beloved to care about jetlag or lack of sleep the night before her arrival. As soon as she caught sight of her handsome airman, she dropped her backpack onto the floor and flung herself into his arms.

"You're finally here Fancy Face," he whispered in her ear as he held her athletic body tightly against his and breathed in the scent of her hair. How he'd missed that – her smell, her touch, her warmth, and the way she looked at him whenever he strummed her a song on his guitar. Phone calls were fine, but they just couldn't compare to the real thing.

"I've missed you so much," she sighed, before they melted into a passionate kiss right there in front of a bunch of strangers.

"C'mon, let's get your stuff and get you settled in," he said after they both came up for air. He grabbed her backpack, took her hand, and led her to the baggage area.

Several minutes later, she followed him through the parking lot to a black Toyota truck. "Is this on loan from a friend?"

"No, I didn't tell you but I sold my motorcycle. As much as I love it, it's just not practical right now."

"Alec Russell, are you growing up?" she teased.

"God, I hope not," he laughed.

A few hours later, they were back in his dorm room, picking right up where they'd left off. "How long has it been?" he whispered hoarsely as he ran his hands over her shoulders and tugged at the sleeves of her simple, cotton sundress until it fell to the floor. Her entire body ached in anticipation, but before she could answer, he lifted her in his arms and laid her down on the bed in one smooth move. The rest of the world faded away in a symphony of stimulating touch, decadent kisses, and indescribable ecstasy. Sam cried out in ecstasy as her entire body convulsed in reaction to his artful lovemaking. When both were spent, they settled back down into the pillows and lingered in the waning sunlight filtering through the window.

Over the long weekend, the couple took in the area's most celebrated sights, including the breathtaking redwood trees, and even attended an Oakland Raiders game against the San Diego Chargers, courtesy of an Air Force buddy of Alec's whose family had season tickets. If his intention had been to keep her guessing, he was doing an excellent job. She couldn't shake the feeling a proposal was imminent but as each day passed without one, she began to wonder if that inner voice was trustworthy.

And after an especially passionate lovemaking interlude on Labor Day afternoon, Sam had decided to release all expectations and savor whatever time they had left. Soon enough, he'd drive her to the airport and she'd board a plane bound for Charlotte, where she'd hop into her car and head back to her own base.

As they held each other in his bed, she would've been happy to stay wrapped in his arms all night, but Alec had other ideas.

"C'mon Sam, we have to get dressed," he urged.

"Where are we going? I need a shower first," she insisted.

"Ok, ok, but hurry. We have reservations tonight. We're going out for a nice dinner."

"Ooh, that sounds wonderful."

"Well then, let's go," he laughed as he pulled her out of bed.

Once showered, she pulled on a special dress for the occasion, one she'd saved up to buy ever since spotting it in the window at Belk's Department Store. Made of crushed velvet in a deep shade of rose, it came down in a tasteful décolletage that displayed just a hint of cleavage. She slipped into a pair of wedge sandals, added a simple gold necklace and earrings, and smoothed her hair until it hung down her back in a shiny cascade.

"You look beautiful," he complimented when she walked back into the room.

"You look pretty handsome yourself," she replied as she took in the sight of him in a crisp, buttoned down shirt and nice jeans.

Moments later, they cruised down Pacific Coast Highway, where Sam gazed out in wonder at the sight of the rocky cliffs and majestic ocean.

"Alec, this place is incredible. Almost makes the distance worth dealing with."

"It is pretty spectacular but I wouldn't go that far," he laughed. Then he pulled the truck into the parking lot of a quaint little restaurant overlooking Half Moon Bay.

"This is stunning," she gasped as they settled into a romantic table for two.

"Nothing but the best for my girl," he replied with a wink. Notwithstanding her earlier resolution, Sam's intuition kept telling her a proposal was on its way this evening. It just *had* to be. Still, she ignored the butterflies in her stomach and did her best to focus on being present in the moment. Here she was, not yet 20 years old, dining in an upscale restaurant in one of the country's most renowned destinations. She had to pinch herself to make sure it was real.

After a delicious seafood dinner, she and Alec strolled arm-in-arm along the water, under an endless sky dotted with luminous stars and a bright, full moon. The next thing she knew, he was down on one knee.

Oh, my God. I was right, she thought as her heart thumped in her chest.

Alec looked up at her with his big, dark eyes. "Samantha Townsend, will you marry me?"

With that, he pulled out an old, worn gold band with a tiny, *barely-there* diamond. She stared at it for a moment before meeting his gaze again.

"Oh Alec, of course I'll marry you," she gushed.

"Sam, I know this ring is old. It's my mom's. When I told her I was going to ask you to marry me, she shipped it out to me so I could give it to you. Back when my dad proposed to my mom, this was all he could afford. And I know you deserve better, and you will have better. Someday when I can afford it, I'll – "

"It's perfect, I love it," she enthused.

It filled her with sheer joy that his mother had thought enough of her to go to the trouble of mailing such a significant treasure to her son. Maybe it wasn't worth much by jewelers' standards, but Sam knew how important it was to Beth, a woman with whom she'd only had limited phone interaction but already loved. This sweet gesture proved that his parents loved her because their son did, and their acceptance of Alec and Sam's romance countered the resistance she often experienced from her own family.

He stood up and slipped the vintage ring on her finger. Then he tilted her head up for an intoxicating kiss to seal the deal while the moonlight danced on the water. Later, on the car ride home, a hyperactive Sam raved on in staccato breaths about planning her wedding with Shannon, picking out the perfect gown, and involving her dad in selecting the right venue, based on his years of experience as the county's most sought after photographer for milestone events.

"Oh, my God, I *cannot* wait to tell them!" she exclaimed.

"Uh, Sam," he finally spoke up, "I think we should get married tomorrow. The court house is open. Let's get married for the paperwork and have our real wedding later. If you're comfortable with that?"

"Absolutely," she answered without hesitation.

"Are you sure? You seemed pretty excited just now about planning a fancy wedding, Fancy Face," he replied skeptically.

"Yes, it's *fine* with me, babe," she soothed. "I mean, yeah, every girl dreams of her fairytale wedding. That's normal. I guess for me, especially after losing my mom, I always thought I'd wear her gown when I walked down the aisle with my dad. But things change. When I enlisted, I never imagined I was going to meet you and fall in love. I figured I'd survive basic training, put in my four years with the Air Force, find a good civilian job and then bump into Mr. Right. All of this still feels like a dream – you and me together – and as long as we're together and in love, I don't care what kind of ceremony we have. It doesn't matter. I just want to be your wife. Besides, I don't want to put my dad or your parents through the expense of a formal wedding and all the stuff that goes with it."

Alec pondered her words as he pulled the truck into a parking space in front of his dorm building. Taking her hands in his, he turned to look at her. "You're sure you won't be mad at me later, like five years from now when we're hanging out with other married friends and one of them decides to show you her wedding pictures with a gazillion bridesmaids and a flower girl? How are you going to feel then?"

Sam leaned in close and whispered. "Alec Russell, I cannot believe the guy who lives for the moment, drives too fast and breaks every rule he doesn't like is sitting here worrying about some mythical future scenario."

"Sam, I'm serious," he protested.

"Well, I am too," she countered. "What's important to me is being your wife and living with you on base as soon as possible. I love you, Alec. And I don't want to spend any more time apart than necessary. The sooner we get married, the sooner we can be together. And the more often we can do things like this."

With that, she pulled his body close to hers and pressed her soft lips to his. Their passion reignited, he felt the familiar urge to make love to her as if tomorrow would never come; the thought of sleeping with her every night in their marital bed removed all traces of doubt about her sincerity regarding the method by which they would legally become husband and wife.

"So, have I convinced you?" she asked sweetly when they finally pulled away.

Gazing longingly into her eyes, he spoke in a hoarse whisper. "Yes, ma'am." He touched his forehead to hers and ran his fingers through her soft hair.

"Uh, I do have one question though," she continued. "Don't we have to make an appointment? I mean, can we have a civil ceremony at the court house on such short notice?"

"Yeah, I looked into it and they have this Express Marriage Ceremony thing. As long as we get there between 10:30 in the morning and 3:30 in the afternoon, they take walk-ins. We just have to buy a marriage license first."

"How much does that cost?"

"Oh, don't worry about that, Fancy Face. I've got it covered. Been thinking about this for a long time. Sam shivered with excitement. "So, it's a deal?" he asked.

She sighed. "Yes, on one condition. Let's just let everyone believe we're engaged for now. We have plenty of time before the Air Force relocates us to the same base and I don't want to hurt anyone. We can figure out later how to tell them we're married."

"OK by me," he agreed, moving in for another kiss. Before he could taste her mouth again, she interrupted with another question, spurred on by a sudden thought.

"What should we wear tomorrow? I'm not sure I have anything appropriate for a marriage ceremony and since I already spilled wine on this dress, I can't —"

"Jeans and tee shirts. Let's just wear jeans and tee-shirts."

She nodded in agreement, knowing that no choice of attire could possibly impact the significance of their union.

"Now please, let me take you inside and give you a preview of what our nights will be like as a married couple." She giggled as he opened the driver's side door, placed his arm securely around her waist, and scooped her out of the truck and into the balmy night air.

✎

Santa Clara County Court House greeted them the next morning with stately columns and ornamental arches surrounding long, rectangular windows. Holding her hand firmly in Alec's, Sam felt a surge of nervous energy as they ascended the impressive stairs.

Fittingly, the court house reminded her a bit of New Orleans, further supporting their relationship's star-crossed Bo and Hope soap opera narrative. In her heart, she felt calm and at peace with her decision, though her serenity was tempered with a twinge of guilt. *Would her dad understand and forgive her when the time came? Would Shannon ever speak to her again?*

Sam pushed such disconcerting thoughts away and forced herself to concentrate on what was about to transpire, just as Alec opened the ornately carved wooden door for her. As she proceeded through the grand entrance, she was struck by the formal ambiance of the place and regretted showing up in matching white tee shirts and blue jeans. But she smiled at her soon-to-be husband as he extended his arm and led her in the direction of the service window, bringing her full attention back to their reason for being there.

Oddly enough, despite the fact it was the day after a federal holiday, there were fewer people in line than they'd anticipated; within minutes, it was their turn to purchase a marriage license.

"That'll be seventy dollars," the female clerk announced.

"Yes, ma'am," Alec replied. He opened his wallet and pulled out four twenty-dollar bills. "Do you have change?" She nodded her head before sliding a ten beneath the opening in the glass.

"This must be your lucky day," she commented.

"Excuse me, ma'am?"

"Normally, when couples don't have an appointment and want to get married right away, they have to do the Express Marriage Ceremony right here at the window. And that costs a hundred dollars. But since we're not that busy, I can get you a private ceremony for eighty. That is, if you have a witness."

Sam's heart sank. *How could they have forgotten about that crucial aspect of a wedding ceremony?* She and Alec exchanged worried glances.

"Uh, ma'am, we don't have a witness," he finally admitted.

"Oh, that's no problem. For an additional ten dollars, we can provide one." Alec returned the bill he'd just taken from her with a chuckle. "Guess I won't be needing this after all," he noted. Then he retrieved a crisp Benjamin from his wallet and slid it under the glass window. "Now I can take back one of those twenties I just gave you," he joked. The clerk smiled and, after completing the necessary paperwork, directed them down the long hallway, where they met up with another county employee who escorted them to the marriage ceremony room.

Unsure of what she'd find, Sam tentatively walked through the doors and breathed a sigh of relief as she looked around. Far from being stark and clinical, the space had a high tray ceiling and shiny hardwood floors. An assortment of plain, but comfortably cushioned cream-colored chairs formed a makeshift aisle in an angled grouping. Ahead of them stood a decorated archway with two connected columns on either side and a no-frills podium in the middle. In between the columns that flanked the podium, two larger arrangements of pink, white, and red artificial roses complemented their counterparts intertwined the archway.

"At least there are flowers, even if they aren't real," she whispered in Alec's ear as they sat down.

"Nothing but the best for my girl," he teased, taking her hand in his and squeezing it tightly.

A few minutes later, a kindly older gentleman with snow white hair, dressed in a long, black robe walked through the door to the right of the podium. Painted the same neutral color as the walls, the door had been camouflaged so well that Sam was noticeably startled when she saw it move, prompting Alec to laugh out loud. She elbowed him sharply as they stood up and regained their composure, making their best effort to demonstrate the maturity befitting the occasion.

"Hello, I'm Judge Ralph Andrews. You must be Samantha Townsend and Alec Russell." He extended his hand to each of them, then engaged in brief, polite conversation while they awaited the court-appointed witness. Within minutes, another clerk appeared.

With all the necessary elements accounted for, Judge Andrews took his place behind the podium and invited them to come forward before starting the brief ceremony. The elated couple beamed at each other as they held hands and followed his instructions. When Sam murmured, "I do," she felt a shift take place on the inside, as if the utterance of those two simple words had somehow transformed her from innocent girl to worldly woman – even though she'd given herself fully to Alec almost a year earlier. Still, with the official commitment made, everything seemed new, different, and even more exhilarating. With one sweet kiss, the deal was sealed; somehow, she'd live with this secret until the time was right to break the news to her family. Afterward, Judge Andrews indulged their request to take their photo holding their marriage license.

The next day, the young couple eagerly filed the appropriate paperwork with the United States Air Force to get the ball rolling on their relocation to the same base. Thinking that bureaucracy had its advantages, Sam was grateful to have plenty of time to rehearse the right words to let her family down gently. Once she announced her engagement, she knew they'd insist on a formal wedding – Walter's anticipated displeasure aside – and she needed the next several months to come up with a plan. For now, she could gush to them about her engagement and no one would be the wiser.

Chapter Two

"What about this one?" Shannon asked brightly as she held up yet another lace-and-sequined concoction. Her shimmery blue nail polish created a stark contrast against the pure white fabric. An exhausted Sam stared at her little sister with a combination of admiration and exasperation. Shannon's enthusiasm hadn't dissipated from the moment they left the Days Inn in Goldsboro in Sam's Mitzubishi, bound for Raleigh at eight o'clock that morning. After several hours spent wandering in and out of just about every bridal boutique in the metro area, where she'd found fault with every gown she'd tried on, Sam was nearly out of patience. Between the overeager saleswomen, uptight brides-to-be, and her own guilt, she was starting to wonder if she and Alec should just come clean.

Why put themselves through the aggravation of this expensive charade when they'd already committed to their love for each other forever? It wasn't fair to them, and it sure as hell wasn't fair to their parents.

It had been hard enough at Christmastime to feign excitement when Walter surprised them with a plane ticket and hotel reservation for Shannon so they could engage in the ritual of searching for the perfect gown together. Bless his heart, he was making a genuine effort after the initial shock and anger at their engagement had worn off. Upon returning to Seymour Johnson a secretly married woman, Sam had summoned the courage to pick up the phone and tell her father about her engagement. Fully prepared for his reaction, she'd listened patiently as he rattled off a laundry list of reasons why Alec would break her heart – all predicated on fatherly instincts and concern – ranging from their young ages to the future groom's *bad boy* tendencies.

In truth, she couldn't deny her father's accurate characterization, but she trusted in the fact that Alec was the one who proposed. If he wanted to be a playboy his entire life, why would he get married now? Besides, he was the product of two people who'd met when they were just slightly younger than Alec and Sam, and married right out of high school. They'd already weathered imminent financial ruin, the rebuilding of a business, and their own son's well-documented high school rebellion. Surely with such a strong example of love and devotion, Alec was ready for a long-term commitment.

During the conversation, when Walter had inquired about a timeframe for their impending nuptials, Sam had given a vague, noncommittal answer in the hope of delaying the inevitable. Of course, she knew she had two options: either be honest and risk the fallout, or keep up the charade and find a way to live with the remorse of lying. Then Walter gave her the shock of her life on Christmas morning – a clear indication that she had no choice but to keep up the pretense.

"Dad, we haven't even set a date yet," she'd protested meekly as she watched Shannon practically knock him over in her zeal to express her gratitude with a big hug.

"I know. I just thought it would be fun for you two to spend a weekend together. This family finally has something to celebrate," he added. Walter's eyes glistened with tears. "Without your mother here, it's bittersweet, but I want you two to enjoy yourselves and do all the girly stuff that goes along with a wedding. Stuff your boring old dad wouldn't understand."

"Sam, it's gonna be a blast," Shannon squealed, embracing her. Sam stared up at her father as she wrapped her arms around her sister. How could she possibly say no?

"Earth to Samantha!" Shannon's voice penetrated her eardrum, forcing a return to the present moment.

"What? Oh, I'm sorry Shannon." She blinked her eyes, wishing the gesture could somehow transport her out of the busy bridal outlet and back to the comforting confines of her dorm room.

"What is wrong with you?"

"Huh? Nothing, I'm just a little tired."

"Well, what do you think of the gown?"

"It's…nice." She shrugged her shoulders.

"Geez," Shannon rolled he eyes and sighed. "What is with you? Do you even want to get married? Because you're sure not acting like a bride-to-be."

"I-I'm sorry," Sam stammered. "I guess I'm just not feeling it today."

"What? Dad paid for me to come down here and gave us his credit card to buy your dress and you're not into it? It doesn't make any sense."

"Maybe I'm just sick of being around Bridezillas and pushy salespeople. Did you ever think of that?" Sam snapped.

Shannon's face lit up. Sam could almost hear the wheels turning in her platinum blonde head as she stared at her heavy eye makeup application and sexy school girl ensemble, complete with heavy black tights, tight red sweater, and tartan mini-skirt. As predicted, Shannon had been garnering judgmental looks from mothers, grandmothers, and boutique owners all day, but none of their clucks of disapproval had fazed her in the least.

Shannon returned the dress to the rack. "Oh…my…God. That's it!" she deduced. Sam braced herself for what was coming next.

"What are you talking about?" Her nerves were on edge as Shannon's penetrating blue eyes gave her the once-over.

"You barely ate breakfast or lunch. You hate just about every gown you try on, if you even bother to do that. You don't act like you're excited about getting married even though the guy is hot and totally into you. You're pregnant, aren't you?"

"What?"

"Well, it's the only thing that makes any sense."

"Lower your voice," Sam ordered. She took her by the arm and led her to a quiet corner toward the back of the retail outlet. "No, Shannon, I am *not* pregnant. My God. How could you think something like that?"

"Uh, because I know about the birds and the bees?"

"Yeah, well, so do I. And like I've told you a million times, I even know how to prevent a pregnancy."

"Fine. If you're not pregnant, what the hell is wrong with you? Why aren't you happy? Is it because of Mom?"

Sam was momentarily taken aback. She and her mother hadn't been particularly close, but she couldn't help but imagine their relationship would have smoothed out as Sam grew into young adulthood. Sometimes, she even fantasized about her expressing pride in her eldest daughter for making the mature decision to enlist in the Air Force, instead of forcing Walter to waste money on college. Now, the memory of her mother was like the elephant in the room every time she had a conversation with her father. The thought of his wife not being there to see their daughter's wedding must have been weighing on Walter's mind. But if it was, he kept it to himself, save for an occasional reference. Or maybe it was something he reserved for private chats with Patricia, with whom he still had an ongoing personal and professional relationship.

"Wait a second," Sam stated, ignoring her sister's question. "Did Patricia say something to dad that I could be pregnant? I know she never liked Alec and I'm not even sure she likes *me* very much. She and dad must've had one heck of a conversation after he found out I was engaged."

Shannon shrugged. "Beats me. If he did, I never heard about it. Probably talked about it when I wasn't around. Besides, they just saw you last month."

"Well so did you. Did I look pregnant to you then? How about now?" She opened her tweed winter coat, and lifted her black sweater to reveal flat, tight abs.

"Fine, I get it. You're not pregnant. But something is wrong. Did you and lover boy have a fight?"

"No...I-I'm just not sure if I want the whole traditional church wedding and big reception, that's all. You know dad; he'll invite the whole stupid county. And when was the last time I even set foot in a church? I'll feel like such a hypocrite." Satisfied with her off-the-cuff explanation, Sam forced herself to stop talking before she revealed too much. *At least it's not a total lie*, she rationalized, since she couldn't even remember the last time she attended services.

"Eh, you're too hard on yourself. One thing I know for sure is that Dad wants to give you your dream wedding. He's really proud of you Sam." Though her words were meant to be soothing, they had the opposite effect. Besieged by another heaping dose of guilt, Sam nevertheless managed to keep a poker face.

"Thank you," she finally breathed out, pulling Shannon into a hug. "It means a lot to me that he feels that way."

"Oh, my God, I'm such an idiot." Shannon's voice was muffled against Sam's red-knit winter scarf. "Mom's not here for this. *Of course,* you'd be sad. I wasn't trying to be mean or anything, I swear."

"I know," Sam sniveled.

"Wait, I know what you could do. And I think it would make Dad really happy."

"What?"

Shannon pulled back to face her sister. "Wear Mom's wedding gown. You're built just like she was, I'm sure it'll fit. And since you don't like anything in the store, that might be the way to go."

A fresh wave of angst consumed her. "Well, yeah, I guess I could do that," Sam at last spoke. "And it would save Dad some money, too."

"That's my practical older sister," Shannon teased. "So…is it a deal? Let's shake on it, in honor of Dad and Mom."

Sam cracked a smile as she shook hands with her sister and wondered what to do next.

৯৯

"Hey babe, what's up?"

"Hey, it sounds noisy. You in the car?"

"Yeah, I just dropped Shannon off at Raleigh Airport and I'm heading back to base. I was going to call you when I got home."

"Well, I couldn't wait to tell you the good news," Alec continued. "My dad took on a second job so he could pay for us to have a honeymoon. Isn't that awesome?!"

"What?!"

She was at a loss for words. Tom and Beth had barely gotten their business back off the ground, which already demanded most of their time. How the *heck* was he managing a second job? And for the sole purpose of sending them on a honeymoon? She felt guilty and grateful at the same time.

"Yeah, he wants to send us on one of those Carnival Cruises out of Miami. You know, a four-or-five-day thing. We're gonna have a blast!"

"Sounds fun," she concurred.

"Hey, you don't sound too excited. If you don't want to do a cruise, we can do something else. I'm sure my dad won't mind."

"No, Alec, it's not that. It's just that I was going to talk to you tonight about our little secret and how we should just come clean because it's killing me to lie. And now your dad takes on another job just to send us on a honeymoon? There's no way we can tell them the truth."

"Can you hang in there for a little while longer?"

"I'm gonna have to. You should see how excited my little sister is. Man, she dragged me all over Raleigh trying to find the right dress. I hated everything, so I'm going to wear my mom's gown and Patricia was nice enough to offer to make a matching lace train. I had no idea she even sewed, but when we called my father to tell him, she was there. Walter even went to the church to ask about dates and it turns out there's an opening in April on the same day Stowe Mountain Resort has one. Boom! Church and reception scheduled. There's no way I can let anyone down now."

"So, we get to officially tie the knot in front of God and witnesses in less than four months? Cool!"

"It doesn't bother you at all that they have no idea we're already married, does it?"

"Ah, Sam, all I can think about is watching you walk down the aisle in your wedding dress. You're gonna make a beautiful bride. And look, they just want to make us happy. Why ruin it? We're in this secret and there's no turning back. Let's just enjoy it, OK?"

"Easy for you to say. You're not dealing with a nosy little sister who asks a million questions every time we talk."

"You can handle it Fancy Face," he laughed.

"Thanks a lot," she joked.

"Sam?"

"Yes?"

"Since we're all-in with our secret and doing the formal wedding thing, do you think Walter would let us use the Stingray?"

"I don't see why not. I mean, he trusted you to fix it last year. Poor guy, he'll probably wash and wax it six times a month instead of four up until the day of the wedding." Then, with another thought, "My God, I hope it doesn't rain and it's not freezing cold.

April is an iffy month in New England to be riding around in a convertible."

"Ah Sam, you worry way too much. You know how good we're gonna look as bride and groom in that awesome car? I can't wait!"

"Yeah, well, let's just get Walter's official permission before you celebrate too much."

"Better get used to it, sweetheart. I always expect the best."

෨

Saturday, April 19 dawned overcast and chilly over the sleepy berg of Morristown Vermont. Nestled under her childhood bed's soft, plush comforter, a dazed Sam lazily hit the button to silence her blaring alarm clock, momentarily forgetting the significance of this brand-new day. As she sank her head into the downy pillow, she drifted back toward blissful unconsciousness until a sudden, forceful movement startled her. For a split-second, she panicked at the presence of a figure laying down next to her until a familiar voice squealed, "Oh my God, today's the big day! Sam, c'mon, wake up, it's your wedding day."

"Go away, it's too early," she replied groggily as she turned onto her side.

"Samantha Townsend, wake up," Shannon persisted, shaking her shoulder. "You're getting married today!"

Little do you know it's already Russell, she thought. Then as her senses awakened, she asked, "Is that coffee I smell already?"

"Yep. Dad is making a nice breakfast, just for the three of us, so rise and shine sleepyhead!" She yanked back the comforter and forced her sister to sit up.

Sam rubbed her eyes and looked out the window at the barren landscape. Although the buds on the trees were present, they were still in the early stages of transformation into colorful blooms. Against the grey sky, even the hue of the green grass seemed dull. "Man, it's so ugly out," she lamented. "I hope it doesn't rain hard like the weather guy predicted." She shivered. "Damn, I wish we could have had this wedding in June. I've been down South so long I'd forgotten it takes forever for spring to arrive up here."

"Ok, enough whining *Hope Brady*," Shannon retorted. "This will be the last time the three of us eat together with Dad while you and I are both single. We need to enjoy it."

"What about Patricia? When is she coming over?"

"Not until late-morning. Don't worry, she'll be here with your train in plenty of time. C'mon, get up and I'll meet you downstairs. I'm going to help Dad with the eggs and pancakes."

Sam raised an eyebrow in disbelief. "You? Help with cooking?"

"Fine, I'll just set the table. Now get your butt out of bed already. Geez, you're about to marry one of the hottest guys on the planet. Show a little enthusiasm."

"Ok, ok." Sam let out a nervous laugh.

"See you downstairs in a minute?"

"Yes ma'am."

"Alrighty then; I'm outta here." In a flash, Shannon sprang from the bed and out into the hallway; a second later, Sam could hear her quick footsteps against the back wooden stairs leading to the kitchen. She got out of bed, threw on her robe and made her way into the hall bathroom. Flicking on the light, she inspected her face in the mirror, where she noted the absence of any nerve-induced blemishes with gratitude. Eyes closed, she splashed cool, invigorating water on her skin, washed her face with Cetaphil and then gently patted it dry with a clean face towel.

Why am I nervous? she thought as she dabbed her cheeks with moisturizer and used her fingertips to smooth it over her forehead, around her eyes, and down her neck. *We pulled it off. In only a few more hours, we won't have to pretend anymore; everyone will know we're husband and wife.*

Her morning ritual completed, she headed downstairs, where Walter greeted her in the dining room with tear-stained eyes and a big bear hug. For a moment, she felt like a little girl again as she breathed in the scent of his Brut aftershave and felt the warmth his fleshy arms encircling her.

"I'm so proud of you, Samantha," he choked out. "Your mother would be proud of you, too."

"Thanks, Dad," she managed to whisper. They held each other in silence until a loud crash in the kitchen startled them.

"I'm sorry," Shannon stammered when they rushed in to discover shattered pieces of what was once their mother's favorite China platter sprawled out all over the ceramic tile floor. "I don't know how I dropped it; I was just going to spoon the scrambled eggs onto it and it slipped out of my hands. I'm so sorry."

Wordlessly, Walter extended his arm and drew her and Sam into another embrace as the determined sun filtered through the heavy cloud layer and filmy white curtains above the farm sink, enfolding them in its glow.

❧

Sam stared in awe at her reflection in the hand-carved, full-length mahogany mirror. She hardly recognized the image of the statuesque woman in white looking back at her as she stood there in the simple, form-fitting, vintage lace gown worn by her own mother 27 years prior. Its classic 1970-style complemented her toned, athletic body, with a mermaid cut that flared out at the bottom. Twisting slightly at the waist for another perspective, she admired the matching lace train, fashioned with care and precision by Patricia.

Despite their inauspicious beginning, the relationship between Sam and Patricia had developed into one of mutual respect, if not maternal affection. Having experienced for herself the indescribable joy and peace that comes from companionship with the right person, Sam appreciated Patricia's presence in her father's life. And when Patricia had offered her sewing talents to add a new design element to Sam's wedding gown to make it uniquely hers, she was genuinely touched.

While she continued to gaze in the mirror, she admired her simple pearl earrings – a gift from her thoughtful in-laws – then ran her fingertips lightly over her bare skin and subtle décolletage, exposed by the gown's V-neck. With a sigh, she rethought her opposition to wearing a strand of pearls.

In the next moment, she heard a quiet knock on the door.

"Come in," she responded, her voice barely above a whisper.

"You look incredible…so much like your mother," Walter marveled. He extended his arms to take her hands in his, then leaned in to place a kiss on her cheek. Sam blinked back a tear. *Wow, this was happening*. She couldn't help but feel a twinge of guilt as she contemplated the events of the last several months. It hadn't been easy to go along with the charade, no matter how justified she and Alec had felt about keeping their court house nuptials a closely guarded secret. But now, as she witnessed her father's genuine pride and joy, she immersed herself fully in the role of firstborn daughter and bride in their immediate family circle.

"Thank you, Dad," she choked out.

"Look, I know I didn't approve of this wedding at first," he began. "As your lovable, over-protective dad, it's my job to look out for you. But I must say, Alec has proven me wrong. I'm still young enough to remember what it feels like to be madly in love and know what that looks like. And I can tell Alec loves you. I know he'll take good care of you. That's all I want Sam. Your happiness – always."

"Aw, Dad, you're making me cry," she half-joked, placing her arms about him and drawing him into an affectionate, yet cautious hug, mindful of the placement of his red rose boutonniere.

"I love you, Sam. I'm very proud of you. I know your mother would have been too."

"I love you, Dad. Thank you for everything." Her pangs of guilt dissipated, she savored the moment. For a while, nostalgia blanketed them in silence until the telltale pitter-patter sound against the bedroom's picture window broke the spell. A worried Sam pulled away from the embrace as she looked out at the front yard.

"Ugh, I hope this rain holds off at least until we're in church," she lamented. "Thank goodness I don't have a veil to worry about on top of everything else." She lightly touched the top of her head and felt the uncharacteristic stiffness of her hair, thanks to Shannon's insistence on using extra-hold hairspray. Pulled back at the crown with the rest falling in shiny waves past her shoulders, the hairdo satisfied Sam's desire for simple elegance.

"No matter what happens, this is going to be the wedding of your dreams," Walter assured her. "You look incredible, Sam. No amount of rain is going to change that. Besides, everyone knows when it rains on your wedding day it's good luck."

She shot him a skeptical look, but before she could utter another word, Shannon entered the room.

"Absolutely," her exuberant voice chimed in. Wearing a strapless red satin number in a similar mermaid style, she looked as if she'd stepped out of the latest copy of *In-Style Magazine*. Her messy blonde up-do perfectly accentuated artful makeup application.

"Wow, Shannon," Sam raved. "You look amazing."

"Thank you," she enthused, turning all the way around in a dramatic gesture so they could admire her from every angle. "I'm so glad you let me get this dress, Sam. It's so me." She showed restraint in keeping her thoughts to herself regarding Derek's anticipated reaction, although she secretly prayed he'd show up later as promised.

"Yes, it is," she agreed with a laugh, noticing their father's reaction – a combination of surprise, alarm, and grudging approval.

"I hope you have a wrap to wear in church," he finally said.

"Don't worry Dad, Sam made sure I'd be respectfully covered," she teased. "C'mon you two; Mr. Crawford will be here any second. It's time to get this show on the road."

"Where's Patricia?" Sam inquired as Shannon scuttled behind her to pick up her train.

"Oh, she'll be meeting us at church," Walter answered.

"Dad, she could have ridden with us in Mr. Crawford's limo," Sam reprimanded. "That would have been more than okay with me you know."

"I know sweetheart," he explained. "I just wanted this to be a special memory for the three of us of your special day."

She felt as if she would burst into tears. "You're the best dad in the world."

"Alright, alright, enough of the mushy stuff, we're going to be late," Shannon admonished. She hustled them out of the room and down the front stairs into the house's small foyer just as the doorbell rang. Walter opened the door to the sight of his old buddy, dressed in his Sunday finest, holding an umbrella. A dismayed Sam shivered as a rush of cold, moist air enveloped her and the sound of torrential rainfall assaulted her eardrums.

"Great timing," Gary Crawford chuckled. The two men exchanged pleasantries before the limo driver turned his attention to the bride. Noting her striking resemblance to her mother, he stared at her in awe. "Forgive me, Sam, but it feels like déjà vu. And you are just as beautiful today as your mother was on her wedding day. Hard to believe it was so long ago; I remember it like it was yesterday."

She gave him a peck on the cheek. "Thank you."

"Don't you worry about this weather," he continued. "I've got a huge umbrella here and I'll make sure you and your dress stay nice and dry." With that, he extended an arm and ushered her out the door.

As they traveled across the picturesque Vermont countryside in the white stretch limo, a slow, steady rain drenched the rolling green hills and washed away the remaining vestiges of dirty snow from red covered bridges. Sam took in the scene with a heavy heart, forcing back tears, lest she ruin the subtle makeup artistry Shannon had painstakingly applied. That's when she felt Walter's arm around her shoulder.

"Hey," he consoled, "it's good luck, remember?" Dressed in his formal black tuxedo, he didn't seem to have a care in the world. Sam nodded dutifully as she forced a smile.

When they finally caught sight of the soaring steeple of Stowe Community Church, she blinked her eyes in disbelief. *Was it glimmering in the sunlight?* Impossible as it might have seemed on the ride over, the dark, ominous clouds began to dissipate over the small, traditional structure flanked by verdant mountains.

She let out a deep sigh of relief as Walter playfully poked her in the side. "See, I told you it was good luck. Now let's go make you and Alec a married couple."

After pulling up to the entrance, their driver exited the limo and opened the back door. He first extended a hand for Shannon, who adjusted her satin wrap around her shoulders before carefully extricating herself from the vehicle.

"Thanks Mr. Crawford," she called as she hurried into the vestibule to meet Patricia and the florist.

Next, he helped Sam onto the walkway, which led to a grand entrance featuring full-length, three-step stairs, floor-to-ceiling windows, and ionic columns.

She smiled as she watched Walter shake his hand.

"Thank you, my friend."

Gary pulled him into a bear hug. "Anytime."

The joyful bride tucked her arm into her father's, and, as they made their way into the church, tilted her head up to look up at the black clock embedded in the steeple; its gold minute and hour hands displayed the time as 2:30. She shivered in breathless anticipation. In just thirty minutes, she'd walk down the aisle toward her handsome groom and embark upon a new life. *Let the fairy tale begin*, she thought, her heart filled with gratitude.

❧

Sam closed her eyes and let out a squeal of excitement as Alec pressed down on the accelerator of the black Stingray convertible. Wedding formalities behind them, she welcomed the feel of the cool wind caressing her face and rustling her hair before the last rays of sunshine disappeared over the horizon. Just as her new husband had predicted, Walter let them use his prized antique car to transport them from church to their formal reception at Stowe Mountain Resort. In another act of kindness, Patricia loaned her a short, white fur wrap to keep her warm on the ride over.

With one hand firmly on the wheel and the other on Sam's, Alec expertly navigated the mountainous terrain, glancing every so often as his new bride with a wink and a dimpled smile. After the ceremony, the giddy couple had complied with Walter's request for formal photos in front of the altar and on the steps of the country church, until the minister politely indicated it was time to move on.

From the moment she and her father started their walk down the aisle, Sam had felt like a spectator outside of her body, watching herself formally become Mrs. Alec Russell. She noticed the familiar faces of her high school friends, family members, and practically every resident of Lamoille County who'd attended the nuptials, mostly out of respect and affection for Walter. Although her face hurt from smiling, she could not stop herself from nonverbally expressing her inner joy, especially when she caught sight of her new in-laws beaming back at her. But that feeling paled in comparison to seeing Alec waiting at the altar – dressed in his formal black tux and standing at attention, his dark eyes transfixed upon her. In that moment, their entire courtship flashed through her mind's eye, from their unlikely meeting in the Air Force base laundry room to their first exquisite night together. She stifled a laugh, remembering the angry sergeant escorting him out of the building to get back to work.

She vaguely remembered saying, "I do," followed by a tasteful kiss and an eruption of applause that echoed throughout the tiny church. And after the ceremony, as they rushed down the aisle holding hands to more clapping and cheering, she lost any remaining vestiges of guilt. Keeping their secret had resulted in a proper celebration of their love and uplifted everyone who cared about them.

As Alec made a sharp turn toward the majestic entrance for the Stowe Mountain Resort, a gust of frigid   air forced Sam to clutch the fur wrap closer to her body. But as her eyes caught sight of the luxurious Alpine building flanked by stunning mountains, she shivered with excitement.

"Oh Alec, it's so beautiful," she sighed. "I know I complained a lot about keeping our secret, but now I know it was worth the effort. This place is incredible. It's even better than anything I ever imagined as kid playing dress-up."

He smiled and kissed her hand as he drove the Stingray around the circular entryway, where a young uniformed valet immediate ran out to meet them.

"Take good care of this car," Alec warned him. "I want to stay on good terms with my father-in-law...and believe me, you do too."

"Yes, sir," he replied stiffly.

Sam stifled a giggle, realizing the valet was probably around their same age. They watched for a moment as the Stingray slowly moved toward an enclosed parking garage featuring the same alpine aesthetic.

"Are you ready to go inside and have some fun?" he asked, extending his arm.

"I am *so* ready," she laughed. "I just don't want it to go by too fast. Already, it feels like it's flying by."

He cracked up.

"Sam, we just got here. Cocktail hour hasn't even started yet."

"I know, it's silly. I'm just trying to experience every moment so I can remember it forever."

He kissed her tenderly on the lips.

"Me, too. C'mon beautiful. Let's go celebrate with our guests."

The Mansfield Ballroom was a setting fit for a royal couple, with its vaulted cathedral ceiling and walls of arched windows showcasing stunning natural views. Enhanced by the glow of the setting sun behind them, the mountains provided a luminous natural backdrop to the adjacent Terrace Garden, where formally attired servers offered hors d'oeuvres from silver platters. A few long tables bearing vegetable, fruit and cheese trays were spaced out in different areas, with an open bar set up at one end. Well-placed torches kept the multitude of wedding guests comfortable as they chatted enthusiastically about the loveliness of the ceremony, their admiration for the young couple, and the beauty of their surroundings.

From their assigned place inside the ballroom, a live band serenaded the crowd with uplifting music, blending old standards like *Fly Me to the Moon* by Frank Sinatra with contemporary ballads from current country artists including Shania Twain and Trisha Yearwood.

Sam caught sight of her new in-laws as she and Alec approached the reception. She hadn't fully noticed until now, but Beth looked stunning in her beaded illusion champagne-colored gown, her dark hair swept up in a French twist. Standing beside her tuxedo-clad husband, she exuded timeless elegance. Upon catching sight of the bride and groom, the Russell's beamed with pride.

"Oh, you two are so precious," Beth choked out, throwing her arms around them. "Welcome to the family Sam. Tom and I couldn't be prouder to have you as our daughter-in-law."

Sam breathed in the scent of Coco Chanel, Beth's favorite perfume, as she basked in the comfort of maternal affection. "I-I'm so lucky to be a part of your family," she murmured, thankful for waterproof mascara. In her mind, she saw images of future happy holidays together spent cooking, eating, laughing over funny family stories and watching football games. It was hard to believe that with one decision to enlist, she had shaped the course of the rest of her life.

"Thank you, Mom and Dad, for putting up with me," Alec half-joked.

"Son, you have done us proud," Tom countered. "Your mother and I love you. And we love your new bride. We're thankful you found her at a young age. Seems like history is repeating itself, thank God." He winked at his wife.

The foursome was soon joined by Walter, Patricia and Shannon, who promptly announced, "I don't know about the rest of you, but I sure am ready for a drink!"

"Yes, well, it'll be club soda for you, young lady," Walter retorted. Everyone laughed as she strode off in a huff toward the terrace with the father-of-the bride and his date following closely behind.

"Shall we go in?" Sam asked. "I'm starved all of the sudden and those hors d'oeuvres sure smell good. I mean, it's ok for us to go out there, isn't it? I know they're going to announce us before dinner."

"Sweetheart, it's your day. You can do anything you want," Alec replied. "Besides, it's no fun to play by the rules all the time."

"Yes, don't I know," she winked.

He laughed as he led her by the hand into the main ballroom.

గ

"Ladies and Gentlemen, presenting Mr. and Mrs. Alec Russell!"

Sam felt tingles up and down her spine as they made their grand entrance to hearty cheers, whistles, and applause. Try as she might to imprint every second of the evening in her memory, it felt surreal as she attempted to focus on the smiling faces of family and friends. She vaguely heard the emcee announce their first dance as bride and groom before the band broke into *I'll Still Be Loving You* by Restless Heart.

She looked up at Alec and gazed into his dark eyes, oblivious to the flashes of light pulsating from the cameras of onlookers, including Walter's part-time employee, whom he'd hired for the reception at Sam's insistence. She wanted her father and his date to enjoy themselves, not spend the evening working.

The next thing she knew, Walter tapped Alec on the shoulder. Her eyes filled up when she heard them play *Child of Mine* by Carole King.

"Oh Dad," she whispered as they slowly moved to the music, "I remember when you used to sing this to me at bedtime. Wow, I haven't heard it in so long. Thank you…thank you for remembering."

"Ah Sam, I never forgot," he whispered. "I know it might have seemed that way. I'm sorry."

She squeezed his arm. "No, Dad. There's nothing to apologize for. Nothing. You did a great job. You're the best father any girl could ask for." She looked him squarely in the eyes. "And you deserve to be happy too. I *want* you to be happy. Okay?"

He smiled and nodded. "Okay, Samantha. But right now, I'm happy knowing you are married to a good man who loves you. Just remember I'm always here for you if you need me. You'll always be my little girl, no matter what. I love you."

"I love you, Dad."

They swayed easily to the music until the song came to an end, prompting their appreciative guests to clap with approval. Sam dabbed her eyes lightly with her fingertips as she stood beside an uncharacteristically sentimental Shannon, who tried to pretend she hadn't been crying. She slipped her arm around her sister's waist as they watched Alec and Beth take their turn on the dance floor.

"*Songbird*?" Shannon asked with surprise. "I thought Alec was into country?"

"Well, his mom loves Fleetwood Mac," Sam explained. "He wanted to make her happy. Besides, she used to sing this to him when he was little."

"Aww, look at them. They are adorable."

Sam sighed as she watched the obvious love between her new husband and his mom expressed through this beloved wedding tradition. Observing Beth's joy and the pride on her husband Tom's face as he took in the sight moved her to tears. She gazed around the room at all the smiling faces of family and friends and felt a twinge of sadness for the absence of her mother.

Would she have been proud that Sam chose to wear her gown? Would she have approved of her daughter getting married so young?

A hand on her shoulder interrupted her musings. She looked up at the beaming face of her handsome groom.

"Dance floor is open for everyone now, sweetheart," he explained as he reached for her hand. "I want to dance with my bride again."

Her heart fluttered.

"Go ahead, Sam. It's your big day," Shannon insisted. "Go celebrate." She waved her arms toward the dance floor.

But like a rush of cold water, an upsetting thought popped into Sam's head and temporarily disrupted the magic. "Where's Derek?" she asked, squeezing Alec's hand to temporarily stop their progression. "Wasn't he supposed to make it to the reception?

"Oh…ah, he's not here yet. But he promised he would be. Probably running late. Don't worry about me; you two go enjoy yourselves."

Sam offered a reassuring smile as Alec pulled her away. For a fleeting moment, she hoped her little sister's loser boyfriend wouldn't let her down *this* time. But as she felt her groom's strong arms around her and heard the sultry sounds of the ballad *Valentine* by Martina McBride, she forgot about everything else but her own fairytale ending.

ക

As Sam predicted, the evening went by in a blur of joyful activity. The blissful newlyweds indulged their guests with all the wedding rituals, most notably, kissing in response to the near-constant clanging of silverware against glasses, courtesy of Alec's high school buddies who happily imbibed the open bar's generous offerings. Although it made her blush each time, Sam embraced the corny tradition, too grateful for having found her man early in life to care about what some of the older guests in attendance might be thinking.

When the emcee announced a break from dancing to initiate the cake-cutting ceremony, the bride and groom followed his instructions and walked toward the far end of the ballroom. Sam nearly burst into tears at the sight of her magnificent wedding cake, a four-tiered concoction made of white buttercream icing with a cascade of intricately detailed red roses down one side. Lovingly designed by the owners of a local Morristown bakery Walter had known for years, the father of the bride had taken great pleasure in hiding it until the perfect moment.

As the couple stood in front of the dessert table, Sam caught her fathers' eye. "It's beautiful, thank you," she mouthed to him over *It Had to Be You*, by Harry Connick, Jr. Then, she joined Alec in making the first slice as camera bulbs flashed all around them.

Although slightly embarrassed, she giggled when Alec smashed a small piece in her face and returned the gesture while the crowd cheered them on. He bent down to give her a sweet kiss, prompting more catcalls from the young guys in attendance.

"I'm going to clean myself up real quick," she whispered to her groom, unsatisfied with the job a dry napkin had done. "My face feels sticky. I'll be right back."

When Sam entered the Ladies Room, she found her sister crying in the sitting area, slumped over the vanity table with her head resting on her arms. A twinge of shame shot through her as she realized she hadn't even noticed her absence just moments before. Gently, she placed a hand on Shannon's bare shoulder.

"Hey," she whispered.

"Hey," Shannon blubbered, momentarily startled. She lifted her head to gaze into the mirror and caught sight of the remnants of icing on Sam's face. "I see Alec got his way. I knew he would."

"Yeah, yeah, he did. Guess it's not as bad as it could have been. I came in here to wash it off."

"I'm sorry I missed it."

Sam pulled out a cushioned stool from under the counter and situated herself on top of it. Then she took Shannon's hand in hers.

"Hey, it's OK. I know you're upset and I'm sorry. I just hope you know you are way too good for that jerk. I'd like to say I can't believe he didn't show up, but that's what he does – he hurts you over and over again because he knows he can get away with it. Guess I was just hoping he wouldn't disappoint you today of all days because I know how much this wedding meant to you. I know how much you were looking forward to him seeing you all dressed up in your gorgeous gown. I can't tell you how thankful I am to have you as my little sister, Shannon. Thank you for everything you've done to make this the best day of my life. I love you."

She pulled her into a warm embrace, prompting her to burst into tears once more.

"Shh, don't cry," Sam comforted. "You're young, beautiful and smart. If Derek doesn't see how lucky he is, he's a loser. Besides, there are so many cute single guys here to take your mind off him. Don't try to deny it because I saw you dancing with them. It sure looked like you were having fun."

"I know, I know, I was," came the muffled reply. "It just hurts, that's all."

Sam reached for a clean tissue and dried her sister's eyes. "C'mon," she urged, taking her by the elbow and guiding them both to their feet. "We're going to get cleaned up so we can go back to the party. I want to see you laughing and dancing the rest of the night. It's all going to be over before we know it and I want us to enjoy what's left. Okay?"

"Okay," she grudgingly agreed. "Sam?"

"Yes?"

"Are you doing that stupid bouquet toss to the single girls? 'Cause if you are, I'll wait here until it's over."

"Ugh," she sighed, rolling her eyes. "I'll let you in on a little secret; I don't want to. I love my bouquet and I want to keep it. Besides, who says we must follow every dumb wedding custom, anyway?"

"Oh, I don't know. Maybe your new in-laws? Alec has more relatives than Vermont has citizens."

Sam cracked up. "Yes, he does. It's kind of nice to think I get to be a part of it now." Then, as an afterthought, she clarified, "You and dad will always be my family. I just meant that we can all have bigger holidays. Manchester isn't that far away and I'm sure Tom and Beth will be happy to include you both…and Patricia."

"Sam?"

"Yeah?"

"Do you think Dad will marry her?"

"I don't know. You're the one who still lives at home. What do you think?"

"Not sure. I mean, yeah, she's nicer now and everything. But dad never talks about where it's going. Some days, I don't think he's ever going to get over what happened to Mom. But who can blame him? I don't think I will either."

Sam sighed. "I get it, Shannon. Honestly, I do. And I miss her just as much as you and Dad. But we're still here, whether it's fair or not. And life is meant to be lived. We'll never forget her, but we need to move on with our lives. For whatever it's worth, I told Dad I want him to be happy. Maybe that means he marries Patricia, or maybe it doesn't. Only he knows what's best for him. And only you know what's best for you, although as your big sister, I reserve the right to give you my unsolicited opinion. If I were you, I'd dump Derek. The guy's a bum. You can do so much better."

"Yeah, because there are so many available guys in our stupid little town."

"Who says you have to stay in Morristown your whole life?"

"Ugh, Sam, I'm not like you; there's no way I'm enlisting."

She cracked up. "Do you think that's your only option? There are plenty of other things you can do, you know."

"Like what?"

"Well, you love to do hair and makeup and you're really good at it. Maybe you could go to beautician school?"

"Seriously?"

"Why not? You glammed me up for my wedding. Who'd have ever thought I could look so elegant?"

"Well…you may have a point." Shannon broke into a big grin while Sam removed the last remnant of smeared mascara from her face.

"There's my beautiful little sister," she announced with pride.

"Not quite yet, gotta touch-up my make-up." She strode back to the vanity table where she'd left her duffle bag containing every beauty accessory she owned. Sam smiled as she watched her retouch her eye-shadow, blush and lipstick.

Before she could finish, however, they heard the emcee announce the tossing of the bouquet.

"Oh God," Sam groaned. "Guess there's no turning back now."

"Sam, wait! I mean, you *do* want to keep your bouquet, right?"

"Yes."

"Then, make sure you throw it right at me. C'mon, let's go," she squealed. She jumped up, grabbed her sister's hand and led her out of the Ladies Room, feeling revitalized.

⤸

The early morning sun rose over the green mountains, its light penetrating the exposed portion of the window in the Russell's complimentary suite. Beneath the soft, velour covers, the couple lay entwined in each other's arms, their warm, bare bodies satiated from an extended love-making session. Sam lay with her arm draped around his chest and her head tucked into the crook of his arm. As Alec smoothed his hand over her silky hair, watching her gradually awaken from slumber, a slow smile spread across her face.

"Good morning, Fancy Face," he whispered coarsely.

"Mm, good morning, Beauregard" she murmured, tracing his chest with her fingertips.

"So? Did it feel any different now that everyone watched us become Mr. and Mrs.?" He kissed her on the forehead.

"Well," she teased in a mock Southern accent, "you certainly do know how to make a girl feel good. But last night was especially… uh…satisfactory."

"Nothing but the best for my girl." He shifted his body and pulled her on top of him, bringing their foreheads together. "Sam, you are incredible. I can't believe I get to spend the rest of my life with you. I promise, I'll do everything in my power every single day to make you glad you married me. I love you."

"I love you too, Alec."

"It sure feels like we have it all, doesn't it?"

She nodded her head. "I hope we're always as happy as your mom and dad. They made it through some tough times and they're still so much in love. They inspire me."

"Yeah, well, dealing with me was probably the worst of it," he joked. They both laughed until the sentiment triggered a worried thought in Sam's mind.

"Hey babe, we never really talked about this with them, but you don't think they expect us to have kids right away, do you? I mean, we're way too young for that and we have our whole lives ahead of us to be parents. I'm just curious because I don't want to disappoint them if they think we're giving them grandchildren anytime soon."

"Nah, I wouldn't worry about it. We gotta finish our Air Force sentence, then get jobs and hopefully a nice house. They get that."

"Hey," she teased, "don't pick on the Air Force. If not for them, we never would have met."

"That *is* true," he conceded. "But now that I have you, I cannot wait to be done with it. I'm sick of answering to morons in uniform who wouldn't be able to hold down a job anywhere else."

"Just be thankful you have so much going for you it's not going to be your long-term career. You're much too smart, ambitious and sexy for that."

"Oh really?" he remarked, his voice thick with desire. "Sexy, huh? What makes you think that?"

"Oh, I don't know…I seem to remember you showing me not so long ago."

"Well, I think it's about time I showed you again Mrs. Russell."

With that, he drew her into a passionate kiss, running his hands up and down her soft skin until, consumed with passion, he moved her onto her back. She sank her head back into the plush, downy pillow and moaned with pleasure as his lips and tongue danced their way tantalizingly down her neck until finally reaching her breasts. She writhed involuntarily as he took turns sucking and licking each nipple while his hands explored every part of her body, her fingers clutching his thick, dark hair. Then she felt him move her legs apart before slowly entering her, while he described in husky whispers how much she turned him on. She massaged the taut muscles of his back and chest as they rocked rhythmically in ecstasy before Sam screamed out in pleasure. Once spent, they held each other close as the sunlight flooded through the sheer curtains.

Overcome with love and gratitude, Sam closed her eyes and snuggled against Alec's warm body. *Thank you, God, that he's mine forever*, she prayed silently.

Chapter Three

Sam arrived home to the familiar rhythms of Alec's guitar. As per her habit, she closed the door softly behind her to lose herself in the mesmerizing melody of his original composition and avoid disrupting his concentration. Since the Air Force had relocated him to Seymour Johnson in June, the couple had happily settled into married life, opting for a one-bedroom apartment off-base when military housing was not available. Although their housing stipend didn't quite cover their entire rent, Alec didn't care.

"When we get done with work, we are off this base," he'd informed her. "I have no desire to see these idiots outside of that. I don't care if I have to spend an extra $200 every month. I want to be as far away from military culture as possible." Since Sam couldn't have cared less either way, there had been no further discussion on the matter.

The summer flew by as they settled into their roles as satellite communications engineers, which didn't involve much more than making sure all telecom equipment was ready to be deployed at any time. For Sam, the daily commute back and forth to work together more than compensated for the mundane aspects of earning a paycheck. After a long year spent on opposite coasts, she felt nothing but gratitude for the gift of every waking moment with her beloved.

During the week, they cooked dinner and worked out together, and on weekends, indulged in drinking and dancing at Morgan's Bar on Ash Street, their favorite local hangout. As she'd predicted, her husband's penchant for speeding resulted in losing his license due to points. But instead of being angry about having to drive him everywhere, Sam saw it as another opportunity to spend time together. For the most part, their schedules were in sync anyway.

Alec's passion for country music had taken on new life as he felt inspired to write his own lyrics and create his own chords, aside from playing old standards and the latest hits. Sam could listen to him sing to her for hours, a nightly ritual that took place in their living room. She wondered how one human being could have been blessed with such an abundance of talent and intelligence. Upon awakening every morning in his arms, she would silently thank God for the gift of her husband's love and their blissful union. She knew she was living the dream and vowed to never take that for granted.

Now as she quietly watched and listened to him strum his guitar, her conflicted emotions tortured her as she contemplated how to break the news: after only five months of living together in marital bliss, they were about to be separated again – this time by much more than just a continent.

"Hey Fancy Face, how long have you been standing there?" he asked with a sheepish grin as he glanced up at her. "Just been sitting here practicing while I was waiting for you to get back."

Her heart leaped in her chest. "It sounds fantastic. I wish I hadn't interrupted."

"Ah, thanks. It needs more work, but it's coming along." He carefully set the guitar down on the tile floor. "Well don't just stand there, gorgeous, come sit next to me," he urged with a wink, patting the empty space on the sofa next to him.

He drew her into a long, satisfying kiss as she settled in. *He sure isn't making this easy*, she thought.

Sensing hesitation, he stopped to take her face in his hands.

"What's wrong, baby?"

"I have some news," she sighed. "You're not going to like it. In fact, you'll hate it as much as I do. But I don't have a choice."

"Where are they deploying you?" he demanded with a frown.

"What? How'd you – "

"Sam, it was only a matter of time until one of us got the orders. So, tell me, where and when?" he repeated in an agitated voice.

"Saudi Arabia," she sighed.

"No. *No*. You are *not* going to Saudi Arabia. Not without me," he declared. "I'm going with you."

"What? Will our Sergeants even allow that?"

"Hell, yeah. We're gonna talk to them first thing Monday morning. There is no way I'm letting you go halfway around the world without me, for God knows how long." His dark eyes reflected determination and resolve. He pulled her close to him and buried his head in her hair.

"Oh Alec, I hope they let you. I can't stand the thought of being away from you again either," she sobbed.

"They'll let me."

"You sound awfully confident. Just promise you'll behave when we talk to them. Be respectful, OK? No matter what the answer is."

"I promise, Fancy Face. For you, I will. Fighting authority all the time gets tiring anyway."

She let out a muffled laugh. "I'm sure it does."

To their great surprise, the following Monday after speaking with both of their Sergeants, their request was granted. Out of the 19 others in Sam's squadron with whom Alec could have switched places, her Sergeant selected a newly married guy whose wife was scheduled to give birth the following month. What had begun as a perceived hardship for the newlyweds turned out to be a serendipitous turn of events for everyone involved.

Before leaving on their four-month assignment overseas, Sam called her family to say goodbye. But as she spoke with her father, she sensed concern over more than just her upcoming Middle East adventure.

"Dad, what else is going on?" she asked.

"I'm worried about your sister. You know, I take your advice and do my best not to butt in with her and Derek. Someday when you're a parent you'll understand, but it's killing me. I keep hoping she'll dump him but so far, she's hanging in there even though he's not my idea of a good boyfriend. I'm starting to wonder if I should step in."

"What happened? I mean, besides the usual?"

"Nothing I can really pinpoint; just that she's not happy. I've caught her crying several times, but when I ask what's wrong or if I can help, she shuts down. This is her last year in high school and she doesn't even want to talk about her future. Every time I bring up the subject, she cuts me off. I'd love nothing more than for Shannon to join me in the business, if that's what she wanted. But I know she's sick of Morristown and I don't expect her to stay if she wants something more out of life. I'd even pay for her to go away to college and I've told her that over and over. The problem is, she has no direction. She doesn't know what she wants, other than Derek for some strange reason. It's like he has a hold over her. That guy's a bad influence on my daughter and I don't know what to do about it. Has she said anything to you, Sam?"

"Not really, no," she admitted. "I get the feeling she pretends everything is great with him whenever we talk because she doesn't want my honest opinion. I told her the night of my wedding that she could do so much better. Heck, there were a ton of nice, single guys there, but she didn't have any real interest in any of them. Is she home now, Dad? Can I talk to her? I'm hoping I get to say goodbye tonight because I doubt I'll be able to communicate much over the next few months."

"I'm embarrassed to say I don't even know," Walter groaned. "Let me check to see if she's in her room."

In the background, Sam could hear his heavy footsteps mounting the stairs. *Please God, let her be there so I can talk some sense into her.* A second later, she heard her father's forceful raps on the bedroom door.

"Shannon? Are you in there? Your sister needs to talk to you."

"Ooh, yes," came the exuberant reply. *Well, at least she's excited to speak with me*, Sam thought, settling down into the plump pillows on her Queen-sized bed. She inhaled deeply and released the breath, grateful Alec was out with his buddies for the evening, with the promise they would drop him off at a reasonable time.

Walter handed the cordless phone to Shannon after professing his love for his elder daughter and urging her and Alec to be careful in the desert. Then he headed downstairs to the kitchen, where a leaky faucet needed his attention.

"Sam!" Shannon squealed as she closed her door and flopped onto the bed.

"You sound awfully excited. What's going on?"

"I have some news for you. I am so psyched I get to talk to you before you leave for the Middle East."

Sam wasn't sure if she should be afraid or excited, until a sick feeling in the pit of her stomach signaled an answer.

"Shannon, just tell me," she ordered.

"Okay, okay, it's about Derek and me. We're going to get married."

Sam swallowed hard to suppress a wave of nausea. "What?"

"Yeah, he asked me to marry him and I said 'yes'! Isn't that exciting?"

"When?"

"When did he propose? Oh this past –"

"No, I mean when are you getting married?" The real question was *why*, but with time of the essence, Sam had to prioritize.

"Oh, not until after graduation. And since I love the fall, I was hoping for an October wedding when the leaves are so colorful and pretty. Hopefully, we won't get any snow until December, just in case we have to set a date in November."

Thank God, there's time, Sam thought. *I have a year to talk her out of it.*

"Sam, say something. Aren't you happy for me? You know I want you to be my matron of honor. Please say you will."

"Of course, I'm happy for you," she replied, mustering as much enthusiasm as she could while retaining a semblance of sincerity. "I'm just a little surprised, that's all. I would love to be your matron of honor."

"Oh, thank you. It wouldn't be the same without you and Alec."

"Have you told Dad?"

"No…not yet. I'm going to wait a while."

"That's a good idea. In fact, if Derek wants Dad's blessing, he should ask Dad in person if he can marry you…when the time is right."

"Like Alec did with you? Come on, Sam, that is so old-fashioned."

"Hey, I'm just trying to give you some good advice since Derek hasn't exactly been a model boyfriend. And don't try to deny it because you know I'm right. Remember how he stood you up for my wedding?"

For a few moments, there was nothing but silence.

"Shannon?"

"Okay, fine. You're right," she conceded. "But he's changed since then, Sam. He's sorry about what he did. And he wants to make it up to me."

"Well, if he's serious about that, he'll ask Dad if he can marry you. But if I were you, I'd wait until you can somehow get Derek to spend more time with him. You know, getting to know him better, proving he's worthy of you, maybe sharing his career plans to show he can be a good provider. Graduation may seem like a long way off, but it will be here before you know it. If Derek loves you, he'll have no problem with it. You need to ask him."

"Fine, I will."

"Shannon?"

"Yes?"

"I thought you wanted to get out of Morristown. Why the rush to get married?"

"I just want to live in my own place," she explained to her skeptical sister. "Living in this town will be so much better when

I have my own house and husband. I'm tired of being under dad's roof where I have to do whatever he tells me...and God forbid I drive one of his precious cars."

"Okay, I get it. You want to be independent and make your own decisions. How do you plan to pay for your own place?"

"I'll get a job."

"What kind of job?"

"I don't know; one that pays the bills."

"That's kind of vague, Shannon."

"C'mon, Sam, give me a break. I'm not you," she countered. "The perfect one who always does everything right – oh except that one time when you got married in a court house and pretended you were engaged for a year to have a fancy wedding."

"What?!" Sam couldn't decide what surprised her more: the fact that Shannon found out or that she'd managed to keep her mouth shut.

"Yeah, I knew. I figured it out, but I kept your little secret because I didn't want to ruin your big day. It was the least I could do after Alec saved my butt with Dad when I crashed the Stingray. But please don't lecture me about doing what I think is best for my life."

"Shannon, I'm only giving you advice because I care about you and I want you to be happy. Would you do me a favor and just think about going to beautician school? You can do that and get married, you know. There's a good school in Williston. It would be an easy commute."

"I don't know, Sam."

"Why? You love to do hair and make-up and you're good at it. Don't you want to get paid to do something you love?"

"You mean like you, who has to spend the next five months in the middle of nowhere?"

Sam laughed. "Sometimes, Shannon, being an adult means having to make sacrifices for a greater goal. Once I'm out of the Air Force, I'm going to school for business and see where it takes me. I didn't know what I wanted to do or what I was good at when I was in high school. You do. All I'm saying is, don't give up your dream, okay?"

"Okay," she sighed.

Sam couldn't shake the feeling there was more to the story, but figured she could get to the bottom of it when she returned in the spring. She suddenly wished Alec would get home so they could spend some quality time together in bed before embarking upon a long tour of duty that would require living in separate tents for males and females.

"Okay, then. I'm not sure how much I'll be able to communicate while I'm gone, but I'll be thinking about you. Don't do anything impulsive while I'm away, you hear me?"

Shannon giggled. "I won't," she promised.

"I love you, crazy little sister."

"I love you, Sam. Stay safe."

છ

She closed her eyes and sank into the firm mattress, relishing the decadence of upscale bedding. Soon, she'd be stationed halfway around the world, living in a tent in the desert and sleeping on a rudimentary cot. It felt surreal that the Air Force was sending her to Saudi Arabia, a country she knew little about, except that its culture and traditions stood in stark contrast to everything she'd ever known. She could not even imagine the panic she'd be experiencing right now had Alec not been granted permission to go. Bad enough she had to quell her apprehension by telling herself their mission would keep them so busy, they wouldn't have time to miss the United States. At least her work overseas would be interesting, unlike the daily grind at the base, where all they did was check and re-check equipment, save for the occasional practice drill in the woods.

The sound of a key turning in the lock startled her for a second, until she heard his voice calling for her. A moment later, her husband walked in, looking as hot as ever in his jeans and buttoned-down shirt. He kissed her sweetly on the lips before sitting down next to her on the bed.

"How was your evening, Bo? Did you behave?" she teased.

"I did, only because I couldn't wait to get home to you, Fancy Face," he replied in a seductive tone. "You do realize, this might be our last night to enjoy each other's company for a really long time." With that, he moved in closer to kiss her again, his lips and tongue probing while his hands slipped beneath her tank top. She sighed with pleasure as he caressed her breasts and teased her nipples with his fingers until they became stiff. In that moment, all thoughts of military responsibilities, foreign lands, and sisterly concerns melted away, powerless against raw passion and all-consuming desire.

Sam raised her arms and felt the cotton fabric move swiftly against her skin as Alec freed her from her top. Before she could reach out to unbutton his shirt, he laid her against the bed. As he sat back on his knees, he whispered, "I just want to make this all about you for a little while."

Fully lost in the moment, all she could do was nod as she felt the welcome, warm sensations in her body. She felt him reach for the drawstring of her sweat pants and slowly untie the bow. Then, just to tease her a little more, he leaned in and placed soft, wet kisses on her skin, beginning at her neck and working his way down to her waist, while she moaned in pleasure.

"You are so beautiful Sam," he whispered. "Damn, I'm gonna miss this while we're away."

"Then don't waste any more time," she urged softly, a slow smile spreading across her face. He grinned at her as he unbuttoned and removed his shirt to reveal taut abs and sculpted arms – her reward for evenings spent at the gym in their apartment complex lifting weights and doing cardio on the treadmill. While it lacked the variety and scope of a professional gym, it sufficed to keep them both in shape and, as per Sam's insistence, saved them an unnecessary outlay of cash every month.

As she extended her palms to touch his bare torso, she felt the heat emanating from him skin. Hands trembling with desire, she released his belt buckle and unzipped his jeans in a provocative motion. Alec lowered himself on top of her as she pulled the remainder of his clothing off. His jeans made a rustling noise as they drifted to the floor. She reached down to caress his throbbing, stiff manhood in the manner he'd taught her from their first coupling at Brittany's apartment. A far cry from the innocent, virginal girl of that faraway evening, under Alec's loving tutelage she had developed impressive skills in the art of lovemaking.

As a wife, she embraced her power as the woman her man looked to for his sexual satisfaction. Once, she'd overheard the conversation of two strange ladies in a supermarket – not much older than 30 – complaining about their husband's constant need for sex. It had both startled her and strengthened her resolve to satisfy her own man in every way. *How could these women not like sex with their husbands? Had it become too routine?* Sam had vowed in that moment to keep the flame alive at every age until death did they part.

Now, as Alec brought her to the height of ecstasy with his artful tongue, she screamed out with pleasure while her body convulsed – a sight that always filled him with pride and anticipation of the moment when he'd enter her slowly at first, the better to fully experience her warmth and wetness closing around him, before initiating a frenzied dance that would culminate in a mutually satisfying release. Perhaps because this would be their last connubial interlude for an extended period, every touch, kiss, and gaze took on a new level of intensity. Once fully spent, they held each other in the darkness, their legs and arms intertwined. As Alec nodded off to sleep, Sam closed her eyes and imprinted the memory of this exquisite experience in her psyche, ready to be summoned for her comfort when life in the desert became monotonous.

৵

"Looks like another evening in paradise," Alec joked. The assembled group sitting around their makeshift camp in Tent City let out a collective groan.

"Just shut up and play Russell," one of the guys ordered, prompting Sam to giggle out loud.

"Oh, so you think that's funny Fancy Face, do ya?" he teased.

"C'mon, don't pretend you haven't been basking in all the attention and praise everyone's been giving you over the past few months. You know you love hearing what a great singer and guitar player you are." She patted him playfully on the butt as he lowered himself into the chair next to her with his guitar in tow.

"Guilty as charged," he laughed. "Ok, what's everyone want to hear tonight? Aw, hell, let's start with a classic." He answered his own question as he began to play an old standard from Merle Haggard.

"Seriously, dude, *The Bottle Let Me Down*? I'm missing my wife like crazy, can you keep it up tempo please?" another guy in the group complained.

Alec feigned offense. "Tough crowd," he opined. "Alright, I get it. How 'bout this?" With that, he broke into *Hello Texas* by Jimmy Buffet, to the delight of his desert audience. They clapped and sang along as he belted out one standard after another, until his voice was nearly worn out.

"Seriously, Alec, you are so talented, you could make a career out of country music. Have you thought -about it?" one of Sam's tentmates asked.

He glanced at his wife. "Nah, not really. I mean, not in any meaningful way. I guess it would be cool to play on weekends at Morgan's because we go there almost every Saturday night. Besides, the choice had already been made *for* me. After high school, it was either join the military or go to Nashville. And since I didn't even have the money for a one-way bus ticket, my ass is sitting here in the middle of this godforsaken place entertaining all of you idiots."

Everyone erupted in laughter, much to Sam's relief. Still, she noticed a hint of regret in his voice, which she attributed to the manic pace they'd been keeping ever since their arrival. It appeared the Universe had responded to her complaints about her boring base job by presenting her with one that never stopped. Whether a soldier's malfunctioning computer or a General's glitchy phone, there was always something to fix.

On one hand, the unrelenting demands of their work distracted them from the unpleasant reality of their crude living conditions in sex-segregated, desert-sand-colored canvas tents shared with strangers. Upon their arrival, Sam had visibly shuddered at the sight of her accommodations, which featured five cots lined up on each side and basic lighting consisting of a few light bulb strands that ran up to the top of the tent. To her dismay, there were no dressers, nor any type of partition between each cot that would have provided a decent amount of privacy. Instead, she and her roommates improvised by employing a clothes line and clothes pins to hold up blankets and quilts as barriers. And, with no other options available, she soon became accustomed to living out of her duffle bag.

Although she and Alec reported to different units, they had the benefit of shared workouts and evening meals together, aside from what soon became the most anticipated part of everyone's day: Alec's country music concerts under the nighttime sky.

As they immersed themselves in his professional-quality renditions, for a blissful moment, all was well. In their minds, they were home, basking in its creature comforts and modern amenities. Alec's talent possessed the power to make them forget about the glorified port-a-johns and the segregated shower tents with nasty, concrete floors, shower hoses, and flimsy curtains separating six stalls.

"At least the water is warm," Sam had muttered during her first experience with this makeshift method of personal hygiene.

Challenging as it had been, her time in Saudi Arabia had given her an opportunity to contemplate her own future. One starry night, as she watched her husband perform with an outward display of interest on her face, her thoughts wandered off to her little sister.

Much as she hated to admit it to herself, Shannon wasn't the only one who needed to get her shit together; Sam knew she had to take her own advice and figure out her own professional life. It wasn't enough to decide *not* to make a career out of the military. She'd done the right thing by enlisting, but now that an honorable discharge was less than two years away, it was time to be proactive.

Thankfully, she and Alec had agreed about postponing parenthood until at least their late-20s, which gave her plenty of options. Should she go back to school part-time or full-time once she fulfilled her commitment to the Air Force? Why study business? What exactly did she want to accomplish with a business degree?

In this depressing environment, the questions took on a new sense of urgency. She had no doubts that her straight-A student husband would land a high-paying job once discharged – if she could keep him on the straight-and-narrow until then. But deciding on her own career path was a much more daunting task. All she knew with certainty was that she was never coming back to this horrible place again, once she fulfilled her obligation.

Sam thought about her dad and the long-ago $50 bet that ultimately led to her extended stay in Tent City, halfway around the world in a culture that seemed as foreign to her as the distant planets. Back then, that innocent, eight-year-old child could never have anticipated the ramifications of one simple decision. As she gazed at her handsome husband and basked in the sound of his sexy baritone voice, she shivered with love, desire and gratitude. Of all the consequences of her fateful choice, he'd been the least expected and most welcome. In about another month, their dry spell would come to a merciful end, freeing them to make love with abandon once again.

Yet, there was something else, a feeling she couldn't quite pinpoint. She brushed it aside, preferring to marvel instead at Alec's ability to transport his appreciative listeners to another dimension, thereby providing a welcome reprieve from their otherwise dreary desert existence. Sam convinced herself that her husband's unmistakable passion for playing and singing was merely a survival mechanism; a pleasant way to endure harsh reality until the Air Force saw fit to bring them home.

Home.

How she missed it. Even their humble little one-bedroom apartment felt like an upscale luxury penthouse compared to where they were serving their tour of duty. Never again would she complain about Alec's music sheets cluttering up their living room, or his clothes taking up too much space in their shared closet. From now on, she would just be thankful. Besides, she knew that in less than two years, they'd move on to a more spacious place with at least two bedrooms, one of which Alec could use as a music room. And once she'd obtained her degree and charted her career course, what was to stop them from buying a house? The possibilities were as expansive as the stars twinkling down on her from the panoramic sky.

Sam's thoughts turned to her mother. Did she approve of the close relationship she had forged with Beth, her beloved mother-in-law? She felt a twinge a guilt as she realized how much she had grown to love her husband's parents, with whom she engaged in regular conversation. She couldn't wait to spend the next Thanksgiving and Christmas with them, as discussed in detail over the course of countless conversations.

In the next moment, excitement transformed into self-reproach as she reflected upon her talk with   Shannon the night of her wedding reception and realized she hadn't even asked the Russell's if her family could be included in the planned holiday festivities. Which led to another panicked thought: what were Tom and Beth's unspoken expectations? How long before their patience ran out and they started demanding grandchildren? Would they start pressuring them for a newborn in the year following their honorable discharge from military service?

Suddenly, the sounds of raucous laughter shocked her back to the present moment, where she was now the center of unwanted attention.

"Uh, Earth to Samantha?" Alec teased as he snapped his fingers in front of her. "Did you even hear my question?"

"O-oh my gosh…I'm so embarrassed," she stammered as she felt her cheeks blush. "No…I…sorry, guess I drifted off there for a second." She let out a nervous laugh.

"Guess my wife is my toughest critic after all," he joked to their assembled Air Force friends. "You were a million miles away, sweetheart. And here I thought you loved my singing."

"Uh…no. I mean, yes, I love your singing. Sorry, I must've gotten wrapped up in the glamour of this place," she remarked facetiously.

"Well, these fine folks made a bet with me," continued. "They dared me to sign up for the talent contest at Morgan's when we get back home. You know it's coming up this summer."

Sam nodded.

"If I win, it's a thousand bucks and a shot at a regular gig on the weekends. Plus, I'd probably get enough exposure to win some gigs around Goldsboro. I wondered if you'd be on-board with that."

"Hey babe, if that's what you want, go for it," she replied confidently, ignoring a profound sense of foreboding. "You know I love your singing and it might be fun to be married to a local celebrity."

"Yeah, well, just be careful," another Airman warned. "Groupies are everywhere, even at the lowest levels of fame."

Sam couldn't help but view his words as a warning, notwithstanding her faith in her husband. She drew in a deep breath in preparation for a response, but Alec beat her to it.

"Seriously, Bucci?" he snarled, a clear indication that the laid-back mood had shifted with just one word of warning.

"Hey man, not saying you would…just saying be careful. Chicks dig a guy who can sing…and some will even ignore a wedding band if it means a chance to score."

"What are you implying?" Alec demanded, his dark eyes flashing. He laid down his guitar and strode over to where Airman Bucci was sitting.

"Alec, calm down," Sam ordered in a firm, measured voice as she gained her composure. She rose from her chair, ready to step in should things escalate. The last thing any of them needed was a reprimand from a commanding officer.

"Dude, chill out. I'm not looking for a fight with you," Airman Bucci scolded. Sam swallowed hard as she watched him stand up and get in Alec's face. "Look, we're all tired of being here," he continued. "Thanks to you, it has been more bearable, but that doesn't give you the right to be an asshole when all I was trying to do was give you sound advice. You've got a great woman there who supports you. Just don't screw it up. I'm older than you; I may know a thing or two from my own experience. And now, I'm calling it a night."

He turned and walked toward the male sleeping tent as everyone watched in stunned silence. A moment later, they began to take their leave one by one, until Sam and Alec stood alone in the desolate environment, now devoid of the music and laughter that had transformed it into a romantic setting just moments before.

She walked up behind him and reached up to place her hands on his shoulders.

"What just happened?" she whispered in his ear. He slowly turned to face her.

"Ah, Sam, I'm so sorry," he admitted. "I don't know what got into me. I'm just so sick of this hellhole."

"I know, me too," she comforted, pulling him into a tight embrace and resting her head against his chest. "It won't be long now. We're almost done."

"Thank God."

"Alec, you do know that he was right? I do support you in whatever you want to do with your life. And if you want to try out for that contest, I think you should go for it."

He pulled her closer, awakening a longing that had not been fulfilled in what felt like an eternity. "I love you, Sam. And I promise, no groupie will ever come between us."

"I know that, silly. Only the military has the power to do that," she teased.

He laughed out loud.

"Damn, I miss being with you."

"Tell me about it. We'll have to focus on how we'll make up for lost time once we're back home."

"Oh, I have a few ideas Fancy Face."

"I figured you would," she chuckled.

As they made their way to their respective tents, she imagined what it might be like to be the wife of a famous country music star, even as she continued to suppress a persistent feeling of apprehension.

ৡ

"Oh, Beth, I'm so disappointed we can't be there for Thanksgiving," Sam complained to her mother-in-law on the phone. "Gosh, I knew military life would be tough, but who'd have thought we'd get shipped back to Saudi Arabia a year later? I was really looking forward to coming to Manchester."

"We were too, honey," she replied. "But at least they let you switch with someone in Alec's squad so the two of you can be together. History is repeating itself."

"Yeah, I'm happy about that. I wasn't sure if they'd do that again, but I'm thankful to the Sergeants. Ugh, I am not looking forward to going back there, though."

Beth laughed. "Soon, you will both be discharged and you won't have to worry about it anymore."

"Oh yeah, I can't wait for that day. I can't really complain, though, because this deployment came just in time to stop my little sister from making a huge mistake. Without me being there to be her maid of honor, she postponed the wedding, thank God. My dad is so relieved, he didn't care about losing his deposit on the reception hall. And I suppose I could find some use for my gown or maybe put it in consignment."

"Well, it's a small price to pay, given everything you told me about Derek."

"I just hope Shannon comes to her senses and dumps him for good," Sam sighed. "I feel blessed to have found Alec and I know there's someone amazing out there for her, too. If she could just focus on getting her life together, everything else would fall into place. I hope she's saving her money since she's working for my dad right now and living at home."

"One thing I know for sure is that you are a wonderful sister," Beth noted. "Alec has always told me that. And I can see how much you love Shannon and your dad."

"Aw, thanks. I try my best."

"Sam, I know it has been tough growing up without a mother. I just want you to know you can confide in me any time. I may not have all the answers, but I promise I'm a good listener."

"Thank you," she replied softly, touched by the genuine sentiment.

"So, is my son around? I'd love to remind him how lucky he is to have you."

She cracked up. "No, he had a gig at Morgan's tonight. A couple of his buddies picked him up since I had a few things to do around here. I told them I'd meet them later."

"My son, the country music star. I'm not surprised he won that contest." Although light and playful, Sam detected a tinge of regret in her voice.

"Me, either. If not for Alec, I'm not sure how we would have survived in the desert. It was the one thing we had to look forward to every night after running around servicing equipment all day long. He's going to miss the live crowds around Goldsboro, but at least he'll have 19 people to play for."

"He sure loves his music. It's been his passion since he was a little boy. I'm just sorry we had to stop his formal training when the business went south. Then again, if he hadn't joined the Air

Force, he never would have met you. I suppose everything works out the way it should."

"I believe that, too. Who'd have thought we'd bump into each other in a laundry room of all places? It's crazy when you think about it. But no matter how many bars Alec gets to play in, I'm lucky to be his private audience of one every night. I'm so proud of him. Really, he is the most talented, intelligent person I know. He can pretty much do anything with his life."

"Sam," Beth continued in a more serious tone, "has he talked about his plans for after the military?"

"N-no, not really. I think we're both just counting the days until we're out for good. I mean, I'm planning to go to school and get a business degree once we land somewhere. A lot of our friends are talking about heading to Charlotte to interview for telecom jobs. Apparently, it's the place to be for that industry and from what I've heard, companies are offering excellent money to start out. Guess we'll have plenty of time to talk about it every night in Saudi Arabia."

"That's good to know," she replied. "Just think, the two of you could have it all soon – great careers, a nice house, kids. I'm so proud of you both. And wherever you end up, we will come visit. Don't worry…we'll be the best grandparents ever. You'll have reliable babysitters any time you need them."

Sam felt her stomach tighten into knots. "Thanks, we'll keep that in mind," she replied airily.

"Honey, I'm sorry; I didn't mean to pressure you. I know I'm getting ahead of myself. When you and Alec are ready, whether its five years or 10 years down the road, we'll be there to help. Right now, I just want you both to stay safe. If my prayers are answered, this will be your last deployment."

"Amen to that," Sam laughed.

"Sam?"

"Yes?"

"No matter what, always remember how much my son loves you. Even if this country music thing ends up going somewhere, you'll be right by his side. Just don't forget us when you make it big in Nashville."

"We won't, I promise." Knowing the next several months would test her resolve, envisioning a glamorous life in the country music capital provided a welcome respite from reality. Still, that familiar sense of foreboding lingered throughout her psyche, much to her consternation. Beth sounded as if she was only half-joking.

"Well, I'd better let you go so you can catch up with that handsome husband of yours. Tell him to give us a call when he's finished. We don't care how late it is."

"Will do," Sam promised.

She hung up the phone and opened her closet to search for the perfect outfit, at last deciding on a pair of comfy jeans paired with the blue cashmere sweater she'd worn on their first date. *Looks as good as new*, she thought. Prior to taking Beth's call, she'd applied an anti-frizz serum Shannon had recommended and blown out her freshly shampooed hair. Now, after a few measured strokes from her naturally bristled brush, it fell in shimmering waves down her back. As she gave herself the once-over in the mirror, she decided to add a bit of foundation, blush, and mascara, figuring it would be her last time to engage in such *girlie* activities for a while.

As she lightly painted her lips with a subtle gloss, her mind wandered. *Samantha Russell, wife of country music superstar Alec Russell, attends the CMA Awards with her husband, wearing a Calvin Klein original*, she imagined a tabloid headline announcing.

Then she chided herself out loud, "Don't be ridiculous, Samantha. You're about to do another tour of duty in the freaking desert, not walk down some glamorous red carpet. Get a grip."

But as she locked the apartment door behind her and headed out to her car, the sense of foreboding followed.

෨

"Babe, I'm so proud of you," Sam enthused. "You nailed it after one interview; why am I not surprised?" As she spoke, she piled more belongings into a moving box in preparation to join her husband in Charlotte in two weeks, once she was officially discharged.

"Yeah, who'd have thunk it? Alec Russell, telecom executive," he laughed. "I'm still trying to wrap my head around making it through the Air Force with an honorable discharge. Now here I am, Senior Engineer with World Telecom, making the big bucks. Got a hot wife, a great career, and a happenin' city. I'm the king of the world," he joked, referencing Leonardo DiCaprio's character Jack in the blockbuster film *Titanic*.

Sam giggled. "I can't wait to get there. I hope you got us a nice apartment Russell."

"Hey, I'm making 90K now, Fancy Face. Only the best for my girl and me. Seriously, our new place is awesome – two big bedrooms, a nice living room and kitchen, plus a balcony with a great view of the skyline. You're gonna love it. Oh – and I hope you don't mind, but I got a regular gig on Saturday nights at one of the downtown bars. I start this weekend."

Sam took a gulp of air. "Wow, you have definitely accomplished a lot in a few days."

"Hey," he consoled her, "singing is just part of who I am babe. You know I'm only there for the music. Besides, the extra money will help us save for a nice house. You don't want to live in apartments the rest of your life, do you? If I'm gonna put a suit and tie on every day, I'm at least gonna make it count. From what I know, there are some nice developments going up all around Charlotte. I want to buy you your dream house."

"Alec, as long as we're together, I don't care where we live. Wait, what do you mean a suit and tie every day? Won't you have to go out and fix cell tower signals?"

"That's the best part of the deal – I get to dispatch other people out in the field to do the hard stuff while I sit in my corner office looking important."

"Ah, I see, Mr. Executive," she laughed. "But I don't think we need to rush out and buy a big house for just the two of us. We're not having kids anytime soon and – "

"Well, I do. You deserve the best of everything, Fancy Face. If not for you, I would not have made it through the past four years. And don't forget, you have a father-in-law who's in the construction business. I wouldn't buy anything without him checking it out first. We'll get a great deal on the best house out there."

She realized she'd lost the argument.

"Alright, but before we do any of that, I want to register for classes. And I need to get a job."

"Oh, I figured that out too," he informed her. "That is, if you don't mind."

"What do you mean?"

"Turns out, Coyote Joe's needs a new bartender. I figured you could work at night and take classes during the day. I already checked and you don't have to be licensed to sell alcohol in North Carolina."

"My husband, the overachiever," she giggled.

"Sam, I just want us both to have a little fun. It'll be just like our Saturday nights at Morgan's, except now I'll be playing for a bigger crowd. At least we can still be together…or at least under the same roof. And I can dedicate original songs to you on stage, so everyone there knows you're my girl. C'mon, what do you think?"

"Alec, I've never bartended before."

"Uh, Fancy Face, you've handled obnoxious Generals, crappy tent living in the desert in the middle of nowhere, and me, for God's sake. I'm sure you can handle bartending. Besides, with your looks and personality, you'll have those good ol' boys tipping you well."

"As long as they understand I'm a married woman…and that goes for your little groupies too."

"You've got nothing to worry about sweetheart. I promise."

Sam stared in awe at the majestic lobby of the Ballantyne Hotel. It felt as if she had walked into *Gone with the Wind* as she took in the sight of the massive crystal chandelier hanging from a soaring ceiling, surrounded by a stately, antebellum staircase and floor-to-ceiling arched windows. Beneath her open-toed, high-heeled black sling-backs, rich marble flooring completed the ambiance of pure opulence and Southern charm. Here they were, two 24-year-olds, about to ring in the New Year in Charlotte's most prestigious, four-star hotel. It felt like a fairytale, much like their beautiful Vermont wedding, which seemed to have taken place a lifetime ago.

But here it was, New Year's Eve 2000, with the promise of even greater things to come. Since their move to Charlotte, Alec had not only embraced his career as telecom executive, he'd become a local celebrity, thanks to his weekend appearances at Coyote

Joe's. Within weeks, he'd formed his own band and attracted unprecedented crowds to the bar – a number that only increased after he was featured in *Charlotte Magazine.*

Sam had eagerly applied herself to business classes at Queens University by day and bartending at Coyote Joe's by night. Her joyful personality and remarkable ability to multi-task paid off in the form of abundant cash tips, which she responsibly deposited into their savings account, along with Alec's annual bonuses.

While their two-and-a-half years in The Queen City had been a merry-go-round of work, school, and the daily tasks of life, Sam and Alec made a conscious effort to keep their marriage fresh and exciting. As promised, he wrote, composed and dedicated an original song to her entitled *Fancy Face,* to put the Coyote Joe's groupies on notice. And she was featured prominently in his Charlotte Magazine interview, which included the beaming couple's wedding photo, along with a fun casual shot of the two of them laughing while Alec held her in a piggyback pose.

While Sam appreciated her husband's fulfillment of his promises, she often bristled at the antics of some of the women in the crowd who didn't seem to care about marriage vows – especially after the effects of alcohol took hold. Yet every night in the privacy of their bedroom sanctuary, Alec assuaged her fears with his intense, soulful love-making – drowning out the little nagging voice within and its warning of impending doom.

Unknown to Sam, one of her regular customers – a middle-aged gentleman she knew only by his first name, Rick, and his weekly Tuesday appearances at the bar to order the same beer and burger – had been keeping a close eye on her in the professional sense.

The VP of a communications company, Rick had been impressed by Sam's consistent customer service and ability to up-sell menu offerings like specialty drinks and desserts. As time went on, they developed a friendly rapport, to the point where she felt comfortable confiding in him about her classes and undetermined future.

One night, he caught her off guard during a particularly busy shift. "Sam, have you ever thought about sales?"

"Sales? Hmm, I'm not so sure about that," she replied as she placed his cold beer on top of a coaster.

"Well, I am after all this time spent watching you excel at your job. I'm in town now hiring for a sales position for Frontier Communications and I think you'd be really great at it." He reached into his pocket. "Here's my card. Write down the name of the hiring manager, call him, and tell him I recommended you. It's business-to-business sales, with a base salary and generous commission. We have a great new product called WebEx. It's a web conferencing service. Don't worry, we offer paid training too."

"Well, thank you," she enthused, encouraged by his words. "I'm definitely going to give him a call tomorrow."

Just as predicted, her interview a few days later had simply been a matter of going through the motions. "If the VP sent you in, you have the job," the hiring manager informed her. "Welcome to Frontier Communications."

It felt like a miracle – the teenage girl who'd joined the military to save her father the expense of college and accrue some life experience had transformed into a competent, successful businesswoman who exceeded her quotas every month and brought home a significant share of the bacon. Best of all, having established her long-term career trajectory, she no longer had to devote every week night to bartending at Coyote Joe's. Life was amazing.

In a strange way, growing up in a small town where everyone knew her family had prepared her for the local celebrity status Alec's musical performances created.

How many women are lucky enough to find a handsome, loving, faithful, and multi-talented husband like mine?

It was a question Sam asked herself every day; a verbal "pinch" to remind herself this was not a dream, but her own magnificent reality. And with the establishment of an abundant dual-income household, Alec's thoughts soon turned to the acquisition of their dream home. His strong case for building equity, securing their future, and having an expansive place to host family holidays and entertain friends wore down Sam's resistance. Despite her earlier fears, she had to concede to the benefits only a house could provide – including a sound-proof music room where Alec's band could practice every week.

Soon, they fell into a Sunday routine of house-hunting in Charlotte's most upscale communities, where they toured model homes and perused countless floor plans and upgrade options. Tile or hardwood? Granite or quartz countertops? Two-story colonial or craftsman? Maybe a one-story ranch? The possibilities made her head swim.

Then, right after Labor Day in the year 2000, Beth and Tom flew down to spend a few weeks helping the young couple make the right decision. At the time, Sam and Alec were torn between a new build – a traditional, two-story, four-bedroom brick house in the Allyson Park neighborhood of Ballantyne, and a charming, newly renovated bungalow in Dilworth. In Sam's mind, the latter option, with its proximity to uptown, more than satisfied their needs and desires. She loved its quintessentially Southern front porch, hardwood floors and manageable living space of just seventeen-hundred square feet. And with state-of-the-art speakers, three bedrooms and two-and-a-half baths, there were plenty of accommodations for band practice and out-of-state guests.

But if she'd believed her in-laws' passion for grandchildren had waned during their final years in the Air Force, she'd soon discover it was back with a vengeance since Sam and Alec had settled into upwardly mobile careers, with her husband's local celebrity status providing additional income and prestige.

After picking Beth and Tom up at Charlotte Douglas International Airport, the quartet drove to Dilworth to give them a tour of Sam's preferred option.

"Isn't it just beautiful?" she gushed as she took Beth's arm and led her up the four steps to the front porch. "The owners just renovated the entire place, so we wouldn't have to do a thing to it… just move in. And I love that it's so close to work and everything we want to do."

"It certainly is charming, no doubt about that. But do you think it's big enough to raise a family?"

Before Sam could reply, Alec slipped an arm around her waist. "Mom, you know that's years away still, don't you? We want to have kids…just not now."

"But why buy a house you'll only outgrow after you start having babies?" Beth insisted. "Don't you agree, Tom?"

"Well, yes, I do," he chimed in. "You'd be surprised how small seventeen-hundred square feet will feel once it's filled with all the stuff you'll need to take care of a baby. And that's just if you have one. Why not get a place that's already big enough? That way…

when the time is right…you can grow into it and not have to move again."

"Mom and Dad, do me a favor," Alec asked, "just wait until the realtor gets here to give us a tour of the inside before you pass judgement. Who knows? You might even like it."

To Sam's relief, a moment later their realtor's bubbly voice and perky disposition prevented the tension from escalating.

"I am sorry I am runnin' a bit late," she apologized. "You must be Tom and Beth. How are y'all doing? I hope you had a good flight." They exchanged pleasantries before she entered the code into the lockbox to begin their tour.

By the end of the day, Sam found herself signing paperwork for the new build in Ballantyne, to be completed before the end of February of the following year. The smile on her face betrayed her inner turmoil as the stroke of a pen committed her to a home she did not quite feel ready for, but couldn't exactly understand why.

૭

"10-9-8-7-6-5-4-3-2-1…Happy New Year!" the entire ballroom erupted at the stroke of midnight, while a cascade of confetti, multi-colored metallic ribbons, and gold-and-silver balloons rained down upon them.

Alec pulled his wife close to him and gazed into her deep blue eyes. "This is our year, Fancy Face. If you thought 2000 was great, just wait until you get a load of 2001. All of your dreams are coming true."

"Oh Alec, they already have," she answered.

"Oh, you ain't seen nothin' yet," he grinned before drawing her into a passionate New Year's kiss with a tantalizing preview of what awaited them once they returned to The Presidential Suite

– an obscene indulgence that Alec had insisted on upgrading to. Considering his status as Charlotte's promising new country music voice, The Ballantyne Hotel had no problems accommodating the request, even on their busiest night of the year.

"Well, Fancy Face, are you ready to ring in 2001 in private?" he asked, after coming up for air. A nod and a smile told him everything he wanted to know. After saying goodnight to their friends with a promise to see them later that morning for a breakfast buffet, they held hands as they walked out of the grand ballroom on their way to the lobby elevators.

A few minutes later, Sam gasped as her husband opened the double doors.

"Wow, this place is even better than our honeymoon suite," she observed, taking in the sight of the crown molding, built-ins, and columns.

"Let's check out the bedroom," he suggested with a wink. The intimate space welcomed them with sky-blue-painted walls and a King size bed adorned with white Egyptian sheets and a stunning sky-blue-and-cream-colored tapestry. Another doorway framed by white molding led into a luxurious marble master bath with dual vanities, a jacuzzi and walk-in shower. In the closet hung two his-and-her Turkish terry cloth robes.

For a moment, Sam stood transfixed, until she felt her husband's arms wrap around her from behind. Her entire body shivered as she felt him move her hair to one side and begin to nibble her ear and neck as they faced the large, gold bathroom mirror.

"You know what I like most about this Vera Wang dress?" She could feel his hot breath in her ear. "Watching it fall to the floor." With that he slowly unzipped it before placing his hands on the spaghetti straps on her shoulders to peel it away from her body. She felt the soft material pool around her feet, which were still trapped in her high-heeled sling backs. But all thoughts of releasing them melted away while her husband tantalized her by freeing her breasts from the confines of her strapless bra.

"God, Sam, you are so beautiful," he whispered, his hands cupping them gently at first as they both continued to stare in the mirror. "You...are...the...only...woman...for...me," his husky voice repeated as his caresses escalated in intensity, causing her to lose all sense of time and place as she leaned back against him and moaned. She immersed herself in his touch as his fingers lingered over her nipples until they hardened against his skin. Then his skillful hands ran down her taut abs and tiny waist before slipping under her silk panties and feeling the moisture and heat emanating from the most intimate part of her body.

When her knees grew weak, he picked her up in his arms and carried her to the bed, where they savored each other's company and dreamed of an even brighter future.

Chapter Four

Alec drove his Cadillac Escalade past the neighborhood's wrought-iron-and-brick entrance which bore a plaque emblazoned with the words, "Allyson Park," and a gold cut-out of a majestic oak tree. Although late January, the presence of a large, golden sun amid a clear blue sky neutralized the chill in the air just enough to ride with the windows halfway down. On the radio, Sara Evans' latest release, *Born to Fly*, blasted through the speakers.

Caught up in the euphoria of meeting his wife to make their final decisions on upgrades for their brand-new home, he resisted the urge to speed through the tree-lined streets, an effort made easier by the ubiquitous presence of construction equipment and workers. He smiled as he turned onto the cul-de-sac and saw their majestic, two-story brick house, the last one to be completed in this section.

"If only the drill sergeants could see me now," he remarked out loud in a voice laced with arrogance and condescension. But when he noticed Sam smiling and waving to him in the driveway, his mood changed. He shifted the car into park and jumped out to greet her.

"Hey Fancy Face, how was your day?" He kissed her on the lips and pulled her into a hug.

"Awesome! And it's about to get even better," she giggled. "I'm so excited to be in the final stretch of this home-building process. I can't believe we'll be moving in in just a few weeks."

"You excited?"

"Of course, I am."

"It's just that I know this wasn't your first choice, that's all."

"Yeah, but the more I think about it, your parents were right. This is a house we can grow into…when we're ready. And even though it's been fun picking out paint colors and all the other stuff, I don't really want to do it again anytime soon. I want us to grow old together, right here."

"I hear ya," he laughed.

They strolled arm-in-arm up the landscaped walkway to the white double-doors with gold knobs that led to a grand foyer with a vaulted ceiling and a curved staircase. Here, the builder's sales representative met with them to finalize upgrades like granite countertops, crown molding, wainscoting and custom cabinetry. As the numbers added up, Sam felt a sick feeling in the pit of her stomach, but reminded herself that they could easily afford it, thanks to their thriving corporate careers and Alec's singing. After all, this was an investment in their future, the home in which they'd spend the rest of their lives. Wasn't this the reason she'd carefully saved their bonuses and annual increases? Why keep throwing money away on rent when they had the capability to buy their version of the American Dream?

And a few weeks later, when Alec carried her through the threshold, her lingering insecurities vanished amid the aroma of new paint and the vision of stainless-steel appliances, hardwood floors, and upscale finishes. She'd sure come a long way from her simple home in the Vermont countryside. To celebrate, the couple threw themselves into planning a house-warming party. In addition to family and friends, the guest list included a writer and photographer from *Charlotte Magazine*, since the publication had contacted them to run a story about the Russell's new home in the city's most desirable new neighborhood.

To prepare for the arrival of Walter, Patricia, Shannon, Tom, and Beth, the couple selected bedroom furniture and accessories from Atlantic Bedding and Furniture on Harris Boulevard. Every time she watched her husband pull out his credit card to pay for a purchase, Sam reminded herself that these were necessities, not luxuries. If they wanted family to visit often, they had to have comfortable accommodations. Besides, both of their jobs were going well; there was no reason to suspect anything would change for the worse in their financial situation. Between them, they were earning a healthy six-figure income, while many of their peers were still agonizing over what to do with their lives.

One of them was Shannon. Although she worked hard in Walter's photography business, she felt trapped by her circumstances. This problem was compounded by her tumultuous relationship with Patricia, which often put her at odds with her father. Sam did her best to broker peace long-distance, without much success. She almost felt guilty inviting Shannon to the house-warming party and purchasing her airline ticket, but hoped the visit would give them an opportunity to have a meaningful conversation in person.

When Sam arrived at Charlotte-Douglas Airport to pick them up after work on a Friday evening, she noticed someone was missing.

"Dad, where's Patricia?" she asked after giving him a big hug and a kiss on the cheek.

"Oh, she decided to stay behind and keep an eye on things at the shop," he answered nonchalantly. She eyed him suspiciously, but did not pursue the matter further, preferring instead to savor the company of two of her favorite people.

"Sam, I'm so excited to see your new place. It looks gorgeous!" Shannon squealed.

"Yes, well, you'd better come and visit often," she teased. "There's enough room for an army in there."

"So, uh, when are you and Alec going to get busy creating that army?" Walter teased.

"Ugh, not you too, Dad," she sighed as they made their way to baggage claim.

"Oh, believe me, sweetheart, I know better than to pressure you like that. When you set your mind to do or *not* do something, I know you mean it."

"I just wish Tom and Beth did. When they got to the house last night, the first thing they said was, "Oh, you guys have a huge house with four bedrooms now. When do you think we're gonna have some grandkids? How many times do we have to tell them we are not there? AT ALL," she added for emphasis. "We are *nowhere* near ready to have kids. My husband lives for his weekends playing at Coyote Joe's and now he's getting gigs all over Charlotte. Soon, he's going to end up playing in bigger cities like Atlanta, I just know it. I'm not having babies until he and I are both ready to take on the responsibility."

Walter and Shannon listened in silence and allowed her to vent her frustrations. When he was certain she was finished, her father replied calmly, "Sam, you are only 24 years old. That sounds perfectly reasonable to me. You have sound judgement and you work hard. You have every right to enjoy your life right now. You're young; you have plenty of time to be a mother."

"Thanks, Dad. I appreciate your support. I'm sorry for going off on you both like that; I guess the pressure is starting to get to me a little. Thank God, they live in another state. I love my in-laws, but I can only take so much."

"Well, what does Alec say?" Shannon questioned. "I mean, he does support you in front of them, doesn't he?"

"Yeah, we're totally on the same page. And they love that his country music hobby seems to be turning into a promising thing. I mean, you just never know where it'll lead because it's so competitive, but I'm proud of what he's accomplished so far. If it ever came down to packing up and relocating to Nashville, I'd go with him in a heartbeat. Tom and Beth just think it's no big deal to throw a baby or two into the mix because they can't wait to be grandparents. I get it. But I'm not ready to give them what they want yet."

"Well, then, you just keep standing up for yourself," Shannon encouraged her. "But I gotta tell you, I can't wait to be a crazy auntie," she giggled. "You can take me along on the tour bus and I'll babysit."

As Sam surveyed her little sister's purple-streaked hair and dramatic make-up, she couldn't help but grin. Placing an arm around her, she joked, "That sounds good. But you're not doing their make-up or buying them clothes until they are at least eighteen."

"Smart-ass," Shannon laughed. "That's OK; if Alec hits the big-time, I'll be more interested in hanging out with some hot country music guys than being a bad fashion influence on your kids...I'll just sympathize with them having to be dressed like dorks."

"I'm sure they'll appreciate that." Sam winked at her. "Oh, by the way, there may be a few hot single guys at the party, so keep an open mind. Who knows? Maybe I'll get you down to Charlotte soon. I know you would love it here."

⁓

Sam threw her keys on the coffee table and flopped onto the couch. Happy, but exhausted after a busy weekend of celebrating, she'd just returned from dropping everyone off at the airport and looked forward to a relaxing evening with her husband in their new home.

As her eyelids grew heavy, she drifted off into a contented, dream-filled sleep, where visions of the future featured cherubic babies, career advancement, and even a summer getaway home in Wilmington. She watched herself play with her giggling toddler in the waves, gently rocking her on her hip while the warm water swirled and danced around them, her father capturing the magical moment with his camera. Lost in this intoxicating fantasy, she didn't hear Alec calling to her from behind, his voice building in intensity with every utterance of her name.

"Sam, Sam, wake up. *Sam.*"

She felt a firm nudge on her shoulder, abruptly ending her enchanted interlude. Up until that moment, it had felt as real as his urgent touch. She shot up on the couch and rubbed her eyes.

"I'm sorry, I must have drifted off, I'm so tired. What's wrong?" her heart sank as she noticed his hollow expression.

"I got laid off, Sam. Company cut-backs." His entire demeanor exuded devastation and fear – two emotions she was unaccustomed to seeing.

"Oh, babe…I'm so sorry. But you're young, intelligent…it's just a matter of time before you'll find something even better, don't worry." She reached up and caressed his cheek with her hand.

"Great timing," he snarled. "Why couldn't it have happened before the closing? Now we have a mortgage to deal with."

"Hey, I have a job," she assured him. "And you're still singing at the bar. That'll help." She wrapped her arms around him and laid her head on his chest. "It's going to be okay; you'll see."

Alec slowly folded his arms around her and buried his head in her shoulder. "Is it? I don't know, Sam. I don't even know what I want to do in life anymore."

Like a menace, the foreboding feeling returned with a vengeance, tormenting her as she whispered over and over that everything would be alright. She pulled him closer and prayed to God for something even better to come along.

But as the weeks passed by, Sam struggled to maintain a cheerful façade while she watched her husband's transformation from confident go-getter to catatonic couch potato who barely spoke to her and couldn't even be bothered to shave. Worse, his emotional distance translated into a lack of interest in being a husband in every sense of the word. Not only would he reject her advances, he'd refuse to even hold her as they slept, often preferring to spend the night downstairs on the leather recliner in the living room. Even his prized guitar languished alone in his state-of-the-art music room, the sound of silence flooding the house with a palpable sense of impending doom.

One evening, after a stressful day at the office, Sam arrived home to find him staring blankly at the wall, unshaven and scruffy in his flannel pajamas.

"Alec," she whispered, gently tapping his shoulder. "Hey, babe, I'm home." He remained unmoved by her presence, much to her annoyance. Despite her best efforts, her patience was wearing thin, thanks to their dwindling savings account and his glaring lack of motivation to improve the situation. He'd even given up his singing gigs at Coyote Joe's, which put him in danger of violating his contract and ruining his reputation.

"Alec, c'mon. Talk to me. I can't keep doing this alone."

"Look what arrived today," he announced. He held up a copy of Charlotte Magazine, with several pages curled back to reveal a glossy photo of the two of them, taken at their recent housewarming party. It bore the headline, *All American Couple Alec and Samantha 'Sam' Russell Have It All: Thriving Careers, A Passion for Country Music and Each Other...and a Gorgeous New Home in Charlotte's Most Desired Zip Code.* Their facial expressions radiated with pure love and joy.

Sam's eyes filled with tears remembering the jubilant occasion; it was just a short time ago that she was living a dream life. Now her entire world was collapsing around her and she had no clue how to put it all back together.

"Oh...my," her voice caught in her throat. "What happened to this happy couple, Alec? Where did they go?"

"I don't know, Sam. The guy in that picture...it's not me. Because I just don't know what I want to do with my life anymore. I know I'm not where I want to be. I'm 24 and I feel like I'm 44. I feel too old. I want to pursue my personal dreams."

"But you are pursuing them. Look how far you've come. Today it's Charlotte Magazine, tomorrow it could be Country Music Magazine. You have the drive and the talent. What do you want to do? Want to pack up and move to Nashville together? I'm ready.

Don't you get it? I support your dreams," she replied, fighting back the tears.

But nothing could have prepared her for his reaction.

"Well, yes, I do want to go to Nashville, but I need some time and space to figure it out."

His use of the words "time and space" pierced her soul. For the past six years, they'd lived as a crazy-in-love team that did everything together. *Time and space?*

"Space from me? We're a team. What do you mean, space?" she finally managed to say.

"When I move to Nashville, it's not gonna be with you."

He might as well have punctured her heart with a stake. She felt her knees buckle and grabbed onto the back of the chair to steady herself, lest she crumble to the floor in a hot mess of hysteria. Drawing in a deep breath of air, she forced herself to exhale slowly while her life with Alec flashed before her in a haze of tender kisses, romantic serenades, and unforgettable milestones, from their original Santa Clara court house nuptials to their lavish New England wedding.

Then, she felt the bile rise in her throat and ran upstairs to the master bathroom, where she spent the rest of the evening curled up in a ball on the rug, immune to her husband's pleas to come out from the other side of the door. By the time the sun rose the next morning, Alec was gone, as were many of his possessions.

Somehow, Sam pulled herself together to make it into the office, looking bedraggled and defeated. At every opportunity, she called her husband on his cell phone, only to get voice mail. By 2 PM, she told her boss she was ill and needed to go home.

Home? Did she even have one anymore?

Her thoughts tortured her as she pulled into the driveway in her new Honda Accord and stared at the stately entrance of what now felt like someone else's dream. The red brick construction, black shutters, and ornamental white columns she had once adored now seemed to mock her sorrow, along with the hydrangeas that lined the walkway to the front doors.

After fumbling for her house keys, she walked through the grand foyer and into the gourmet kitchen that had once filled her with pride and excitement. As she threw her purse on the granite counter, she accidentally toppled a crystal vase filled with fresh flowers from Harris-Teeter – one of Sam's earlier attempts to create a cheerful atmosphere. It exploded when it hit the ceramic tile, splashing water, scattering pink roses and white lilies, and shattering glass everywhere.

She shrieked in horror, then turned and ran back toward the foyer to front door. Halfway there, she bumped into Alec's broad chest and felt his strong biceps encircling her.

"Let me go, let me go," she cried. "I don't even want to see you. I don't know what to do. What's happening? What do you want from me?" She pounded his chest as her tears soaked his tee shirt. Although his heart ached for her, his resolution never wavered.

For a few moments, he just held her until rage wore her out.

"C'mon, let's sit down on the sofa," he whispered as they walked arm-in-arm toward the living room.

"Sam, I want you to know, you didn't do anything wrong. I gotta figure out my shit and I just need space. That's why I'm moving out."

Her heart caught in her throat.

"W-what?"

"I'm moving in with Ted."

"From the band?"

"Yeah. I have to get back at it if I'm going to have a country music career. I'm starting back at Coyote Joe's this weekend, too. The last thing I need is a legal mess following me into Nashville and ruining any chance I have to make it big."

"So, it's all about you and to hell with how it affects me – the woman who is willing to pick up her entire life and move with you."

"Sam, please. I just need some time alone to figure things out."

"And I'm supposed to – what? Keep up a façade that everything's okay? Have you even told your parents what you're doing?"

He nodded sheepishly, recalling that difficult conversation. As expected, they supported his goal, but not his method for achieving it.

"Have you told Walter and Shannon anything?"

"No, not yet. Not until I understood myself what was going on. What exactly *is* going on, Alec? Is this a temporary separation? What's your plan?"

"Sam," he sighed. "I just don't know. Like I said, I need time to figure it all out. For now, I'm moving in with Ted to concentrate on my music without any distractions."

She winced at his words. "Distractions? Like me? Like a brand-new house with a mortgage?" He shuddered at the increasing bitterness of her tone.

"I'm heading out," he finally announced. "I'll be back later for the rest of my stuff."

With that, he rose from the couch and strode out the front door, leaving her alone to wallow in the aroma of new paint and carpet while she wondered what to do next.

As days turned into weeks, Sam kept up the charade of a happily married woman for the benefit of her family and co-workers. Each night, as she lay alone in their King size bed, she'd reminisce about better times and reconsider her father's initial misgivings about her Air Force boyfriend. After Walter had come around and thrown the most elegant wedding Sam could imagine, she didn't have the heart to break the news to him. How could she when she'd hadn't even accepted it herself? While there was the slightest chance of Alec coming back to her and renewing his commitment to their marriage, she preferred to remain silent. If her father and Shannon knew about the pain he was inflicting on her, they'd probably lose all respect for him, even if they did manage to reconcile.

But maintaining the façade had all but drained every ounce of energy she had. Her days consisted of getting up and going to work, then coming home immediately afterward. She could barely force herself to eat and couldn't remember the last time she'd even worked out. Here she was, living in one of the most prestigious neighborhoods in Charlotte and her home felt more like a gilded cage than a lovers' haven from the outside world. Without Alec, it meant nothing more than shelter from the elements.

To make matters worse, occasionally she'd arrive at the house at the end of the day to find him there, gathering more of his belongings. If returning to their marriage was even a possibility to begin with, it was becoming an increasingly remote outcome to this entire drama.

After pulling into the driveway one evening to see his Escalade there yet again, Sam knew exactly what needed to be done.

"Alec," she called after closing the front door behind her. "I need to talk to you."

A minute later, he appeared at the top of the stairway, carrying a box of clothing. "Hey," he greeted her.

"Hey. Can you come down here for a minute?"

He complied and followed her into the living room. Sam took a deep breath, then began. "What is going on? Are we breaking up? Do you not want to be with me anymore? I'm so confused."

"I don't know what I want, Sam. I can't figure out my life with you because I need space. It's not fair to stay married to you while I pursue my dreams and I don't want to hold you back. At the same time, I love you and I don't want to lose you. I wish I could hit the pause button on our relationship for three or four years. I'm trying to figure my life out. I really do think I want to go to Nashville and try to make it in country music."

"Ok, then let's go. I've told you a million times, I support your dream. If you want to move to Nashville, let's pack up and move to Nashville. We'll put the house up for sale and go."

Alec remained silent, his eyes cast downward.

"Look, Alec, you have to make a decision. There is no 'pause' button in real life. Either I'm part of your life or I'm not. Either you move back in and we start working on things, or you move out and do your thing, but I can't live in limbo anymore. I've been living all alone in this house for two months." Sam laughed bitterly. "I don't even know how to refer to it anymore. Is it my house? Your house? Our house? Are we selling it? I just don't know what to do."

"I'm sorry, Sam."

"Alec, stop apologizing and just make your choice; either I am part of your life and I support you in your country music career, or I'm not. It's that simple."

"If that's the choice, you're not. Because I have to figure my life out. I have to do my own thing."

As she pondered the significance of his words, Sam felt as if she'd been the target of a prank played on her by a sadistic Universe that took pleasure in her pain. Why else had their relationship unfolded with such ease and serendipity, only to crash and burn in the worst way imaginable? There was no other woman, at least none that she was aware of. It was much worse than that. Her husband, who had vowed to love her forever, simply didn't want her to be his partner anymore as he pursued a dream she fully supported. It didn't make any sense.

Her knees buckled as she dissolved into anguished tears on the sofa. While the sight of her crying tugged at his heart, Alec made no move to comfort her. After a few minutes of listening to her sobs, he announced, "I want a divorce."

ॐ

"Hello, Samantha, I'm Sean McIlveen. I'll be overseeing today's proceedings."

Sam mumbled a response as she forced herself to shake hands with the man who would file the paperwork to erase the most significant part of the last seven years of her life. From the moment she'd awakened that morning, she'd felt dead inside. She couldn't even remember any detail about the ride to the attorney's office, her mind too busy replaying the events of the past few months. But try as she might, she couldn't figure out how it had all gone wrong while she gazed out through the windshield and steered her car in the direction of an unfamiliar corporate center. Somehow, she arrived at her destination in one piece.

After Alec had declared his intention to divorce her, she made the decision not to prolong the agony by engaging in a nasty fight over material possessions. When he came to the house a few weeks prior to making it official, she'd put up a strong front in response to his questions.

"What do you want, Sam? How do you want this to work? What do you want to walk away with? I don't want to screw you; I don't want to be unfair."

Unfair. Was he kidding? Just six months ago, he promised her 2001 would be their most incredible year yet. How did they arrive at ugly breakup and divorce from unending marital bliss? What else could she have possibly done to demonstrate her full commitment to him and his dreams?

Her stomach twisted as she attempted to answer these questions with any degree of satisfaction – an impossible feat, given the surreal nature of the situation and its detrimental effects on her mind, body, and soul. Shouldn't an impending divorce come with more tangible warning signs?

"Look, Alec, I am not going to fight you for alimony. You can have the house. I don't want it; I can't afford the mortgage payments and even if I could, there's no way I'd want to stay here. All I want is my car and my stuff and move into an apartment. You can have everything else."

"What? Are you sure?" He reached out to take her hand in his, but she drew back from him in a clear signal that he was never to touch her again. Alec understood. God knew, he'd just pulled the rug out from under her. It was too soon to expect that they could even be friends.

"Yes. I'm just gonna take my car and my personal stuff. That's all I want."

"Sam, I know how hard this is for you. And that's fine; if that's all you want, I'm cool with it. But I hope you'll accept something else from me." With that, he pulled out his checkbook and walked over to the kitchen table. She watched from a distance as he scribbled something, then walked back into the living room to hand it to her.

"Please take this," he pleaded. "It'll help you buy some furniture for your new place."

She looked down to read the signed check, made out to her for three-thousand dollars, and resisted the urge to perform a dramatic act of defiance by ripping it up. He'd just broken her heart into a million pieces with zero consequences; the least he could do was cough up a few grand for her expenses. As if abandoning their marriage wasn't bad enough, Sam had recently been subjected to internet and tabloid rumors of her soon-to-be-ex-husband's affair with a Coyote Joe's groupie. She thought back to Airman Bucci's sobering speech in the desert and shuddered. Had that been a clear warning sign she'd chosen to ignore?

Whatever the case, here she was, sitting in a divorce attorney's conference room, just weeks after spending her 25th birthday alone, conducting an inner monologue about maintaining her self-control. But her outward display of strength and resilience disintegrated at the sight of the massive stack of papers awaiting her signature. Unrestrained tears began to flow as the divorce attorney began to disseminate the legal documents and explain where to sign each one. She could barely make out the signature lines through her tears or hear the explanation given for each piece of paper as she participated in the dissolution of her marriage through written consent. Every so often, she'd glance at Alec and could tell he was fighting a battle within himself to remain stoic. Though his dark eyes were filled with moisture, he maintained his composure; Sam's intermittent sobs were the only other sound punctuating the room.

After about 30 minutes, the attorney announced, "Ok, Sam, that's all you need."

"That's it?"

"Yes, it's done. We'll file it with the judge, but as far as you're concerned, it's pretty much done. That's it."

Easy for you to say when we're talking about my life, she thought.

Consumed by anger and hurt feelings, she rose from the table and walked out without saying another word or looking back at the man who'd once promised her the world but had proven himself incapable of the task.

When she exited the revolving glass doors, the early summer sun bathed her in its intense heat in stark contrast to the conference room's frigid air-conditioning. She squinted and sighed in frustration as she fumbled through her purse in search of her sunglasses and keys while walking as fast as she could from the scene.

Then she saw it.

Alec's six-month-old Escalade parked in a shaded area in a remote corner of the lot. She glanced behind her at the building entrance, but there was no sign of him or anyone else. Emboldened, she picked up her pace, incited by a fresh wave of undiluted rage. Although a desire for revenge had never been part of her intrinsic make-up, the finality of the morning's events had triggered new and overpowering emotions that won out over lingering heartache and depression. She'd just allowed this man to walk away unscathed after he rewarded her devotion by making her a divorcee at an age when most of her friends hadn't yet married for the first time. He deserved some sort of punishment.

She approached the passenger side at the back bumper and, before she could change her mind, dragged her key across the length of the car. Shaking, she stood at the front bumper for a moment to inspect her handiwork before the slam of a door a few feet behind her brought her back to reality. Heart pounding, she spun around and was relieved to discover it was nothing more than two business people engrossed in their own conversation as they headed toward the office building. She exhaled deeply, then proceeded in the direction of her Accord before her new ex-husband could discover what she'd done.

A little while later, Sam arrived back at her one-bedroom apartment in Strawberry Hill, grateful for having taken a full day off from her job. She lit some candles and settled into a warm bath, planning to relax as much as she could before she met up with a co-worker for drinks. But every time she closed her eyes, a movie played in the theater of her mind, featuring her and Alec in the starring roles, reenacting every moment spent together since meeting at Keesler.

"Damn it," she muttered. Having given up on her plans to create a home spa experience, she held onto the side of the tub to steady herself as she got on her feet and reached for a nearby towel. Wrapping it snugly around her body, she walked into the bedroom just as her cell phone rang on the night stand.

"H-hello?"

"Sam, thank God. Are you okay? I've been trying to reach you for hours," Shannon's panicked voice responded. "Dad and I have been worried sick."

"I'm sorry, Shannon. It's been a rough morning…I just needed some time alone."

"No, time alone is not what you need right now, Sam. You need your family…which is why I'm calling. Dad got me a plane ticket. I'm boarding in a few minutes and should be there by 6 PM."

Sam's heart fluttered. "Really?" she choked out.

"Of course, silly. I would have gotten there sooner, except it's been busy around here with graduations and stuff. But now that the rush is over, Dad can spare me for a few days. Screw Alec; you and I need to go out on the town and have some fun."

Fun. It felt like a distant memory.

"Okay, well my girlfriend from work and I already had plans. I'll pick you up at the airport and we'll meet her at the bar."

"Excellent. I'll see you soon. And Sam? You'll get through this, you'll see. By the way, where are we going?"

"Oh, this place called the Tin Roof. It's in Uptown in the middle of everything. Live music and great food, supposedly."

"Live music? No chance of running into Alec, is there?"

"Nah, as far as I know he's pretty tied to Coyote Joe's. I'm not worried."

"Okay, see you soon."

"Shannon?"

"Yeah?"

"T-Thank you. I don't know what I'd do without you."

"Hey, that's what little sisters are for. I'm furious at Alec for hurting you like this. Who the hell does he think he is, anyway? He'd better pray we don't bump into each while I'm in town…and he's damn lucky Dad can't get away from the business right now. If you think I'm mad, you should hear dad. I've never seen him this angry. Not even Patricia can calm him down."

"Oh, no. I hope he's taking care of himself. I don't want anything bad happening to him because of me." She barely got the words out before she broke down again.

"He's fine physically, Sam, don't worry. And it's not your fault. Trust me, if something were to happen to Dad – and I'm not saying it is – I would hold Alec responsible. Mister 'I want to hit the pause button.' What a jackass. You were too good for him. Someday, he'll realize it and by then you'll have moved on with some hot new guy who is capable of honoring his commitment."

"Just get here soon," Sam whispered. After writing down the flight number, she ended the call, curled up in a fetal position on the bed, and at last gave in to exhaustion.

∾

The three women entered the trendy Uptown establishment to the tantalizing smells of Carolina barbeque and the familiar sounds of Pam Tillis crooning, *Let That Pony Run*. The irony was not lost on Sam, who appeared visibly shaken. Shannon gave her shoulder a squeeze.

"It's going to get better, Sam, I promise."

"Let's just get to the bar," she demanded. "I need a drink now more than ever." The three women elbowed their way through the dense after-work crowd until they arrived at the long, wooden structure set up on one side of the room. Sam nudged her way to the front and got the attention of one of the harried bartenders as he walked by.

"Hey, I'm hungry too," Shannon reminded her. "They didn't give us anything on the plane."

"Fine, let's get our drinks and then find a table," Sam replied. "I need a beer. What do you two want?"

"Ah, Merlot for me," Laura requested.

As her server came into view, Sam's heart sank when she recognized one of her former co-workers from Coyote Joe's.

"Hey, Sam." His smile oozed sympathy, which only irritated her even more.

"Hey, Ron." Ignoring her discomfort, she forced herself to smile back and engage in small talk. "Are you working here now?"

"Yeah, I needed a change of pace and this is closer to my day job, so, here I am. Hey, Sam, I'm sorry about you and Alec. For whatever it's worth, she doesn't hold a candle to you."

Sam felt her knees go weak and tightened her grip on the bar to maintain her balance.

"I'm sorry, what?"

"That groupie that's been hanging around Alec." Then, picking up her on confusion, he added, "Oh, my God, you didn't know. I'm sorry, it was all the gossip at the old place and it's all over the internet. We just assumed you knew and it was one of the reasons for the divorce. Everyone thinks he's crazy to let someone like you go."

So, the rumors were true.

As he watched the color drain from her face, he patted her on the hand. "You know what? I'm sorry, Sam. I should never have brought it up. The first round is on me. What will it be for all of you?"

An astute Shannon answered his question. Although she hadn't heard their exchange, she assumed her sister had been hit by another wave of heartache in an endless grieving process. A few minutes later, they found a free booth by the stage and settled in.

Behind the stage, which was set up with drums, microphones and music stands, an exposed brick wall bore the flashing neon words, *A Live Music Joint.*

"I don't know why they call this place a live music joint when we're still listening to studio music," Shannon remarked. "Guess I'll check out the menu while we wait."

"Don't worry, the live bands will be coming on any minute now," Laura assured her. "There's one from Raleigh that's supposed to be excellent." The statuesque blonde had recently relocated from the D.C. area to become a marketing director at Frontier and had already settled into the Charlotte social scene.

Sam remained quiet, preferring to swig her beer with gusto to numb the pain. It hurt badly enough when the affair was clouded in rumor and innuendo; receiving this unexpected confirmation ripped open a fresh, gaping wound.

"Hey," Shannon interjected. "Let's have a toast first. To new beginnings and better things to come."

"I'll drink to that," Laura joined in.

Sam appreciated the sentiment, but remained fixated on what she'd just discovered. *A groupie? You left me for a groupie – me, the woman who would have uprooted her entire life to make you happy.* Is she why you wanted to hit the pause button? So you could try another piece of ass?

"Sam?"

"Huh?"

"What're you having?" Shannon asked. "The waitress is on her way."

"Just another beer for me."

As the benefits of alcohol kicked in, Sam transformed into a giddy young professional, mirroring her peers who comprised the bulk of the Tin Roof crowd. The passion of the live bands revived her spirits as she joined in the sing-along and even got up to dance alongside her sister.

But when the second band was announced, it felt like a forceful, deliberate kick in the stomach.

"Ladies and gentlemen, please welcome Alec Russell and Red County."

She watched in horror as her ex took the stage, looking radiant, free and ready to party the night away. "Hello Tin Roof, how's it going?" he greeted his audience from behind the mic and strummed his guitar. "It's great to be in a new venue tonight with some new people. I hope y'all enjoy our music."

With that, the band broke into one of their signature songs she'd heard them practice several times over the past few months. An onset of intense nausea consumed her as she ran for the ladies' room, with Shannon close behind. Sam pushed open an unlocked stall and gave in to the inevitable as she knelt in front of the toilet.

"Sam, I'm so sorry...that...that...son of a bitch," she heard Shannon say. "How dare he? I could kill him with my bare hands, I – "

A loud flush drowned out her voice. Shannon moved aside as a scantily clad woman with ample cleavage and dramatic eye make-up approached the sink to wash her hands, just as Sam emerged to catch sight of her.

"Oh, my God. It's you."

The flashy blonde eyed Sam from the full-length mirror. "Well, aren't you the ex-Mrs. Russell?" she replied in a tone dripping with condescension.

"W-what's going on?" Shannon demanded in full defense mode.

"What's the matter, honey? Upset because you couldn't hold onto your man? I guess that Charlotte Magazine feature was a bit premature, huh?"

Shannon's protective instincts kicked in with a vengeance as she stepped in between the women. "You shut the fuck up, you hear me?" she shouted in the groupie's face. "Stay the hell away from my sister. Come on, Sam. We're leaving. I thought this was a high-class establishment, but clearly, I was wrong if they let trash like her in here." With that, she wrapped an arm around her sister and pulled her toward the exit before something could happen that would just add fuel to the fire in the local tabloids.

"Let's get Laura and go," Shannon ordered as they made their way through the dense crowd back to the table. Alec and his band were still performing; Sam couldn't bear to watch him looking so carefree mere   hours after legally ending their marriage. Were those crocodile tears she'd noticed in his eyes as they sat at the conference table? Because he sure didn't look like a guy in emotional distress. For a brief second, she swore he'd caught sight of her as she stared at the stage moments before her sister forced her to turn around and walk back out through the main entrance.

As the summer progressed, Sam threw herself into her account manager position at Frontier, understanding that now more than ever, career advancement was critical. Once Shannon returned to Vermont, she decided to take on a waitressing job in the evenings to combat her loneliness and help her save more money for the future – one that now felt uncertain and scary.

Every day, she prayed for the strength to move on, heal from the hurt, and get beyond the anger. But with her ex sowing his oats in such a public way, the task seemed insurmountable. Although she and Alec stopped all communication, Sam kept in touch with

Beth, who insisted that her son was simply going through a phase. Every time they spoke, Beth would remind Sam of how much he loved her and express her opinion that his country music success on the local scene had gone to his head. Sam would patiently repeat her standard reply that she had been more than willing to give up her career and move to Nashville with him, but that wasn't good enough. She'd remind Beth that she never wanted the divorce, but could not live in limbo. It just wasn't fair. A disheartened and embarrassed Beth would sigh and agree.

One night, after an especially draining call, Sam came to a decision. She opened her dresser drawer and retrieved her engagement ring – Beth's original that she had lovingly sent to her son when he proposed. Somehow in the unfolding drama, she'd never gotten around to returning it to Alec, but now she knew what to do. The next morning, she wrapped it up for priority shipment and sent it off to her former mother-in-law, along with a note expressing her gratitude. She hoped the gesture would provide Beth the closure she needed; holding out hope for a reconciliation was pointless and delusional, and no matter how much Sam appreciated the support, there was no way she could move forward if this pattern continued. Eventually, she would stop all communication, but for now, this was a good first step.

Then an unexpected phone call on a humid July morning rocked her world again.

"Hello?" Her voice quivered slightly, knowing who was on the other end.

"Sam, I gotta ask you something. Did you key my car on your way out of the attorney's office? I figured it was you, but I didn't want to – "

"I don't know what the hell you're talking about," she cut him off. "But I did meet your little groupie in the ladies' room at Coyote Joe's. Tell me, Alec, when exactly did you break our marriage vows? When we were picking out paint colors for the house? Planning our housewarming party? When did you start screwing her? Should I be visiting my doctor to get tested, just in case? Or did you use protection?"

Her rapid-fire words caught him off-guard, but he knew he'd deserved the verbal onslaught.

"I'm sorry I called," he mumbled, before hanging up.

She felt a strange but welcome sense of satisfaction as she flipped her phone shut and headed out the door.

୭

"How are classes going at community college?"

"Ugh, don't ask," Shannon answered. "I'm bored as hell and I still don't know what to do with my life."

"Yes, you do," Sam reminded her. "Remember, beautician school? You're a natural; you just need some professional training to make a career out of it."

"Yeah, whatever." Shannon rolled over on her bed and stared at the ceiling. "What going on with you? I can tell there's something you want to tell me."

"Well, yeah," Sam admitted with some enthusiasm. It felt amazing to feel happy about something again as she told her little sister about an upcoming conference her company was sending her to in Washington.

"D.C.? Wow, look at you, all grown up and going on your first business trip. That's awesome. Screw Alec and his trashy chick; maybe you'll meet some hot new guy in D.C."

"Yeah, my first *big girl* convention," Sam laughed. "I can't wait. And I need a break from Charlotte. It'll be nice to get away for a while."

"When is it?"

"We fly up on September 10, but the trade show actually starts on September 11."

"We?"

"Yeah, remember Laura from marketing? She's coming with me."

"Ah yes, the high-powered chick with the red Mercedes who thinks her shit don't stink."

Sam giggled. "Shannon!"

"Oh, come on. You know I'm right. Are you sharing a room with her? 'Cause I can't imagine what that's gonna be like."

"Hey, I'm a big girl, remember? I can handle it. Besides, we're only there to sleep and shower. Most of the time we'll be at the convention meeting other people. It'll be fine."

Little did she know, getting along with a roommate would be the least of her problems.

The morning of September 10 dawned bright and beautiful as Sam and Laura boarded their plane and arrived in the nation's capital a few hours later. After they checked into the Marriott Marquis, they headed to the ballroom to set up their booth. Whatever Laura's faults, Sam appreciated the fact that she, too, was a perfectionist with a strong work ethic. With the common goal of creating a successful event, the two of them joined forces to accomplish a perfect set-up. Once their task was complete, they walked over to the Corduroy Restaurant, one of Laura's favorite D.C. establishments.

For the first time since June, Sam realized she had gone several hours without thinking about Alec or reliving any aspect of their history. When she fell into bed that night after enjoying a hot shower, she drifted off into a deep, relaxed sleep, hopeful that the events of the following day would present unexpected and welcome opportunities.

She woke up ahead of the alarm clock the next morning, eager to experience everything awaiting her. Rubbing the sleep out of her eyes, she walked over to the window to peek out through the filmy white curtains.

"Looks like another gorgeous September day," she noted to Laura, who emerged from the bathroom in a thick terrycloth robe, hair and make-up expertly done.

"It's all yours," she announced.

A few minutes later, she called out from the other side of the door, "Sam, I'm all dressed. I'll meet you down in the lobby for coffee, okay?"

"Sounds good," she called back as she applied a bit of liquid foundation. Since it was going to be a long day, Sam decided to use more make-up than usual, recalling Shannon's expert tips. Once satisfied with her work, she opened the door and headed toward the closet to get her business clothes together. Then she switched on the *Today* show to keep her company while she finished dressing. It wasn't until she heard the words "plane" and "World Trade Center" that her ears perked up. She zipped up her skirt quickly and hurried over to the TV screen.

"Oh, my God," she breathed when she saw footage of the mass of thick, angry black smoke erupting from one of the world's most famous skyscrapers. "That can't possibly be from a private plane." As she tuned into the reporting to discover it had been a commercial airliner, her heart began to pound in her chest. A minute later, her cell phone rang.

"H-hello?"

"Sam, it's Beth. Are you alright? Where are you?"

"Uh, yeah. I'm still in my hotel room in D.C. I just turned on the news and heard about the World Trade Center. Oh, my God. It's so awful."

"Sam, please just stay safe. Don't leave your room yet."

"Beth, what's going on?" The panic in her voice escalated. She knew that sound was still emanating from the television, but couldn't focus on what was being said.

"I don't know, I – "

"Oh, my God. I can see the smoke from the World Trade Center outside my window. It must really be bad. The smoke from the towers is already down here."

"Sam, I don't think the smoke would already be that thick down there."

"But I can see it. It's pouring out all over the skyline."

"Sam, you have the news on, right?"

She spun around to look at the screen just in time to view the footage of the Pentagon.

"Oh, my goodness, the plane hit here in D.C. *That's* the smoke I'm seeing." She started to sob. "What should I do Beth? What should I do? What's going on? I'm so scared."

Just as her former mother-in-law began to comfort her, another call clicked in.

"Beth? It's Alec. I want to talk to him." She ended the call and greeted her ex with a shaky voice.

"I didn't know you were in D.C."

"Yeah, I'm up here for a work thing."

"Just be safe, Sam." She detected palpable fear and concern his voice. "Are you there alone?"

"No, I have a co-worker with me."

"Good. At least you're not by yourself. Go find her, okay? And please call me later. I need to know you're alright."

As the day's frightful events unfolded, Sam felt as if she'd entered The Twilight Zone. Her scalp tingled and her legs felt as if they would crumble with each step she took. Every face she made eye contact with around the hotel told the same story of anxiety, fear, and uncertainty. To make matters worse, Laura announced that she was leaving to go stay with family and didn't even bother to invite Sam along. Now she was all alone in a strange place, waiting for the other shoe to drop.

At one point, she ventured outside to discover that the bustling city she'd experienced the night before had been transformed into a ghost town in a matter of hours. As she walked the lonely streets, she saw nothing but vacant storefronts and "Closed" signs in display windows.

Good God, 2001 can't end fast enough, she thought. Another chill ran up and down her spine. She picked up the pace and walked as fast as she could back to the hotel.

Once ensconced in the safety of her room, she flipped on the television, threw on a pair of sweatpants and crawled under the covers. Then her phone rang.

"Hello?"

"Sam, it's Alec again. I just wanted to check in on you. When can you get back to Charlotte?"

"Get back to Charlotte – Alec all of the flights are grounded and my roommate just left me in the lurch to go stay with her family. How the hell am I supposed to get home?" She broke down in sobs.

"Shh, it's okay, Sam. I'm going to help. You know what? I'm driving up there to get you. I want you home where it's safe. You need to be down here."

Safe. What did that even mean anymore?

"No, no, Alec, just give me a day or so. I'll check in with Laura and we'll get a rental car."

"I'll give you until Thursday" he declared. "That's it. If you don't have a rental car booked by Thursday, I'm coming to get you because you can't just be stuck in D.C. for days or weeks."

She let out a nervous laugh. "Well, you did promise me 2001 would be a year I'd never forget. I just never expected it to be like this."

"I'm sorry, Sam." She detected a hint of regret in his voice and, for a fleeting moment, wondered if an unforeseen act of war could serve as a catalyst for the renewal of their relationship. She brushed the thought aside to focus on the present.

"Well, I'll call Laura now and work on getting a rental. I'll keep you posted."

By Thursday, after several fruitless attempts, the two women secured a sedan to drive back to the rental company's Charlotte location. They drove with determination and resolve down I-95 on their way to I-77, which would lead them all the way home. The heavy traffic felt oddly comforting to Sam; signs of life in the aftermath of terror. She didn't care that more cars meant extra hours for their commute.

"So, how do you feel about Alec calling you?" Laura inquired.

"I don't know," she sighed. "I don't know what to think anymore, except that this has been the craziest year of my life."

"Well, it seems he still cares for you if he was willing to drive all the way to D.C. to get you."

"Maybe that's the problem. Maybe it's not about caring about me as much as it's about doing what he wants. I don't know. Everything feels so raw right now."

"Yeah, people get emotional in the aftermath of tragedy. But what if you get back and he tells you he wants to reconcile?"

Her heart fluttered again at the thought, but was tempered by a sobering gut feeling.

"I'll never say never," she replied. "But one thing's for sure, I'm proceeding with caution."

When they arrived at Enterprise Rental Car, Alec was there to greet them. Recognizing Laura from the night at the Tin Roof, he felt a little embarrassed as Sam made the introductions. After dropping her co-worker off, they headed toward Sam's apartment in Strawberry Hill.

"Uh, listen, Sam. About that woman…"

"You mean your little groupie?"

"Yeah, her name is Kimberly. She's nothin.' I just hang out with her because she comes to all our shows."

"Right. And the two of you just hold hands, I'm sure."

"Look, Sam, I want you to know I didn't sleep with her before the divorce. I was never unfaithful to you."

Maybe not physically, she thought.

"You do believe me, right?" he asked.

"Yes, I believe you."

For better or for worse, the erstwhile couple resumed their friendship and began to meet on a regular basis for coffee, lunch, or dinner, depending on their schedules. They stuck to "safe," out-of-the-way public environments where they could avoid temptation and focus on catching up on each other's lives. Sam listened as he shared the latest happenings with the band, noting the sparkle in his eyes as he described their expanded venues throughout North Carolina, with plans to start playing in Atlanta by the end of the year. He listened with pride as Sam recounted her latest promotion, raise and increased responsibilities at work.

"I'm happy for you, Sam. You deserve the best," he noted one morning over coffee at Starbucks.

"Alec, does Kimberly even know that you meet me for coffee?"

He smirked. "That's not something she needs to know."

She couldn't figure out whether to be relieved or disgusted, but refrained from commenting as she took another sip of her Caramel Macchiato.

৶

Several weeks later, on a dull November morning, as Sam and Laura sat in the company conference room discussing their latest marketing campaign, there was an urgent knock on the door. The women exchanged surprised glances; they'd informed their respective teams that they were not to be disturbed, which meant whoever was on the other side must have something earth-shattering to share. Or maybe because of recent world events they were still on high-alert, though neither would admit it.

"Come in," Sam responded. The door opened to reveal the presence of her grey-haired Senior Manager Tom Parker, standing next to a tall, skinny guy.

"Forgive the interruption, ladies. I know you're working on a campaign and I don't intend to take up too much of your time. I just wanted to introduce you both to David Chapman, our new benefits manager. David, this is our sales manager Samantha Russell, and our marketing director Laura Graham."

"Oh hi, it's nice to meet you, David," Sam enthused, extending her hand. She flinched inside when he gave her a wimpy handshake – one of her pet peeves – but maintained her outer professionalism. After a few minutes of small talk, the men left them alone again.

"Okay, I'm just gonna say it," Laura announced without apology. "That's guy's a real nerd. Did you notice how awkward he was?"

Sam laughed. "Yeah, he was pretty stiff. Can't say I'm surprised he's a benefits manager."

"I'm not surprised he's from the Midwest."

"What do you mean?"

"You know; good people, nose-to-the-grindstone types," Laura explained. "But in my experience, all work and no play. I worked with quite a few Midwesterners back in D.C."

"Speaking of work, let's get back to it. I'm not from the Midwest, but I can relate to the nose-to-the-grindstone thing. Don't hold it against me," Sam joked.

"You're different, Sam. You have a great personality and a lot of interests. Personally, I don't know why you leave here to go work as a waitress every night. You should take up a class or join a runners group or do something interesting and fun."

"Hey, I'm a divorcee remember? I gotta supplement my income and besides, I like being a waitress. It keeps me humble and I get to observe interesting people."

"Well, I'm sure it provides endless entertainment. But with any luck, this campaign will be a huge success for both of us, with bigger paychecks and perks. Then you won't have to work a second job, so you can go out and find Mr. Wonderful. I'm pretty sure it's not David Chapman," she chuckled.

"Uh, probably not."

Sam shrugged as she clicked on her mouse to get to the next screen in her PowerPoint presentation. As she and Laura resumed their business, she didn't give the tall, skinny, nerdy guy another thought.

ço

A biting wind howled all around them in the darkness of the early hour as a light layer of snow dusted the windshield of Shannon's Honda Civic. The two girls tossed the last of the bags in the trunk, slammed it shut and ran for the shelter of the running car to bask in its heat.

"Damn, I was hoping we'd miss the storm if we got on the road early enough." Sam sighed as she slid in behind the wheel, in keeping with her promise to drive for the first several hours of their southbound journey.

"Hey, it's 6 AM. Early enough," Shannon insisted. "Can't believe I even agreed to that. This was the most boring New Year's I've had since I was six, thanks to you." She brought her silver travel mug to her lips and drew in a careful sip of steaming hot coffee.

"Hey, you'll forgive me once you get to Charlotte and start building your new life...rent-free and bills-free for an entire year, I might add," Sam reminded her.

"I know," she replied. "And I don't mean to sound ungrateful, Sam. You have been so generous and I'm excited about starting beauty school at Empire. I appreciate everything you're doing for me. God knows I'm looking forward to living in a warmer climate.

I won't miss long, depressing Vermont winters, that's for sure. I know Charlotte's not a tropical paradise, but compared to here, it'll probably feel like one."

"Ha! I know the feeling. It won't be as drastic as going from Vermont to the Mississippi Gulf, but trust me, you won't have to deal with much snow at all."

"Well…let's get moving, then. If I let you drag my butt out of bed at this ungodly hour, I want a good reason."

Sam laughed and threw the car into reverse. But just as she was about take her foot off the brake, she noticed her father rushing toward them, clad in his thick bathrobe, flannel pajamas, and bedroom slippers. She put it back in park and rolled down the window.

"Dad, it's freezing and the storm is picking up; you're going to catch pneumonia out here," she scolded. Her demeanor softened when she noticed his tear-stained eyes.

"I'm sorry. I just had to see my girls one last time…and to give you this." He handed her an envelope filled with five 20-dollar bills. "I wish I could do more, but that should help pay for gas," he explained.

"Aw, Dad, you're the best. You didn't have to – "

"I wanted to." He leaned in through the open window to address Shannon. "I want you to know, I support your decision and I'm very proud of you for going after your dreams."

"Thanks, Dad," she choked out. "I love you. And I love Sam for making this possible."

"I love you both. You're my girls. Always remember that. And please, call me along the way to let me know you're alright. Your old dad worries, you know."

The Townsend sisters nodded their agreement as their father moved away from the vehicle to allow them to back out of the driveway. They waved at him for a few moments, watching the snowflakes swirl around him until he vanished from sight altogether when they reached the end and turned onto the street.

"I'm gonna miss him," Shannon sniffed.

"Yeah, me too. Who knows? Maybe someday he'll join us."

"Maybe. If his girlfriend approves. Don't know if she loves him enough to relocate."

Sam grunted and shook her head.

"What?" Shannon demanded.

"Oh, nothing. Life is unpredictable, that's all. I loved Alec as much as humanly possible and look what happened. A year ago, we rang in the New Year in high society while he swore the best was yet to come. Now here I am, driving in a snowstorm with you back to Charlotte…no offense. Guess there's no guarantee."

"Well, if it's any consolation, I hope Dad's predictions for 2002 happen for all of us."

"Me, too."

"Sam?"

"Yes?"

"We're sisters, forever. That means nothing – not even a man – will ever come between us. I'm sorry about lecturing you about Alec last night. You're an adult and if you want to meet up with him, it's your business, especially if you decide to sleep with him for old time's sake. I just don't want you to get your heart broken all over again. But just in case that happens, at least I'll be close by."

"You have no idea how excited I am that you're moving with me. And believe me, I get it. I know it's crazy, but even after everything he's put me through, I like seeing him. Then, I remember he's with Kimberly and I want to vomit even though he's just using her for sex. Would I feel worse if he'd fallen in love with her? I don't know…I guess he really was just a player at heart and his time with me was – "

"The real thing? Because it *was*, Sam. I'm sure he loved you."

"Now you sound like Beth."

"She still calling you?"

"Not so much anymore. I think she got the message because I stopped taking her calls once I mailed her ring back to her. I love the woman dearly, but it was just too hard to move on with her insisting that Alec loved me and was going to come around sooner or later. I didn't want to hurt her by being all snarky about Kimberly and risk saying something I couldn't take back."

She glanced briefly at Shannon, who regarded her with skepticism.

"Yeah, I know – then why am I still meeting him for coffee? I have no good answer."

Shannon placed her travel mug back into the cup holder. "Well, you'll know when it's time to put an end to it. Or, maybe he'll announce he finally worked up the guts to go to Nashville like he's been promising for months and that'll do it. He cracks me up; he's so damn cocky, yet can't seem to work up the nerve to go for it. Personally, I think Mr. Pause Button likes being a big fish in a small pond because his big fat ego probably can't take rejection… and don't go defending him. It's one thing to talk to him, but I'm not going to let you demean yourself by – "

"Okay, enough," Sam interrupted, her hands tightening around the steering wheel. "I need to concentrate on the road and the snow is really coming down. She set the wipers to the highest speed and focused her full attention on the highway.

Shannon said no more as she watched her sister navigate through the blizzard. They continued for several hours until stopping for gas shortly after turning onto Interstate 95 in Connecticut. By then, the worst of the storm had dissipated and the sun began to filter through the thick cloud cover. The rest of their conversation on their way to The Queen City centered around beauty school, Shannon's agreement to waitress at Sam's restaurant, and divvying up the chores around the two-bedroom apartment Sam had secured at Strawberry Hill once Shannon had taken her up on her offer.

୨

"Wanna meet for lunch tomorrow?"

As usual, Alec sounded upbeat and carefree. Sam frowned as she flipped through the stack of mail she'd pulled out of her box just before her cell phone rang.

"No, I-I can't tomorrow. Sorry."

"What's wrong Fancy Face? I can tell you're distracted."

"I'd appreciate it if you didn't call me that. And nothing's wrong; I'm just a little stressed out from work, that's all."

"I'd like to help," he offered. "Let me guess…Laura Graham is giving you a hard time."

"What?"

"C'mon Sam, you complain about her all the time. What did she do now?"

It bothered her that he could still read her so well, but the last thing she wanted to do was cry on his shoulder. Not after all these months of proving her strength and ability.

"Nothing. I'm just tired; it's been a long day and I have to get to my other job soon." *As soon as Shannon gets back with her car,* she thought.

"Sam, I know something's wrong. Is it Shannon? Are you two having problems?"

"No as a matter of fact it's not Shannon. Yes, I had a stressful day at the office and on top of that, I had to take my car to the shop at lunchtime. Turns out, I need four new tires for the bargain price of $350." She sighed as she ripped open a bill and looked at the amount due. "And if that wasn't enough, my goddamn cable bill just went up by $20 a month. Is this my reward for taking on a bigger apartment and paying my sister's way for a year? Happy New Year to me!"

"Sam…I'm sorry. What can I do to help? Want me to give you a ride to work tonight? Need some money to pay for the car? Whatever you need, you got it."

"No, no. Thank you. Shannon will be back from class soon and we'll take her car to work."

"Are you sure?"

"Yes, I'm positive. Thanks for the offer. I'll be fine."

"Okay, then. I've got to get to band practice before our show tonight. If you change your mind, just call me."

"Goodbye, Alec."

She flipped her phone shut and ran up the stairs to her room, noting with disdain the mess of laundry piles and assorted items that littered the floor of Shannon's bedroom. *The least she could do is close the door so I don't have to look at her freaking mess,* Sam thought. Then, she reconsidered. Their two-bedroom apartment featured a bathroom in each bedroom, which spared her the aggravation of having to reprimand her sister for her poor housekeeping skills. She had to concede that so far, Shannon was honoring her rules for the common areas; if she wanted her personal space to be a pigsty, that was her business. Besides, having Shannon around gave Sam a sense of peace and comfort that far surpassed any negatives.

She opened her closet and pulled out her freshly ironed work uniform – khaki pants with a white buttoned-down shirt bearing the Red Rocks Café logo – and took a deep, cleansing breath. Since it was Friday, the place was guaranteed to be busy, which meant hours on her feet along with the reward of bountiful tips. Now more than ever, she could use the money.

After a hectic and harried shift, Sam and Shannon arrived home just after midnight, completely exhausted. "Goodnight, Sam," her sister whispered when they reached the top of the stairs. "Between school and work today, I've had it. I can't wait to be horizontal."

"Goodnight," Sam murmured before closing the door on her bedroom sanctuary. She'd barely finished her nightly ritual of brushing her teeth and washing and moisturizing her face when a loud knock at the door startled her. Heart racing, she threw her robe over her cotton pajamas and worked her way down the stairs as quietly and quickly as possible before the raps on the door resumed and awakened her sister.

"Who is it?" she asked in a loud whisper, grabbing an umbrella from the stand.

"Someone who cares about you. Let me in, Sam."

She hesitated for only a moment before opening the door, where she looked upon the sight of her ex-husband in all his masculine glory, holding a brown bag in his hand and grinning at her with his full, sexy lips while his dark eyes sparkled with life.

"Hey, Fancy Face, I know you had a bad day so I brought a little something to cheer you up," he announced. With that, he pulled a gallon of rocky road ice cream out of the bag.

She felt a mixture of gratitude, hope, and excitement, though she did her best to temper her outward reaction. For the first time since their break-up, she didn't even mind that he used his special term of endearment for her.

"Oh my gosh…you're…crazy," she laughed. "Come on in."

"Hey, we may be divorced but I still care about you. And I still remember this is your favorite. What do you say we grab two spoons and talk?"

"Sounds good to me. Give me two seconds." She ran into the kitchen for the utensils, then led him up the stairs after placing her finger to her lips to indicate the need for quiet. He followed her into her bedroom, closed the door behind him, and joined her on top of the bed, where, in muted tones, they laughed and talked until the wee hours of the morning.

༆

A late-fall rain pelted against the panoramic windows of the conference room as Sam gathered with other mid-level managers and senior staff per Tom Parker's urgent email. As she sat next to Laura, she did her best to tune out the speculative chatter all around her, but as evidenced by her queasy stomach, she couldn't deny that she shared their same concerns about impending lay-offs.

And a few minutes later Tom Parker arrived, accompanied by David Chapman, to confirm everyone's worst fears: Frontier Communications was relocating its headquarters to Chicago. Those who wished to remain with the company would have to relocate; otherwise, as David explained in detail, they would receive a severance package. As he described the terms, Sam experienced a combination of regret and relief. Had she not talked her sister into relocating, she would have jumped at the chance to move to The Windy City and truly start over. But with Shannon settled into the Charlotte scene and nearing the end of her formal training, she didn't have the heart to abandon her. Frontier's generous package, along with her waitressing job, would keep her going until she could secure another full-time position.

To her great surprise, David ended his presentation with an invitation to his house for a party, where all employees were welcome. He also promised to do everything he could to help those who chose to remain in Charlotte find new employment. As she watched him, she was struck by the sincerity in his voice. Afterward, back in Laura's office behind closed doors, her soon-to-be former colleague declared her intention of moving with the company to Chicago.

"I wish you all the best," Sam replied. I've learned a lot from working with you, Laura."

"Same here. And I have no doubt you'll find something even better right here in Charlotte."

"Thanks."

"So? Are you going to David's party?"

"Ugh, I don't know. Thanks to you and Shannon convincing me to set up a profile on Match.com, I have a date that night. But maybe I could push it back an hour to put in an appearance. I'm sure it'll be boring and I won't want to stay, but I think I should at least show my face."

"You've got a date? Good for you. I knew it wouldn't take long," Laura remarked happily, ignoring the part about David. "You know, maybe this is a good thing – new job, new boyfriend. A fresh start. It's the only way to get Alec out of your heart and your life for good."

"Well, it helps that he's out of town most of the time playing in Atlanta," Sam remarked. It was a half-truth, but she figured it was no one's business that she and her ex were still meeting regularly.

"You'd better keep in touch," Laura pleaded. "I'll be long gone by then and I want to hear details."

Sam reached out to embrace her. "Of course, I will. Best of luck to you in Chicago. I know you're going places in this company. I'll be keeping an eye on your blossoming career."

"Thank you, Sam. All the best."

Sam let out a groan as she parallel parked on the residential street. Defying her expectations, the circular driveway in front of David's ranch house had reached full capacity.

Best to get this over with, she thought as she glanced in the rearview mirror and applied a light coating of lip gloss. In preparation for her date later that evening, she'd chosen to wear a business casual type of outfit with a black cashmere twin-set, beige slacks, and black pumps. To her surprise, David greeted her with a warm smile and a peck on the cheek.

"Sam, I'm really glad you could make it."

"Me, too. Thanks for doing this. It's really nice of you."

"Well, it's the least I could do for everybody. C'mon, the party is in the basement."

She followed him through a small foyer, noting the frat house feel of the home's outdated interior, complete with 70s style wood paneling and linoleum floors. As if reading her mind, he offered, "This is just a starter house for me. When I got here from Wisconsin, I didn't have much time to house hunt. I answered an online ad and moved in with two other housemates. I'm just glad I have my own bathroom in my bedroom."

Sam laughed. "I know the feeling, believe me." When David opened the door to the basement, the previously muted sounds took clear form – a cacophony of loud country music, laughter, and animated voices. To her chagrin, they were accompanied by thick cigarette smoke, but she decided not to let that bother her. These people had just lost their jobs, after all. They were entitled to have a little fun.

As she made her way through the crowd, she greeted her colleagues with hugs and smiles. David led her to the bar, where large kegs of beer and an assortment of wine bottles awaited. She opted for a beer, then accepted his invitation to play darts.

"I have to warn you, I'm probably not very good at this. I haven't played darts in forever."

"No problem, I'm happy to teach you. When you grow up in Wisconsin, it's the only way to deal with winter," he explained with a chuckle.

Sam fully immersed herself in the art of the game, though she was no match for David's remarkable precision. Still, he didn't seem to mind that his novice teammate caused them to lose most of the matches they played that evening. She appreciated his graciousness and sportsmanship, taking note of the way in which he interacted with everyone in attendance. He truly appeared to care about helping them with resumes and job placement – a topic that inevitably came up despite everyone's efforts to simply enjoy the party and deal with the more serious aspects of life the following Monday.

The hours passed by quickly. It wasn't until she took a break in the powder room that Sam looked at her phone and determined she'd blown off her date, whom she'd been scheduled to meet almost an hour-and-a-half earlier. She shrugged as she glanced in the mirror and pulled a small brush out of her purse. Running it carefully through her shiny waves, she realized she was having a wonderful time.

Then she noticed a text message on her phone from Shannon.

"Having a good time on your date or do you need back-up?" it read.

Sam immediately responded, "No. I'm still at David's, having a blast."

"?????" came her sister's expected reply.

Sam giggled. "I'll fill you in later," she typed out before snapping her phone shut and heading back out to play another game of darts.

By the time midnight rolled around, she was ready to head out. After saying her goodbyes to the remaining partiers in attendance, she spotted their host by the bar and approached him.

"Hey David, I need to get going," she announced. "Thanks, I had a great time."

"I'm glad you came, Samantha. Let me walk you out."

They stepped out into the cool night air. When they reached her car on the street, David asked for her phone number, causing her to laugh out loud. "I'm on the list, remember?" She was referring to the contact form that he himself had passed around earlier.

"Oh yeah, that's right," he grinned, feeling slightly embarrassed. "But what I meant to ask was, would you like to go out on a date… with me?"

She hesitated only for a moment as she noted the sincerity in his hazel eyes. "Umm, yeah. I think that would be nice. I guess I could do that."

"Great, I'll be in touch."

"Sounds good. Here, let me." He motioned for her keys, then opened the driver's side door for her.

"Thank you," she replied, impressed by the gesture. "And thanks again for a great party. I enjoyed myself."

"You're welcome."

She drove off into the night, wondering if she could surrender her heart and learn to love someone who was the opposite of Alec in every way imaginable.

؏

"Hey, just a reminder I have a softball game after work," Sam informed her sister.

"Wow."

"What?"

"Just seems so funny, that's all…a softball game in November. That's something we could never do in Morristown. Is David going to be there?"

"Of course, he's the one who arranged it. Part of the company's efforts to ease the pain of lay-offs."

"Interesting."

"What?"

"Oh…you never know. I mean, he's a little nerdy, but there's something kind of hot about him," she teased.

"Shannon, c'mon."

"Hey, you're the one who blew off a perfectly good date to hang out at his house. I'm just sayin' you should keep an open mind about his offer."

"Says the girl who hasn't dated since she got here almost a year ago."

"Well, I'm a grown-up, now," Shannon protested. "I'm focused on finishing school, so I can work full-time at a salon and get my own place. My time is almost up, you know."

"Shannon, you know I'm not going to throw you out. If you want to stay, I just need you to start paying rent once you get your real job."

"Well, I want you to know I've been saving my money. Dad would be so proud…your influence finally rubbed off."

Sam laughed. "Good. But you are welcome to stay past January if you want. I've gotten used to having you around."

"It's been fun," Shannon agreed. "But we both need our own place. One of your interviews will pan out, I just know it. Then you'll have a good, steady income again."

"I hope you're right," she sighed. "Thanks for the vote of confidence. I'll see you later."

When Sam arrived at the field, David was there to greet her with a big smile and a hug. For the first time, she noticed the uniqueness of his eye color – hazel, with flecks of brown – though he still seemed awkward in his tall, lanky frame. It was as if he was still adjusting to his body, even though by her estimation, he was easily in his early 30s. Over the next few hours, in between turns at bat, Sam confirmed his age to be 33 and learned more about the guy she'd only interacted with a handful of times at the office.

An only child, David was the product of an ambitious CEO father and an emotionally distant mother. Because his father traveled most of the time and his mother couldn't be bothered with mundane and maternal activities, he had been raised by a nanny before his parents shipped him off to a boarding school several hours away from their home in Lake Geneva Wisconsin.

His story tugged at Sam's heart and made her appreciate her own father even more. As she listened to David, she found herself wishing that Walter would make the move to Charlotte, something she discussed with him often. She missed his goofy sense of humor and joyful spirit.

At the end of the game, David escorted her to her car. "I really enjoyed hanging out with you, Sam. You're much better at softball than darts," he joked.

"Am I now?" she feigned offense but couldn't help but crack up. "Okay, I'll let you in on a little secret. I was a jock in high school. Guess I've still got it."

"Yes, you do," he agreed in a soft voice. Before she knew it, he leaned down to pull her into a kiss, wrapping his arms around her waist. His lips felt soft and warm as she responded, realizing it had been too long since she'd experienced this kind of intimacy. True, it lacked the intensity and passion of Alec but she enjoyed it nonetheless.

After a few moments, he backed away and held her hands in his. "I hope that wasn't too presumptuous of me."

"No...no. I – it was really nice," she replied sincerely, her eyes meeting his.

"Well, you drive safely and I hope we can see each other again soon...I mean, outside of the office," he clarified. They had one more week to go before the Charlotte location shut down for good.

"That's up to you." She smiled as she got into her car. He closed the driver's side door and watched as she clicked her seatbelt into place.

"In that case, I'll see you soon, Samantha," he promised, before turning around and walking back toward the field to pick up the remaining equipment. He wondered if he could ever compete for her heart with a rising country music star even though her words and actions filled him with hope. She was about a mile from home when her cell phone alerted her to a new text message. She waited until the traffic light turned red before looking at it.

"Dinner tomorrow night?"

For the first time in forever, Sam felt excited about something. When she pulled into the parking spot in front of her apartment, she texted David back, "Yes."

The following day, the typical late-fall weather returned with a vengeance, bringing torrential downpours and 40-degree temperatures back to The Queen City. Sam looked out her bedroom window with dismay, having hoped by now the rain would have tapered off to a drizzle. With David scheduled to pick her up in a half-hour, that outcome seemed unlikely. She turned her attention back to the ensembles spread across her bed, trying to figure out what to wear. He was taking her to The Village Tavern, an upscale eatery in Uptown, not far from the Tin Roof, where Alec was scheduled to play.

She chided herself for thinking of her ex when this new guy seemed genuinely interested. After a few more minutes of deliberation, she decided on a simple black sheath dress with a matching, long-sleeved jacket. Inspecting herself in the mirror, she was satisfied with her choice. It wasn't her usual attire, but she didn't mind wearing panty hose and pumps occasionally; she had to admit it was nice to look and feel feminine for a man again.

A few minutes later, there was a knock on the door. Sam grabbed her purse and raincoat and briskly strode down the stairs. At first, she bristled at the rush of cool, moist air but smiled when she laid eyes on her six-foot-four date dressed in a grey raincoat, holding a huge umbrella over his head.

"Good evening, Samantha," he greeted her. "This is not exactly the weather I would have liked for our first date, but I promise we'll have a good time anyway."

She laughed. "Come on in for minute. It's cold out there."

David closed the umbrella and braced it against the wall before helping her into her coat.

"Thank you," she said.

"Shall we go?"

"Yes, I'm ready."

He picked up the umbrella and carefully opened it against the powerful, bracing wind before reaching for Sam's arm and escorting her to his running Audi A4 Sedan. He opened the passenger-side door and she settled in to the heated seat, impressed by his thoughtfulness. As the evening progressed, David continued to behave like a gentleman, holding doors and standing up when Sam excused herself at one point to use the Ladies Room.

When they arrived The Village Tavern and he removed his outer coat to reveal a dorky tie with a mismatched shirt and pants, she bristled at his obvious lack of fashion sense. Yet Sam forced herself to overlook appearances and focus on David's inner qualities like any mature woman would do. As they conversed about a multitude of topics, it was clear that he was a solid, stable individual – one who was content with corporate life, steady paychecks, and a house in the suburbs. She thought back to her father's initial concerns about Alec, particularly his ability to be a good father. She had no such misgivings about David in the few interactions she'd had with him, and now that she was approaching her late 20s, her biological clock was ticking.

If his mere presence didn't elicit tingles up and down her spine, so what?

Maybe that kind of passion was overrated, anyway. She and Alec had all of that and more and it wasn't enough to keep them together despite her eagerness to support him in every way as his dutiful wife. Could she have overlooked more important qualities when it came to choosing a husband? Sam was willing to admit to her own foolishness as a young girl madly in love with a guy who hadn't yet lived enough to understand the meaning of the word.

By early December, Sam and David had gone out a few times. But the more hours she spent in his company, the more dramatic the differences between him and Alec became. Stability and maturity aside, she missed that passion and questioned whether it had to be an either/or proposition. Wasn't it possible to find a combination of Alec and David in someone else? Could Alec just need another year or two of sowing his oats before coming back to her? With every ounce of her being, she wanted to believe it could happen. One night, as if reading her mind, David asked some pointed questions as they sat in a small bistro sipping cappuccino after seeing *The Santa Clause 2* with Tim Allen.

"Sam, I hope you don't mind my asking, but what is the nature of your relationship with Alec? I know you see him from time to time and I was just wondering if you were hoping to work things out with him. I'm just a regular guy, not an up-and-coming country music singer, and I don't want to hang out with you if you're still in love with your ex-husband."

She experienced a powerful twinge of guilt. In fact, not only had she been fantasizing about Alec, she'd seen him several times since she and David had begun dating. Torn over how to explain their relationship to him, she'd chosen to avoid the topic altogether. But now that he'd confronted her directly, it was time to address the situation. She took a deep breath.

"Look, David, there's nothing going on between Alec and me. We're truly just friends. We were married for five years and we've kinda been through a lot of life together, but we're not reconciling. I'm on my own path; he's on his own path. For all I know, he'll be heading to Nashville tomorrow for his big break. And I do know he's been enjoying the companionship of groupies, if you know what I mean. There's nothing you need to worry about." As she spoke the words, she wondered who she was trying to convince more.

"Okay, Samantha," he replied when she finished. "I believe you. Thank you for being honest."

"You're welcome."

Her stomach twisted into knots as she smiled back at him.

The next day, Sam made an important phone call.

"Hello?"

"Hi Alec, can you come over to my apartment for few minutes? I really need to talk to you."

"Sure, I've got some time before I have to meet up with the guys. What's going on?"

"I'll explain when you get here. And don't worry…Shannon's at work."

He laughed. "Alright, I'll see you in a few."

When he arrived, Sam did her best to ignore the feel of his strong, rippling muscles as he pulled her into a bear hug. She took his hand and led him to the living room, eager to get the conversation over with. Once they settled into the sofa, she began.

"Alec, I need you to be honest with me if there's any chance of you and I having a future together. We've been divorced for a while and we have this great friendship and everything else. If you think there's a chance of you and I getting back together, I need to know now. Because I'm finally starting to see this guy David and he has potential. He could be somebody that I might have a future with and if that's the case, it's not fair to him that you and I have this weird friendship on the side. If you have any interest in us getting back together, tell me now. Because if you don't, I really want to try to move on from you. And part of moving on from you is not seeing you. Not having these midnight ice-cream or beer-drinking visits because I can see that that would be very uncomfortable for a new man in my life."

She breathed in deeply and steeled herself for his reply. He reached out and took one of her hands in his.

"As much as I love you Sam, I still don't think I'm ready to get married again or even date you again. If you've found somebody else you think you want to pursue and date, go for it. Because I'm just not ready to step back up to the plate…and I don't know if I ever will be. I'm not trying to confuse you into thinking we have more than we already have. I'm sorry if it felt that way."

His words had the effect of transporting her back in time to another painful day in the recent past, when he announced his decision to leave. She swallowed hard and forced herself not to cry.

"Okay, then, thank you. That was all I needed to know."

By the spring of 2003, Sam had immersed herself in her relationship with David, determined to be a grown-up and focus on what really mattered in a potential mate. She'd also found a job as a sales manager for another telecommunications company, making close to six figures. Shannon's career as a beautician was off to an excellent start with an employment offer from one of the city's most upscale salons. It enabled the sisters to secure their own apartments – close enough to visit whenever they wanted, yet far enough away to give them each the privacy they craved.

Somewhere along the way, Sam and David became physically intimate. Although she'd been wary about their first time together, he had pleasantly surprised her with his giving nature and genuine desire to make her happy. Although his lovemaking lacked the burning desire and intensity of Alec, it exceeded her expectations and left her satisfied. Making love with David was nice, if not as meaningful as it was with Alec, but that ship had sailed. It was time to appreciate this new man and the unique gifts he brought into her life.

Okay, he can handle himself in the bedroom, she thought.

Then one night while doing the laundry, Sam received an unexpected text from Alec asking her to dinner. Her heart pounded as she read the message. They hadn't met up in person since their serious conversation in Sam's living room the previous December; something had to be up.

Could he finally have gotten a record deal in Nashville? Worse, had he fallen in love with a new woman he planned to marry?

She contemplated the menacing possibilities the entire ride to the Mexican restaurant where they'd agreed to meet over dinner and margaritas. Sure enough, when she saw him, she could tell he was nervous about whatever news he wanted to share. Yet despite multiple attempts to pry the truth out of him, he never budged. Instead, he focused the conversation on Sam – her relationship with David, her new job, and her goals for the future.

"Alec, come on, I know you didn't invite me to dinner just to hear about my life. I know you well enough to know there's something you want to tell me. Why don't you just spill it? Whatever it is, I'm a big girl and I can handle it. I've handled the worst from you, remember?"

Although his face turned red, he denied the accusation again. Sam shrugged. "Alrighty, then. I'm just gonna enjoy this for what it is…dinner with a friend." But, an hour later as she was driving home after they said their goodbyes, he called her on her cell phone.

"Hey Sam, want to continue our evening?"

"Uh, sure. What did you have in mind?"

"Don't think I'm nuts but I don't want to end up in a bar where people will recognize me. It's a nice night and I really do need to talk to you. How about we meet at Marathon gas station on Trade Street? Do you know which one I'm talking about?"

"Yes."

"Let's meet there. They have a convenience store. We can grab two forties and talk."

"Okay, I'll see you there."

Much to her consternation, her heart beat with hope for a renewal of their relationship even though her intuition predicted a much different outcome. By the time she arrived the their agreed-upon location, Alec was already holding a bag and leaning against the trunk of his Escalade, waiting for her.

When she got out of her car, he handed her a forty of Colt 45 Malt Liquor. "This was all they had," he explained apologetically.

"That's fine," she chuckled and accepted the gift. Then they walked over to a secluded curb and sat down to talk while the stars twinkled above in a clear sky. Under any other circumstances, it would have been a romantic setting.

"Ah Sam," he sighed, his eyes filling with tears. "I've hurt you so much and I'm sorry. I want you to know I loved you very much. I still do."

Her heart pounded in her chest.

"I still love you, too, Alec," she admitted. "Even though I've been with David all these months, I can't get you out of my mind. It's not fair to him." She began to sob. "I've tried so hard...so hard to move on from you...I have to know...is there any chance still of us getting back together? If not, I gotta move on...somehow... it's so completely unfair to David. It's like he has no idea he's competing with the memory of you."

Alec put his arms around her and held her close, just as he'd done countless times before. She closed her eyes and relished his familiar warmth and scent. "Sam, I just wish – gah, timing is everything in life, isn't it? You're the perfect woman for me at the wrong time. Especially now."

"W-what do you mean?" She looked up at him with puffy, tear-stained eyes. He took a deep breath.

"Sam, it finally happened. My big break, I mean. I – I mean, the *band* and I, we got a record deal and we're all moving to Nashville. It's over between you and me...whatever...this...whatever you want to call what we've been doing since the divorce, it's done. There's no hope for a reconciliation because I'm just not ready for the responsibility of marriage. That's why I didn't want you to come with me in the first place. It's the whole reason why I wanted the divorce. And now that you have David in your life, I feel better about leaving town. I'm just sorry for hurting you. I never, ever meant to do that. I just wish we'd met later in life. But I guess we don't get to decide those things. I'm thankful for everything we've shared. And in case you're wondering, no, Kimberly is not coming with me. She never meant anything to me, Sam. But you...you did. In another time, another place, you would be the woman for me. I'll always love you. I just can't be the man you deserve."

Once again, his words sliced through her heart like a knife. It felt like déjà vu as she sat there and listened to his honest confession while her entire body crumbled under the weight of sorrow. This time, however, she let him hold her while she processed the finality of what she now knew for certain: the Alec Russell phase of her life was finally over.

Chapter Five

Sam felt the balmy breeze caress her cheeks as she stepped out into the sunshine and onto the red-brick patio through the French doors, wearing a simple white gown made of filmy fabric. In her hands, she carried a small bouquet of peonies. Once again, Shannon honored her request for an understated look, so minimal make-up enhanced her natural features, as did her hairstyle. Pulled loosely at the crown with the rest cascading midway down her back, it accentuated her cheekbones and framed her deep blue eyes.

As the bride gazed upon the gazebo in the distance, impeccably decorated with white lilies and ribbons, she smiled at the success of the backyard's transformation into the perfect wedding venue. She took a deep breath before proceeding down the length of the long, white runner that led the way down three wide steps, then over the verdant lawn to her waiting groom. As Sam approached her destination, she caught sight of happy, familiar faces, including her beloved sister and father, her new in-laws, and her closest friends and colleagues, while The Wedding March emanated through a state-of-the-art sound system provided by a local deejay.

With David's approval, she'd arranged for an intimate, outdoor occasion at home. Although it was his first time tying the knot, he preferred to keep things low-key and in fact, had been relieved when Sam described her vision – especially since he'd just spent a good chunk of money renovating his ranch house after purchasing it via his lease-to-own contract. Once his roommates moved out, he and Sam embarked upon the hard work of knocking down walls, repainting, and gutting the kitchen, bedrooms, bathrooms and common areas. The entire effort had taken the better part of a year to complete but by the time they finished, it was like having a brand-new home in which to begin their married life and raise a family – at least while their children were young. By the time their expanding family would require a larger place, they'd have amassed plenty of equity in the ranch house, making it easier for them to afford a larger home. That was the plan, anyway.

After Alec left for Nashville, Sam released all lingering hope of reuniting with him and focused her attention on her new man. Despite the unique challenges this relationship posed, whenever a doubt would come up in her mind, she'd push it aside and remind herself that reliability was the quality she most needed in a partner at this point in her life. She accepted the fact that if she wanted David to dress appropriately, she would have to buy his wardrobe, then lay the appropriate attire for the occasion on the bed. *It wasn't so bad*, she told herself. *At least he's receptive to it.*

As a lover, David continued to be thoughtful and fully focused on Sam, though his prowess at providing oral pleasure was often his way of compensating for his inability to have or sustain an erection. At best, they engaged in routine sex once a week – and always in the bedroom. Still, it was fun and Sam enjoyed it. Her days of wild abandon were over; she was a responsible woman now and she'd made a connection with a mature man who shared her dreams of parenthood. Divorce wasn't the outcome she'd intended when she entered her first marriage, but she could never have predicted that the irresistible lure of country music fame would shatter her dreams of forever with her first love. Thankfully, with David, there were no hidden factors. He represented a second chance and for that Sam was grateful. Having built a fulfilling career, all she wanted now was a family and a stable home life. If that meant accepting certain trade-offs, so be it.

"May I cut in?" Walter asked as the bride and groom ended their first dance under the tent to *Off White* by Pam Tillis. The sun had just begun to set, painting the sky with a color palette of orange, pink, and yellow while the light humidity in the air began to wane.

Sam smiled at her dad. "Of course." Walter patted his new son-in-law on the shoulder with a look of pride in his eyes as he released his new wife to the waiting arms of her father.

"You know, Sam, this one's definitely a keeper," he whispered in her ear. "All I want is for you to be happy. I know David is the guy who can provide everything you deserve. It's about time you had a solid, stable guy in your life who's in it for the long haul."

"You really like him, don't you Dad?"

"I love him like a son, Sam. I can breathe easy, knowing what kind of man he is…and I'd be lying if I said I wasn't excited to be a grandfather. When you two are ready, of course."

She chuckled. "I am so ready to be a mother. I'm one-hundred percent committed to this marriage and I can't wait to have kids. It's an amazing thing to feel secure like this. I know my husband is never going to surprise me one day with an announcement that he's leaving to pursue some adolescent dream of fame."

Although neither one verbalized it, each briefly wondered what had become of Alec. Sam made it a point not to search for him online and so far, had not heard a song from him on the radio. Of course, the entertainment industry was fickle and complicated; it wasn't out of the question that he'd achieve full-fledged stardom years from now. Many others before him toiled in obscurity before their big break finally came.

Don't even go there, she thought. *This is a fresh start with a good man who loves you. And you finally got to have the wedding of your dreams, not someone else's. On your list of qualities of your perfect man, you must admit David hits 23 out of 25. He's the man who will stand by you, the man you will grow old with. Passion is fleeting, but what you and David have is forever.*

She smiled up at her father as they swayed to *Hero* by Mariah Carey. She noticed the moisture in his sparkly blue eyes and placed a hand on his cheek.

"Thank you, Dad. For everything," she sighed. On that magical evening, all was right with the world.

Following their backyard nuptials, the couple settled into married life, each focused on upward mobility at the office while they continued to try for their first baby at home. After a year, Sam was elated to discover she was finally pregnant. But before she reached the end of her first trimester, something terrible happened. She and David were sitting around the dinner table talking when she felt a searing pain in her stomach and screamed in agony. Then came the horrific rush of blood.

"Sam…oh my God…Sam, what is it?" Her panicked husband grabbed the phone and dialed 911.

By the time she arrived home from the hospital with Shannon two days later, only her physical wounds had begun to heal. "Come on, Sam, let's get you situated. Do you want to stay out here on the couch in the living room or go to the bedroom?"

"I-I don't care," she mumbled.

"In that case, I think the bedroom is probably best; at least the bathroom is right there." Shannon held an arm around her as they slowly made their way down the hallway. "I'm glad I could be here to help you. I can't believe David didn't take the day off work, but least he went grocery shopping last night."

Sam said nothing, too immersed in her own sorrow to comment. After Shannon helped her into bed, she got to work in the kitchen making meals for the next few days before heading to the pharmacy to fill Sam's prescriptions. By the time she came back to say goodbye, her sister had fallen asleep. Shannon bent down and kissed her on the forehead.

"Just rest, Sam," she whispered. "Take as long as you need to grieve. I'm here for you. Call me anytime you need me." With that, she proceeded out to the driveway in time to catch David pulling up in his Audi.

"Hey."

"Hey," he greeted her. "How is Sam?"

"She's resting. Doctor says she'll be fine, but I'm more worried about her emotional state. She needs you David."

He eyed her with skepticism in his usual manner, noticing the green and purple streaks in her platinum hair. It was difficult for him to take her seriously as Shannon well knew, not that she cared in the least.

"You did get her medicine, right?"

"Oh yeah, she's all set." *This dork thinks I'm an idiot*, she thought. "I even cooked some meals for the two of you with the groceries you bought. I'm just glad it was my day off today so I could help." She wanted to add, *since picking up your wife from the hospital after a miscarriage didn't rate taking one goddamned day off work*, but resisted the urge. Instead, she asked, "How are things at the office?"

"Good. Always busy, but that's to be expected. They don't pay me to sit around and twiddle my thumbs." He pulled his briefcase out of the back seat. "Even brought some home with me."

Shannon bit her tongue to prevent an altercation. *Was this jackass going to spend the night working when his wife just lost their baby?*

"Well, don't work too hard. I told Sam I'm just a phone call away if she needs me. Gotta be at the salon early tomorrow, but I could swing by at night on my way home."

"I don't think that's necessary as long as she has everything she needs.

Yeah, well, I'm not so sure about that.

"Alright then," Shannon announced. "I'm heading out. See you later." She shook her head in disgust as she watched him walk into the house. "God, please let him do the right thing by my sister," she sighed as she started her engine.

David closed the door behind him and heard his wife's cries from the bedroom. "David? Is that you? I need you."

"I'll be right there," he replied with a trace of annoyance, setting his briefcase by the kitchen table. When he entered the room, she was sitting up in bed, dabbing her red, puffy eyes with a tissue. "What can I do for you, Samantha? Do you need your medicine? Are you hungry?"

It never entered his mind to wrap his arms around her and offer words of comfort. Instead, he stood there stiffly, like an impatient server at a restaurant waiting for a customer to make up their mind between two entrees on a menu. After a few moments of stunned silence, she finally answered in a whisper.

"N-no…I don't need anything like that. Could you…could you just stay with me awhile? I don't want to be alone."

"Sam, I'm sorry, but I've got a pile of paperwork waiting for me. As it is, I'll probably be working until 2 AM."

"Oh," she sobbed. "I thought maybe we could…never mind." *Had he always been this detached?*

"I see your glass is empty," he remarked with a glance at the nightstand. "I'll get you some more ice and water. Would you like some hot tea, too? I can make some. I'll bring you some dinner if you'd like to eat in here. Whatever Shannon made smells good."

She stared at him blankly. "Uh…no. No, just bring me some water." He nodded and left the room, leaving her to contemplate where their marriage went from here as she pulled the covers over her head.

❦

Sam held the precious bundle in her arms and stared at her in wonder. "My beautiful baby girl. You're finally here," she cooed. She was over the moon to be a mother, especially after the pain of losing her first child. *I'm finally a mom*, she thought. *I'm so in love with this baby.*

"Hey, hey!" Shannon burst into the room, bearing a gigantic stuffed teddy bear and a pink Mylar balloon bearing the words, *It's A Girl.*

Sam looked up at her and smiled. "Guess what, Madison? Your Auntie Shannon is here. I know you're going to love her."

"Ooh, Sam, she's so precious," Shannon gushed. She set the teddy bear in the chair next to the bed, then tied the balloon around its wooden arm rest.

"Isn't she, though? I can't believe she's mine."

"I'm so happy for you. Where's her daddy?"

She watched her sister's smile fade away. "Where else? Back at the office."

"What? You just had her a few hours ago. Couldn't they give him the day off?"

"I wish I could blame it on the company, but he wanted to go back to work."

Changing the subject, Shannon announced, "Well, Dad is on his way to see his new granddaughter. I'm picking him up at the airport later. He's beyond thrilled."

Sam broke into a grin. "He's going to be the best grandfather any little girl could ask for. I can't wait for him to meet her. Is Patricia coming with him?"

"Yes, I think so. He's got somebody taking care of the business for the next week while they're away."

"Great. The guest room is ready for them."

"Why am I not surprised?" Shannon teased. "If you decide to give up on corporate sales, I'm sure you could find a job with Martha Stewart."

Sam chuckled, then snuggled Madison closer. "For now, all I want to do is spend my time with this little one."

As expected, Walter embraced his new role with unconditional love and enthusiasm, doting on Madison for most of his visit. Sam appreciated the help as she adjusted to life as a stay-at-home mom – a decision she and David mutually agreed to before their firstborn's arrival. Given the severity of her depression after the miscarriage, she wanted to savor every moment with her new baby. Having her father and Patricia around for that first week helped her to make a successful transition, though at times she wondered if her father's significant other felt a bit of resentment. Sam thought she sensed an aloofness in Patricia she hadn't seen since before her first wedding to Alec when she offered to make her a matching train for her wedding gown. But such thoughts were fleeting and scattered amid maternal joy.

When forced to say goodbye after only a week, Walter couldn't hide his sadness and dejection. "I hate to leave my girls," he whispered as he pulled his daughter into a hug. "Especially this little one," he continued, with a nod toward the baby fast asleep in her bassinette. "They change so fast; I hate to miss everything."

If only my daughter's father felt the same way. She pushed the thought aside as her heart swelled with love for her dad, whom she comforted with the reminder that he was welcome to visit anytime he wanted and the promise of calling him regularly to apprise him of Madison's milestones. A few hours later, as the wheels of his plane lifted off the runway, Walter's mind raced with possibilities for the future.

Madison's father, on the other hand, displayed an alarming indifference to her arrival in his life. To her horror, Sam observed her husband's lack of interest in his beautiful new baby; while she immersed herself fully in motherhood, David refused to feed, bathe or snuggle their infant. As expected, he continued to provide for their every need, but demonstrated through his words and actions that fatherhood had little to no effect on him.

After the failure of her first pregnancy, Sam's intense gratitude for the blessing of a healthy daughter had erased any previous reservations she might have had about relinquishing the perks of a high-powered, upper management job and accompanying salary. Besides, her lifelong practice of financial discipline had yielded a bountiful savings account for an extra measure of security. She could easily afford to throw herself into motherhood full-time.

Once she'd given birth, it was hard to imagine what her life was like without a child.

But as the months went by, David's emotional distance from his daughter worsened, showing Sam a side of her husband she'd never experienced before. By the time Madison reached nine months of age, she'd grown impatient with his failures as a father – and a husband. One evening, when she could no longer overlook the obvious, Sam and David had their first big fight.

"What is wrong with you?" she demanded. "You are the father of a beautiful baby and you want nothing to do with her. Hell, you don't even change her diaper unless I ask you to. Your daughter is now sitting up in the bathtub, splashing and playing and you're missing out. Don't you want to connect with your own child? Don't you want to be a part of her life? You're missing all these moments because you're sitting on the couch."

"Well, you're such a good mom, you've got it under control."

"David, it's not about me having her under control. It's about you wanting to bond with your daughter. You need to get involved."

"I pay the bills. I am involved."

"Ugh; you just don't get it, do you? It's not just about paying for things, David. Don't you want to be there to experience her first tooth? Watching her figure out how to crawl or take her first steps? That's what being a parent is all about…and you're missing it. How can you not be involved with this child? Don't you *want* a relationship with her?"

"I am not having this conversation with you, Samantha. I do care about my daughter. That's why I go to work every day – to keep her and you – housed and fed."

"Is that all we are to you? An obligation? Oh, my God," She threw her arms up in defeat and stormed into the master bathroom to take a shower while her husband watched her with genuine confusion and anger. Lacking any fundamental understanding of his wife's point of view, he strode back into his office to tackle some paperwork, though he did think of taking the baby monitor with him. As the pulsating, hot water rained down on Sam, she squeezed some shower gel into a puff and ran it over her athletic body in a slow, deliberate motion. Under the scrutiny of her purposeful gaze, she confirmed that she had lost most of the baby weight and regained her muscle tone, thanks to daily power walks with Madison in tow.

But could that be an illusion? Was her body unattractive to her husband now? Did that explain why he never touched or kissed her anymore? Her insecurity was compounded by the fact that David hadn't suggested or made plans for a date night in over a year. *Was their marriage beginning to unravel now that they were parents?* Such burning questions remained unspoken and unanswered that evening; her altercation with David ended in an impasse, with Sam spending the night in her daughter's room after rocking her to sleep. The next day, Shannon joined her and Madison on a walk in the park on her day off from the salon.

"Sam, what's going on? You look awful," she blurted out as she emerged from her car and took note of her sister's disheveled appearance. Dressed in an old pair of sweatpants coupled with a worn-out sweatshirt, Sam's hair was pulled back in a messy ponytail. Dark circles under her eyes complemented the harried expression on her face. Madison, of course, looked impeccable in her pink and white footies, complete with a matching knit hat that emphasized her big blue eyes and rosy cheeks.

"Ugh, I don't know what to do," Sam began as Shannon moved behind the stroller and began to push. They walked toward the pathway as the sun shone down on them through the majestic trees. "It's like I'm living with a total stranger. Ever since I had the baby, David has been completely absent. He wants nothing to do with her, and if that's not bad enough, he has no interest in me, either. We haven't been out on date in forever. I'm overcompensating for his parental deficiencies by spending all of my time with her."

She nodded toward the baby, who was looking around with wonder at her surroundings. "Don't get me wrong; I love Madison more than life and I'm thrilled to finally be a mom. But I'm frustrated. My husband has no interest in our child or me, I have no sex life, and I don't even have the satisfaction of making money at a job where people respect me. I don't know what to do."

"I have an idea," Shannon suggested. "I'm off on Wednesdays. Let's make Tuesday nights our girls' night to get you out of the house. You just tell David, 'Madison is all yours on Tuesday nights. I'm going to hang out with Shannon.' If you do that, he'll have to step up to the plate."

Sam sighed. "I don't know. I'm nervous about leaving her with him. He's already missed her first tooth and her first step. Will he even know what to do with her?"

"Hey, you'll be a phone call away. And it'll force him to learn out of necessity."

"Yeah," Sam contemplated the benefits in her mind. "You know, the more I think about it, the more I know you're right. And I gotta get out and do some adult things. I'm going stir-crazy at home."

"What about that mom's group Diana suggested when we were at the family reunion in Vermont this summer? Have you given any thought to that?" Shannon was referring to their cousin, the one whose wedding Sam had skipped out on years before to fly to

California to be with Alec. Now the mother of a baby boy, Diana had greeted the Townsend girls warmly, bearing no ill will toward Sam, who'd been relieved. But Diana wasn't the type to hold grudges or take joy in others' pain and heartache. Instead, after listening to her cousin's dilemma, she suggested that Sam do an online search for moms' groups in her area to make new friends with shared interests.

At first, Sam dismissed the idea. "That's sounds lame. A dating site for moms."

"No, seriously, you'll make new friends. It's been great for me," Diana countered.

Now, with Madison approaching her first birthday and her patience wearing thin, she was reconsidering her resistance to the idea as they strolled around the park.

"Sam, just do it. What do you have to lose?" Shannon encouraged.

"You have a point. I can't go on like this, that's for sure. After all these years of constantly working a full-time job and for most of that, *two* jobs, this is a total let-down. I love Madison more than anything, but I need something more. Remember when you babysat for me a few weeks ago so I could meet up with work friends?" Shannon nodded. "Ugh, I never told you, but all they did was complain about their husbands wanting too much sex. Meanwhile, here I am, a married woman living like a nun. I told them to stop complaining and just be happy their husbands found them attractive. I'd give anything to feel David's hands on me again. I miss that kind of human touch, but he has zero interest. I don't know if it's my body – "

"Sam, stop it. Have you looked in the mirror lately? You're in awesome shape. No one would even guess you had a baby."

"Then what other reason could he possibly have? This is personal, I know, but you're my baby sister and I tell you everything. And I'm telling you, my husband hasn't made love to me since Madison was conceived. Do you have any idea how frustrating that is?"

Shannon stifled the urge to confess her own personal secret. A recent interlude with a promising new beau flashed through her mind, though she hadn't yet revealed his presence in her life to her Sam. Since she planned to keep it that way until he became a serious contender, she brushed the thought of him aside and focused back on her big sister's problem. "I get it. I mean, I can *imagine* how you feel," she sympathized. "You're married for crying out loud. But that's the thing about joining one of those groups. I bet you'll meet other women who have the same problems. Maybe you can help each other. Would be cheaper than therapy."

They took a break to sit down on a bench. Sam pulled two water bottles from the back of the stroller and handed one to her sister. "You know, you have a point. I'm going to check it out when I get home."

That afternoon, Sam created an account on MeetUp.com and found a group in her area. Perusing their page, she stared at the endless photos of outings to places like Chuck E. Cheese – featuring perky, well-dressed women and beaming, energetic children – and felt a knot in the pit of her stomach.

"This is so not my scene," she sighed. She forced herself to compose an email to one of the group's founders to introduce herself and receive more information. Within a day, a response came inviting her to participate in a smaller gathering within the larger membership, for mothers whose children were within a few months of each other in age. Once every two weeks, they met at someone's house for coffee and donuts; the babies played while the moms talked.

"Okay, that doesn't sound so bad. I'm open to that," she affirmed aloud as she sat at her kitchen table with her laptop. She was all alone, save for Madison, who was playing contentedly in her crib. But when the follow-up email revealed the location of the next meeting – a gorgeous, red-brick home in Sam's old neighborhood of Allyson Park – she flinched a little. *Get a hold of yourself,* she thought. *That was a lifetime ago and you have moved on. For goodness' sake, you're a married mother now.*

The following week, Sam and Madison pulled into the driveway of an impressive, six-bedroom house that appeared to be close to 6,000 square feet. "Gosh, they definitely make more money than we do," she whispered to herself as she helped the baby out of her car seat. Then, like a bolt out of the blue, she experienced a flash of memory where two young newlyweds giggled and kissed while they toured Charlotte's most talked about new neighborhood to decide on their first house together. She froze for a moment, but shook it off and returned to the present when she heard Madison say "Mama?"

"C'mon honey," she coaxed, taking the child's small hand in hers. "We're going to meet some new friends here today." *I may be an introvert, but I can do this; I have to do this,* she thought.

Within five minutes, however, Sam was ready to escape. While she attempted to converse with these new women as they sat around the kitchen table over coffee and donuts, she was disgusted by the sight of their one-year-olds pushing their heads under their mothers' shirts, trying to get breast milk.

Are you fricking kidding? she thought when two of the moms began to nurse their toddlers. *That is beyond gross.* Although Sam had breast-fed Madison as a newborn, now that her child was able to walk around and hold a donut in her hand, she couldn't imagine doing such a thing.

"Excuse me for just a second," she announced, forcing a smile. Then she went into the powder room to call David.

"These women are crazy. Turns out, they are part of the La Leche Club. This is so outside my comfort zone. These moms are nothing like me," she lamented.

"Sam, I'm really sorry. I was kinda hoping it would work out," he replied sincerely.

"Me, too, but this is just awful. I can't stay here another second. There is no way I can do this."

But a month later, she resolved to give it another try. "At least I know what to expect now," she rationalized. This time, she struck up a conversation with two new women in attendance who seemed to be much cooler than the others, and better aligned with her outlook and interests. As the trio laughed and talked about their husbands and families, one of them, a woman named Christina, pulled a photo out of her purse.

"Y'all, I rarely ever do this, but I just have to show you how cute this picture is," she gushed. "My husband fell asleep on the couch last week with our son. It was so sweet, I couldn't resist. Aren't they adorable?"

"They sure are," Melissa, the other woman, agreed.

Sam nodded her head. Staring at the image of a grown man snuggling with his baby, she felt a twinge of envy. *David never does things like fall asleep on the couch with Madison*, she thought. *What is wrong with him?*

She smiled as she handed the photo back to Christina.

The next day, Melissa sent out a text: "Hey, do you guys want to get together and take the kids for a walk in the park tomorrow?"

That simple request marked the beginning of their breakaway from the rest of the group. It was officially confirmed when, during their stroll around the pathway, Christina verbalized what the three of them were feeling.

"Okay y'all, I gotta ask; what's the deal with the crazy nursing mothers?" Her voice inflection, combined with her Southern accent, prompted the others to break out into laughter.

"Oh, my God, you feel that way, too?" Sam chimed in. "I thought it was just me."

"Uh, no," Melissa assured her. "It is most definitely not just you."

"My gosh, I'm so relieved. The first meeting I went to, I was so disgusted I had to excuse myself to call my husband. I couldn't get out of there fast enough."

"Well, let me make a proposal," Christina continued. "I say we start our own thing. We meet up once a week at alternating houses and break open a bottle of wine while we keep the kids locked in the basement. What do y'all think?"

"It's a deal," Sam and Melissa responded in unison.

That bonding moment forged strong friendships that expanded to include spouses and fun family outings. Sam was grateful to have followed her intuition and returned for a second meeting despite her unpleasant initiation; if not, she never would have met them. Fulfilling Shannon's prediction, the women often discussed the challenges of paying bills, balancing quality family time with marriage time, and saving for their kids' college educations. Funny, but Melissa and Christina's entry into her life improved it in unexpected ways, too. Shortly after connecting with them,

Sam received a phone call from her former boss, asking if she'd like to do some recruiting out of her home – an offer she happily accepted.

Getting back into the professional swing of things filled her with a sense of renewed purpose. She'd missed working and with the option of doing her job from the house, there was no need to pay a babysitter or put Madison in daycare. She was a happy child who, for the most part, obeyed her mother and played quietly in her room. For Sam, it meant having the best of both worlds.

Miraculously, some normalcy had even returned to Sam and David's marriage, with her husband once again seeking out sex sporadically. While it was just as routine as before, Sam welcomed his overtures whenever they came with enthusiasm and relief, holding out hope that someday she wouldn't have to wait weeks or even months before their next physical encounter. Despite the irregularity of their lovemaking, she found herself pregnant again before Madison's second birthday.

§

"How's my patient doing?" Dr. Randall asked as he entered the examination room, where Sam, now 38 weeks pregnant, lay on the table in a hospital gown.

"Doctor Randall, I'm actually concerned. I thought it was strange that I wasn't gaining much weight this time around, but since everything else seemed okay with my check-ups, I put it out of my mind. But now I've noticed this baby is not moving. I'm scared."

"Alright, let's get you on a monitor," he replied. A few minutes later, he frowned when he noticed that the baby's heart rate was dropping every few seconds. "Something's not right," he announced. "I think the umbilical cord is wrapped around the neck in the womb and that's what's causing the low activity. Let's get you over the hospital so you can deliver today. We'll induce labor but there's a chance you may need a C-section. They're going to ask you to sign the release forms."

"That's fine. I just want my baby to be okay." Her heart raced as she texted David, Shannon, and Walter with the update, then closed her eyes and uttered a silent prayer.

Thankfully, a C-section proved unnecessary but when little Zach made his debut into the world several hours later, he couldn't breathe. His lungs had not fully developed, a natural occurrence that usually takes place at 32 weeks of pregnancy. But in a rare and random phenomenon, Sam's placenta had shut down at 30 weeks gestation, essentially starving the baby to death in her womb. She listened in shock as the doctor explained that had she waited three more days, he would have been a stillborn. This condition, called "placental insufficiency," also prevented her from gaining a normal amount of weight. When Sam delivered, her placenta looked like a piece of tissue paper – rather than a robust piece of meat – because it had deteriorated so dramatically.

But the outcome was far from settled as the scrawny, five-pound, bony baby fought for his life on a ventilator in the NICU while his frantic mother sought emotional support from her family. As usual, her husband could not be counted on.

"What do I need to do today with Madison?" David asked when she called him from the hospital with the news.

"What do you mean; she's a freaking two-year-old and you're her father, for God's sake. Just take care of her while I'm here," Sam snapped. "Our son is fighting for his life. There's no way I'm leaving." Then she added, "It would be nice if his father could stop by to see him too while he's in intensive care."

Goddamn it, what will it take for him to show some emotion? Does our baby have to die?

She tossed her phone in anger as she dissolved into tears in her hospital bed, but a moment later, she smelled Shannon's signature perfume and felt her arms encircle her. "Hey, Sam, don't worry. Dad is on his way. He wants to take care of Madison while you stay with Zach," she soothed. "I just came from the chapel; he's going to be okay. I just know it." Once Shannon had apprised him of the latest happenings, Walter boarded the first available flight to Charlotte with the intention of staying with Madison at home while his daughter kept a round-the-clock vigil at the hospital. Since Madison adored her grandfather, Sam could have the peace of mind she needed to be there for her new son while he remained in the NICU.

The first three days of Zach's life felt like a punishment to his mother. Not only was his life in jeopardy, his medical team refused to let her hold him, due to fear of infection. All she could do was stare at her vulnerable baby helplessly as his tiny chest heaved up and down, his frail body connected to a network of imposing tubes and machines. By 2 AM on the fourth night, Sam was at her wits' end. Her husband, whose office was located just ten minutes away, had not even bothered to visit the NICU, leaving her alone to cope with an overwhelming burden of fear, exacerbated by a lack of sleep and tormented thoughts of worst-case scenarios.

"I'd give anything to take you home, baby," she whispered. "Please keep fighting. Please stay with us. I love you so much." *I don't know how I'll go on if he doesn't make it. God, I cannot bury a child. Please, please make him well*, she pleaded.

Finally, on the fourth day, a nurse placed him in Sam's waiting arms, and after eight agonizing days, Zach was well enough to be transferred to the maternity ward, where he would remain another day for observation. Shannon, who had taken a half-day off from work, stopped by to pick up her sister. "Sam, let me take you home so you can take a hot shower and get some rest. I'll come back and see the baby, but from what they told me, he's fine now. You need a break."

"Okay," she complied. "I'm exhausted."

"Dad is taking Madison to the park for the afternoon, so you can sleep. If she sees you, you'll never be able to."

"How is she?"

"She misses her mommy, but other than that, she's fine. And you should see dad; he's loving it. They are so cute together."

"He's a better father to her than her own father. Can you believe David never once stopped by the NICU to see Zach? I'm so angry right now, I can't even tell you. If I wasn't so tired, I'd go right over to his office and ream him out. Ten freaking minutes away, his son close to dying and my husband couldn't inconvenience himself to show his face, if only for a couple of minutes. Do you know how embarrassing it was for me to try to explain his absence to the nurses? They probably think I'm married to an unfeeling zombie."

Displaying uncharacteristic restraint, Shannon simply listened and sympathized as they made their way through the midday traffic, bound for Sam and David's new craftsman style home in Dilworth. By early evening, Sam emerged from her retreat feeling refreshed. After checking in on Zach at the hospital, she   walked down the stairs through the short hallway toward the kitchen, where she heard her daughter giggling with her grandpa, and inhaled the enticing aroma of Italian food. For the first time in forever, she recognized the gnawing feeling of hunger in her stomach.

"Mommy!" Madison squealed upon catching sight of her.

"Hey, baby, how are you? Mommy missed you so much," she cooed as she scooped her up in her arms. Suddenly, she looked so grown up. Sam kissed her blonde curls and breathed in the sweet scent of baby shampoo.

"There's my girl," Walter greeted her with a bear hug, encircling both Mom and daughter.

"Dad, I can't thank you enough for everything," Sam choked up.

"Hey, we're family," he stated. "There is nowhere else I'd rather be. How's the little guy?"

Sam gave him the latest update as Walter prepared a tossed salad and put some garlic bread in the oven. Then he sat down next to her at the kitchen table while Madison watched cartoons in the living room. "I have something to tell you, Sam," he announced. "I've been wanting to do it for a long time, but after this ordeal, it's settled. I'm selling the business to Patricia and moving to Charlotte. Nothing is more important to me than my family."

"D-dad, are you sure? I've been waiting to hear you say that for so long, but I didn't want you to uproot your whole life for me."

"Bah; my life is wherever I decide it is. And I'm ready for a change."

"I take it Patricia doesn't want to move? What's going to happen with you two?"

"We're over, Sam."

"I'm sorry."

"Don't be; it's the right decision for everyone involved. I want to watch my grandkids grow up. I want to be there for them...and for you and Shannon. Besides, I'm sick of Vermont winters too," he half-joked.

"Oh Dad, I'm so happy to hear this." She cried tears of joy as she threw her arms around him.

༄

"Are you telling me you haven't had sex for a year?" a horrified Christina blurted out.

"Shh, lower your voice," Melissa admonished, blushing a little. The three women were seated in a corner table at a new bistro in Ballantyne enjoying a farewell lunch for Melissa, who was moving to Seattle, thanks to her husband's job transfer.

"Not since Zach was born...and we just celebrated his first birthday, as you know," Sam sighed. "Believe me, I've done everything I can think of to entice him. At first, I was so angry about David's indifference with the baby being in the NICU, I didn't care if we ever did it again. But once we brought Zach home, I was so grateful and excited, I wanted to celebrate with my husband, who, for once, consented and went the distance." She paused for a minute. "TMI?" she asked.

"N-no, this is fascinating," Christina replied. "Go on...I mean, if you want to."

Sam laughed. "You know, I trust you. Never thought I'd find another confidant besides my poor sister, who has spent her life listening to my stuff. Who'd have guessed I'd find *two* amazing women to talk to."

"Alright, enough with the flattery; just tell us," Melissa urged, cracking them all up.

"Okay, okay. Anyway, after that one time, I thought we'd turned a corner and I wanted more. I thought David did too. But I was wrong. I spent the next three months trying to get him to touch and kiss me again, only to be rejected every single time. Then, I started to wonder: was it me? Was my body turning him off and he didn't know how to tell me? That's the main reason why I joined the Cross-Fit gym in the first place. Now I'm stronger and fitter than I've ever been in my life…and that's saying something. But David still didn't want sex. I tried everything…parading around the bedroom in Victoria's Secret lingerie, leaving sexy notes in his briefcase, letting the kids have sleepovers at Grandpa's house so we could have privacy. Nothing worked. I might as well be living with my brother or a platonic roommate. Yes, he's a good provider, but so am I. I have a great job and I could support my kids on my own if I had to. I'm frustrated and confused because my husband doesn't want me and I just don't know what else to do," she lamented.

Melissa and Christina exchanged knowing glances. "Sam, I hate to even bring this up, but do you think David is having an affair?" Melissa finally asked. "I mean, you're an attractive, vibrant woman. Why *wouldn't* he want to be with you?"

She sighed. "I've already asked him; he flat-out denied it and I believe him. During one of our fights, I said, 'How can you go a year without having sex with your wife?' I truly wanted to know. He told me he just has a low sex drive. I suggested that he go to his doctor to get checked out, but he refused. These days, there are all kinds of things they can do to fix these kinds of problems, but my husband can't be bothered. He's happy with the status quo and doesn't give a damn about my feelings…he has no regard for me at all. And don't get me started about his lack of affection for the kids. He's totally disconnected from them, too. It's like he doesn't know how to just be a regular dad. They're toddlers, for crying out loud. How hard is it to play ball with them in the backyard or horse around with them in the living room? Thank God, my father moved here…they get to do that stuff with him. But it doesn't excuse David."

"Well, you did tell us about his upbringing with detached parents. Guess without a good example, it's hard for him to know what to do," Christina offered.

"Yeah, and that should have been a red flag for me. It's awful for me to say this now because I have Madison and Zach, but I wonder if I made a big mistake in choosing security over passion. I married a man who is incapable of intimate relationships; all he wants to do is work. He's almost 40; I doubt he's going to change."

"Not without therapy, anyway," Melissa suggested.

"If he's willing to go," Christina countered. "Have you asked him about that?"

"Not yet, but it's my next step. If he's not willing to see a medical doctor, he's for damn sure going to see a marriage therapist. I'm struggling to keep my family together and I can't do it alone. I'm sorry his parents weren't involved with him when he was growing up, but he's an adult now and he needs to step up. Our kids deserve better…and so do I."

Then, remembering their reason for getting together, she changed the subject. "Alright, enough about me. Here's to Melissa and Doug, and their new life in Seattle." The trio clinked wine glasses in a bittersweet moment of celebration.

෨

"So, David, did you complete the assignment I gave you last week, the one where you were to plan a date night with Sam?" their marriage counselor Susan inquired. While she awaited his answer, his wife sat in her comfortable chair in the doctor's office, fighting to hide her disgust. After a year of weekly professional sessions, nothing had changed.

"No, I'm afraid I did not," David admitted.

"Why not?"

"Uh, I just got busy…you know, with work and other demands of life."

"David, counseling is a two-way street. It's not up to me to save your marriage. It's up to you. Do you want to improve your relationship with Sam?"

He nodded.

"Well, if that's the case, I advise you to follow through when I give you an assignment. It's not meant to be a punishment, but a way of helping you reconnect with her and rebuild your marriage. You do want that, right?"

"Of course."

Sam could no longer hold back. "It sure doesn't feel that way to me, David, when I'm the only one making the effort, here. Do you know why I joined the gym? Because I was worried that after two kids, my body wasn't attractive to you anymore. I got into the best shape of my life and you still don't want to touch me. My God, you don't even want to vacation with us." She turned her gaze from him to look at Susan. "Do you know, I take the kids to Vermont every summer with my father because their own father can't be bothered? He's happy to stay home and work. I'm even willing to take them to Wisconsin to visit his parents since they never get to see their grandkids and he has no interest. Now that Madison and Zach are old enough to understand what's going on, they ask me why their friends' daddies do things with them, while theirs spends all his time at the office. I don't even know what to tell them anymore."

"Yes, well, I'm thinking about their education and keeping a roof over their head," he replied.

"And of course, those things are important, David. Sam, do you appreciate the fact that your husband provides well for your family?"

She drew in a deep, cleansing breath, recognizing the therapist's attempt to avoid ganging up on him in favor of fostering an open dialogue. *Respond, don't react*, she thought. "David," Sam began, reaching out to take one of his hands in hers, "I do appreciate that you provide so well for our family. I love our home in Dilworth and I know you love Madison and Zach. I'm just trying to communicate that we miss you. I miss private time with my husband, and the kids…well, they would be thrilled if you would just take some time to hug them, play with them, or read them a bedtime story. All we're asking for is a little quality time with you. As for me, the lack of intimacy in our marriage makes me wonder if you still want me at all. Do you?"

She thought she detected some moisture in his eyes, but it was hard to know for sure as he sat with his head bowed down, staring at the floor.

"David?" Susan intervened.

"Yes, Sam, I –"

"David, please look at your wife as you speak to her," their counselor requested in a calm, measured voice.

He stared into her eyes, "Sam, yes, of course I love you. And I love our children."

"I love you, too, David. That's why I'm here. I want to resolve our problems, but I can't do it alone. I need your help. Will you meet me halfway?"

"Yes." Like every previous counseling interaction, Sam swore she detected sincerity in his tone and prayed that *this* time, his actions would match his words.

"Good," Susan proclaimed. "David, I would like you to make plans for a date night with your wife this coming week. When I see you both for our next session, I want to hear all about it."

"Oh, I won't be able to this week," he explained. "I'm travelling to San Antonio for work. I'll be gone for seven days."

"I see. Well, then, I suggest you stay in touch with her while you're gone. Can you FaceTime Sam and the kids in the evening, even if just for a few minutes?"

"Oh, ah, that's okay because I'm going to be away at a work thing myself," Sam fibbed. "I mean...definitely do that with the kids. My dad is babysitting while we're both gone," she explained to the therapist.

Sam figured it was no one else's business that she'd scheduled a breast augmentation in a last-ditch attempt to entice her husband. If that didn't work, she was prepared to take the next step of legal separation and file for divorce because of irreconcilable differences. If nothing else, perky boobs would complement her hard-earned body and make her feel good about herself again. God knew, these counseling sessions weren't making a difference, despite Susan's competence. But not even a skilled, seasoned marriage therapist could work miracles; if David couldn't find the motivation to change for his wife and family, there was only one place this unhappy union was headed. She hated the idea of being divorced for a second time, but couldn't deny her own feelings.

She was still a young woman with a healthy sex drive and she wasn't prepared to live out the rest of her married life in celibacy.

A week later, with Madison and Zach spending the night at their grandfather's house, Sam prepared for her big debut. Since David would be home in the early evening, she told him to expect a special dinner upon his return. She cleaned up the house, bought some fresh flowers for the dining room table, and lit candles in the bedroom to create an aura of romance. *If this doesn't work, I give up*, she thought as she pulled the filet mignon out of the oven. The aroma of seasoned meat wafted through the air as her husband entered through the front door. When Sam heard his key turn in the lock, she smoothed her pencil skirt and unfastened another button on her loose Lycra-and-cotton red blouse to display her newly enhanced cleavage. Beneath the fabric, her breasts were still bandaged, but she looked forward to removing them in front of her husband after their meal. If all went according to plan, the two of them would spend the rest of the evening in bed.

"Hey," she greeted him brightly in the foyer. "I'm glad you're home." He set down his briefcase and slowly put his arms around her. Sam closed her eyes and pressed her body against his.

"Something sure smells good," he remarked. "What's cooking?"

"Oh...filet mignon, one of your favorites." She pulled away from the hug and led him into the dining room. "You must be hungry. Everything's ready; sit down and I'll bring it out."

She bristled at the awkwardness she felt around her own husband, but remained focused on her goal. Throughout their dinner, she ignored his apparent lack of enthusiasm and channeled her energy into engaging him in conversation about work, his favorite topic, after apprising him that the kids were safely at Grandpa's for the evening. Later, after coffee and dessert, she boldly took him by the hand and led him up the stairs.

"Sam, I need to tell you, I'm pretty worn out," he announced, signaling his acknowledgement of her expectations.

"Well, just give me a chance. You may feel energized when I show the surprise I have in store for you," she teased.

When they reached the master suite at the end of the hallway, she led him to a plush recliner chair in the sitting area, with the instructions to sit down. After he complied, she stood closely in front of him and, with all the playfulness she could muster, began to slowly undress herself, beginning with her skirt, figuring she'd save her full, robust B-cups for the finale. As she slid the form-fitting skirt down her toned, muscular legs, she thought she saw a flicker of desire in his eyes as he caught sight of her black G-string. Once the material fell to the floor, Sam reached for the bottom button of her blouse, teasingly working her way up to reveal, first the underside of her breasts, then a full view as she let the garment fall from her shoulders and pool around her high-heeled black pumps.

"The doctor says it's okay to remove the bandages," she whispered. "Do you want to help me?" With that, she pulled him to his feet. Then, reaching for his hands, she placed one on each of her covered nipples. "How does that feel to you?" she whispered. "Please, David, I want you to remove the bandages. I want to feel you caress and kiss my breasts again. I want you to make love to me."

Much to her dismay, he offered no reaction to her advances, save for annoyance and embarrassment.

"So, this is what you did while I was away at the convention? Get a boob job?"

Her heart sank. "No, David, I'm trying to save our marriage," she snapped as she picked her clothes up and headed into her closet, where she threw on a terry-cloth robe before confronting him again. "I'm doing everything I can to turn you on, but I'm obviously failing when the sight of me naked doesn't even give you an erection. What will it take, exactly? Tell me. What do you need from me to be a husband again?" she cried out in frustration.

"Like I've told you a million times, I just have a low sex drive. It's not you. And I just got home from a long business trip. All I want to do is sleep, Sam. I'm sorry."

"Most men can't wait to get home to their wives after they've been away that long. Not you, though. You don't give a damn about my needs. You are content to live with your nonexistent libido when a simple visit to the doctor could fix the problem."

"It's not a problem, Sam. It's just the way I am. I'm sorry if you can't live with that."

"David, we're husband and wife and we're living like siblings, for God's sake. This is not normal…and it's not how I want my marriage to be. Don't you get it? We have to resolve this before – "

"Before what? You have an affair? File for divorce?"

"Affair? What are you talking about?"

"Am I supposed to believe you spend most of your free time at the gym just to work out?"

It was as if he was reading her mind. Truth be told, Sam had struck up a friendship with a cool guy who worked out at Cross-Fit, but up until now, she'd never entertained the idea of cheating on David with anyone…let alone Logan Nash. From what she'd observed, he was a big flirt who enjoyed the company of women, although the men there all seemed to like him, too. He was one of those people with a larger-than-life personality whose joiede-vivre attracted everyone around him. Though aware he was married, Sam had never seen his wife at the gym and had hardly given a thought to the state of his marriage, other than lending a sympathetic ear – possibly because Logan's stocky build and average height stood in direct contrast to what usually attracted her to a man. When she saw him, they'd laugh and talk as they worked out, but other than a good friendship and a welcome reprieve from her own problems, nothing was going on between them.

"Well?" David demanded.

"Well, I don't know what you're talking about. I joined the gym to get my body in shape for you. Now it's become a release for me since my own husband wants nothing to do with me. And yes, there are guys there, but all I do is work out with them. I haven't been unfaithful to you, David, but you are violating our marriage vows in another way. You've abandoned me."

"I haven't abandoned you, Sam. I live here with you and our kids in a lovely home in one of the nicest areas of Charlotte. I go to work and pay for everything you need. I'm sorry if that's not enough for you. Now, I really need some sleep, so I'm spending the night in the guest room."

With that, he turned on his heel and strode out of the room, leaving his dumbfounded wife to wonder what to do next as she flopped onto her bed and cried tears of pure frustration into her pillow.

౨

Sam slid behind the wheel of her Pathfinder and put on her favorite country music station. Her professional tasks completed for the day, she had just enough time to head to the gym and work out for an hour before picking up the kids from school. As she drove through the winding, tree-lined streets, she recalled the previous night's fight with her husband and tried to make sense of it all.

It was true that over the past few years, the Cross-Fit gym had been her saving grace. What began as a vehicle for toning her body transformed into an outlet for pent-up frustration. Rather than have an affair, she redirected her sexual energy into the kind of training reminiscent of military boot camp, where recruits are pushed beyond their limits to mold them into paragons of mental, emotional, and physical strength. In her case, the results spoke for themselves; she exceeded her fitness goals and felt pride in her accomplishment of a body that rivaled women half her age. Now, with the added benefit of a breast augmentation, she felt more confident than ever about her looks, despite her husband's indifference.

But somewhere along the way, the gym began to offer much more than just a place to maintain her hard-earned peak physical condition. Over time, she developed solid friendships with the other regulars, though most of their interactions were confined to the Cross-Fit walls since most, like Sam, were busy professionals with families. On rare occasions, a few of them would head out for drinks or a quick bite to eat afterward, but such opportunities were few and far between.

Logan Nash, the longtime member whose reputation preceded him, was among these new friends. When Sam first signed up, she felt as if she already knew him even before laying eyes on him in person, because she'd heard so many funny stories about him from her other workout partners. One afternoon, she experienced his exuberant personality for the first time when he burst through the doors, greeting everyone there with jokes and high-fives. Upon being introduced, Sam felt a kinship with the married father of two boys, though the idea of an affair never crossed her mind. She was fully focused on her initial purpose for being there: to save her own marriage by making herself more attractive to David. Besides, Logan didn't turn her on in that way…at least not until recently. Perhaps it was due to the easy rapport they shared over relatable difficulties in their relationships with their spouses.

So why would David insinuate such a thing? Was he picking up on something she herself hadn't even acknowledged? Was he spying on her somehow?

"Okay, now you are just being ridiculous," she admonished herself out loud as she braked for a traffic stop. "David's probably just jumping to conclusions, knowing I'm frustrated with our lack of a sex life. You have done nothing wrong." She took a gulp of air as the light turned green. Then she heard the deejay announce a debut song on the radio from Nashville's newest talent and nearly plowed into the car in front of her when a familiar voice, melody and lyrics emanated through the Pathfinder's speakers.

Fancy Face. He finally broke out with the song he wrote for me a lifetime ago.

She didn't know whether to laugh or cry as she took it all in. Reaching Cross-Fit's parking lot, she pulled into a space, threw the car in park, and put her head down on the wheel. Alec's sexy, baritone voice was even more appealing than she remembered; with the accompaniment of professional musicians, the beautiful ballad had the words "Number One Hit" written all over it. It felt surreal to have been the inspiration for what was sure to become his signature song.

Her mind wandered back to happier days when two newlyweds couldn't keep their hands off each other as they embarked upon the adventure of life with the passion and wildness of youth. How she missed the feeling of being irresistible to her man and the experience of him wanting her anywhere, anytime with reckless abandon. Yes, she was a grown-up with two children now, but surely, she could still have even just a fraction of the sexual intensity she and Alec had once shared? She wept as she thought of David. *Why did it have to be such a chore to seduce him? Why couldn't he see her point of view and get help for his problems? Why couldn't she and Alec have worked out their other issues and moved forward?*

Such thoughts clouded her mind and weighed heavy on her heart as the song ended. She inhaled deeply, dried her eyes, and decided what to do next as she got out of the car and headed for the gym entrance.

ॐ

"H-hello?"

"Samantha Townsend, how are you?" the enthusiastic male voice on the other end greeted her.

"I'm great, how are you, country music star? Congratulations!"

"Aw, shucks, ma'am," Alec teased. "Thank you. You of all people know it's been a long, twisted road."

"Yes, and I want to hear all about it. I've got plenty of time." It was mid-morning on a Thursday and she was sitting in her home office, alone. David was at work and the kids were on a play date.

"I'd love to darlin' and that's why I'm calling. I'm coming through Charlotte in a few weeks and I'd like to meet up with you somewhere to talk, if it's alright with you. You can even come to my hotel suite, so we can have some privacy. I swear, I just want to catch up with an old friend, nothing more than that. I know you're a married mama now."

"Oh, Alec, that would be great, thank you."

"You have no idea how excited I was when our web guy showed me your message. Since I'm the opening act for Garth's upcoming concert in Charlotte, it seems like fate."

"Oh, my God, you're opening for Garth Brooks? Wow, you really have made it…good for you."

"None of it would have happened without you, Sam. I can't wait to see you…in a respectful way, of course."

"Of course. I'm looking forward to seeing you, too. It's been way too long." After they hung up, she added his private number to her contacts in her smartphone, using the alias, *A. Keesler*. The name could easily be referenced as a work contact, should David somehow discover it and ask questions. There was no reason for him to know it reminded her of falling in love for the first time at Keesler Air Force Base.

A few weeks later, Sam dropped the kids off at Walter's house after school, on the pretext of meeting with a boss who had flown in from Atlanta for dinner. Not even Shannon knew the real reason for her visit to the Omni Charlotte Hotel; as much as she loved and trusted her sister, Sam decided it best to keep her meeting with Alec a secret. Not that it was easy.

Once *Fancy Face* began to climb the charts, her family took notice. Shannon took a special interest in Sam's reaction to Alec's re-emergence into her life, if only as a public figure. During one of their Tuesday night outings, she grilled her sister about it.

"Oh, my God, I remember when he wrote the song for you. Back then, it was so sweet. It must feel surreal that all these years later it's a country music hit. Does it bother you at all?" Shannon took a sip of her dirty martini as they sat at the Tin Roof bar.

"Eh, not really. At first, I was shocked, you know, when it came on the radio. But I'm sure I'm not the first jilted wife to inspire a hit song…this is country music, after all," she replied with a laugh.

"I know, I just wondered, since you and David are having problems, if…" Shannon's voice trailed off.

"It's okay, you can say it," Sam sighed. "If, I've thought of my marriage to Alec and how much better it was than what I have now. Between you and me, yeah, it brought back memories and made me miss what he and I once shared. With him, I never had to question my attractiveness or wonder when he would want me again. In that regard, we were completely in sync. And I would have followed him anywhere to pursue his dream, but it just wasn't meant to be, I guess. God, listen to me. I have two beautiful kids now and this kind of talk is pointless."

"Sam, you're stuck in a marriage with a man who won't even try to change to make you happy. You're doing all the work you can think of to keep it together and he's totally indifferent. I wouldn't blame you if you'd fantasized about Alec, especially now that his love song for you is a national hit. I mean, it's pretty amazing to think you were once married to a hot new country music star."

"Emphasis on *once*," she retorted. "He left me, remember? And if David and I were in a good place, hearing that song on the radio would have been nothing more than a nice surprise. I would have been excited for an old friend and thought it was cool that his breakout song was originally written for me. As it is, it just brings back memories of what is was like to have a husband who made love to me all the time and makes me more frustrated with my marriage."

"That's what worries me, Sam. You're vulnerable. And if Alec somehow gets in touch with you, then what? Or has he already?"

"Okay, I have a confession to make: I talked to him. We had a friendly conversation, where I congratulated him on his success and that was that," she lied. "He did tell me he's coming through Charlotte soon with the Garth Brooks tour, and who knows? Maybe he'll even play at Coyote Joe's for old time's sake." Sam did her best to sound nonchalant.

"And? Are you planning to see him?"

"Of course not. Look, no matter how much trouble my marriage is in, I'm still a married woman with two young kids who need me. I'm not looking for a scandal here. And, honestly, I don't want to put myself through more heartbreak. It's hard enough hearing *Fancy Face* on the radio and dealing with David's reaction to it."

"Has he suspected anything?"

"He questioned me about how I feel about it. It reminded me of when we first started dating and he perceived Alec as a threat, which he kinda was at the time. But I told him that was then, and this is now. I'm happy for Alec and that's about it. The irony is that if David would just meet me halfway, we could restore our marriage. That's my first preference. But between you and me, I don't know how much longer I can go on like this. I'm a physical person. I love sex. I want to have lots of sex with my husband and he…well, he just doesn't. I'm not sure where that leaves me."

Shannon listened without judgement. Since meeting her boyfriend Rick right around the time Sam gave birth to Madison, she'd begun attending regular church services with him – something she never thought she'd do in a million years. But despite her initial misgivings, weekly attendance had given her a new perspective on life and strengthened their relationship. Unlike Derek before him, Rick was respectful, kind, considerate, and loving. Shannon was grateful for his presence in her life; he'd also shown her the value of living one's life with a moral standard.

Shannon patted Sam's hand. "Whatever happens, promise me you'll get a divorce first before doing something crazy like having an affair. If you decide you've run out of options, no one would blame you. You can't fix your marriage by yourself. But you owe it to yourself and your kids to end things the right way, that's all."

Sam nodded her head and suddenly thought of Logan. Like her, he was stuck in a loveless marriage and devoted to two children – his sons Tyler and Nolan. During their workouts together, he confided and commiserated with Sam as their friendship developed. It seemed inevitable that two lonely people who wanted to do right by their families would form a solid, platonic bond where each became the other's sounding board. For Sam, it was comforting to have a safe person she could turn to in her life, aside from her marriage therapist; the fact that Logan was dealing with similar problems provided a measure of credibility she could not get from anyone else.

But since summer was his busy season in the landscaping business, Logan's attendance at Cross-Fit had been hit-or-miss lately, denying Sam the opportunity to confide in him about *Fancy Face* and the dormant feelings it had awakened within her. She'd thought about calling him to talk, but never followed through. Besides, she didn't need anyone else's advice on the matter; she was going to deal with Alec in person and put an end to it. Now that he'd achieved his goal, she would have to adjust to hearing more of him on the radio and seeing him online and in the tabloids…no doubt with a new woman. Thus far, there had been no news on that front, but knowing Alec, he wasn't living a life of celibacy.

"Sam? Did you hear me?" Shannon repeated.

"Y-yes, you are absolutely right," she agreed, raising her martini glass. "Let's drink to that. I promise, when I have reached the end with David, I'll file for divorce before I get involved with another man." But as they clinked glasses, she wondered if she could keep that vow.

ॐ

"Samantha Townsend, look at you," Alec gushed, wrapping her in a bear hug while the security detail around his suite at the Omni Charlotte Hotel looked on. "You haven't changed a bit...except you're even hotter if that's possible."

"Still the charmer, I see," she joked. When he released her, she looked up to gaze at his big dark eyes and full, sensual lips, noting he was just as handsome now as he was during their Keesler days. "You don't look so bad yourself," she added.

"Well, come on, girl, get in here so we can have a drink." He gestured toward the sitting area, where a bar stood by the wall to the right. "Sit down and make yourself comfortable," he instructed. "Want a beer? A glass of wine?"

"Uh, a beer is fine." She sat down on a plush love seat and took in the view of the city from the panoramic windows. A minute later, he handed her a bottle of Bud Light as he sat down next to her. Her heart fluttered in her chest as she briefly wondered if coming here was the right thing to do. She shifted her body closer to the arm rest.

"Don't worry, Sam," he said, noticing her discomfort. "This is not a booty call. I have way too much respect for you for that. This is just two old friends who have shared a bunch of life experience getting together for old time's sake. I hope it doesn't bother you that my manager chose *Fancy Face*. He knew it would be a hit and he was right. I want you to know, I meant every word when I wrote that for you."

She nodded her head, unable to speak.

"It's kinda cool when you think about it," he went on. "I mean, you were the inspiration for the song that launched my career. You were great, Sam. I have no regrets about what we shared, and I hope you don't either, despite everything that happened. I'm sorry I hurt you."

"I know," she managed to say, taking another swig of beer.

"But, uh, I have a feeling you did get even with me back in the day. C'mon Sam, why don't you just admit that you were the one who keyed my car?"

His question worked as intended; her mood shifted from sadness to feistiness. "You know what? I did key your goddamned car," she admitted. "And you deserved it."

With that, they both dissolved into unbridled laughter. "No argument from me, Fancy Face," he remarked a few minutes later. The awkwardness broken, they spent the rest of the evening engaged in genuine conversation about their lives, with Alec showing an interest in her ongoing problems with David. She surprised herself by confessing to a strange attraction to a guy friend at the gym who seemed to like her in a romantic sense, possibly because of their shared misery in their respective marriages. But she couldn't be completely sure since he flirted with all the women there.

"Sam, just be careful," he advised. "Don't do anything until you decide about David. Personally, I think the guy is crazy for not getting his ass to a doctor to figure out why he has no interest in a sexy woman like you."

"Yeah, well do me a favor? Don't turn our marital woes into your next hit ballad, okay?"

They cracked up again. "I won't, I promise. But Sam, take things slow with Logan. From what you told me about his wife, Heather Raines, and her family, you could be asking for trouble. I've seen a million commercials for the Raines Law Firm on TV since I got here. Now that I think about it, I remember hearing about that personal injury firm way back when, when you and I first moved to Charlotte. Just be careful."

A strong sense of foreboding shot through her – the same feeling she experienced often during her ill-fated marriage to Alec. Sam shuddered. "Believe me, I will. It's not just about me anymore. I have two beautiful kids who need me. I won't do anything to ruin their lives."

"You've always had a good head on your shoulders, Samantha Townsend. I know you'll do the right thing."

"Thank you. And please give your parents my best. I'll always remember them and the wonderful times we spent together. They must be so proud of you." She patted him playfully on the cheek before glancing at her phone. "Oh my, I gotta get going. My kids and my father are going to think I abandoned them," she chuckled.

They ended the evening with a hug and a promise to stay in touch, but Sam knew it would be their final interaction. From this point on, Alec would be someone she used to love and a celebrity she read about online. She gave him a quick kiss on the cheek and wished him the best before heading down the hallway to the elevator, eager to see Madison and Zach.

৯

Chapter Six

Sam sighed as she read the latest text from Logan in the privacy of her home office.

"Hey partner, I had a great time working out with you today… although I have to admit it's hard to concentrate when I can't take my eyes off of you. You looked smokin' hot today!"

"LOL, thanks. It was a hard workout today, I'm glad you were there to push me through it. I'll be going at noon tomorrow, you?"

"It's a date, see you then. ☺"

Then, knowing he would be spending the next several hours with his family, she leaned back in her leather swivel chair, closed her eyes and reminisced about the events of the previous several months. After leaving Alec's hotel room that evening, she felt a renewed sense of purpose and determination, inspired by his example of never giving up. Sam knew what she wanted out of life: a man who adored her, a stable home, and the opportunity to see her own children grow into well-adjusted adults with dreams of their own.

She could face herself in the mirror with a clear conscience, knowing she'd done everything in her power to restore her broken marriage. Time and time again, David had proven he did not share the same desire to rekindle whatever passion had existed between them before they became parents, or express any sort of affection in the form of a hug, touch, or term of endearment. Their therapy sessions felt more like a charade than anything else, a way for Sam to smoothly pave the way for the inevitable, for the sake of her kids. Week after week, whether neglecting to follow through on Susan's "homework," make love to his wife, or attend Zach's lacrosse games, David failed her and the kids, leaving his frustrated wife no choice but to accept reality: her marriage was a lost cause. She could not want more for David than he wanted for himself. If the drive to become a better, more fully present husband and father did not exist within the depths of his soul, there was no way he was going to transform into the man she'd fantasized about.

All that was left was to help Madison and Zach with the upcoming transition, whenever the time felt right, now that her initial shame at the prospect of a second divorce had dissolved into quiet resignation. She was still young, vibrant, and full of life. And there was no way she was going to settle for less than she deserved. Yet she wanted to move through the process deliberately, not only for her children, but her father.

Over the years, Walter and David had forged a symbiotic relationship, each fulfilling a role in the other's life. For Walter, David felt like the son he'd never had, and for David, Walter showed him what it meant to have a caring, interested father. David felt most at ease when family outings involved Grandpa, whose quick wit and spontaneous personality created a natural buffer and relieved his discomfort about how to interact with his two joyful, healthy, high-energy kids.

Meanwhile, Sam continued to channel her relentless sexual energy into increasingly more difficult workouts at the gym, where her flirtatious interludes with Logan began to take on a new intensity. Although she'd dismissed him at first for not being her type, the more she got to know him, the stronger her attraction became. What started as two friends commiserating over their loveless marriages in a safe, public space gradually evolved into something more. She didn't know exactly when it happened, but at some point, she realized she could no longer deny the sensations within her that simmered beneath the surface, ready to express themselves in a fury of supercharged emotion and primal instinct. If her intuition about Logan proved to be accurate, it was only a matter of time before she gave into temptation. Like her impending divorce, it felt destined to happen.

After weeks of suggestive conversations at the gym and exchanges of secret texts, the day of reckoning arrived. Sam dropped the kids off at school, then returned home to complete a few hours of work before taking a shower and preparing to meet Logan for lunch. As she stood under the pulsating hot water, every inch of her body felt electric, her womanly urges palpable. It felt like forever since a man had touched her; she couldn't wait to feel the warmth of Logan's bare body against hers, and experience his hunger as he reawakened her suppressed desires. Having spoken often about their unfulfilling marriages, they understood each other's frustration. Both feeling stuck and unloved, they were persevering out of their love for their children. And though ready to find solace in each other's arms, they remained on high-alert about the severity of the consequences, should the wrong people uncover their affair.

To his credit, Logan informed her upfront that he would not leave his wife, despite his intense physical and emotional attraction, and his desire to explore the possibilities of their unexpected relationship. Aside from his consideration for his sons' well-being, his powerful father-in-law was running for Senate, creating another layer of scrutiny and peril. He swore to her he'd deny the affair and commit to saving his marriage, if, God forbid, they were ever outed by someone in the media, another Cross-Fit member, or anyone else seeking their fifteen minutes of fame. None of it deterred Sam in the least. After what she'd been through in her relationships with men and marriage, she was in no rush to jump into anything more than a secret love affair – something she could hold onto when the nights felt cold and lonely.

She finished applying a coat of mascara and took one last glimpse in the mirror before deciding on a well-fitting pair of jeans and a light, flowy yellow top. She slipped on a pair of sandals, ran a brush through her long, silky hair, and headed off for her "date" with Logan. When she turned into the parking lot of Dos Amigos, the Mexican restaurant they had selected, her heart pounded in her chest at the familiar sight of his Range Rover. She sent him a quick text to let him know she was parking and he promptly responded, "Come on in, Beautiful." Suddenly, her nerves kicked in as her palms started to sweat.

"Just breathe, Samantha," she told herself. She inhaled, held it for a few seconds, then exhaled deeply before proceeding out of the car and striding confidently toward the main entrance.

She walked in to find Logan sitting comfortably at the bar. Sensing her presence, he turned his head to look at her and a huge smile appeared on his face.

"Damn, you clean up well," he announced, before pulling her into a big bear hug. Sam inhaled the musky scent of his cologne, causing her knees to go weak.

"Is it okay if we sit at the bar?" he asked, pulling out a chair.

"Yeah, this is perfect," she replied, noting that his margarita glass appeared to be almost empty. She wondered how long he'd been waiting for her.

For the next hour, they shared stories and laughs, an intoxicating familiarity infusing their conversation; it felt as if they'd known each other their entire lives. Sam's initial butterflies subsided within minutes of seeing him face-to-face at the bar, replaced by an overwhelming feeling of happiness. To her chagrin, when she finally glanced at her smartphone to check the time, she realized she had to get going.

"Ah, Logan, I hate to bring this to an end, but my kids will be getting off the bus soon and I need to go meet them."

He flashed her a hopeful smile. "Can't a neighbor get them for you today?"

"Well, I guess I could ask," she replied. "Let me send her a quick text." A minute later, she received a response that her friend would be happy to greet Madison and Zach at the bus. Sam's heart began to race at the possibilities.

"Okay, my neighbor will meet them, but I do need to be home by five p.m.," she announced.

"Perfect," he remarked in a sexy, masculine tone.

They sat at the bar for 20 more minutes, laughing and talking before Logan suggested something that would forever change the course of their relationship and their lives.

"Sam, I am having such a good time with you. I've have more fun with you in a couple of hours than I've had with Heather in years," he confessed. She smiled and blushed a little at the compliment. He continued, "I don't want to rush things, but I'd love to have a little more privacy with you before we wrap up our afternoon. My mom's house is only about two miles from here, in Heydon Hall. She's in Florida for the month...would you be interested in having one last drink there?"

Her heart began to pump so furiously she was certain he could see the nervous energy that had overtaken her whole body. But in her response, there was no hesitation.

"Sure, I'd like that," she answered in a tone of confidence.

A few minutes later as she followed his car into his mother's exclusive gated community in South Charlotte, Sam couldn't help but imagine that they were about to share more than just a drink. Oddly, she wasn't nervous or scared, but filled with pure excitement. When they pulled into the majestic driveway of the massive red-brick house, Logan entered the garage code, where Sam parked her Pathfinder safely inside, next to his Range Rover. He disabled the alarm system before ushering her into a large, gourmet kitchen with Carrera marble countertops, dark hardwood floors, and stainless steel, state-of-the-art appliances.

"Let's see here, she usually has some wine around the house," he observed as he walked toward an elongated island which housed a small wine fridge. While he bent down to inspect its contents, Sam looked around in awe of the beauty, warmth, and comfort of the place. It was decorated impeccably, with all the accoutrements of an upper-middle-class existence, yet it resonated with Southern charm and family love.

"This is such a beautiful home," she gushed as she wandered into the family room.

"Yeah, Mama has a knack for decorating," he agreed, opening a bottle of Chardonnay before filling two elegant wine glasses. She smiled as she walked around observing the myriad of family photos placed throughout the rooms. Most of them featured his mother's grandchildren and her late husband. Although Logan had mentioned his dad's passing before, he never disclosed when or how it had happened. In the photos, Sam saw the story of an adventurous couple that had traveled the world in their love and passion for life. She felt a palpable tinge of sadness for Logan's mom, realizing how much she must miss her late husband.

"Here you go." He handed her a glass of wine. She took a sip and savored its oaky taste and coolness.

"Come on, let's sit on the back porch, the view of the golf course is great from there." He led her out through the back door, where a large porch swing awaited them. They sat down on it with a gentle rocking motion as they resumed the easy flow of conversation and laughter.

"Your eyes are so pretty, Sam," he almost whispered. She felt the warmth of her cheeks blushing.

"Thanks," she responded with a shy smile.

Before she could fully process his genuine words, he leaned in for a kiss. The softness of his lips took her by surprise; there was a longing there she had not experienced in ages. As their tongues explored each other's mouths, Sam scooted closer to him on the swing, feeling every nerve ending in her body responding to his touch. There was no doubt they were about to cross a dangerous line. Time seemed to stand still as they made out with wild abandon, reveling in the exquisiteness of authentic, passionate kisses – a sensation that had eluded each of them for what felt like an eternity. But it was Sam who suddenly broke the spell when the internal voice of reason barraged her with thoughts of kids, home, and responsibilities.

"Uh, Logan…I don't want to…but I probably better go," she reluctantly announced, releasing herself from his embrace. Things were getting a little too steamy and though she still had plenty of time, she knew what would happen if she failed to summon the discipline to leave.

"Nooo…fifteen more minutes, please," he whined and flashed her a pouty face.

"Ha! Okay, but I do need to go soon," she warned. They spent several more minutes snuggled together on the porch, feeling totally at peace as the cool breeze blew through their hair.

"I think you need to pinch me," he admitted. "I have not felt so happy, so appreciated in such a long time – I must be dreaming. Sam, I've been living like a zombie, just surviving each day at home. Don't get me wrong; I love my boys and I spend every possible second with them, but I haven't felt like this in years…or maybe ever."

He paused and gazed into her big, blue eyes; it was obvious she felt the exact same way. "Come with me," he encouraged, standing up and grabbing her hand. Giving in to destiny, she followed him through the house, up a large, winding staircase and down a long hallway to a welcoming guestroom. Somewhere along the way, her lingering doubts vanished, allowing her to lose herself in the moment. She was vaguely aware of her surroundings – the coolness of the air on the second floor, the framed family photos scattered throughout the guest room, and the plethora of plump, decorative pillows arranged on the perfectly made-up bed. For a moment, they lingered in the doorway in silence. Then Logan spoke up.

"Sam, if this is too much, then I'll stop right here. I love hanging out with you; it's like you have reawakened me. I know it's risky in so many ways, but I feel so connected to you. I want to make love to you, I want to be close to you, I want…"

She cut him off with a deep, probing kiss, putting an end to any further discussion on the matter.

"Me too," she whispered, when she came up for air. She felt his strong arms pull her tightly against his body as they resumed their kissing. Her hands massaged the back of his neck while her fingers wandered through his hair. Her whole body tingled as his hands slipped under her top and began to caress her back. Then, in one smooth motion, he unclasped her bra and pulled her billowy blouse over her head, revealing the full breasts he'd been longing to ogle and touch ever since laying eyes on her at the gym. As she stood before him, he paused for a moment and allowed his gaze to linger.

"Sam, you are absolutely beautiful," he whispered hoarsely. She smiled nervously at the compliment, feeling almost like a teenager again. How long had it been since a man had uttered those words to her during such an intimate moment? True, for weeks Logan had been complimenting her appearance at the gym, but she didn't take it seriously until now. And yet, his reaction still took her by surprise.

Under his appreciative stare, she unbuttoned her jeans and let them slide to the floor. Logan pulled her close and kissed her neck, working his way down her toned, firm body. She let out a deep moan as his lips took one of her breasts into his mouth, while his fingers grazed her nipples. Their passion rising, he picked her up and laid her down on the bed. As he lowered himself on top of her, she tugged his shirt off. When he unbuckled his belt and removed his jeans, giving her an up-close view of his body, she marveled at his fitness and athleticism, normally hidden under shorts and tee shirts at the gym. But his sculpted abs and upper thighs were not the only body parts that impressed her: an obvious bulge protruding from his black boxer briefs revealed the intensity of his pure lust and filled her with a sense of validation.

They exchanged the most electrifying of kisses as he lowered his body down on top of her. She massaged his strong back and shoulders, feeling the ache in her hips and the burning desire to feel him move inside of her while their passion drove them over the edge. Logan stopped for a few seconds to stare into her mesmerizing eyes.

"Sam, I am completely crazy about you," he whispered. "I have been imagining this moment for weeks; it feels incredible to finally be skin-to-skin with you, to smell your body, to taste your lips. I gotta say, the real thing…it is far beyond my wildest dreams." He covered her neck in soft kisses, then worked his way down to her taut stomach, where his tongue tickled and teased her. But when he peeled her panties off and tossed them to the floor, she tingled in anticipation of what was about to transpire.

When his warm mouth greeted her clit, she couldn't help but let out an audible moan. Within a minute, he brought her to climax, her entire body flooded with the satisfaction and enjoyment of her orgasm as she lay there for a blissful moment, fully immersed in the experience. Then, she felt the rush of Logan entering her, his body strong and heavy on top of hers. He took his time making love to her, bringing her to orgasm a second time before unleashing himself inside of her. The new lovers spent the next hour tangled in each other's arms, neither one wanting to end their exquisite afternoon together.

ം

Sam gazed out the window of her home office, lost in thoughts of Logan. It was the third-month anniversary of their first official date and consummation of their relationship at his mother's home, and try as she might, she couldn't quite concentrate on work.

Though she'd spent time with her lover that morning at the gym, a mandatory conference call with an important client had prevented her from indulging in the luxury of an extended love-making session with him in the afternoon.

She glanced at her phone and sighed. It was almost time for her to dial in to conduct the sales training. With fingers flying, she typed out a quick text message to her man, who'd promised her a night on the town that coming Friday, if he could figure out his wife's plans. With her father's campaign in full swing, it was possible Heather expected him to be somewhere, though the thought of it made him sick.

"I miss you already! You are my happiness. Hope you don't get into trouble," Sam texted.

"I'm fine…and you are fine…as in hot, unbelievable, beautiful, intelligent, an incredible Mom, an incredible lover, a gorgeous soul," came Logan's reply.

"I LOVE you! So fucking happy!" she added a few heart emojis for emphasis.

"With you in my life, I'm happier, sexier, smarter, stronger, sweeter, calmer. You have had such an incredible impact on me in three short months!"

"Let me know about Friday. I can get sitter if needed, or maybe my dad can watch the kids."

"OK. Pretty sure Heather will be away on a work trip. Really hoping it's not some BS political event. Gotta go. I'll be in touch. Love you!"

A chill of foreboding shot through her body as she read the last line of the message, but she shook it off and focused on business for the rest of the afternoon until it was time to meet Madison and Zach at the bus stop.

❦

"Happy birthday to you, happy birthday to you, happy birthday dear Logan, happy birthday to you," Sam sang as he emerged from the shower with a thick towel wrapped around his waist. They had just made love again at his mother's house and she'd hidden the surprise – a special fancy cupcake just for him – until the moment was right. Her heart was filled with love and tenderness as she noticed his eyes glistening with tears.

"Oh Sam, I truly don't remember the last time someone gave me a cake or cupcake for my birthday. My wife hasn't done this for me, ever. Hell, she doesn't even do it for her own kids. Why would she do it for me? I'm the one who makes the boys' birthdays special. I'm the one who buys the gifts, gets the cakes, plans the party. If not for me, we wouldn't even have Christmas presents or decorations at our house. But hey, as far as the media knows, we're all just one big happy family," he snarked.

"Well, Logan Nash, as far as I'm concerned, you deserve to be celebrated on your birthday and every day," she whispered, placing the cupcake back on the nightstand to pull him into a long, lingering embrace. She pressed her head against his chest and closed her eyes, ignoring the familiar feeling of dread that had begun to plague her again. But as she listened to his strong heartbeat and savored the strength and warmth of his body, she brushed all thoughts of impending doom aside.

"Thank you, Beautiful. From the bottom of my heart, thank you," he whispered over and over. "I love you so much, Sam."

"I love you, too."

She lost herself in the sweetness of the moment, not knowing it would soon become a bittersweet memory.

❧

"I know I drove her away. I'm willing to change," David announced to their marriage therapist as he and Sam sat in her uptown office. *Whatever*, Sam thought.

"Sam, I'm sorry for embarrassing you the way I did a when I found out about the affair. I was so enraged when I read those private Facebook messages on your phone, I couldn't see straight. But threatening to change the locks and keep you from the kids if you didn't fly home from Florida right away after calling everyone to confess – "

"David, I know, it was completely out-of-character for you," she replied evenly.

Her mind wandered back to that fateful day. The plane had barely touched down in Fort Lauderdale for the Cross-Fit competition when her scorned husband called her with the news that she and Logan had been busted, ruining her much-anticipated weekend for which she'd spent countless hours in grueling workouts. Her trip had thankfully coincided with Logan and Heather's anniversary, which of course, involved a lavish party thrown by Edward Raines, with a lapdog media in attendance. Sam was grateful to be out of town, but could never have anticipated this outcome.

Just days before, as they laid tangled up in the sheets, Logan had informed her, "When you're a powerful attorney running for Senate, every personal event must be transformed into a media circus. I'm just thankful I have you in my life now, Sam. Makes it so much easier to bear all this insanity."

"Logan, what happens if he wins?" she'd inquired, feeling a knot in the pit of her stomach.

"Nothing. My wonderful in-laws will spend more time in D.C., thank God. With any luck, my wife will join them to play the socialite and rub elbows with the elite. But I have the perfect excuse of not wanting to disrupt the boys' schooling or my landscape business. Don't worry, baby, it might end up being a good thing for us."

"I'm not so sure about that," she confessed. "Heather doesn't give a damn about your business. She thinks it's a joke. And with all the social events going on up there, she is going to demand you escort her to everything. Your role as dutiful husband...it's never going to be over if her father wins the election. As it is, we're walking a dangerous line." It hadn't occurred to Sam in that moment that her own spouse would be the first one to out them, due to her own carelessness in leaving behind her old smartphone without removing the Facebook private messenger app.

"Sam," Logan whispered, "our time together is precious. Please, I don't want to waste it with anymore talk of Edward or Heather. All I want to do is make love to you – my beautiful, sexy, gorgeous woman." With that, he shifted his body on top of hers and stared deeply into her eyes.

"I love you, Sam. I'm sorry this is all I can give you right now."

Her heart fluttered in her chest as she caressed his cheek. "I love you, too, Logan. I never thought I could feel this way again, but you have awakened me...my soul, my body, everything."

He felt the blood rush to loins as he took in the meaning of her words and gazed at her glorious, naked form. She gasped when he could no longer restrain himself and took one of her nipples in his mouth while his hands cupped and massaged her perfect, full breasts, the ones he could not get enough of. She sank her head into the pillows, arched her back, and stretched her arms over her head, losing herself in ecstasy.

He smothered her stomach in soft, wet kisses as his hands moved over her tight muscles before spreading her legs apart. She released a guttural moan when his fingers entered her, gently at first, then with more intensity as they explored her warm, inner layers, preparing the way for his artful tongue. It flickered and lingered within her as Logan delighted in her taste and scent, the sounds of her rapture encouraging him on, until she screamed out with pleasure. A moment later, she wrapped her legs around his back as he thrust inside of her, the two of them moving together in harmony, their passion rising to a crescendo and obliterating all thoughts of the outside world.

"Sam?" David's voice brought her back to the present moment. Embarrassed and slightly annoyed, she adjusted her body in the cushioned chair and tucked her hair behind her ear. *God, I'd give anything to be with Logan right now instead of this stupid counseling office with David*, she thought.

"Yes?" she answered.

"Sam, I did it because…I wanted you to hurt as much as I did. In those messages I could tell what was going on between the two of you was so much more than an affair. I wanted payback. Now I can't believe I forced you to tell your dad about it to shatter his illusion of you as his perfect little girl. Making you confess to my own father…I don't know what got into me. I was wrong, Sam. I'm sorry."

While he appeared to be genuinely remorseful, she had no desire to offer absolution.

"David, I don't get it. For years, I did everything I could think of to save our marriage. You're the reason I went to the Cross-Fit gym in the first place. I didn't set out to have an affair. I thought if I made myself more attractive to you, we could somehow work it out. But you had no interest. Do you have any idea how it feels to be rejected by your husband repeatedly when all you want is some affection? Some love? Some consideration? Let me tell you, it makes a person feel shitty…not to mention your detachment from you own kids, who just want to spend time with you. They don't need expensive trips to Disney World; they need a dad who can run around in the backyard with them, go to their games, and help with homework. What is so hard about that?"

She stopped short of verbalizing her belief that a divorce most likely would not feel much different for them since they barely knew their father anyway. Given the visceral anger she harbored, it was a monumental effort. She thought back to her horrific fight with her father, who did not take kindly to the news of her and Logan's affair. More than anything, Walter's expression of profound disappointment in his eldest daughter, the one for whom he'd always held the deepest respect and pride, had nearly shattered her. Sam had no idea how long it would take to repair their relationship, but she was determined to help him see her point of view. David was neither a victim, nor a villain, yet he did play an integral part in the dissolution of their marriage. Once Walter worked through his initial shock and anger, she planned to have an in-depth, face-to-face conversation. Right now, protecting her kids was her top priority.

"I-I'm sorry, Sam. If it makes you feel any better, the fact that my dad blew the whole thing off as if it was nothing, hurt me. 'These things happen?' Guess he doesn't think much of me or my feelings."

Though she felt a twinge of sadness for her estranged husband, she remained silent. Her father-in-law's strange reaction had taken her by surprise too, though the man had never expressed affection or loyalty for his only son. Perhaps if she hadn't completely fallen out of love with David, she might give a damn and suggest that David explore his *daddy issues* one-on-one with a professional. But as she participated in this necessary game, she put on her best show. For the time being, she needed David to believe she was, in his words, "doing the right thing," by ending the affair and working on their marriage.

"Alright," Susan spoke up. "We're here to deal with your relationship with each other, not your parents. We need to talk about the news at hand, that Sam has decided that she's ready for a separation and divorce. David, I know this will be a difficult conversation but it's one that is best had in the safety of this office. Let's keep in mind that as the next few weeks unfold that the goal is to put the children first and not to lash out at each other. I know this is a lot to digest today so let's wrap up and plan to meet again later in the week to talk about what this news means. In the meantime, please try your best to act "normal" at home around the kids. We will discuss when the time is right to share this adult news with them."

The next day, David approached her as she sat at her desk in her home office, preparing a report on the computer.

"Sam, I am really sorry that our relationship has come to this."

"I know, I am too," Sam responded and a wave of hurt washed over her seeing the sadness in his eyes.

"I don't want to be that bitter divorced couple, so I will continue to go to the sessions with Susan and let her lead us how to navigate this change for our family. I suppose I need to start looking for a new place to live."

"Remember David, we are going to take this slow. You aren't going to move out next week or anything so take your time making any decisions like that."

"Yeah, I know. Okay, well I need to get into the office, I'll talk to you later."

Sam knew that the next few weeks would be challenging for them as they needed to talk through things like finances and who gets the kids for what holidays. She was determined to keep things between them as amicable as possible when those difficult conversations happened.

҈

"She is mine. She is soft. She is hard. Confident and quiet, with eyes like the sea and lips like rose petals. She is front seat petting, she is back seat loving. She is cold sheets, tequila, whiskey, and beer. Sharing shots and songs and knowing glances. Smart as a whip, sugar-sweet, she is love-sent notes and heart-melting smiles. Daring and risky, porn-star hot, supermodel hot, she's my rock and my conscience, my smile and my strength, my everything. She's mine."

With a heart bursting with love, she texted her reply, "{Biggest smile ever}. Thank you, I love reading your beautiful words! I'll see you later!" Sam replied to Logan's text before finishing her morning cup of coffee.

It has been three weeks since she and David had the open conversation about their impending divorce. Things had been unfolding rather quickly and seemingly smoothly. They had managed to work out the parenting plan and child support as well as hire an attorney. It was now just a matter of time before David was out of the house and Sam would be able to have a freer conscience about her love for Logan.

"You know, baby, it's kind of mean not to remind a father about his son's birthday." Logan's voice was soft and persuasive in her ear as they cuddled beneath the sheets. She savored the strength and warmth of his bare chest against her back and the feel of his arms encircling her protectively. After a strenuous workout at the gym, they'd retreated to MaryAnn Nash's house, where they indulged in a hot, steamy shower before an extended love-making session in the guest room.

"Babe, I appreciate your input, but believe me, I know what I'm doing. How is David ever going to learn to remember these things on his own once we're divorced if he doesn't start now? You have no idea what it felt like when I read his email about entertaining clients on Zach's birthday. What a dumbass. It's bad enough to forget any child's birthday, but our son's? He almost didn't make it, for God's sake. Of course, I don't know why I'm surprised since he never even came to the hospital to see him while he was fighting for his life. Thank God for my dad and sister, even though neither one is speaking to me much right now."

"Ugh, I'm sorry about that, Sam. I know how much they mean to you. They'll come around, you'll see." He pulled her closer and placed soft, comforting kisses on her head.

"I hope so. I miss them so much. I mean, they're here in Charlotte and they might as well live in Australia. The only time I see my dad is when he picks up the kids from school or takes them out on a Saturday. And even then, he just goes through the motions with me, so they don't notice the tension between us. And Shannon…now that she has Rick, she's completely changed. I mean, it's for the better. She needed to calm down and grow up in many ways, and he's been a stabilizing influence on her. He even has her going to church. And if you knew my little sister, you'd understand what a miracle that is. God, if someone had predicted that I never would have believed them. I just miss her, you know? We used to go out for a girls' night every week. Now we barely talk. And if she knew about us, she'd – "

"Shh, Sam, please don't beat yourself up. Someday, I hope to tell the whole world you are mine – my perfect, sexy, hot, gorgeous woman with a heart of gold. But for now, let's enjoy this secret, sacred time together. I'm thankful we have the chance to spend as much time together as we do. I love you so much."

"Ah Logan, I love you too," she sighed. "And I'm grateful we have a place to connect, where no one can find us. Besides being the most amazing man, ever, you're the only one I can confide in. You have no idea how much that means to me."

"I'll always be here for you, Sam."

"Logan?"

"Yes?"

"Are you absolutely sure Heather bought your 'I'm just a flirt' excuse?"

"Oh yeah. She has no idea about us…not that she would care. Well, she'd care about the political fallout, but other than that why would she give a damn? It's not like she cares about our marriage. She hasn't made any effort to improve anything about our relationship since my boys were born. It's like she fulfilled her obligation to her parents and we're just living our lives for show."

"Good," Sam sighed. "It's bad enough my family knows about us, but given your situation, it would be a disaster. It's hard enough to put up a front with David without the added burden of a media spotlight. Been there, done that with my first husband when he was just starting out with his country music career, except I thought we were solid. I would have followed him anywhere in pursuit of his dreams. Funny how life works out, isn't it?"

"At least you got a hit single out of it," he joked. But when he felt her stiffen a bit in his arms, his tone became serious. "Hey, Beautiful, this is our special time, remember? Let's not ruin it with thoughts of the past and just be happy our paths led us here. I know it's not the perfect scenario, Sam, but I really do love you. I promise you, someday, when my boys are grown, I'll tell the entire world you are my woman forever. For now, I just want to focus on the present and enjoy every second we have alone together. Because when I'm not with you, this is all I can think about – holding you, touching you, kissing you, being loved by you. It's unlike anything I've ever experienced."

"Me too," she whispered.

"So then, let's not waste another second of this precious time talking when we could be doing something so much better."

With that, he turned her body toward him and drew her into another mesmerizing kiss that dissolved all awareness of the outside world as passion consumed them once again.

Sam put the finishing touches on Zach's last birthday present and arranged several gift-wrapped boxes at his place on the kitchen table. She smiled at her handiwork, knowing how much he would love the bright, multi-colored paper featuring footballs, baseballs, hockey pucks, and basketballs – perfect for a boy who adored sports. After leaving Logan's mother's place that afternoon, she'd stopped at the store to pick up a few more items in preparation for her son's birthday the following day. Per her tradition, she and Madison would sing *Happy Birthday* to him in the morning when he came down for a special breakfast of pancakes, then he'd open his presents before heading off to school. That evening, they'd have dinner at Bonefish, his favorite restaurant, and Sam would bring a birthday cake from her favorite Charlotte bakery, the same place where she found Logan's fancy cupcake.

As she inspected the mound of presents sitting on the table, she glanced over at David, who had been staring intently at his iPad in the next room the whole time, oblivious to her presence. *You're so disconnected, you didn't even bother to ask me what I was doing*, she thought. When she entered the kitchen at the crack of dawn the next morning, she found her husband pouring coffee into a travel mug. They mumbled a perfunctory greeting before he headed out the door to work. If he'd noticed Zach's presents sitting on the table, he didn't acknowledge them.

To Sam's surprise, David called her several hours later after seeing her emotional Facebook post about Zach, accompanied by photos of him excitedly opening his presents and digging into his pancakes. After his tumultuous birth and near death as a fragile infant, she thanked God every day for his robust health. Her son was growing, developing, and reaching every milestone right on time and for that, she was profoundly grateful. His birthday gave her the perfect opportunity to remind him how much she loved him and share his story with the world.

"I forgot Zach's birthday," David announced.

No shit, you idiot. "Uh, yes, it's today," she forced herself to reply politely, Logan's words ringing in her ears. "I'm not sure if you saw me wrapping his presents last night, but we're going to

Bonefish for dinner if you would like to join us. I know you said you have to entertain clients; I just wanted to extend the invitation."

"Ah, sure. Sure, I think I can make it. You know what? I'll just reschedule with them."

"Great, we'll meet you there at 6:30."

After hanging up with David, Sam scrolled through her text messages from Logan – an activity she often indulged in during the day when thoughts of her beloved overwhelmed her. Like a schoolgirl with a crush, she'd giggle as she pored over them, grateful to have found the right man at last, even if their forbidden relationship had to remain a secret for the foreseeable future. Whenever the frightening implications of the Raines family somehow discovering their affair sent shivers up and down her spine, Logan's modern-day communications gave her the strength and courage to keep going.

"Your kisses are like heaven," his text message read. "'For it was not into my ear you whispered, but into my heart. It was not my lips you kissed, but my soul.'"

"I love this! I love you! {Smiling Heart}," Sam had replied.

Her heart fluttered as she scrolled down to read the next one.

"Hey, Sam?"

"Yes, Logan?"

"I ♥ U!"

"And I love you, dear Logan," she uttered aloud, ignoring her computer's notification of a new work email. How she wished they could be together that day, even if only for an hour, but between their jobs and family obligations, it wasn't possible. Sam wasn't even sure she could make it to the gym for her daily workout. And yet, all she wanted to do was keep reading his texts.

"My heart when I'm with you."

"My heart when I'm not."

"My smile when I'm with you."

"My smile when I'm not."

"My weenie when I'm with you." She laughed out loud looking at his crude depiction of an erect penis. It still cracked her up after all these months.

"My weenie when I'm not." By now, Sam was in tears laughing at Logan's silly, simple drawing of a flaccid penis. She wiped her eyes and took a few deep breaths to regain her composure before moving on to the next one.

"Have I told you today how happy you made me? I LOVED laying in your lap, with your beautiful fingers stroking my hair and chest, and listening to you work. 'She's here with me when life's not fair. She runs her fingers through my hair. She warms my heart, she makes it whole. As she runs her fingers through my soul.'"

"Someday Logan, someday we'll be free to declare our love to the world," she declared aloud in a tone of determined resignation. But she couldn't deny the sick feeling of doom in the pit of her stomach, though she couldn't figure out what it was trying to warn her about. Would they be caught up in a public   scandal, despite every precaution taken? Would she end up losing her job, her kids, and the support of her family?

Sam pushed these panicked thoughts aside and focused her attention back on the day's work. It was Zach's birthday and she was determined to make it special. Besides, after everything she'd dealt with in her life, she felt confident she could handle whatever this affair with Logan was leading her into.

Chapter Seven

"Ding dong" the chime of the doorbell alarmed sending Madison and Zach running to the door.

"Daddy!" they shouted in unison as David opened the door.

It was a Friday night and the first weekend that David would be taking the kids to his new place. In the two months since Zach's birthday they had managed to file for divorce and they even worked together on selecting David's new place and getting it ready for the kids. They were excited to see their new rooms and to order a pizza for dinner. David collected the kids bags as they each gave Sam a big hug before rushing off to his car with excitement. After they left, it was a strange feeling for Sam to be in the house alone. The house felt eerily quiet. She was thankful for Logan's texts that night checking in on her and how she was doing.

Sunday had started out like any other, except for the fact it had been Sam's first official weekend without the kids. Upon awakening alone in the stillness of a brand-new morning, same checked her phone and thought it was strange to not have one from Logan. He had been out with Heather the night before and Sam knew they had a long night, but he tended to text her even the shortest "goodnight" when they would get in. Quickly dismissing it, she decided to get dressed for the Sunday services at Waypoint Community Church. At the suggestion of Shannon's boyfriend, she had adopted the habit of weekly attendance about six months prior – much to her sister's delight. In the aftermath of David's outing of her affair with Logan, Shannon and Rick had gently nudged her in that direction, believing she would benefit from developing a deeper and more meaningful relationship with God. It was safe to say that neither Shannon, nor Rick condoned Sam's actions, which was partly why she never shared many details. There was no point in rhapsodizing about finding true love after two failed marriages, though she'd certainly done everything in her power to make her previous unions work. At first, Sam listened mostly out of respect, but one day she took their advice to heart and met up with them for her first Waypoint experience.

She remained skeptical about regular church attendance on the drive over, but once she stepped through the doors of Waypoint, "The church for people who dislike church," she felt right at home. Yes, she acknowledged her blatant hypocrisy – here she was, carrying on a clandestine affair with a married man and father of two young boys – but once surrounded by the warmth of the community and the sounds of joyful worship, all was forgotten. It was as if stepping through the church doors transported her to another dimension where only love, forgiveness, and peace awaited her.

Of course, the irony hadn't been lost on David. "What, you had this affair and now you're going to church? I don't even know who you are anymore," he'd snidely remarked. *If you only knew*, Sam had thought to herself. Back then, David was blissfully unaware that his soon-to-be ex had not fulfilled her promise to end things with Logan. In fact, the intensity of their love and longing for each other had only increased since the *private messenger* incident the weekend of Sam's Cross-Fit competition in Fort Lauderdale.

But somewhere amid divorce proceedings she had convinced David to start going to Waypoint, believing he could benefit from the support. Among other things, the church had an active men's club where he could meet and hang out with other divorced guys in a safe, nonjudgmental environment. Once David gave in, he embraced this new practice with as much enthusiasm as Sam. It satisfied his own spiritual needs and provided an opportunity to bond with his children in the Christian faith.

Logan, on the other hand, fully supported and appreciated Sam's commitment. His father had been a devout Southern Baptist who read the Bible every morning and pulled out a specific verse for daily guidance and wisdom. Every Sunday without fail, Logan Nash Senior took his wife and kids to church. As an adult, Logan Junior had fallen out of the practice of weekly church attendance, though he often brought the matter up to Heather since he wanted them to go as a family. She would just blow him off and claim that she didn't have time for it. Still, he maintained a good spiritual connection, thanks in part to his dad's example.

"I love that you're starting to go to church," he responded when Sam confided in him. "I wish I could take my own family, but my wife is apparently too busy."

For whatever reason, this little exchange came to mind as Sam finished brushing her hair and prepared to head out the door. She smiled when she thought of Logan – a down-home country boy at heart – having to put on a tuxedo and play the role of devoted husband and son-in-law at the previous evening's swanky gala. She imagined he'd looked hot all dressed up in formal attire and wished she'd been the one on his arm.

Someday, we'll have the chance to share our love with the world.

But as she walked out to the driveway, she couldn't ignore the nagging feeling that something was wrong; she hadn't received a text from him since late Saturday afternoon, which was unusual. No matter what else was going on, Logan always found the time to communicate. True, they'd been forced to be much more careful after David discovered their secret, but the incident had only made them more determined. Was something wrong or was he just exhausted from drinking and schmoozing with the upper-crust of Charlotte? As she pulled out of her development and onto the main road, these concerns preoccupied her mind.

A few hours later, Sam inspected the contents of her kitchen cupboards and realized the necessity of a trip to Kroger. Knowing the kids would be back at dinnertime she wanted to make them one of their favorite meals – lasagna – but didn't have all the ingredients on-hand. It felt like déjà vu when she approached the end of her development and prepared to turn onto the highway; the anxieties prompted by Logan's lack of communication returned, this time with more intensity. Then, out of the blue, her smartphone blared out its familiar ringtone from its perch on the passenger seat. When she saw the name on the screen, her heart lurched: she knew the call had something to do with Logan. There was no other reason in the world for this gym trainer to reach out to her.

"Ah, maybe it's just another DUI, or maybe Heather uncovered some more incriminating evidence," she mused out loud before touching the button to answer.

"Hello?"

"Hey Sam, where are you right now?"

"I'm in my car. What's up?" She tried to sound casual and ignore her rising panic.

"Can you please pull over. I have something to tell you. Are the kids with you?"

"No. What's this about?" She maneuvered her white Nissan Pathfinder safely to the side of the road.

"Are you pulled over?"

"Yes, yes I'm pulled over. Just tell me what it is…please, Katie."

I just want to let you know that Logan Nash is dead."

An electric current of shock jolted her from head to toe.

"W-w-what do you mean he's dead?"

Katie broke down in tears. "Sam, I don't have a lot of the details; I really don't know what's going on. I just got the call from somebody else at the gym who said they found his body in the creek near his house. It's gonna go around; people are going to start talking about it and I didn't want you to find out from just anyone or by seeing it on social media."

Sam began to sob. "What happened? Who knows the details?"

"Sam, I'm sorry, I just don't know anything more. I'm so sorry; I know how close you guys were. I am so, so sorry," she kept repeating.

"Thank you for letting me know," she managed to blurt out before hanging up. She placed her palms over her face and cried her eyes out on the side of the road for what felt like an eternity. Then another couple from the gym with whom Logan was close came to mind. She reached for her phone and found their number in her contacts list. A few seconds later, the wife answered.

"Holly, it's Sam. Do you know what happened?" No further clarification was needed as the two women wept together in shared sorrow.

"I'm so sorry, but I don't have any more details. I wish I could tell you more."

"I don't know if you guys knew or not, but Logan and I were having an affair."

"Sam, we knew. Logan told us. I know this is going to be hard but let us know if there's anything we can do."

Sam pressed her for information about the funeral, but Holly insisted nobody knew anything yet. After they hung up, she sat in the car sobbing for a few more minutes before another thought popped into her head, *I need to see this creek*. She imagined that maybe the police would still be there, that she could somehow see his body. But as she composed herself enough to start driving in that direction, she felt an overwhelming compulsion to reach out to MaryAnn.

Oh, my goodness, she was in Marco Island. She must be on a plane trying to get home right now, all alone and devastated. She and Logan had such a strong connection. She's going to lose it, she thought to herself. Sam focused intently on the road ahead. The more she thought of MaryAnn, the more desperately she wanted to find her and give her a hug even though that was impossible. No doubt, the woman hadn't even arrived back in Charlotte yet.

Rather than visit the creek alone, Sam called Shannon. Through tears and hysteria, she shared the news with her stunned sister, who naturally wanted more information. "I wish I knew more," Sam sniveled. "No one seems to know anything." Then in the next breath, "Shannon, can I come over? I really need to see you right now."

"Of course. Get over here."

A few minutes later, Sam parked her Pathfinder at her sister's place. When she got out, she collapsed onto the front lawn and curled up in a fetal position on the grass. Wondering what was taking so long, Shannon raced out to the front lawn, where the sight she beheld filled her with indescribable tenderness.

"Come on Sam, let's get inside," she urged in a soft voice as she helped her to her feet. They walked arm-in-arm into the house and settled into Shannon's plush, comfy living room sofa. At first the two women didn't do much talking because Sam didn't know any of the circumstances of Logan's demise. But after some time spent alternating between weeping and blowing her nose, she finally came clean to her sister about the extent of their love affair. Suddenly, it felt supremely important to confide all.

"Shannon, this was a deep connection. This was a love; it was something so much bigger than just two people getting together to have sex a few times a week. Even though I know that's what it looked like to everyone else who knew."

Shannon stroked her hair and silently nodded.

"Look," Sam continued, picking up her phone. "Look at these texts and pictures. There was a real bond between us." Shannon obliged her and together they pored over countless 21st century-style communiques of love and passion, including one of Sam's favorites:

"You're my peaceful nirvana; my tropical Copacabana; my I'm gonna; my sweat hot sauna; my I wanna; my pet iguana; my tasty Benihana; my premium marijuana; my biting piranha; my talented Madonna; my Playa de Tijuana!"

As she perused these intensely personal, genuine declarations of raw human emotion, Shannon couldn't decide what was worse:

believing her sister had a tawdry affair or knowing she'd lost the true love of her life.

After a while, Sam remembered her obligations. "Oh my God, I have to call David. He has the kids and thinks I'm at the grocery store right now, buying stuff to make lasagna. He's bringing them back for dinner." When he answered, she declared, "Just so you know, I'm not home and I won't be for several more hours. I'm not at the grocery store, I'm at Shannon's house. I just got a phone call that Logan Nash is dead."

"Sam, I am so sorry," he responded. To her surprise, he sounded sincere. "Listen, take all the time you need; I've got the kids. I'll take care of getting them dinner. Stay with Shannon for as long as you need and just let me know when you want me to bring them back. I can even keep them overnight and drive them to school tomorrow morning. Whatever you want."

Grateful for his sympathetic reaction and generous offer, she pondered it for a moment. "No, no David I want them home. I need to see them."

"Ok, I'll have them back at dinnertime."

"Thanks, I really appreciate it," she choked out. As she touched the screen to end the call, she felt a twinge of guilt, along with worry. Since David still thought their affair had ended nine months ago, he had to be wondering why she was so torn up. She knew they'd have to have a heart-to-heart at some point but wasn't ready for it just yet.

"Sam," Shannon began. "Is there anything you want to do? Is there anywhere you want to go? Do you want me to drive you somewhere? Wanna go to the creek? What do you want to do?"

Without missing a beat, she answered, "I want to get a margarita at Dos Amigos." It was the last place she'd seen him alive only two days ago – a spot that held significance for the two of them.

‿

The entire ride to the restaurant was populated with memory triggers for Sam, who kept pointing out various landmarks and informing her sister, "That's the road that leads to his parents' house," and "That's the park where we used to walk after the gym." In the aftermath of his passing, Logan seemed to be everywhere. And now that he was gone, she couldn't silence the impulse to share the truth of their relationship with everyone who would listen. When they walked into Dos Amigos, she recalled that she and Logan had to sit at the bar the other day instead of their usual booth because the place was crazy busy. "I want to sit on the same barstools Logan and I sat on the other day," she announced.

The girls settled on two stools at the end and ordered margaritas. When Sam asked their bartender if Armando, their regular server, was working that day, he informed her that he'd be in at four p.m., which meant they had about thirty minutes to wait. Sam spent the entire time vacillating between sips and sobs while she and Shannon sat in silence, their somber mood contrasting with the upbeat rhythms and festive décor of their environment. She didn't care how long she had to wait; she just needed to be around someone who'd known of their connection. Someone who knew that what they'd shared went far beyond physical attraction and gratification.

As their regular Dos Amigos server, Armando had borne witness to Logan and Sam's love with all its sentimental expressions: staring longingly into each other's eyes, giggling like teenagers, and Logan insisting on holding Sam's foot under the table just because. The tears spilled down her cheeks as the memories kept on coming.

At last, she spotted him. When he caught her eye, he seemed to look at her as if to say, "Why are you here on a weekend?" As Shannon watched, Sam sprang from her barstool, ran up to the heavyset waiter and gave him a hug, though she was barely able to wrap her arms fully around him as she cried into his chest.

After a moment, she pulled away to look at him. "You know Logan, the guy I come in here and have lunch with?"

"Si, si" he replied with his thick, Mexican accent.

"He's dead. He died today," she squeaked out.

Armando's eyes teared up. "Oh senorita, I am so sorry," he consoled, pulling her into another hug. "You need another margarita with a shot of Grand, don't you?"

"It's okay, I already have one."

"Senorita, let me buy you another. It's on me. It's the least I can do. Logan was my favorite customer. He always took the time to talk to me. I remember how much he loved to talk about his kids."

Sam nodded. "Yes, that's the kind of guy he was."

"Well you two can stay here as long as you want. The Grand Marnier Margaritas are on me," he reiterated with a nod to Shannon. "I have to get to work now but I'll send them out for you."

The two sisters hung out at the bar for about an hour. As they prepared to leave, Sam said goodbye to Armando and told him he was probably going to see her in there every day from now on. "I don't know where else I would go for lunch. We came here all the time," she explained.

Despite her prediction, it would be a long time before Sam would set foot in there again.

◦

"Wow, I don't see anything," Shannon observed as they drove over the creek. "No evidence of a crime   scene, nothing roped off."

Sam stared out the window at the gathering of assorted people on the pedestrian bridge. Some of them were walking dogs but all seemed to be peering down as they talked to one other; it was plain to see that they were discussing what had happened. Once the Miata reached the other side, Shannon turned into a parking lot in preparation to head back home.

"Hey, do you want to get out and walk across? I can pick you up on the other side," she offered. Sam considered it for a moment, then shook her head.

"No, no thanks. I think I just want to go home and see the kids." Shannon floored the accelerator and they headed back across town. Once in the security of her home, Sam felt comforted by the sight of Madison and Zach joyfully running around the living room. As soon as they spotted her they rushed into her arms, eager to tell their mommy all about their adventures of their first weekend at David's house.

Sam held them tightly to her chest for a moment and inhaled the sweet scent of their hair as she kissed them. She listened with the rapt attention of a devoted mom as they regaled her with story after story while their dad looked on in silence.

When they were finally talked out Sam announced, "Mommy's not feeling well. I'm going upstairs to take a bath. Daddy's gonna get you some dinner, give you your baths and tuck you in, okay?" She and David exchanged knowing glances.

"Thank you," Sam whispered as she walked by him on her way to the staircase.

After a long, hot bath in her soaker tub, she threw on her favorite pair of cotton pajamas and crawled into bed, knowing David would tend to the kids well.

As she lingered in the twilight between full consciousness and restful slumber, Sam became incrementally aware of a persistent ringing sound, which she recognized a few seconds later as her smartphone. She rummaged under a few fluffy pillows before locating it where it was lodged in the tiny space between the headboard and mattress. Squinting at the screen she touched it to answer.

"Shannon, what's up?" she asked groggily.

"Where's David?" her sister asked in an urgent tone.

"He's taking care of the kids for me while I rest."

"Look, Sam, I just got off the phone with Dad. We were talking about how suspicious everything is…and he, well both us…we're wondering if you're sure David was with the kids the entire weekend. Is it possible he might have left them with a sitter Saturday night?"

"Shannon, what are you suggesting? That David murdered Logan?"

"Well, he is a jilted husband. And if he did it, we don't think staying in the house is the safest thing for you or the kids."

"Whoa!" Sam exclaimed, now fully awake. "I know it how bad it looks but I don't believe for a second that David could murder anyone – not even his wife's lover. That's really a stretch, don't you think?"

"Who knows? Maybe it hit him all the sudden. Think about it: his first weekend divorced and out of the house, dealing with the kids totally alone for the first time. Maybe under his calm, bland exterior was simmering resentment that none of us saw. You see this kind of stuff in the news all the time."

"Shannon, seriously? Come on, we're talking about David. Don't you think you're being just a little dramatic?"

"*Samantha*," she retorted impatiently, "it is not out of the realm of possibility. How many times do you hear neighbors of a convicted murderer say stuff like 'He was such a nice guy; we can't believe he'd do something like this.' Maybe he snapped and in some twisted way, thought it would be fun to murder his wife's lover on the night of a high-profile political gala on Halloween weekend."

Try as she might, she couldn't bring herself to imagine mild-mannered, impotent David murdering anyone for sport. Besides, as far as he knew their affair had ended months ago. And in terms of their marriage, they'd reached the point of irreconcilable differences long before Logan Nash arrived on the scene. It just didn't make any sense.

"Shannon, I appreciate you and Dad being concerned about me, but honestly, there is no way David is responsible for Logan's death. No way. And why wouldn't the kids have mentioned daddy leaving them with a sitter to go out Saturday night?"

"Maybe it was late. Maybe they were already sleeping."

"Ugh. You don't give up, do you?"

"Not where you and the kids are concerned, no."

But before Sam could utter another word, there was a tentative knock on her bedroom door.

"Sam? It's David."

"I gotta go," she whispered into the phone before ending the call.

"Come in," she responded.

"Hey, I just wanted to tell you again how sorry I am," he offered. He stood in the doorway with his hand on the knob and one foot in the hallway, hesitant to fully enter the room they once shared as a married couple. As she gazed at his tall, skinny frame Sam pondered Shannon's scenario yet still couldn't wrap her head around its validity. *But why was he so hesitant to enter the bedroom?*

"Thank you," she answered softly. "You know, can come all the way in if you want." She offered a sincere, if fleeting smile. David took another step until he was completely inside but remained right in front of the doorway. They looked at each other in awkward silence for a moment.

"Is there something else on your mind?" she asked. Sam felt a twinge of anxiety – not because of Shannon's theory that he'd snapped and gone to the dark side, but because of the secret she'd been keeping from him. She had a sinking feeling it was time to reveal the truth.

"Sam, just out of curiosity. When was the last time you saw Logan?"

Her heart lurched in her chest as she embraced her pillow tightly and prepared to come clean.

"I just saw him on Friday," she admitted.

"This past Friday? The day I picked up the kids from school and took them home with me for the weekend?"

She nodded.

A few moments of silence passed before she spoke up again. "Okay, you're not going to like what I'm about to share with you," she began. "But Logan and I never really stopped seeing each other. He was someone so important and so special to me that even if we'd tried to end our affair even after you busted us we just couldn't do it. So yeah, I saw him on Friday. We had lunch together. And I'm literally still in shock and heartbroken. I can't even describe to you how heartbroken I am right now."

With that she dissolved into tears. David didn't flinch as he watched her, strangely moved by her palpable emotion and honesty. "I can't believe you've been seeing him this whole time," he finally uttered with genuine curiosity. There wasn't a hint of malice or resentment in his tone, which surprised her a little.

She patiently answered his questions and filled him in on the depth of her love for Logan, knowing it was probably more than he wanted to hear. But in keeping with her compulsion in the aftermath of this shocking tragedy to share their love story with anyone who would listen, Sam bared her soul.

"Was he going to leave his wife?" David inquired when she finished. "Were the two of you planning to get married and run off together?"

"No," she stated forthrightly. "He was very clear that if he ever left Heather it wouldn't be until the boys were done with high school. I did not divorce you so that he and I could run away together next month. That wasn't in the cards. I divorced you for many other reasons and everything else we talked about in counseling, and yes, he was a factor but no, we were not planning to go public with our relationship and to hell with everyone else. It wasn't like that."

They spent the next hour engaged in honest, heartfelt conversation interrupted only by David's trip to the bathroom to get a glass of water and a fresh box of tissues for his distraught ex-wife. His sweet, caring gestures solidified Sam's belief that he was no way responsible for Logan's death though she remained suspicious about it for various other reasons. Consequently, she refrained from even questioning him about his whereabouts late Saturday evening and early Sunday morning.

During another period of calm, David glanced at his watch and announced, "Well it's getting late and I should probably get going." He made a motion to get up from the cushioned chair he'd been sitting on, then in the next breath added, "Is there anything else you need, Sam? If you want me to stay, I can go sleep on the couch downstairs."

She was visibly moved by his genuine concern and decided to take a leap of faith. "Can you just lay here with me and hold my hand? I just need some level of comfort right now."

"Of course," he agreed softly. He walked over to the other side of the bed, climbed in, and laid down beside her. In an innocent, pure gesture of love, he grabbed her hand and held it in his, causing her to break down again while all the pain and anguish poured out from the depths of her being. In a rare display of emotion, David cried with her. For a while neither one of them spoke.

When Sam had calmed down enough to talk again, she informed him, "You know, I heard a powerful message today in church; that we should all try to love like God. That God wants us to love somebody even when they don't deserve it. Thank you, David, for loving me that way tonight."

He turned his head to look her in the eye. "Honestly, if I hadn't taken the kids to services today and heard that message I'm not sure I'd have been able to do this. To lay here with you and listen to the truth…it would have been way too painful, Sam. I know I couldn't have done it," he confessed.

"Well in that case, I'm really glad you went to church. Because if there was ever a time God acted through another human being, He is surely acting through you right now, David. I don't know how I would get through this lonely, horrible night if I didn't have someone here with me. And I know I don't deserve it. But here you are, comforting me and holding my hand because my whole world has just been blown apart," she spoke through staccato breaths.

He kissed her forehead. "I'm glad I can be that person for you. God really does work in mysterious ways."

॰

It was hard to believe how much had changed in just 48 hours.

Sam looked in the full-length mirror that hung in the entryway of her house and adjusted her bright yellow *Old Navy* tee shirt. She'd selected her favorite dark boot-legged jeans along with a pair of her most comfortable flip flops to complete her outfit. Even now, as she was approaching middle age, her dislike for *girly* things like make-up and fussy up-dos remained intact, Shannon's efforts notwithstanding. Sam still preferred an au naturel face and a simple hairstyle. The only thing lending color to her pale complexion this morning were her weepy red eyes, which she'd been dabbing at continuously with tissues. Her thick, brown hair hung straight to her mid-back. Fortunately for Sam, the city of Charlotte had been experiencing an extended Indian Summer, saving her the effort of wearing a heavy coat, hat and closed-toe shoes. Under the circumstances, the ability to comfortably dress in lightweight clothing offered a small measure of peace.

Glancing at her smartphone, she noted the time and moved into her home office where her laptop sat open on her desk right where she'd left it. In the aftermath of Logan's unexpected death two days ago, she'd spent last night typing out her feelings out on the monitor. Taking a deep breath, she sat down to read:

I feel lost. I am in shock. Logan was my best friend, lover, companion, support, happiness, laughter, everything! Never before has a man been the perfect blend of the sex appeal and friendship for me. He was perfect to me. He was beautiful to me. He was exactly the person I dreamed of growing old with in this life. Whether it was working out at the gym, having lunch together, a quick kiss in the parking lot, hours in bed at his parents' house, or just messages throughout the day – he made my heart happy. He made me feel like the most beautiful creature on the planet. Our love was so natural, so comfortable. It never felt like we were trying, it just happened. Some of my favorite times with him were when we would just lay in each other's arms and share stories. Stories about our past, stories about our kids, stories about our future. Always joking about "meddling" everything…spouses, kids, work, schedules, anything that got in the way of us being together.

Our dream was that one day in years to come we would be able to show our love openly and live out our golden years on a beach somewhere. But even before the big dreams of beach retirement we had lots of little dreams and goals together. One of those dreams was to just spend an entire day and night together…what we felt would be heaven! To have that much time together laughing and enjoying each other and the idea of falling asleep in each other's loving arms was something that we constantly dreamed of. As I'm writing this now my tummy is growling like crazy! Probably because I have not eaten in more than 24 hours – but he always loved kissing my tummy when it growled. He would ask "Are you looking for some loving?" As if my tummy was yelling out to him "Kiss me!" And every time it growled, he kissed it and talked to it, and every time it brought a big smile to my face.

My tummy is growling now – but it's growling in anger because it will never be kissed by his lips again. Logan, I loved you from so early in our relationship. Your beautiful smile, your bright eyes with that scar, your sexy calves, your strong body – I absolutely loved your strong body! You would always tell me you were too fat or too old for me – not true! I loved my manly man. Heaven to me was being wrapped in your strong arms. I will spend the rest of my life looking forward to those arms if that is what heaven holds. I know I will pull myself together and be a great mom and live my life but it saddens me that you're no longer a part of it. I know I will never experience a love like ours again. It was, to use your word, unbelievable! I know that you know how much I loved you. I know that you knew that I felt you were love. I am truly grateful that I got to know such a special side of Logan Nash. A side that probably only a few women got to experience. The side of absolute, true love and appreciation. I can't believe you're gone! I can't believe that I can't put my hands on your scratchy face again! I can't believe that I won't get to do karaoke and experience life, with you! As I said once before, "you are my bucket list." I love that you wanted to help me achieve my goals. I love you, I love you, I love you! I am hurting so badly. I'm hurting for me but I am also hurting for your kids and I hurt for Heather and I hurt for your family. I hope, I pray, that you did not suffer. I wish more than anything that something, anything went differently that night!

౨

"Is *that* what you're wearing?" Shannon raised a skeptical eyebrow as she entered the foyer. In a decision befitting her emotional maturity, she'd selected a demure black dress with matching high-heeled pumps and replaced the purple streaks in her hair with chunks of sun-streaked blonde.

"I didn't know what to wear," Sam shrugged. "I haven't been to one of these things since…well, since Mom died." Shannon softened as she took note of her sister's tear-stained face and trembling hands.

"Well I didn't know what to wear *either*," she sighed. Then with a chuckle added, "Bet you never expected to see me looking so mainstream." Although she appreciated the attempt at humor, all Sam could do was nod her head. "Well, okay then, let's get going." Shannon took her by the hand and maneuvered her out the door. "We don't want to be late since they were nice enough to do this."

A moment later they were cruising down Interstate 77 in Shannon's Miata, where she attempted to engage Sam in conversation for the well-intentioned purpose of aiding her healing process.

"Shannon, please. I appreciate what you're trying to do but I am just not ready to talk about it," she pleaded. "The best thing you did for me was to call the funeral home and set up this special appointment. I can never thank you enough for that."

"You don't have to thank me. No matter what you are still my sister and I hate that you're hurting so bad. Don't you think talking about him might help?"

"No. No, I don't want to talk."

"Alright, we don't have to then," Shannon's tone was soothing.

"Ugh, it might seem really silly but all I can think about right now is this goofy video he sent me a while back of him singing an old 70s song," Sam explained. "God, I loved that stupid video." She succumbed to a fresh eruption of anguish brought on by another fond memory.

"Well we're going to play it right now," Shannon announced. With that, she spoke the words '*Never Been Any Reason* by Head East' into her smartphone; a minute later, its distinctive, hard rock rhythms replaced all other noise, save for the sounds of Sam's mournful sobs.

∾

"May I help you?" A prim, older woman responded to the ring of the doorbell at the funeral home's grand entrance. Her smooth, white hair was pulled back in an old-fashioned chignon that set off her high cheekbones. An impeccably pressed navy suit and sensible pumps finished her ensemble.

Sam cast her eyes downward and fidgeted with a fresh, unopened package of tissues while her empty stomach convulsed in knots.

Are they really going to let me in? What if Heather or another member of the family sees me? What am I, crazy?

Shannon remained calm and composed. "Yes ma'am," she replied politely. "We called yesterday to set up a special appointment for this morning."

"I see. Are you part of the family?"

"Ma'am, I already spoke to the director about this and he told me it was okay for us to visit this morning since the family visitation was last night." Shannon's tone was unyielding but cordial. The woman's face brightened in remembrance.

"Oh yes, he did mention something about that to me. Please, come in."

The two younger women followed their escort through the massive double doorway and into a burgundy carpeted vestibule. "Right this way," she directed, leading them down a wide hallway featuring offices to the left and various viewing rooms on the opposite side. Sam's anxiety increased exponentially with every step that moved her closer to the last door on the right, their destination.

"Here we are," the woman announced as she turned the gold-plated knob. "Take as long as you'd like. I'll be in my office if you need me." She nodded toward the other side of the hall before leaving them alone.

"Ready?" Shannon whispered, slipping her arm into Sam's.

Sam hesitated. In one motion, she pulled her arm away and took a step back.

"I-I don't know if I can look at him like that. I'm scared. Please, can you go in first?"

Wordlessly, Shannon agreed to the request before making her way into the viewing area. Sam leaned up against the wall for support as she felt her knees weaken.

Did she really have the strength to do this?

A moment later she returned with the news that the casket was closed. A relieved Sam followed her back into the room with renewed determined to honor her plans to say a proper goodbye: she owed Logan at least that much.

Sam took her time gazing at her beloved's artifacts while she prepared for the inevitable moment when she'd have to approach his casket for the final farewell. As she stood there staring at the table, two objects caught her attention: a patterned bandanna and a knit skullcap embroidered with the logo of one of their favorite Mexican restaurants. She reached out for the beanie and held it close as she reflected upon its journey from the final remnant of a restaurant franchise's discontinued merchandise to one of Logan's most treasured possessions. A slow smiled formed on her lips. For whatever reason, he had taken a liking to that silly hat the second he'd laid eyes on it. A mutual a friend, a woman who also frequented their Cross-Fit gym regularly, used to wear it often and, much like Sam's ordinary yellow tee shirt, it had captivated him. Logan had been so enthralled by the hat that one day after they'd all worked out he'd impulsively taken it off its owner's head and placed it on his own, inciting reactions ranging from unrestrained disgust to giddy laughter from everyone around him.

That's when Sam had made it her mission to find him the exact same beanie, never dreaming this simple gesture would entail phone calls to the company's corporate office and a long drive to their Statesville restaurant's location. Apparently impressed that anyone would go to these lengths for such a low-ticket item, they'd let her have it for free. But for Sam the extra effort had been worth it to behold the pure joy on Logan's face when she gave it to him. He wore it all winter long, grinning from ear to ear. Suddenly, she was tempted to do something she'd never thought she would in her 40 years of life.

However, after a few minutes of serious consideration, mature sensibility triumphed over raw emotion and she placed the beanie back on the table, feeling a strange sense of gratitude. The significance of these two items was known only to her and Logan, yet they had been part of the showcase. If not overshadowed by senseless tragedy, their inclusion might have even made her laugh.

She took a deep, cleansing breath and slowly walked over to the side of the casket. In a tentative motion, she laid her hand on top of it as tears of sorrow began to flow again. In the next moment, she felt a touch on her upper back, followed by Shannon's low whisper, "Hey, let's open the casket."

A palpable shiver shot up her spine as she recalled the cause of death. Between sobs she asked, "Do you really think that's a good idea? I mean it must be closed for a good reason. It was a shallow creek. I'm sure his face is all cut up and bruised."

"Sam, I know this is hard, but I think it would be best for you in the long run if you can see him one last time. Yeah, I know it's trite to say 'closure' but you won't be able to grieve and move on unless you look at him. I just don't know how we're going to get this gigantic bouquet off. It looks heavy. And I don't mean to sound rude, but who in their right mind chooses pink roses for a man's casket? Weird."

Sam thought of Heather and her blatant disregard for anything that might demonstrate a semblance of affection for her husband. My God, his body had barely been cold for five minutes and she'd already made all the funeral arrangements, forcing his sisters from out of state to make hurried travel plans, along with his widowed mother who'd just returned to her winter home in Marco Island Florida. Knowing Heather, pink roses had probably been the easiest, most convenient choice of arrangement.

The sisters debated back and forth for a few minutes before Shannon announced her intention to find someone to help them. Sam nodded her assent and a few minutes later, Shannon returned with the woman who'd let them in earlier. Her tone was apologetic as she explained the funeral parlor's policy of closing caskets overnight out of respect for the dead.

A while later, as they rode back to Dilworth in silence in Shannon's red Mazda Miata, all Sam could do was ponder the strangeness of Logan's smooth, unblemished face. *Why didn't he at least have a superficial scratch? How could anyone fall face down into a shallow creek and not be scarred?*

None of it added up. Nothing made sense. *Was the official story of his death the true story? Or was something else going on?* As Shannon navigated through the heavy Charlotte traffic, Sam resolved to get answers.

"Are you sure you don't want me to stay with you?" Shannon asked again after putting the car in park in Sam's driveway. The familiar expression of defiance and resolve on her sister's face made her more than a little nervous; she could tell Sam was consumed by much more than just grief.

"Samantha," Shannon intoned with authority, taking her by the shoulders. She softened a little, struck by her sister's look of utter despair. Lowering her voice to a barely audible whisper she pleaded, "Please, please promise me you're not going to do anything crazy, like show up for the funeral. It's Election Day and Edward Raines is running for national office for God's sake – the church will be crawling with media. Do you really want to take a chance of Heather spotting you and causing a scene?"

Sam gazed at her for a moment as she pondered the wisdom of her well-intentioned words. Bad enough that Edward was already the patriarch of one of Charlotte's most influential families and the head of the city's most powerful law firm; he was also on the ballot that day in a bid for United States Senator – a position for which he'd been recruited by some of the biggest moneyed people in North Carolina and the entire country. With a thriving, successful career and her new status as a divorced single mom, she'd be foolish to take such a risk. And yet, she couldn't squelch the desire to go. Her heart not only broke for Logan, it ached for MaryAnn.

MaryAnn.

Logan's devoted, widowed mother with whom he shared a remarkable bond. With his two sisters living out of state and his father passed away, he had eagerly stepped into the role of caretaker whenever MaryAnn needed him – not that she required too much help. As a fiercely independent Southern lady who enjoyed good health for an 80-something-year-old, Logan's "care-taking" mainly consisted of various handyman projects around the house. During the summers when she came back from Florida, they spent many hours together as a family over barbeques, home-cooked meals, and the boys' sporting events. And MaryAnn always came back to Charlotte to spend the Thanksgiving and Christmas Holidays with the family, just as she and her late husband always did before his death. Oftentimes Logan would surprise her in the morning by bursting into the kitchen with a cheery "Hi Mama," and chatting with her over coffee before starting his day. Though they'd never met, Sam felt a strange kinship with the woman, the result of having spent countless hours in her home surrounded by images and keepsakes of all she held dear.

"Uh, Earth to Samantha? Tell me you are not going to that funeral," Shannon repeated.

"Are you crazy? Of course not," Sam lied. "I just really need some time alone. My therapist wants me to keep journaling and I can't do that with someone else around. Please, Shannon? While the kids are at school I really need time by myself to process everything. Thank you," she added, drawing her into a hug. "You've been a great support to me through all of this. I really appreciate it."

"I'm your sister, silly. That's what sisters do."

Shannon released Sam from the embrace. Catching a stray hair on her forehead she smoothed it away, along with a tear that had begun to trickle down her cheek. "Alright, far be it from me to interfere with a therapist's orders. Just know you can call me anytime if you need me. And if you change your mind, I can be here in a heartbeat. I rescheduled all of my customers today just in case."

"You're the best. Thank you for understanding." Sam pecked her on the cheek and exited the car. As Shannon threw the Miata in reverse, she watched her sister march up the brick path to the steps leading to the front porch of her craftsman style house and fumble for her keys in her purse before unlocking the door. Just as she was about to walk into the foyer, Sam turned to wave one last time as if to prove she planned to stay put for the rest of the day. Shannon waved backed and smiled despite the sinking feeling that her good advice was about to be ignored.

Once the door slammed safely behind her, Sam raced up the stairs and pulled the yellow tee shirt over her head as she ran into her walk-in closet. Discarding it to the floor, she then shimmied out of her jeans and began perusing the racks of clothing in search of something suitable. Ever since she'd started working from home after Madison was born, she'd enjoyed the privilege of dressing casually on a regular basis. In fact, most weekdays she dressed in her workout gear to save time once she got to the gym. None of her clients or colleagues would ever guess that the savvy, accomplished sales trainer did most of her business transactions while wearing Lycra-spandex tank tops and shorts, but Sam attributed at least part of her success to the ability to wear comfy clothing. Only on those rare occasions when a big boss came in from Atlanta or when she travelled to an out-of-town convention did she ever bother to wear a suit or a dress.

At last locating the black sheath she was after, she undid its gold back zipper. She stepped into the dress and with significant effort, managed to zip it all the way back up. Turning to her full-length mirror she smoothed the straight skirt, slipped into a pair of matching heels, and wondered what to do with her hair. Knowing Heather could have easily seen her photos online or on social media, she wanted to look as different from real life as possible. She was fully aware that her mere presence at the service could provoke frustration, anger, and hurt feelings on Heather's part – not to mention tabloid fodder for the local and national media.

Since she always wore her long hair down, she decided on a French braid. Trembling fingers notwithstanding, she weaved alternating handfuls using the method Shannon had taught her years ago when they were kids. *Ugh, Shannon. Forgive me, but I just have to do this. For Logan. For MaryAnn. For me.*

She picked up her smartphone and noted the time. Wanting to blend in with the crowd, she debated back and forth with herself about how to be as low-key as possible. She planned to time her arrival a few minutes after the service began, to blend in with the masses of mourners. Hopefully, by then, most of the media would be fully focused on the grieving widow, her would-be senator father, and her socialite mother.

Sam's thoughts returned to MaryAnn, igniting a fresh eruption of sorrow. "God, I just want to hug her," she sobbed. "I just want her to know her son was loved, and that there is another woman who understands her pain. Please, if it be your will, please give me that chance."

The unyielding impulse to reach out to Logan's mother fueled her determination and courage as she drove to Christ Episcopal Church.

∽

Christ Episcopal Church's stately brick exterior was surrounded by a huge, sprawling parking lot to accommodate its large congregation. Yet as she pulled into the entrance, Sam struggled to find an available spot amid a sea of cars. She expected as much but given the risk she was taking, she knew it would not have been possible to arrive any earlier. The sight of various local and national news crews nearly caused her to chicken out until she focused back on MaryAnn and her overwhelming desire to comfort her with the knowledge that her son had indeed experienced true, abiding love. In that instant, she felt renewed courage and determination.

At last, she located an available parking place in a remote corner. After a quick inspection in the rearview mirror she adjusted her sunglasses, grabbed her purse, and stepped out onto the pavement. Scanning the scene, she waited for a group of mourners to pass before following them through the massive red door and into to the main vestibule of the church. The journey felt endless in her black pumps; she was unaccustomed to even wearing them let alone walk any sort of distance. Still, she strode along with head slightly bowed in her attempt to look inconspicuous.

Once inside, she maneuvered her way through the crowd and into the main worship area. Directly above, she heard a cacophony of voices emanating from the large wall-to-wall balcony that housed the church's musicians and media crew. They were obviously preparing to perform the opening song for the funeral, which evidently was running behind. She glanced at her phone and realized it should have started ten minutes ago. As she searched for a safe place to sit, she noticed some familiar faces from the gym. Although tempted to join them, she ultimately chose a spot among strangers in a distant, angled pew where she would be as far away from the main altar as possible.

When the music started with the familiar yet contemporary adaptation of *Amazing Grace*, Sam lost it; her shoulders shook as she sobbed into her tissues. For most of the ceremony, she remained lost in a haze of sorrow and disbelief, barely comprehending the comforting words of the pastor who emphasized the promise of Jesus and the joy of heaven that awaited all believers. Although Logan's best buddy John French gave a heart-wrenching eulogy in which he chronicled their lifelong friendship, she couldn't even absorb its significance or the palpable anguish of the one delivering the message. All she could think about was visually locating MaryAnn once the family followed the casket out of the church at the end of the ceremony.

Finally, the moment arrived. Sam observed from a distance through swollen, tear-stained eyes as a devastated MaryAnn – flanked on either side by each of her daughters – made her way out. Dressed in the proper black attire of her generation, she presented a vision of true grief in stark contrast to a stoic Heather, who walked ahead of her with her parents, Edward and Kathleen, while her two little boys Tyler and Nolan held onto their uncles' hands. Sam's heart ached as she watched this poor woman mourn for her son, a loss no doubt compounded by the death of her husband just a few years prior.

I have to reach out to her. I have to find a way, she thought to herself.

"Sam!" she heard a familiar voice call out. She looked up to see the friends from the gym she'd avoided on the way in. They gathered around her like a warm blanket and offered sincere condolences. As she heard soothing words like, "We are so very sorry. We know how close you guys were," she realized that her and Logan's closely guarded secret was actually common knowledge among their workout buddies. She understood just how lucky they'd been that none of these people had ratted them out to Heather. Particularly with her father running for political office, the fallout would have been a thousand times uglier than David's reaction when he found out. As vindictive as he'd behaved toward her in that moment, it would have paled in comparison to the wrath of the Raines family and their well-connected compadres. Most likely, that scenario would have resulted in public humiliation, the end of the career she'd worked so hard to build, and the necessity of moving to a new city. She shuddered at the thought as they all made their way outside and witnessed the media spectacle surrounding them.

Sam suppressed an urge to vomit as she watched Heather play the role of the grieving widow and daughter of U.S. Senate candidate Edward Raines. Edward stood with his arm about her as they spoke in glowing terms about Logan to the gathering of local and national reporters. She heard them say something about his devotion as a husband, son-in-law, and father, and how they were certain Logan would have wanted them to carry on with Election Day activities. In fact, they were sure his spirit was praying for Edward to win, so he could do good things for the people of Charlotte and North Carolina as their elected senator.

"Ugh, shouldn't they be moving along to the cemetery? How long are they going to keep the rest of Logan's family and the funeral director waiting?" Katie inquired with noticeable sarcasm, expressing Sam's thoughts almost verbatim.

"I don't know but I have to get going," she announced, visibly shaken. If she had to look upon this repulsive scene for one more minute she was sure she would puke all over the pavement. After exchanging a few more hugs, she rushed back to her car, more determined than ever to reach out to MaryAnn.

Wednesday morning started out like every other weekday, with Sam up early to feed and dress Madison and Zach before driving them to school. As she went through the motions, the nagging urge to find MaryAnn intensified. Her practical side fought hard to silence this inner voice with the logical admonitions, "I have to move on with my life. Logan is dead. I have two kids to raise and a career to maintain. I can't keep obsessing over this."

Yet her intuition kept guiding her in another direction; one that involved reaching out to comfort Logan's distraught mother by assuring her that her son did indeed experience the love and appreciation of a devoted woman before he met his untimely end. Despite the extramarital circumstances, she believed with absolute certainty that this knowledge would help MaryAnn's heart to heal. Of course, a parent is never the same after losing a child, particularly when it's a mother and son like MaryAnn and Logan. Sam could relate in one sense, remembering her long-ago miscarriage and Zach's near death, due to placental insufficiency. She shivered as she recalled the traumatic events surrounding his birth and the lonely desperation she experienced. It was only by God's grace, an excellent medical team, and a multitude of prayers that he'd pulled through. She couldn't imagine what her life would feel like now if he hadn't. How much worse it must be for MaryAnn, who'd had the blessing of watching her son grow into a man and become a parent himself.

Although she'd never laid eyes on the woman in person until the funeral, Sam had spent many hours listening to Logan talk about his close upbringing, the unconditional love and support of his parents, and his joyful dedication to looking after his mom in the years following his father's death. She had vicariously experienced their relationship through his lively narrations of funny family stories and special occasions.

But her impulse to find MaryAnn was fueled by more than just compassion. Sam's perception of her as a sharp, smart lady led her to the inevitable conclusion that she must have had the same nagging questions when she saw her son's unblemished face in that casket. Surely MaryAnn was also wondering how someone who sustained a perilous, face-down fall from several feet above into a shallow, two-inch creek could fail to show the evidence in the form of deep cuts and bruises? If so, she wanted her to know she was not alone in her suspicions. Maybe they could team up somehow to figure out what really happened.

Whoa! I have to knock this off.

She turned into the drive-through of her favorite coffee shop and ordered a tall, dark cup of her preferred brew with just a dollop of cream and a hint of Stevia. For a few moments, she sat in her parked Pathfinder taking sips of the hot beverage while trying to figure out her next move. She didn't want to go home and work, nor did she feel like heading to the gym for a training session. Instead, she decided to visit Logan in a new place: Charlotte Memorial Gardens. On the way, she stopped to buy a bouquet of red roses.

Set amid the sparkling waters of a natural lake, the sprawling grounds of the memorial gardens stretched out as far as the eye could see, with manicured green lawns dotted with majestic pine and maple trees. As Sam drove through the entrance after receiving a map and directions from the attendant, she was struck by the pastoral beauty of the place. It helped that the sun had continued to shine over this long stretch of unusual Indian summer temperatures which would inevitably plummet as the November days led up to Thanksgiving.

Still, she felt a welcome sense of serenity as she got closer to her destination, knowing that coming during a weekday morning would offer her the privacy she craved. Funny, in her fog of grief she hadn't even checked online to see if Edward Raines had been elected, but she felt confident that no one from the Raines family would be here. Win or lose, it was safe to say they'd had a late evening. And since there was no political advantage to be gained by visiting Logan's grave the day after his high-profile funeral, Sam felt even safer. Sure, it was a callous viewpoint, but the Raines were cold, calculating people who rarely made a move that didn't advance their agenda in some way.

When she arrived at Logan's designated area, she was relieved to discover there was not a single car in sight. She took a deep breath, grabbed the roses, and headed to his freshly dug grave. Towering piles of brown dirt surrounded by at least twenty flower stands arranged in a rectangle provided the final piece of evidence that her love was gone forever. As she laid her bouquet on top of the mound, she broke down in sobs. Confronting the reality of Logan's final resting place was almost as difficult as receiving that earth-shattering call from Katie just a few days before. When she was cried out she composed herself enough to speak aloud.

"Oh Logan, how am I supposed to go on without you? I miss you so much; my heart just aches for you. I hate this! Why? Why would God just rip you away from me after everything we shared? It's not fair; I can't stop thinking about the dreams we had for our future. Our connection was so powerful, so true. It's already been three days and I am still in denial that you're gone. I'm hurt and sad that we won't get to do any of the things we talked about…so many life experiences we never got to share.

"Still, I don't feel anger yet. Is that weird? What's even weirder is that I'd rather stay stuck at sad. I know anger is the second stage of grief but I'm not ready. I'm not ready to go there. I'm stuck at sad and lonely and missing you. And your poor Mom. I saw her at the church and I just wanted to put my arms around her, to share her grief, to let her know there was another woman who was hurting as much as she was. I really hope I get that chance."

Sam lingered somewhere between fantasy and reality as she stood at his gravesite mourning, remembering, and contemplating how this whole tragedy could have even happened in the first place. After what felt like an hour, she walked slowly back to her car. She blew her nose and blotted her eyes before pulling out of the cemetery. Still in a fog, she drove aimlessly around town. Suddenly, her phone's familiar ring tone brought her back to the present moment.

"Hey, David," she greeted him with a sigh. Her stuffy nose gave her voice a muffled tone.

"Sam, are you alright? I just called to check on you," he replied softly. She refrained from divulging her location as she walked back toward her car and unlocked the passenger door remotely.

"Thanks, that's very sweet," she began as she clicked her seatbelt into place. "I'm still in disbelief. It's so hard to wrap my head around."

"I understand," he sympathized. But Sam had known him long enough to tell when something unspoken was bothering him.

"David? Is everything alright with you?"

She heard him take a deep breath.

"Yeah, I'm fine but I just need to ask you something. Your family doesn't think I had anything to do with it, do they? You know, the scorned husband whose wife was having an affair with the son-in-law of a senator? Well, Edward wasn't a senator the whole time, but you know what I mean. He was running for office."

"Wait, did he win the election?" she asked.

"You haven't heard? He won in a landslide." She felt the bile rise in her throat. No doubt their sickening display of well-acted sorrow had garnered plenty of sympathy votes from a gullible public.

"Anyway Sam, I was thinking it was a good thing my first weekend with the kids happened to be this past one. Otherwise, I might be the number one suspect."

"David, come on. You know I don't think that. You could never murder anyone, no matter how badly you're hurting."

"Maybe not you, but your dad and Shannon? Remember how awful I was to you when I found those social media messages between you and Logan while you were in Florida? My God, I told you I wouldn't even let you see your own kids until you'd called everyone in the family to tell them what you'd done. I was such an asshole, Sam. I'm sorry."

Replaying the whole sordid event in her mind caused her stomach to twist into a knot as she sat in her SUV and stared out at the burial grounds. "David...you know, it's over. We've been through this already. You were hurt. You were angry. It's all in the past. It doesn't matter now."

"I appreciate that Sam. But what about your family?"

Ugh, there's no way I can tell him, she thought. *Even if they were just fleeting accusations.*

Since her conversation with Shannon, her dad had brought it up on a phone call before quickly discarding it as out of the realm of possibility. Eventually, both he and Shannon had thought the better of their unfounded suspicions, but Sam didn't have the heart to tell David that anyone had even entertained the idea.

"No, of course they don't think you had anything to do with it," she assured him. "My God, how long have they known you? Over a decade? I promise you David, no one in my family believes you had anything to do with Logan's accident."

"Even if it is strange his face wasn't marked up?"

"Well we all think there's something off with that, but it still doesn't make you a murderer. David, I know we've had a rocky road, but you are a decent man and a wonderful father. You're a good person."

"You have no idea how much it means to hear you say that, Sam. I really am sorry about what happened. I know how much you're hurting. If you need anything, please just call me."

His kind words ushered in another wave of anguish.

"Thank you," she managed to choke out.

"I mean it," he confirmed before hanging up.

She gave into unrestrained tears once more as the nearby lake glistened in the early afternoon sunlight.

§

She was sitting at a stoplight when it happened: the familiar blue Mercedes convertible with Florida tags drove through the intersection and crossed right in front of her windshield. "Oh, my God, there she is," Sam exclaimed. Running on pure impulse, she began tailing the car the second the light changed to green, convinced it was a sign from God. For the next several minutes she sped through a myriad of intersections, weaving her way through the heavy Charlotte traffic to keep up with MaryAnn.

But when she ran a red light and nearly got herself into accident she snapped back to reality, aided by the obnoxious sounds of honking horns and an irate driver yelling at her from an open window. Shaken, she pulled into the parking lot of the next shopping center she encountered.

Why I am stalking this woman? Am I crazy? I could have gotten myself killed or killed someone else for crying out loud! What is wrong with me? She lowered her head to the steering wheel and wept.

After few moments, she regained her composure and reached for her smartphone. Finding Shannon's number amid her favorites in contacts, she immediately dialed her number and breathed a huge sigh of relief when she answered.

"Thank God you're there," she began. "I almost did something really stupid. Please, help me."

"What's going on, Sam?"

"You're not going to believe this. Remember I told you the other day I had this urge to reach out to MaryAnn? Well today after I visited Logan's grave I happened to see her drive by in her car and decided to follow her around. I almost got myself into an accident."

"Oh Sam…please don't tell me you actually approached her?"

"No, no, no. I didn't approach her, but I nearly had a collision with another car. That's when I pulled over to call you."

"What did you think you were going to do if you did catch up to her? Walk up to her in the shopping center and give her a hug? You are a total stranger to her at this point."

"I don't know, Shannon. All I know is I can't shake this urge to reach out to MaryAnn. She has no one to support her in her grief once her daughters go back home. God knows, Heather doesn't give a damn. It's incredibly important to me that she knows how much Logan was loved before he died – that he didn't die an emotionally abused and neglected husband – but at the same time I don't want to cause any more pain for her or her family. So, I'm struggling with this feeling because the last thing I want to do is hurt the woman even more. She'd probably be devastated if she found out her married son was carrying on this deep love affair with another woman."

"Sam, remember when mom died lots of strangers – people we didn't even know – came by our house, wrote notes, and expressed their condolences. And honestly, I think that outpouring of love from strangers helped me in my grief because I saw just how many people mom influenced. For you to reach out to MaryAnn is not out of the ordinary, even under the circumstances.

"Now I don't suggest following her around town and stalking her, but I do recommend that you write her a little card letting her know that he was someone special you worked out with and you're sorry for her loss. Then drop it in the mail. That will hopefully fulfill this urge you have to make contact and offer her some comfort too."

"Yes, yes that's a great idea," Sam brightened, suddenly motivated to get home as soon as possible.

"Just one word of caution," Shannon added. "Do not attach any expectations, okay? You're doing this for you to honor your need to reach out and comfort MaryAnn. But don't be disappointed if she never responds."

"I understand."

But after she hung up the phone, Sam's heart skipped a beat as she considered the possibilities.

৭০

A little while later back home in her office, she took Beth's advice and reached for her favorite pen and a blank notecard with a floral image on the front. Drawing a deep breath, she wrote:

"Dear Mrs. Nash,

"I have wanted to reach out to you to express my sincere condolences. I was lucky enough to know Logan for only two brief years – but his friendship was powerful!

"I could go on for pages about what an amazing man he was but that is not the purpose of my letter. So, I will keep this brief.

"He loved you and your late husband deeply. He loved to tell me stories about his dad and how he was always there for him when he was growing up. Logan admired him as a man and a father; his face lit up every time he talked about him.

"Mrs. Nash, you were his girl! I could tell from his stories he was a proud 'Momma's Boy.' I'd always get a laugh from the sweet Southern voice he would use whenever he impersonated you. He would show me photos of you and him together at family events and always bragged, 'Isn't my mom beautiful?'

"The last morning he was alive, he sent me a text to tell me he had slept well but was having weird dreams about his grandfather. But he didn't give me any details.

"I'd like to think that maybe his grandfather was reaching out to welcome him to heaven. Logan was happy and very much loved. He'll be missed daily and loved eternally.

"My thoughts and prayers are with you and the rest of the family. Thank you for raising such a wonderful man. My life will be forever changed because of the time I was blessed to share with him.

"God bless you,

"Sam

"Samantha Chapman

"Logan's friend from the gym."

After a few minutes of deliberation, she included her phone number on the note, then scrawled the address on the envelope, added a stamp, and walked it out to her mailbox. Over the next few days, Beth's warning about expectations reverberated through her brain. Theoretically, she knew her letter would reach MaryAnn within a day or two at the most; when several days passed with no communication, it was difficult to deny her disappointment. Worse, she began to second-guess herself, wondering if she'd made the right decision. No doubt, MaryAnn's mailbox was inundated with well-meaning expressions of sympathy; perhaps her overpowering grief prevented her from even opening them? Maybe the cards were just piled up on the office desk in her kitchen unopened, with Sam's lost in the mix while the distraught mother suffered in silence? Or perhaps her daughters were still in town to offer comfort and solace, distracting her from the mundane aspects of life?

An even more distressing thought occurred to Sam: it was highly possible that one of MaryAnn's daughters – assuming one or both remained in Charlotte after the funeral – was intercepting their mother's sympathy cards. True, they both had husbands, kids, and jobs of their own, but they could have decided to stay for a while, at least to get her through the initial shock of the tragedy. If that was the case, would MaryAnn even see her card? What if she'd read it but had no interest in calling? These nagging questions persisted until the following Monday when much to Sam's relief, her phone finally rang.

"Hi Samantha? This is MaryAnn Nash. I received your letter today."

Sam's heart lurched in her chest. *OMG, is she going to be angry? Is she going to be hurt?*

"I just wanted to tell you, thank you so much," she continued.

Before Sam could utter a word, the woman broke down into sobs on the other end. After a few seconds, she continued with labored breaths, "I still can't believe this. It's the worst thing that has ever happened in my entire life; even losing my husband didn't hurt like this. I'm struggling, Samantha. I'm sitting here trying to have my coffee and all I can do is cry. He used to come over all the time for coffee after he took the boys to school and we'd sit and talk about everything. I just can't believe my baby is gone."

Sam's heart ached for her as she listened with genuine sympathy and interest.

"You know, a little while before I called you I was just sitting here with my coffee when I looked up and saw a picture of Logan and the boys hanging on the wall. And it just made me so angry, I threw my mug at it. Samantha, I'm so angry. This isn't right, this isn't fair."

As Sam continued to lend an ear, MaryAnn told her how her cleaning lady had entered the room after she heard the glass shatter. She calmed her down and cleaned up the mess.

"I don't know how to deal with this grief. It is literally killing me."

Her words initiated a flood of tears for Sam, who related to every emotion she expressed.

For a while, the two women cried together before Sam spoke up. "MaryAnn, I am so sorry. He was an amazing man."

"You knew him from the gym?"

"Yeah, I saw him almost every single day. I've only known him for about two years, but he was just an amazing person. I am so sorry for your loss."

Even though a part of her yearned to fully express the extent of her feelings for Logan to his devastated mother, Sam repressed the urge in favor of acting as a sounding board for MaryAnn's profound anger and anguish. She wasn't quite prepared for what happened next.

"How close were the two of you? Did he ever talk to you?" MaryAnn inquired though her sobs.

Sam remained guarded. "Yeah, we talked to each other just a little bit about our lives and stuff like that."

"You know I don't mean to badmouth my daughter-in-law Heather," MaryAnn continued. "But I don't feel that she's hurting. I don't see her grieving. It bothers me that she just lost her husband, *my son*, and she doesn't seem to give a damn. Did you see her on the news at her father's victory party? My God, she'd just buried her husband and she's all smiles for the cameras because Edward Raines won the election? I haven't seen that woman shed a tear. And that just makes me angry."

"Mrs. Nash, I'm so sorry. I'm really, really sorry about that. I can tell you I've been shedding tears over the loss of such a special man." Sam refrained from commenting about the news cameras outside of the church the day of the funeral, although she did extend an invitation. "MaryAnn, if you ever want to talk to somebody, to get out of the house and meet for coffee, you just let me know because I'd be more than happy to sit and talk with you about Logan."

"Oh, I would love that," she replied without hesitation, much to Sam's surprise. "How about Wednesday at 11:00?"

MaryAnn's suggestion of a specific date two days away further surprised and delighted her.

"Um, sure," she accepted without even consulting her calendar. Whatever was on her schedule could be easily rearranged; there was no way she was missing an opportunity to meet Logan's mother in person. And if making the arrangements for such a meeting became overly complicated, she feared it would never come to pass. For all Sam knew, MaryAnn was headed back to Florida or to Tennessee or South Carolina to spend the upcoming holidays with one of her daughters. If she wanted to meet her on Wednesday at 11:00, then she would be there Wednesday at 11:00.

After agreeing on a place, Sam told her how much she looked forward to it.

"Yeah me too," MaryAnn replied sincerely.

With that, their brief but purposeful conversation ended, having initiated a meeting that would take both of their lives in an entirely new direction.

Chapter Eight

The enticing aroma of Arabica beans and freshly baked blueberry muffins greeted Sam as she made her way into the bistro-style coffee house, fifteen minutes ahead of her scheduled meeting with MaryAnn. After ordering a large cup of that day's featured roast and adding her favorite accompaniments at the self-serve station, she settled into one of two oversized chairs surrounding a small round table in an inconspicuous corner facing the front door. She wanted to afford them as much privacy as possible in this public setting and knew she'd recognize MaryAnn right away from her pictures. Although it had crossed her mind briefly, Sam brushed aside any fears that the media might be following MaryAnn around. Since Edward Raines had gotten the election outcome he'd been seeking after shamelessly exploiting a tragedy, it seemed highly unlikely anyone would care about the deceased's grieving mother.

As Sam surveyed the environment, she noticed a mostly Yuppie crowd running in and out for late-morning energy reinforcements, from frothy cappuccinos to dark-roasted espressos. Taking a sip of her own caffeinated beverage, she wondered if MaryAnn would see right through her; if her mother's intuition would kick in the second she laid eyes on her. *Would she know without even having to ask? Would she come out and ask? How would she take it when Sam told her the truth?*

In the next second, her heart jumped in her chest when she spotted MaryAnn's blue Mercedes pulling into a parking space on the other side of the café's large picture window. She stared in admiration as she watched her enter through the front doors and approach her table after Sam smiled and waved. While her face was undeniably etched with sadness, MaryAnn had taken the time to apply tasteful make-up, including lipstick. Her short, frosted hair fell into a perfect pixie, with wispy bangs framing her weepy blue eyes. Her crisp, black pantsuit and tailored blouse were expertly accented with matching gold-and-pearl bracelets, necklaces, and button earrings. A quilted Chanel handbag completed her elegant look.

Sam glanced at her bootleg jeans and simple red sweater, hoping she'd dressed properly for the occasion. But the second MaryAnn reached her, she smiled and extended her arms to wrap her in a warm hug, effectively eliminating any insecurities she'd been experiencing prior to their meeting. It felt surreal as they held each other for a moment in bereaved solidarity.

"Hi MaryAnn, I'm Sam," she said superfluously when they pulled away to look at each other.

"Oh, hi honey," she responded in a warm Southern drawl. "Let me go get my coffee and we can sit down and talk."

When she returned a few minutes later, Sam noticed that the pain on her face had taken on an even greater intensity. She guessed that this little outing was probably her first time out of the house since the funeral. Before either one of them could speak again, MaryAnn broke down.

"I'm so sorry," she sobbed. "I'm just having such a hard time with this. This is the worst thing I've ever been through…I just don't know how to get out of bed in the morning. I don't know how to move on, you know, with healing. This is just so awful. It is hurting so badly."

Tears streamed down Sam's face as she listened and related to every emotion the aggrieved mother expressed. In contrast to her reserved demeanor during their first phone conversation, she didn't even bother to hold back. Hearing MaryAnn detail the intensity of her anguish made it impossible for her to disguise her own. They sat in the corner crying together for several minutes until Sam finally found the strength to say, "I am so sorry for your loss. I hurt too. He was a good friend. This is awful."

To which MaryAnn responded, "Are you the one who was having the affair with him?"

Sam felt a surge of nervous energy. For a moment, she sat there dumbfounded before she finally replied with a simple, "Yes." She braced herself for the possibility that things could get ugly, having no idea if her confession would cause MaryAnn to lash out in anger before getting up from the table, turning on her heel, and storming out. Still, Sam figured she owed the woman the truth; her emotions had already betrayed her. Why insult Logan's mother by pretending?

To her surprise, MaryAnn just sat there in quiet contemplation for a few moments as if absorbing the meaning of this revelation and considering the proper comeback before speaking again. After what felt like forever she explained, "Well, Heather got your Halloween cards."

Another jolt of electricity coursed through her body. *The three cards he never got to open before he died.*

After embarking upon their affair, Sam had gotten into the routine of sending Logan little notes and cards to his business P.O. Box. Whether they centered around a specific occasion or were just simple *Thinking of You* cards, he began to actually look forward to getting his work-related mail because he knew that amid the usual bills and bank statements he'd find a welcome communication from his beloved. Many times, he'd take a picture of the card and send it to her along with a text like, "Thank you so much, sweetie. This just made my day today."

Once she'd received the news he'd died, Sam realized that, given the timing, these three cards would be sitting in his P.O. box unopened, just waiting to out their affair to whomever stopped by to pick up Logan's mail. Of course, she was always careful never to include a return address or use either one of their names in the handwritten portion, but it still made her a little nervous, especially with the election looming.

"Heather did get the cards you sent him, and wouldn't you know, as soon as I went over there to see those kids, the first thing she said to me when I walked through the door was 'Your perfect Logan wasn't so perfect. Did you know he was having an affair? Look at these cards I got from his mistress.' With that, she tossed them on the table for me to read. But I just walked right by them. Then I said to her, 'I don't think you're too perfect either Heather. Didn't you have an affair a couple of months ago yourself?'"

It had been the first time MaryAnn had indicated to Heather the extent to which Logan shared details with her about his marriage. Her mother-in-law's indifference to Heather's revelation momentarily silenced her while she watched MaryAnn go about the business of comforting Logan's sons as only a doting grandmother could. After returning home later that day, she had made the decision to call Sam. Now here they were, crying together in a Charlotte coffee shop, trying to make sense of it all.

Sam was stunned. "So, you knew about Heather's affair?" Although aware of the close relationship Logan and MaryAnn shared, she had no idea he'd confided this intensely personal detail of his troubled marriage with her. *Did that include a rundown of how Logan and Sam figured it out together that fateful day?*

"With her little boy toy attorney? Oh yes, my son told me all about it."

Sam remained silent. As she thought back to the events leading up to the revelation of Heather's infidelity, she wondered how much detail she should provide, notwithstanding the comfort and ease she felt around MaryAnn as they sat at their corner table talking like old friends. But before she could speak again, MaryAnn unknowingly signaled that Logan had omitted Sam's role in the discovery of Heather's extramarital activities when he shared the knowledge with his mother.

"What did he tell you about it?"

At first Sam played it cool, still uncertain as to how much she should divulge. "Just that he'd found out she was having an affair with one of their law firm's young attorneys."

"And? Did he say anything else?" It was clear she craved more detail.

Sam cleared her throat. "He told me it made him angry, which kind of surprised me, but he assured me it wasn't about him feeling like 'Boohoo my wife had an affair.' His heart wasn't broken about it. It was more just anger that she would do something like this, especially since she didn't spend much time being a mother to her own kids. I remember I had to talk him down from wanting to expose this to the media as a way of derailing the Raines' campaign because I was worried about what they might do to him….and I'll be honest, I was worried about what might happen to me and my kids if somehow our affair went public. These people have money and power. God only knows what they're capable of."

MaryAnn rolled her eyes. "I hate to say this because I love my grandchildren but the worst thing my son ever did was get mixed up with those crazy, ruthless people. I told him from the beginning it was a huge mistake, but I guess he loved her enough at the time to marry her, even though she and her parents clearly felt our family was beneath them. It didn't matter that my husband was a successful investment banker with a great reputation, two beautiful homes and three wonderful children. To them, we were just a bunch of commoners."

Sam laughed. "As opposed to dysfunctional and old-moneyed." It warmed her heart when MaryAnn chuckled at her description of the Raines family. She took another sip of coffee, then continued.

"But even with all of that, when Logan found out about Heather's affair it marked a turning point in our relationship. MaryAnn, I want you to know his boys always came first no matter what. From the beginning, he'd made it crystal-clear he was not getting a divorce until those kids were at least in high school – maybe even college, which we know is at least a decade away. I had to explain to him that my divorce had nothing to do with false hope of he and I getting married anytime soon; my marriage was basically over long before Logan came into my life. I did the professional counseling and everything else I could think of to save my marriage to David, but it just wasn't meant to be. My divorce was not about pressuring Logan to divorce his wife.

"But once he discovered Heather's affair, he actually went to talk to a divorce attorney friend of ours from the gym to find out his rights – "

"Yes, I advised him to do that," MaryAnn interjected. "When Logan came to the house to tell me Heather had been cheating on him I was angry; how dare she do this to him and their children. Even knowing how unhappy he was, I was still as mad as a hornet. That girl just thinks she can do anything she wants; everything is always about her. It's never about her husband or her boys who are just an afterthought. She is the shallowest, most self-centered person I've ever met. Having an affair with a much younger man no doubt stoked her ego."

"From what I know of her, I'm sure you're right," Sam agreed.

"I was tired of seeing my son being neglected and treated like a second-class citizen. That's why I advised him to speak to an attorney and find out what his rights were as a father. As much as I know he loved his boys, I hated to watch him suffer in an unhappy marriage with that despicable woman. I was thrilled when he took my advice and talked to someone. Even if nothing would've happened right away, especially because of this stupid election, at least it was progress."

"That's honestly how I felt," Sam confessed. "I knew his path to freedom was in the infantile stages but just the fact that he'd sought out legal counsel in the first place was huge. Up until that point, he'd never considered even having a conversation with a lawyer about it."

"Yes, I remember telling him that day that now was the time to get out because he had one up on her," MaryAnn added. "I didn't give a damn about Edward Raines or his political opponents, but my son feared what they might do, knowing they were not above exploiting their own grandchildren. Still I managed to convince him to talk to someone he could trust."

The two women sat in silence for a moment before MaryAnn spoke up again.

"Did he ever indicate to you that Edward might have threatened him?"

"You mean, if he thought Logan might seek out a divorce after finding out what Heather had been up to? If Edward had said anything to him Logan never told me about it. The only thing he complained to me about was having to show up at various campaign events with Heather, pretending to be a happy couple. I knew the whole political game was getting to him and he couldn't wait for the election to be over. Of course, now that I think about it, it's very possible Edward did threaten him in some way and Logan kept it to himself to spare me any worry. I do know he was hoping Edward would lose in November, so his life could go back to normal...well as normal as it can be when you're stuck in a loveless marriage and having a secret affair."

Suddenly, the two women each had a frightening thought that neither one verbalized. Instead, MaryAnn changed the subject with a simple request.

"Please tell me about your relationship."

Although somewhat apprehensive, Sam felt compelled to disclose the whole truth. There was no sense in lying or putting her through any more emotional upheaval.

Before she could share the story however, MaryAnn had another question.

"When was the last time you saw him?"

"We were together on Friday. We had lunch together."

"Well, when was the last time you heard from him, like on the phone or through a text?"

"Um, well the last time I heard from him was on Saturday when he sent me a couple of text messages from the golf course. I guess he played a few rounds that day before the gala. Anyway, we went back and forth for a while, but he never responded to my last text, which was around 5:30 in the evening. Honestly MaryAnn, this was so out-of-character for him because we used to communicate constantly. Even knowing he had to get home and get ready, I was really surprised he didn't respond to me. We'd spent a lot of time talking about how he didn't want to go and how much he hated these phony kinds of gatherings. I figured maybe he got busy, but I thought for sure he'd text me when he got home even though it was 2 a.m. because he always did whenever he and Heather got back from whatever they were doing. When I never got a text, I wondered if it had something to do with the election, if maybe something happened at the gala like, *God forbid*, someone dropping a bombshell about our affair in the middle of everything. You know, opposition research, the October Surprise."

Sam let out a bitter laugh. "You know in that moment, I thought someone from the opponent's staff outing Logan's and my affair would have been the worst possible thing that could have happened that night. Little did I know…."

With that she broke down in violent sobs, her shoulders shaking. MaryAnn reached out and placed her hand on top of hers. "It was so unsettling to me not to hear from him," Sam choked out.

"Well there are quite a few things that are unsettling to me," MaryAnn stated plainly, which piqued Sam's curiosity. *Could she feel the same way she did about the possibility of foul play?*

She hadn't planned on grilling the woman about the circumstances of Logan's death even though they remained a mystery. Since receiving Katie's devastating call, having a private visitation with Logan's body at the funeral home, and attending his funeral she'd learned absolutely nothing more in terms of specific details, like the actual time he died.

Sam listened attentively as MaryAnn shared how two women walking their dogs early Sunday morning had discovered his body lying in the creek.

"And wouldn't you know, Heather's reaction when the police knocked on her door later that morning to tell her what had happened was, 'Well you know, it doesn't surprise me. He'd get drunk from time to time and you never knew what he would do.'"

Sam's stunned face said it all.

"Yes, I know," MaryAnn's tone transformed from sadness to resentment. "But it's actually in the police report. Can you believe it? A woman who's just been told her husband is dead has that kind of reaction? It just makes me angry."

Sam listened for a while as she shared the limited information she had. When MaryAnn was done, she noted, "I thought it was strange his face didn't have a mark on it. It was perfect. He did not look like a man who'd fallen face-first into a creek."

That was when MaryAnn confessed that she hadn't even gone in to look at him. During visitation hours at the funeral home, she was so overcome with grief, she could not even walk into the room; the thought of laying eyes on her lifeless son in a casket simply overwhelmed her. Instead, she sat outside in the hallway greeting visitors.

"Samantha, I just couldn't do it. I could not see my baby like that."

"I understand," Sam consoled her, pausing for a moment to compose herself before continuing. "If not for my sister, I might not have even seen him, either. But she looked at him first and told me I'd be okay with it. And she was right, he just looked perfect. And that was so weird to me because I expected he would at least look like he had a cut…maybe a broken nose, a black eye, some sort of scrape or gash or something. I even touched his face and there was nothing, *nothing*, that showed evidence he'd fallen into shallow water to his death."

MaryAnn hung on every word. When Sam finished she noted, "You know, my daughter said the same thing. She said, 'Mom, he doesn't look like he just died. He doesn't even have a scratch on his face.' My daughter thought the same thing as you, that it was weird his face was perfect."

For a while the two women engaged in a discussion of circumstances, fully focused on the suspicious nature of Logan's death and the odd timing of it all – the weekend of Edward Raines' upscale political gala preceding that Tuesday's big election, and of course, the media circus outside of Christ Episcopal the day of Logan's funeral. Then, as if having her fill of conspiracy theories, MaryAnn completely shifted gears and repeated her earlier request.

"Sam, please tell me about your relationship with Logan."

By now, Sam felt comfortable unburdening herself. But refocusing the conversation on the love she'd shared with him initiated a fresh flood of tears before she could calm herself enough to speak. She inhaled deeply. "MaryAnn, I want you to know that we were not just having an affair. What Logan and I shared went far beyond just sex; we truly loved each other. If you take away one thing from our meeting today, I hope it's this: that he was loved, and he knew he was loved. He used to thank me for being someone in his life who loved him, supported him, and believed in him. Because he wasn't getting that at home. But I'm telling you, he was loved."

"You know, that's what I wanted to hear. I know how unhappy he was in that marriage and I know how horribly Heather treated him; how she made him feel like less of a man because he wanted to work his landscape business from home, so he could spend more time with the boys. That meant the world to him."

"I hope this isn't too forward of me, but would you like me to read you the text he sent me on our nine-month anniversary?"

"Yes, I would like that very much."

Sam reached for her smartphone and leaned in closer to her companion before reciting the contents of the text in a barely audible voice just above a whisper:

Hi beautiful, sweetest angel and happy 9-month anniversary! I'm pretty sure I did NOT thank you for coming and picking my drunk ass up and taking me all the way home. I probably didn't even make out with you like I should have. If I didn't tell you thank you, if I didn't show you thank you, then please let me apologize. I'm not sure how it came to be that you "saved" me from the back of Hammerheads…but you did. And from the bottom of my heart I truly appreciate it. I truly, deeply, genuinely appreciate ALL, EVERY BIT of the selfless love you've shown me over the last 9 months. It's been truly amazing. And you are truly unbelievable. It pains me not to be able to climb to the top of the nearest mountain and proclaim my love for you! Everything that I bitch and complain about not receiving from my wife, I receive from you – TENFOLD. I have been spoiled over the months by your soft touch, kind words, sincere appreciation, sweet kisses and deep love. Spoiled beyond my expectations and spoiled beyond what I've ever imagined true love to be like. I could not imagine a day without you – without your kind, uplifting complimentary words and actions. You are the most beautiful woman in the entire world! So attractive, unbelievable and unmatched...and that's just on the inside. I cannot begin to tell you how deeply your giant heart has touched mine. Outwardly, your touch, kisses, beautiful face and crazy-hot body leave me speechless and breathless. And I cannot begin to tell you how deeply your crazy-hot affection has awakened my soul. I want you to know that you have touched me – my body, my heart, my soul, and my mind like I've never known was possible. I love you. I'm so thankful for you. You are unbelievable. As tough as this has been on us both, I wouldn't trade it for anything. It's been nothing less than exhilarating! Amazing! You are my happiness. You are my joy. You are my life. I love you and I'm ever-indebted to you for all that you've provided me in our time together. I eagerly look SO forward to giving and receiving continued love to/from you. I was so lost without you. Now, I have a beautiful purpose for which I take each breath. Sleep well, beautiful. Thank you for taking me home tonight. Thank you for loving me. And thank you for giving me something to love. Yours forever....

By the time she reached the end, she could hardly speak; MaryAnn squeezed her hand in a gesture of comfort. "I am so glad I met you. I am so glad you reached out to me." The older woman's genuine compliment soothed her wounded soul.

"Oh MaryAnn, I can't tell you how much I appreciate that. I was incredibly nervous reaching out to you at all and even more nervous about you finding out about the affair because I didn't want to cause any more pain for you or your family," she explained through staccato breaths. Maryann took both of her hands in hers as if to emphasize her next point.

"Absolutely not. I feel you were here for a reason and I am *so* happy to know that he had you. That means a lot to me."

"I'm so glad you called me," Sam managed to reply. "Being able to share my grief with someone who understands; it's such a relief."

"For me too, my dear. Lord knows my daughter-in-law doesn't give a damn. She was so cold during the funeral preparations; all she cared about was having it at Christ Episcopal where her parents are well-known. You know, so they could gin up sympathy a few days before the election. I believe her exact words were, 'I don't care. You guys do whatever you want.' Guess my daughters and I were supposed to be grateful for her generosity," she mused with obvious sarcasm.

"Is that why the funeral was so rushed?"

"Of course. That family doesn't do anything unless it suits their motives. In this case, Edward Raines saw my son's death as an excellent way to exploit their fake grief while the fawning media just lapped it all up. Apparently, so did North Carolina voters. Gah! It makes me so angry….my beloved son is dead and all they could think of was using his death to their advantage." She dissolved into sobs.

"My God; I thought about you and Logan's sisters having to travel on such short notice."

MaryAnn nodded her head before grabbing a tissue from the table and blowing her nose.

"Ugh, I am so sorry," Sam continued. "I mean I saw the media outside of the church that day swarming like vultures. I felt terrible for you and the rest of the family. What a scene."

"You want to know the worst part?"

Sam braced herself. "You mean there's more?" It was hard to imagine.

MaryAnn laughed bitterly.

"Oh yes. Since Logan married into the Raines family, I've learned there are no limits to their cruelty. They didn't even want my son to have a headstone at the memorial gardens. I had to order one myself."

"What?"

"As God is my witness, I ordered and paid for it myself. But I got the last laugh because I intentionally left out the word 'wife.' It reads, 'Logan Nash. In loving memory of our son. Father of Tyler and Nolan.'"

"Wow, that is cold." Sam shook her head in disbelief. "Despite everything Logan shared with me about Heather and her parents, you'd think basic human decency would win out here."

"Honey, I'm afraid they don't even understand the meaning of the word," she sighed. "But you know, in the end I'm happy because my son's headstone is authentic. It's only fitting that the woman who made his life miserable is missing. The only good thing she ever did was to give birth – and that was only because she gave in to pressure from her father and Logan. Edward wanted heirs for his firm and Logan wanted to be a daddy. That's what breaks my heart the most; those sweet little boys will grow up without a father, with a mother who doesn't give a damn about anyone or anything but herself. And who knows how much their lives are going to change now that their grandfather is a senator?

To be honest, I'm worried she's going to stop me from seeing them somehow."

The thought of it drove MaryAnn to tears once more while Sam looked on with sympathy. It was unbelievable how much her heart ached for this woman who, up until today, she had never even met in person. But it was more than just their shared love for Logan that bonded them in friendship and sorrow; Sam truly admired her strength and sincerity. This sweet, gracious lady had already been through hell and she couldn't shake the nagging feeling things were about to get worse. Vindictive behavior like depriving a widowed grandmother of quality time with her dead son's little boys was within the realm of possibility for a woman like Heather.

Still, she refrained from expressing these upsetting thoughts aloud, opting instead to simply listen. She didn't want to add to MaryAnn's distress by feeding the fear; all she could do was pray to God to somehow work within Heather to compel her to do the right thing. If David could manage to show compassion toward her, surely Heather could put her disgust for Logan aside for the sake of her own children.

Ah, who am I kidding? Sam thought.

"Well dear, I think I've taken up enough your time," MaryAnn announced. "Thank you for meeting with me; you have no idea how much it has helped." She rose from the cushioned chair and reached out her arms to Sam, who stood up and embraced her warmly.

"Oh MaryAnn, it was my pleasure. If you ever need to talk, please call me anytime. I'm here for you."

They looked at each other through tear-stained eyes for a moment before the older woman gently caressed her cheek and said, "Thank you for loving my son. It gives me some peace knowing he at least had someone who cared about him before…" Her voice trailed off as Sam nodded her head in acknowledgment.

After another hug, Mary Ann turned and walked out of the coffee shop, leaving Sam alone with her thoughts. As she mulled over the events of the morning, she wiped a few drops of liquid that had fallen on the table with a napkin and tossed her empty coffee cup into the trash receptacle behind her. Glancing at her phone, she figured she had just enough time to pick up some flowers and stop by Logan's grave before returning home to participate in a conference call with a client later that afternoon.

That's when her ears slowly began to tune in to the country song playing in the background; within a few seconds it revealed itself as *The Dance* by Garth Brooks. She froze for a few moments, fully immersing herself in the melancholy lyrics and haunting melody, which, for just a few moments, carried her back to a much simpler time and place.

Chapter Nine

Sam blinked back tears as she read her last text message from Logan for the umpteenth time. It was a clear, blustery early December day at the Memorial Gardens, her regular destination following morning workouts at Cross-Fit. Recently, she'd tapered her daily visits down to a few days per week, now that a month had passed since her true love had been ripped from her forever. Undisturbed by the frosty wind's chill, she scrolled through the communication with gloved hands, replaying the events of that horrific weekend in a never-ending effort to uncover the real cause of Logan's death.

"Hi Gorgeous. On #8, playing like SHIT...but having fun. Not looking forward to the stupid party tonight...will be thinking of you the whole time while I'm hanging out with these phony baloneys who think they're so important. Anyway, hope your day is going great!"

She burst into tears at the attached photo of Logan and his best friend, John French.

"You look so happy! I'm glad you're having fun! Don't think about later...you'll get through it when the time comes. Enjoy this beautiful day!"

"I will. You too, my love!"

"Damn it, Logan, why did you have to leave me? Why God? Why did this have to happen?"

Overcome with emotion, Sam couldn't determine how much time had passed before her phone's distinctive ringtone startled her back to the reality and discomfort of the frigid air as she ran for the shelter of her car. She sank into the driver's seat just in time to start the ignition, turn on the heat, and respond to the caller.

"H-hi MaryAnn," she choked out through staccato breaths.

"Hi honey. Oh, I'm so sorry you are hurting so badly. My girls and me…we're the only other people on the planet who know how you feel. But Sam, that's not why I'm calling. I have some news for you that may lead us to some answers. It's disturbing, I must warn you. Are you by yourself?"

MaryAnn's words incited an overpowering sensation of déjà vu, when the gym trainer inquired if she was alone before breaking the devastating news about Logan.

"Yes, yes, I'm in my car, getting ready to leave the Memorial Gardens."

"You know, maybe it's best if I tell you in person. Can you stop by the house?"

"Of course. I have some time before my conference call. I'll be right over."

A few minutes later, Sam entered MaryAnn's kitchen to the welcoming aroma of freshly brewed coffee and homemade scones.

"Hi," Sam smiled, returning the woman's warm embrace. "I apologize for my appearance. I didn't have time to go home and change after my workout."

"My dear, don't you worry. I didn't give you much notice now, did I? Besides, seeing you like that reminds me of the stories you've told me about you and Logan at the gym with your friends. Does my heart good to know he had many happy moments like that. Please, honey, sit down. I do need to run something by you. It's terrible news, but it may also be a clue as to what really happened that night."

MaryAnn extended her arm toward the large, hand-carved Cherrywood table bearing two white ceramic mugs and dessert plates, accompanied by decorative red linen napkins. Sam took a seat and watched as her hostess poured the steaming coffee for each of them, then pulled the creamer and sweetener toward Sam's place.

"I think I remembered to get the right sweetener for you."

"Oh, MaryAnn, this is wonderful, thank you," she sniffed, still a bit overwhelmed by her kindness and the ease with which they'd developed a good rapport. *Dare she call it friendship?* "So, tell me, what's going on?" Her heart pounded as she contemplated the idea of uncovering the truth.

"Do you know who John French is?"

"Logan's old frat buddy? Yes, he told me all about him and I've seen pictures of him and Logan on the golf course. I know how much they loved to golf together and I was there when John gave the eulogy at the funeral. Why do you ask?"

"Well dear, there's no easy way to say this." She took a deep breath. "John committed suicide last night."

"W-what? How?" Sam felt as if she would faint as she cupped her palms around her mug and focused on its heat.

"I suppose to put it more accurately, he drank himself to death," MaryAnn clarified. "You know, he'd been under strict doctor's orders to stop drinking immediately or else he would die. He didn't have long to live anyway because he'd already abused his body beyond repair with drugs and alcohol. His doctor told him flat-out that nothing could save him, but if he wanted to stick around for as long as possible, he had to lay off the alcohol. It was a no-no. One drink could be fatal."

"Ugh, I remember his eulogy at the funeral. It broke my heart to see how despondent he was, like he lost the only brother he ever had. Do you think it was just grief and depression that made him take a drink? That would make sense, given his state of mind."

"Honey, I've known that young man forever and I pride myself on my intuition. Something tells me there's much more to this than meets the eye. Yes, he was distraught over my son's death, no question about it. But John was also a father and I don't believe he'd kill himself over grief alone. As it was, his time with his kids was going to be limited. I refuse to believe he'd just drink himself to death when he could have made the most of whatever time they had left. No, no, there's more to this story. I feel it in my bones. But I wanted to get your take on it."

Sam sighed. "So much tragedy in just over a month. I don't know…I don't know what to say. Grief can drive people to do drastic things. What would compel him to kill himself, other than that? You're not suggesting – "

"That John had something to do with my son's death? I don't know. I don't want to believe that. They were so close. Do you know if they had any kind of argument, anything that would have made John resentful or angry? Is there anything in your texts and private messages from Logan that might give us a clue?"

Sam closed her eyes and wracked her brain to recall anything in their communications that would shed light on MaryAnn's suspicions. Then her mind wandered back to a different conversation, one she almost divulged during her first meeting with Logan's mother at the coffee shop.

"Okay," Sam began. "This is completely unrelated to John, but I feel I must share it with you. I'm almost embarrassed to tell you, but since you know about our affair and it might help us figure things out, I'm just going to blurt it out."

"Please, Sam, there's no judgment here. I want you to tell me about anything that could be relevant. I need to know what happened to my baby." She broke down in sobs; Sam squeezed her hand in comfort and the two women mourned together for a few moments.

Then MaryAnn reached for the box of tissues on the table and handed it to Sam after taking one for herself. "Thank you," Sam whispered. She wiped her eyes and continued. "Under normal circumstances, an affair with a married man is dangerous enough, you know. But here we had to contend with Heather's father's political campaign and all its implications. I was already out of my comfort zone, though I loved Logan like no other man before him and I knew what I was getting into. We had to be so careful about everything we did. God, I'm even ashamed to be sitting in this house with you, where – "

"Bless your heart, honey, and I mean that sincerely. It's alright. I meant it when I said I am grateful to you for making Logan feel loved in the last days of his life." She slipped her arm around Sam's shoulder.

"Thank you. It's just…sometimes it's all a little too surreal for me, that's all. I appreciate your understanding more than I can tell you. Anyway, as you mentioned to me before, Logan confided in you about Heather's affair. When he first found out, he told me too. I remember, he moved out of their bedroom and into the basement of the house right away. At the time, I teased him about being a hypocrite, but he was happy and relieved to have an excuse to avoid her. Of course, he got his digs in about their mandatory public displays of a happily married couple for the media, which just enraged her more. Anyway, one day, Logan and I were in your basement bedroom…"

She felt the fire in her cheeks. Her face turned bright red as she recalled that whenever MaryAnn was in town, she and Logan would sneak into the basement from the outside door behind the house. And while it felt exhilarating in the moment, describing it to MaryAnn Nash as they sat in her kitchen drinking coffee felt awkward and uncomfortable, notwithstanding the woman's graciousness.

"Please, go on," MaryAnn encouraged. "Anything you can remember might help us."

"Well, Heather was in Denver at the time for a supposed work trip. At least, that's what she swore to Logan. It wasn't a total lie, I guess, because we saw that Ryan Moore was with her. He's the young, hot-shot trial lawyer that works for the Raines Law Firm.

"Yes, yes, I know who he is. Logan filled me in. I'm sure it stoked Heather's ego to have an affair with a man so much younger than she."

Sam let out a nervous laugh. "As it turns out, I wasn't the only one betrayed by technology, even though we already knew about her and Ryan. But Logan suspected there was more to her quote unquote business trip than she let on. So that day in the basement, we used an iPad and…well, you know, we watched the two of them checking into their hotel. And it was obvious by the way they were fawning all over each other that this was more of a pleasure trip than anything else. I'm surprised about how careless they were, but maybe they figured no one in Denver would even know who they were. Still, it seems a little crazy in this age of social media. Guess they got caught up in the moment and let their guard down. Anyway, she looked like a giddy schoolgirl lapping up his attention. It was hard to watch."

"I can only imagine. She's the most self-centered, egotistical woman I know. Did you know, I wasn't even allowed to see my grandsons on Thanksgiving until much later in the evening and only because my girls fought with her about it? Now she's threatening to move them to D.C., can you believe that?"

Sam's heart sank. During the Thanksgiving holiday, she'd focused on her own family while she and David planned an amicable dinner for all of them, including Walter, Shannon, and Rick. David's transformation into a loving, caring father since the divorce never ceased to amaze her and every day she thanked God that her children were happy and healthy. But even during her bitter estrangement from her father in the aftermath of confessing her affair, she never once entertained the idea of keeping Madison and Zach away from their grandfather.

"Oh, MaryAnn, I'm so sorry. It doesn't surprise me, but I am truly sorry. I know how much you love those two little boys. And it's easy to see from the photos how much they adore you."

"Samantha, I can't bear the thought of never seeing them again." The older woman dissolved into unrestrained tears, her shoulders quaking. Sam drew her into a hug and did her best to offer words of comfort, though she knew they were powerless to prevent such a thing unless they could prove Heather was in some way responsible for Logan's death. And thus far, committing adultery with a young lover did not equate to murder.

After a while, MaryAnn pulled herself together and sat up straight in her chair. "So? What about Ryan? Do you suspect he had something to do with what happened to Logan?"

"I don't know for sure, but his relationship with Heather makes him a person of interest, wouldn't you say?"

"It certainly does. Do you know if they are still involved? If she's moving to D.C., I wonder what that means for them. Maybe Edward will promote him to partner since he doesn't have a son?"

"It's possible. I'm curious to know more about their relationship…I mean, if he is truly in love with Heather or if it's just about sex or getting a promotion or God knows what. But, let's say he fell madly in love with her and she was pissed at Logan. Potentially, she could have the power to make him do anything she wanted."

"Like murder my son? Why? He went along with everything and she didn't even know about the two of you until she found those Halloween cards."

"Yeah, well, I wonder about that too," Sam admitted. "When she read my ex-husband's email after he found out about Logan and me, she was suspicious, but she bought Logan's explanation that he was just flirting. You know, like he did with every woman at the gym. He swore to me she had no idea. I believed him, and we continued our relationship while I went to therapy with David, pretending I wanted to save our marriage." A lump formed in her throat. "Ugh, it sounds so ugly when I say it out loud."

"So, you're saying she could have known and was just waiting for the right time to use it against him?"

"Yeah, I mean, she couldn't care less that Logan was cheating on her, other than what it could mean for the Raines' campaign if a reporter were to find out. Of course, if that were to happen, it could threaten to expose her own infidelity and embarrass her publicly. And as we know, Heather is all about her image."

MaryAnn listened intently, processing Sam's theory and pondering what to do next. Without evidence of foul play, there was no point in going to the police. But now she had another angle to consider, though her gut told her John French's suicide still factored into the equation.

"Oh my gosh, look at the time," Sam announced, glancing at her phone. "MaryAnn, I'm so sorry, but I do have to get back to work. Thank you for inviting me over and filling me in on everything. I believe we're getting closer."

"Me too, honey." MaryAnn gave her a hug before she snuggled into her Lands' End jacket and walked out through the garage door.

"I'll let you know if I uncover anything else," she promised, feeling hopeful that they were about to find the closure they both needed.

و

The winter sunset streaked across the sky in bold shades of orange, gold, and pink as Sam drove through the main entrance of Charlotte Memorial Gardens. David had just picked the kids up for his assigned weekend and she wanted to visit Logan before heading out to do some Christmas shopping.

"Hello, my love," she whispered, placing a bouquet of red roses at his stone. She closed her eyes and bowed her head in prayer; other than Waypoint Church, this was the only place that offered her a sense of peace. She hoped that her time spent alone here with Logan might relax her mind and lead her to the discovery of a solid clue she and MaryAnn could use to unravel the rest of the mystery. How exactly, she didn't know, but she remained open to the possibilities.

Suddenly, she was interrupted by her smartphone ringing in her pocket. "Damn, I thought I'd silenced you," she complained aloud, pulling the device out to see who was trying to reach her. She frowned when she noted who it was, but decided to answer.

"Hey Shannon, what's up?"

"Sam, oh my God, I need to talk to you."

"Are you okay?"

"Oh yeah, fine."

"Then why are you whispering?"

"Oh…I'm still at work and calling you from the smock room. Look, Sam, I don't get off until 9 o'clock, but I have to talk to you. Can I meet you at the house later?"

"Sure, I'll be home by then and David has the kids."

"Great; gotta go. See you later!"

Her curiosity piqued, Sam spent the next 30 minutes alternating talking to Logan and wondering aloud what Shannon had to share. Did she and Rick finally get engaged? Why wouldn't she just blurt it out, then plan to celebrate with her later? These questions remained unanswered until the plummeting temperatures forced her back into her car, headed for the Charlotte Premium Outlets.

Hours later, she walked through her foyer carrying several shopping bags bursting with presents for the kids. She plopped them on the living room couch and proceeded into the kitchen, where she poured herself a glass of Merlot and prepared for Shannon's arrival by slicing up some fruit and cheese and arranging the pieces on a serving dish. A plate of chips and guacamole completed the impromptu after-hours happy hour. By the time Shannon arrived, Sam had a slight buzz.

"Hey, sorry I'm late; it took forever to get out of the salon tonight. Gotta love the holidays." Shannon pecked Sam on the check. Then, noticing the food displayed on the coffee table, she flashed a smile as bright as a Christmas tree. "Oh, Sam, this looks great, I'm starving."

"Well, help yourself. It's just us tonight. I can order a pizza or something if you want. I'm not really in the mood to cook."

"No, no, this is fine," Shannon assured her, pouring herself a glass of wine. "It's just what the doctor ordered." She kicked off her cowboy boots and settled into the couch.

"So, what's going on? It sounded important."

"Oh my God, Sam, I don't even know where to begin or what this even means, but I overheard a conversation today at work about Heather Raines."

Sam's ears perked up. Invigorated, she sat at attention, ready to take it all in.

"Really?"

"Yeah, one of the girls has a regular customer, you know, a woman from the upper-crust of Charlotte society. I never paid much attention to her before – I have my own regular contingent of old-moneyed Southern Belles – but anyway, for some reason, I tuned into this lady as my friend was working on her hair in the station next to mine. She went on and on about the election, the Raines' family, all of it. Apparently, she'd been away in Europe with her husband for six weeks, but they voted for the other guy in the race by absentee ballot."

"Okay," a skeptical Sam interrupted, "what does this have to do with anything?"

"I'm getting to that, silly. Just setting the stage for you. This woman and her husband were also big donors to Edward Raines' opponent, so they had some inside scoop. Let's just say, you and I were not the only ones to question Logan's perfect face in the casket. Lots of people found the whole thing suspicious...the big gala, Logan falling to his death in the early morning the following Sunday, the rushed funeral, everything. This woman had tons of dirt on Heather Raines and promised there would be a huge story breaking soon. She was sure there was a cover-up, like either Edward or Heather did something to cause Logan's death. She said some new media reporter was working on it. If I heard her correctly, she and her husband also fund this guy's citizen journalism, which means she knows what she's talking about."

Sam felt tingles up and down her spine. "Did she say anything else?"

"Just some stuff about Heather being a self-absorbed bitch. But we already knew that."

"Did you catch the name of the reporter?"

"No, she just said the story was about to break wide open and could affect Edward's viability as a senator. I mean, if they can prove he caused Logan's death, the only place he'll be heading is jail. But even if he played some role in covering up what really happened, it's still bad. This lady seemed to think Heather murdered Logan, then made it look like an accident, while Edward covered it up."

"You know, as obnoxious as Heather is, I'm not sure she's capable of murder," Sam mused, taking another sip of Merlot.

"Hey, never say never. We're dealing with ruthless people here, not your milquetoast ex-husband who couldn't hurt a fly."

"And yet, you and dad still suspected him."

"A moment of panic," Shannon countered. "Everything was so fresh, and we were worried about you, Madison and Zach. Come on, Sam, David may be aloof, but the Raines are cold, calculating people who wouldn't know real love if it smacked them in the face. All they care about is status and power. It's not that far-fetched."

"True, but there is something else to consider." With that, Sam filled her sister in on John French's suicide and her recent visit to MaryAnn's house.

"Wow, that is weird," Shannon noted. "It's like he felt guilty because Logan was dead. But why?"

"That's the million-dollar question."

"Did he leave a suicide note?"

"Not that I'm aware of."

"You know what? You need to go back to Logan's grave tomorrow."

"Well, I wasn't planning to, but why would you say that?"

"Maybe there's a clue somewhere. I mean, what if John went there and left a note before he went home and drank himself into permanent oblivion?"

"Shannon, I visit all the time and I've never seen anything, other than a golf trophy, but that's been there for a while now…"

Sam's voice trailed off as her heart began to pulsate. She hadn't given much thought as to who would have left the remembrance at Logan's grave, since he golfed with various friends and clients. She couldn't even recall when she first noticed, since most of the time she was lost in her grief.

"What?" Shannon asked.

"Oh my God, maybe it holds the key. I've gotta get over there, first thing in the morning. Shannon, thank you." She pulled her sister into a warm hug. "I think we're about to find out what really happened that night."

౭

Dear Logan,

Forgive me, buddy. I beg for your forgiveness. I never meant for you to end up dead, but here we are, thanks to me and my addictions. Heather, man, she drives a hard bargain. She told me she doubted your story about Sam and never bought the idea it was just a flirtation, especially after your boys asked you why you were so happy. That's when she suspected the affair was real and still going on.

She hated seeing you happy, that's for sure. She told me all about your fight the night of the gala, after she saw Sam's text to you. It validated her suspicions and enraged her, I know. I can only imagine what it was like riding in the car with her on the way to the country club. You know, hell hath no fury like a woman scorned – especially one so politically ambitious.

It was then that I realized I never should have sold her the drugs. She promised me, she promised me she would use them properly. I had no idea why she wanted them, but figured maybe the pressure of her father's campaign was getting to her. If I thought for a second she would use them on you, buddy, I swear, I never would have sold them to her. But my gambling debts...they're out of control and I have two kids to think about. I hope someday they can forgive me too.

When I came over to your house after I heard the news, Heather threatened me about the bookie. My God, I owe him $80,000. How the hell can I ever pay that debt? Oh yeah, she tried to be my friend and warn me that going to the police would only hurt me and my kids. She told me it *wasn't my fault, but that I could go to jail and how would that help with their college tuitions.*

I swear, Logan, she told me it was an accident. She said you took one pill, then mentioned you might take another. But you and I know better. She slipped too many in your drink and now you're gone. It's my fault. And I just can't live with it. I'm so sorry.

Sam paused after reading John French's suicide note aloud to a stunned MaryAnn. "A-are you okay?" she inquired after a minute had passed. The blood drained from the older woman's face, causing Sam to act. "Here, MaryAnn, drink some water," she soothed, handing her a full glass.

"You know, it's what I suspected all along, but hearing you read it from the horse's mouth, getting confirmation that my hunch was right...it's just...shocking, somehow, that's all." Anguished sobs overtook her as Sam placed an arm around her shoulder.

"I know," she whispered. "I feel the same way."

For a few moments, they sat in silence at MaryAnn's kitchen table.

"So, you found this note at the grave?" the older woman asked.

"Yeah, thanks to my sister. If she hadn't overheard that conversation in the salon, I don't know that I would have thought to take a closer look at that golf trophy. I don't know why I never paid much attention to it. Guess I'm too caught up in my pain whenever I visit Logan. But when I lifted it up off the ground, there was the note folded up underneath, partially buried in the ground."

"God works in mysterious ways," MaryAnn mused softly, wiping away a tear. Sam took her hand in hers.

"Where do we go from here?" she finally asked.

"I think we should go to the police, don't you? It's too late for Logan and John, but why should Heather get away with it? She's loving the fact that she has the power to keep me away from Tyler and Nolan, but little does she know not for much longer."

Sam's stomach twisted into knots with the realization that following MaryAnn's suggestion could implicate her in a public way as the other woman in this entire ordeal. No, she wouldn't be charged with a crime, but being outed to the world as an adulteress would pose an even greater punishment than jail. It would rip open a wound that had only begun to heal with her ex-husband and endanger her relationship with her children. No matter how much she'd try to protect them, someday Madison and Zach would have to deal with the humiliation, because the internet was forever. She felt the bile rise in her throat as she imagined a vindictive Heather posting Logan's private texts, emails, and messages online.

"Samantha? Do you agree?"

"Ah, MaryAnn, you know how much I want justice for Logan. It's just…there's no way to protect my kids if this goes public. I guess I have to take responsibility for my actions, but it was hard enough confessing my sins to my family. If my role in this ends up online, someday my kids will see it and be forced to deal with the humiliation. I might even lose them if they decide they'd rather live with their father than their adulteress mother." She dissolved into tears and it was MaryAnn's turn to offer comfort. For a few minutes, neither one spoke. Then a light bulb went off in MaryAnn's head.

"Sam, I just had a thought. Can your sister find out who the woman was at the salon? Maybe we could speak with her. If there's enough evidence against him, perhaps we can strike a deal to force

Edward's resignation before he even takes the oath of office. I doubt Heather acted alone. What do you think?"

A hopeful Sam dabbed her eyes with tissues. "That's a good idea. Yes, Shannon can help. Her co-worker left the salon that night while she was still doing her customer's hair, so she never had a chance to question her. I'm kind of surprised no one has reached out to you if this woman and her husband are funding a new media reporter to get to the bottom of things, but maybe that's next on the agenda. From what Shannon told me, these people are determined to keep Edward from going to the United States Senate."

"Well, honey, so am I. So am I."

Sam and MaryAnn listened to the recording in shock and disbelief as they sat in the living room of the Myers Park mansion owned by William and Sarah Wentworth. Confirming their suspicions, Edward and Heather's voices answered every question they'd harbored about Logan's death.

"Daddy, I don't know what to do. I was mad as a hornet and I couldn't see straight tonight, knowing my husband had an affair with that tramp from the gym. We fought the whole way over and he said some things that made my blood boil. I just couldn't resist putting more drugs in his drink to teach him a lesson. I never meant for this to happen. What are we gonna do? The limo driver who took us home was awfully suspicious because Logan was dead weight when he carried him into the house. The guy kept asking, 'Are you sure he's okay? Is he breathing?' Daddy, I hustled the guy out as fast as could and poo-poohed it, telling him my husband always drank way too much when we went out. I told him how much Logan loved to party. I was trying to convince myself too,

because I knew something was terribly wrong. Oh my God…I never meant for it to go this far! The guy must've called 911 because the next thing I knew the police were at my door, but I didn't answer. Once the limo driver left I shut off all the lights and made it look like no one was home. Thank God, the boys spent the night at their friend's house. Daddy…I think Logan might be dead!"

"Alright, calm down! I'm sending someone over. The election is two days away and we cannot have any scandals. My bodyguards will be right there. I'm going to instruct them to take one of the boy's bikes and Logan to the river. When they find his body, and show up at the house, you tell the police you and Logan had a fight and he was so enraged, he just took one of the boy's bikes because it was the easiest thing to get out of the garage. Tell them you pleaded with him not to do anything crazy, but he wouldn't listen to you. Understand?"

"Yes, yes Daddy, I got it. I'll do exactly what you say."

"Good. The bodyguards will be there in a few minutes. Don't screw this up for me, Heather. I've been planning this campaign for decades and a lot of donors and lobbyists are counting on me."

"That's the end of the recording," William announced. "I'm only sorry we didn't have it in time to impact the election, but technical glitches required sending it to an expert to make it audible. By the time he fixed it, the election was over. Our undercover reporter didn't get video, but he followed Raines' bodyguards to the river, where he watched them break the chain off the bike and leave it at the top of the pedestrian bridge to make it look like a bike wreck."

"And they just placed Logan's body face-down in the creek," Sam choked out. So far, the resolution she'd pursued with fierce determination ever since laying eyes on Logan's body in the casket felt empty and anti-climactic. She felt MaryAnn's arm encircle her.

"Yes, I'm afraid so," William affirmed sympathetically. "I apologize that our reporter didn't go to the police, but when he realized the sound was garbled on the audio, he knew it would just be hearsay. With no evidence to back up his claim and Edward being the powerful man he is, the police would have done nothing. It took a while to fix the problems with the sound to the point where you can hear well enough to know who's speaking."

"So now what?" MaryAnn asked. "Where do we go from here? Angry as I am, I don't want to put Sam through any more pain, but I want them to pay somehow for what happened to my only son."

William and Sarah exchanged knowing glances. Then William offered an alternative to taking their evidence to law enforcement.

"I think we can all agree Edward Raines isn't fit to serve in the Senate. I believe we can force his resignation before he's even sworn in by letting him know we are in possession of damning evidence that could send him and his daughter to jail. We can drive a hard bargain: publicly declare you are resigning for your own health due a recent medical diagnosis or risk us going to the police…or worse, broadcasting this recording all over social media, which in today's day and age would try him in the court of public opinion and force an outcry from constituents who feel they voted for him under false pretenses. Either way, it's not good for him."

"What are the odds he'd go for the first option?" Sam inquired in quivering voice. "Because the second one would definitely blow up in my face if Heather decided to drag me into the court of public opinion as you call it."

"Honey, I have a hunch that old goat will take option number one," MaryAnn answered. "No matter what, being led away in an orange jumpsuit is too much for his Texas-sized ego. As much as it would hurt you to be outed online, it would hurt Edward more to spend God knows how long behind bars…and I can't imagine Heather embracing the idea either. Can you see my vain, self-centered, egotistical former daughter-in-law in a women's correctional facility? No, I think you and I have the perfect opportunity to get what we both want from the Raines family. We can drive a hard bargain: I get to see my grandchildren and you get to keep your privacy. It may require you to put on a good act, as if you don't care about becoming the public face of an adulteress, but we can call their bluff. Then, this winter, you and the kids can come celebrate with Tyler, Nolan and me in Marco Island. What do you say, Sam?"

A slow smile crept across Sam's face as she absorbed the wisdom in the older woman's words. "It's a deal," she replied.

Epilogue

"Hello, my love," Sam whispered, running a gloved hand across Logan's stone. The setting sun bathed the January sky in deep pink, purple and violet hues as the frigid wind accelerated in response to its descent. She bristled at the cold, then quickly tended to her purpose for being there.

"You know, I'm looking forward to taking my kids to visit your incredible mama in Marco Island next month. It's been way too cold around here, lately. I hope you are resting in peace, my dear man, now that we know what really happened that night. I know it won't bring you back, but somehow, I feel a sense of serenity. Sounds insane, right? You're still gone and I'm still here without you. No matter what, nothing can change that.

"I want you to know I will always carry you in my heart. You are a part of me forever, Logan Nash, and I don't regret a single moment with you. And I know you'll understand what I'm about to say because you were an amazing father who loved your kids. Logan, I must move on. It's time for me to focus on Madison and Zach and on living my life, like I promised God I would that day at the funeral parlor. I don't know if that means finding love again. Right now, that feels damn near impossible, because you raised the bar so high for any other man. Still, I need to open myself to the possibilities.

"I'll never forget you, Logan, I promise. As a matter of fact, this is the first time since you left me that I have the strength to head to Dos Amigos and toast to you with a Grand Marnier margarita. I called over there and when they told me Armando was working tonight, I felt like it was a sign. Anyway, I meant what I said; I will always love you, Logan Nash. You are forever in my heart."

She indulged in one final, cleansing cry before drying her tears and offering a prayer for her beloved. Then, she ran for the shelter of her Pathfinder and drove it in the direction of their favorite Mexican restaurant, where moments later, Armand greeted her with a smile, a bear hug and a complimentary drink. With gratitude and joy for having known him, they made a final toast to Logan Nash and spent a good part of the evening sharing stories and laughs. For the first time in what felt like an eternity, Sam mostly reveled in her memories, oblivious to the handsome stranger at the other end of the bar who'd noticed her presence and inquired about her to her and Logan's regular server and friend.

89072830R00200

Made in the USA
Columbia, SC
08 February 2018